RAGING STORM

THE LEGENDS OF THE ÄLFAR BOOK IV

MARKUS HEITZ

Translated by Sorcha McDonagh

Jo Fletcher

BOOKS

First published in Great Britain in 2019 by

Jo Fletcher Books
an imprint of
Quercus Editions Ltd
Carmelite House
50 Victoria Embankment
London EC4Y 0DZ

An Hachette UK company

Die Legenden der Albae: Tobender Sturm
Copyright © 2014 Markus Heitz (www.mahet.de)
Represented by AVA international GmbH, Germany
(www.ava-international.de)
Originally published 2014 by Piper Verlag GmbH, Germany

English Translation © 2019 Sorcha McDonagh

A CIP catalogue record for this book is available from the British Library.

PB ISBN 978 1 78429 444 1
EBOOK ISBN 978 1 78429 443 4

10 9 8 7 6 5 4 3 2 1

Typeset by Jouve (UK), Milton Keynes
Printed and bound in Great Britain by
Clays Ltd, Elcograf S.p.A.

For those who know they must take action when needed.
There should be more people like them.

Dramatis Personae

TARK DRAAN
ÄLFAR

Aiphatòn	emperor of the älfar in Tark Draan and offspring of the Inextinguishables
Carmondai	master of word and image
Firûsha, Sisaroth and Tirîgon	triplets, joint rulers of the northern älfar
Daitolór	älf-warrior with the rank of a benàmoi
Tanóra	veteran-woman
Vonòria	veteran-woman
Ostòras	älf-warrior
Rhogàta	älf-warrior woman
Votòlor	älf-warrior

HUMANS

Mallenia	Queen of Gauragar and Idoslane
Rodario	King of Urgon
Coïra	maga and Queen of Weyurn
Kerjan Münzler	mayor of Güldenwand

Rodîr Bannerman	warrior
Endô	refugee
Sha'taï	his niece, refugee
Lot-Ionan	magus and one-time foster father to Tungdil Goldhand

DWARVES

Secondling Kingdom

Baromir Goldenstein	messenger
Boïndil 'Ireheart' Doubleblade	of the clan of the Axe Swingers, King of the Secondlings

Thirdling Kingdom

Tungdil Goldhand	warrior and scholar

Fifthling Kingdom

Belogar Strifehammer	of the clan of the Boulder Heavers
Gosalyn Landslip	of the clan of the Tunnel Seekers

Freelings

Carâhnios	the last zhadár
Beligata Hardblow	a former Thirdling of the clan of the Bloodshedders, now a free dwarf

ELVES

Fiëa	elf-leader
Ilahín	Fiëa's husband
Phenîlas	elf-leader

ISHÍM VORÓO ÄLFAR

Dsôn Elhàtor

Modôia	monarchess of Dsôn Elhàtor
Ôdaiòn	Modôia's son
Leïóva	Modôia's confidante
Ávoleï	Leïóva's daughter and battleship commander
Olòndôras	cîanoi
Khônatá	top cîanai of the fine art

Dsôn Dâkiòn

Shôtoràs	sovereign of Dsôn Dâkiòn
Irïanora	Shôtoràs' niece
Saitôra	Irïanora's close friend
Bethòras	chief architect and cartographer
Gathalor and Iophâlor	Irïanora's acquaintances
Pasôlor and Horgôra	confidants of the sovereign
Arthâras	bodyguard
Zelája	maid
Vailóras	warrior and tax collector

Lethòras	top cîanoi
Tanôtai	death-dancer
Anûras	master of the death-dancers
Nodûcor	exiled älf

OTHERS

Kôr'losôi	botoican of the Nhatai family
Saî'losôi	botoican-woman of the Nhatai family
Fa'losôi	top botoican-woman in the Nhatai family
Ysor'kenôr	botoican of the Rhâhoi family
Ythan'kenôr	Ysor'kenôr's brother
Cushròk	commander of a tribe of soldiers for hire
Gricks, Tratshka, Nrashq, Obko	Cushròk's soldiers from the tribe of the Dréki
Joako	pub landlord

GLOSSARY

Dsôn Elhàtor	the Magnificent, an älfar town on an island
Dsôn Dâkiòn	the Majestic, an älfar town on a mountain
Tronjor	river that flows from Dâkiòn to the sea
onwú	sea-faring race of humans, enemies of Elhàtor
shintoìt	designation for a child of the Inextinguishables
zhartài	master assassin who declares älfar targets
zhadár	derived from zhartài, älfar word for the Invisibles
benàmoi	officer rank of älfar

cîanai/cîanoi, cîani (plural)	älfar sorceress/sorcerer
botoican	human with magic powers in Ishím Voróo
Dhaïs Akkoor	old capital of the botoican kingdom
Tr'hoo D'tak	capital of the Nhatai kingdom
Ultai t'Ruy	capital of the Rhâhoi kingdom
malméner	breed of beast comprised of troll, ogre and giant
ghaist	creature comprised of magic and souls bound together in human form; wears a distinctive copper helmet
Children of the Smith	dwarves' term for themselves

It is said that they are crueller than any other known tribe.

It is said that their hatred of the elves, people, dwarves and all other creatures flows black through their veins and is revealed when their eyes are exposed to sunlight.

It is said they have devoted their entire lives to death and art.

It is said they are masters of black magic.

It is said they are immortal . . .

Much has been proclaimed about the älfar tribe.

Now read the tales that follow and decide for yourself what is truth and what is not.

These are tales of unspeakable horror, of unimaginable battles, the greatest evil, magnificent triumphs and devastating defeats.

But also of courage, sincerity and valour.

Of friendship.

And love.

These are the legends of the älfar.

Author unknown
Foreword from the banned, truth-twisting books
The Legends of the Älfar, undated

Prologue

It's not long since I wrote these words down.

Some events are touched on in the Forgotten Writings; some facts now appear in a new light. It's odd how everything is connected after all, even if many divisions of unendingness separate things.

It seems the era of false gods is over. They declared themselves superior beings and failed. That was the end of the Inextinguishables.

But the creature they left behind for us behaved very differently. Dutifulness, humility, self-sacrifice – it's barely expected of mortals and not at all from the son of gods, something he was entitled to consider himself.

Aiphatòn was on the march to keep danger at bay, moving from one stormy battle to the next. The storms became more and more powerful until he encountered the most powerful one of all.

And me?

I'm still in the eye of the hurricane, enjoying a rest after so many moments of roaring and noise, of screaming and death.

I can't say how long this calm will last or whether the wind will then tear me to pieces.

If my notes should end, at least I'll have left a legacy that will outlast me.

What irony: to live on, an immortal älf needs thin paper!
Read and understand.

Excerpt from the epic *Aiphatòn*
chronicled by Carmondai, master of word and image

Tark Draan, Älfar realm of Dsôn Bhará, formerly the elf realm Lesinteïl, 5452nd division of unendingness (6491st solar cycle), early summer

Just as I thought: they waited because they don't dare attack us at night.

With the pale rays of the rising sun, Daitolór could clearly see the pathetic band of foes marching towards them across the plain. *We'll kill them one way or another.*

Dust rose up from underneath their boots – the dry spell had made the earth around the crater sandy. Because there was no wind blowing, the telltale brownish clouds curled up into the air, easy to spot even from far away.

'They're coming across the plain from the northwest yet again. About a thousand of them. Half of the barbarians are dressed like warriors, the others farmers,' Daitolór cried down from his lookout point, not sounding worried or nervous. 'What they all have in common is that none of them has any sense.'

Soft laughter rang out at the benàmoi's words.

The älf, who had stuffed his dark hair underneath his helmet, jumped down from a piece of abstract art made of clear varnished bones and rusty iron. He landed neatly in front of the twenty warrior-women and warriors who were wearing toughened, black leather armour.

Daitolór pointed at the approaching enemy. 'Load the smooth

arrowheads and pull the strings back as far as they go. Every arrow must run through at least three of the enemy and kill them. It will save ammunition.'

Having taken their longbows from their shoulders, his soldiers nodded silently.

'As soon as this senseless lot have come within two hundred paces, we'll release two full volleys, then each of you is to look for targets directly in front of you. Off you go.'

The small unit darted behind the many artworks that had once served to make an impression on visitors, with their composition, their strangeness and their uniqueness.

Daitolór's lookout point three paces in the air was resting on a solid pedestal. With its carved bones bound by silver wire, it was modelled on the Inàste's Arrow constellation with all its heavenly bodies, both large and small. All told, the artwork was four by four by four paces; crystals of various sizes on it symbolised the stars and sparkled beautifully in the light of the sun and moon. You could climb some steps up to the top of the pedestal and find yourself in the middle of the replica constellation.

Daitolór's favourite piece, which he stole glances at from time to time, was around ten paces to his left, surrounded by a crowd of statues made from gold, tionium and polished steel. Its simplicity was what marked it out as different and made it eye-catching. A torso seven paces tall had been formed out of bones to look like it was hauling itself out of the earth. The bones were intricately painted and inlaid with precious stones that glimmered and twinkled.

In its right hand, the figure brandished a weapon fitted with eight blades and mounted like a wind-turbine so that the mildest gust of wind could set it moving. When the rune-inscribed blades cut through the air, they whirred and hummed; and the faster they spun, the more hypnotic the overall pattern of sparkling gems became. Daitolór had often caught himself staring and listening to it for too long . . .

Just like right now. He tore his eyes away from the spectacle. *It's a disgrace that the artworks are being used as cover to take the brunt of this.*

The benàmoi watched the warriors in his unit taking up their positions as he loosened the feathered arrow shafts in the quiver slung around his hips. Although each and every member of the unit carried fifty rounds, enough to obliterate the enemy, nobody knew how long it would be until more lunatics launched their next wave of attack. *For every bolt that hits an artwork, I will have my revenge and make the archer pay.*

Daitolór had stopped counting how many dead carried his name.

And yet, things weren't looking good for the northern älfar's realm, no matter how much scum they were killing off.

The power structures were starting to shake but he had no doubt they would triumph. For the benàmoi, it was just a question of arrow supply.

The älfar had ruled large parts of Tark Draan for twenty divisions of unendingness. At first there were just the Dsôn Aklán – the triplets Sisaroth, Tirîgon and Firûsha – as well as the survivors from the Phondrasôn caves. Together they had built Dsôn Bhará and expanded their rule with every sunrise.

Aiphatòn, the son of the Inextinguishables, had come along later with a band of wild älfar who had no sense of decency or appreciation of art, and he had seized full control over the älfar tribe because of his parentage. The magic he commanded bolstered his claim and literally pulverised any resistance. In the north, they hid their hatred of him and his second-rate entourage behind a mask of haughty politeness.

At long last, the triplets had been able to win over the groundling folk from the Thirdling tribe as allies, and this represented a huge step.

It meant that they could tackle the complete conquest of Tark Draan and especially the protection of areas they had captured.

Daitolór remembered the good times that had ended when Tungdil Goldhand turned up. The hero of old, he had led the courageous tribes against the älfar and all the other conquerors the triplets were already fighting a running battle with: from the magus Lot-Ionan to the dragon Lohasbrand and the monster kordrion.

They'll be close enough very soon. Sadly Daitolór couldn't turn a blind eye to the fact that there were hardly any more warrior-women and warriors from his tribe left to hold out against the waves of scum surging towards them. The barbarians attacked the capital relentlessly, spurred on by successes in Dsôn Bhará's hinterlands as well as the rousing words of the elves, groundlings and self-declared heroes with ridiculous names like Mallenia or Rodario.

The commanders obviously kept quiet about how many casualties the attackers had sustained so as not to discourage the barbarians.

There usually wasn't enough time to disembowel the corpses and scour them for the right bones for new artworks. Most of the bodies were dragged away at night by carrion-feeders so the barbarians couldn't work out the true scale of their losses. Sometimes there was just the slightly sweet, acrid stench of rotting flesh hanging in the air from the surrounding foxholes.

The small crowd of barbarians was approaching across the plain at the double. Whatever was making them come here and look for conflict, Daitolór doubted that their impetus was courage. Barbarians usually carried out the greater deeds from greed. There was no doubt that the älfar's wealth was known about in Tark Draan. *The glittering of the artworks will attract them.*

Apparently the so-called southern älfar, who had been commanded by Aiphatòn, had all fallen in battle against Lot-Ionan, along with their emperor. The only son of the Inextinguishables belonged to the past, and Daitolór did not shed any tears over him. The benàmoi was sceptical that Aiphatòn could have killed the all-powerful magus and dragged him into death with him.

Even the Dsôn Aklán, who to him were the true rulers of the älfar, suffered a painful loss: it was said that Firûsha died a long time ago in a battle with a maga and nothing had been heard from her sibling commanders Tirîgon and Sisaroth for a long time. No doubt they were fighting the scum in Tark Draan somewhere. As long as both brothers stood by them, nothing bad could happen.

They led us out of Phondrasôn to one of our biggest victories. They will definitely lead us through the hard times too.

Their enemies exploited the northern älfar's vulnerability and the chaos: just as the troops were going to assemble quickly to defend the capital, rebellions suddenly broke out all over Dsôn Bhará. So the älfar were forced to rally against sparks of resistance in many places at once, extinguishing them with blood.

As Daitolór had learned in the meantime, the groundlings from the Thirdling tribe terminated the alliance pact and charged into battle alongside the rebels. *We will crush them too. And punish them like we have never punished any tribe in Tark Draan before.*

The tramping of boots and the rattle of poorly made armour rang out. They even had cavalry in their small, shabby army. Around a hundred of their soldiers were on horseback, holding long lances upright with colourful pennants fluttering from them.

No groundlings? The älf scrutinised the whole line as they approached. *I hope, Samusin, that we kill some traitors again.*

'Get ready!' he cried and resumed his elevated position. There was a gap between the artwork's intersecting and interlinked bones, and it was through this that he would fire the shots accurately at the enemies.

Daitolór took one of his extra-large black arrows that even thin metal couldn't block and placed it on his bowstring.

The troops started running – but to the astonishment of the benà-moi, none of the attackers drew their weapons. The cavalry trotted casually behind the infantry, the archers having hung their crossbows on their backs.

They don't know that we're lying in wait here! This thought flashed through the älf's mind and a contemptuous smile formed around the corners of his mouth.

The barbarians were probably in a hurry because they could already see the crater and wanted to get into the Black Heart of Dsôn Bhará quickly to tear it out of the kingdom's breast and destroy it.

Because they didn't send a scout on ahead, they're running blindly into our shower of arrows. Oh, they have truly lost their minds. And soon they'll lose their lives too. 'Ready?' he called, pulling his bowstring back a long way and aiming at the cavalryman with the shiniest armour, the rising sun reflecting off it. He was asking to be shot. 'Fire!'

His fingers released the thin cord, and he immediately followed up the arrow aimed at the horseman with another one.

The twenty-one projectiles were still whirring through the air when the next ones followed.

The first hail of impacts and screams was immediately followed by a second. More than a hundred foes fell to the dusty ground mid-movement and some were trampled by the ones who came after them. It seemed as though the army initially didn't grasp what was going on.

Your death is named Daitolór. He saw his barbarian target in the shimmering armour slump abruptly in his saddle and slip off his horse; the rider behind him yelled out and clutched his chest, while a third let go of his lance and fell off. Meanwhile the barbarian to his left lurched backwards out of his saddle and the rider behind grasped his visor, writhing.

Only five? Daitolór wasn't happy with his spoils. *It ought to have been six or more. Since when have they been using thicker iron? Surely they didn't learn?*

Enraged, he fired one arrow after another at the pitiful army which had come to a standstill, making it an even easier target for five or six heartbeats before the cleverest among the simple-minded lot raised their shields.

But the älfar's war arrows ran effortlessly through the shields, piercing one or two more bodies beyond them. Anyone who didn't fall down dead immediately sustained terrible injuries.

Once Daitolór had used up half of his ammunition and scarcely more than forty heartbeats had gone by, not one single member of the barbarian troop was left standing; even their steeds were lying on the ground.

The älfar stopped their bombardment.

Their wounded foes crawled over lifeless bodies, looking for a place safe from the arrows. The benàmoi saw a flurry of movement behind some of the horses' corpses.

The cowards think they're safe there.

'Advance,' he commanded. 'Keep your bows to hand until we're close enough, then take your lances and kill every barbarian who still looks like they have anything resembling life in them.'

Daitolór left his elevated position and strode towards the bloody chaos of barbarian and horse corpses with his twenty warrior-women and warriors.

The älfar didn't encounter any resistance. Not one bolt flew at them.

Deathly afraid and unable to form a coherent thought, the injured fled for their lives much too slowly rather than putting up a fight.

What a pathetic lot. Daitolór's nose was filled with the smell of spilled blood, and the whimpering, agonised screams disgusted him.

He ordered three of his warriors to guard the unit with their bows; he had the rest continue the slaughter to make sure that none of their enemies survived and made off during the night. The long-shafted lances belonging to the slain cavalrymen were perfect for cutting the enemy's throats open without sullying themselves with their blood.

In ten cases, they found barbarians hidden among the fallen soldiers, hoping to escape the älfar's keen eyes. Swift stabs put an end to those cowards; the same went for the ones crouching behind the dead horses who literally begged for mercy. They died under the warriors' disdainful gaze.

The sun wasn't quite at its peak when Daitolór and his defending forces from Dsôn took the lives of the last barbarians.

'Gather the intact arrows wherever you can,' he ordered his troops and removed his helmet from his dark hair to cool himself down. 'Then we'll return to camp and await the next targets. We'll hardly be out of practice!'

Soft, evil laughter rang out again.

'What about the dead, benàmoi?' asked one of the warriors. 'I still need a few nice teeth – I want to resole my boots with them.'

'The entire sole?'

'Yes. They make a wonderful, musical sound when you walk on stone.'

Daitolór raised his hand as a signal of permission to disembowel the bodies. 'I've got to see these boots with tooth soles,' he remarked.

'I'll show you them as soon as I'm done.'

'Benàmoi, a retinue from Dsôn,' came the cry from one of the archers still on guard.

Astonished, Daitolór turned around and made out a band of ten älfar riding towards them on night-mares. His surprise grew when he saw the blood-red runes on the pennant fluttering in the wind on one warrior's lance.

The symbol of the Dsôn Aklán! The benàmoi's heart beat faster. *Is that . . . Firûsha?*

Indeed there was an älf-woman in the middle of the band wearing eye-catching black tionium armour with exquisite inlay. Because the group was tracing an arc as it approached, the extra protective iron ridge along her spine was coming into view. A very long, narrow sword hung at an angle by her night-mare's flank, the massive crossguards jutting out and gleaming.

That's her! She's alive! Oh, Inàste, that is . . . Daitolór's thoughts raced, his joy threatening to overwhelm him. He took a few steps away from the field of corpses and glanced at his boots to check if the leather was sullied with barbarian blood. *What can she want with us? To congratulate us on our victory?*

The riders stopped in front of him, their snorting night-mares churning up the ground with their lightning-surrounded hooves.

Daitolór bowed slightly. His gaze fell on the double-edged daggers affixed to the armour on her thighs, as well as the iron discuses the size of palms on the metal splint armour on her upper arms. 'Dsôn Aklán,' he greeted her. 'We have held the north of the town once again.' He caught a glimpse of her face through the visor and saw she was incredibly attractive.

His troops looked at the älf-woman as if she were a ghost.

Firûsha's piercing black eyes, in which he thought he could detect a hint of blue, were fixed on him. 'You have served us well, benàmoi. As long as my brothers are at war with Lot-Ionan and the rebellious barbarians, they will not be able to devote time to Dsôn's security.' She nodded first to him and then to his small unit, before finally pushing up the visor of her helmet. 'Thank you. Stand your ground.'

She is beautiful. Just like people say. 'We need more arrows, Aklán,' Daitolór ventured to suggest. 'We are so outnumbered by barbarians that we . . .'

Firûsha smiled and swept a strand of her black hair to the side. 'Send one of your people to my quartermaster in town. He's to supply you with the best ammunition.' The älf-woman pointed southeast. 'Meanwhile we will ride towards the enemy and slaughter anything that stands in our way, to allow you a break. Your arms must be tired from the relentless shooting.'

Daitolór couldn't stop staring at her. *She . . .*

Firûsha took a breath. 'Like so many others, you thought I had passed into endingness, didn't you?'

He nodded almost imperceptibly, although that wasn't exactly what he was thinking. 'Forgive me. People said that you had fallen into the hands of a maga and were lying at the bottom of a lake in Weyurn,' he answered truthfully. 'Seeing you in front of me now is the most wonderful present that the Creating Spirit has given me in the last few moments of unendingness.'

A wind sprang up, blowing southwards. It played with the black hair that jutted out from underneath the älf-woman's helmet and fell to her shoulders. It gave off the refreshing smell of fresh confidence; it was unsullied by decay or barbarian blood.

With one hand, Firûsha grasped the hilt of her two-handed sword. 'And I will ride into battle again. A barbarian-woman cannot rob me of immortality, regardless of whether she's a maga,' she said. 'All of you,' she addressed the troops, 'hear this and carry it in your hearts: I, Firûsha, one of the Dsôn Aklán, walk among you and march out to bring death to enemy ranks. Together we will transform the impending doom into victory!'

Daitolór lifted his blood-spattered spear. 'We will not let the enemy advance any further than this point,' he solemnly swore. 'No barbarian, no groundling and no creature other than an älf will set foot in our town.'

The wind picked up a little more and set the artworks moving.

The crystal stars of Inàste's Arrow bobbed and sparkled, the bones gently rubbing against one another and the thin wire creating a high-pitched murmur that sounded like whispering; the eight blades belonging to the figure breaking out of the ground started rotating faster too, and a whistling hum resounded.

A cool shudder ran down Daitolór's spine, despite the heat from the sun. Without meaning to, the benàmoi turned around and let his gaze wander. Something seemed off, and an ominous feeling spread through him.

The night-mares also seemed to sense a change was taking place. Snorting, their red eyes rolled; they thrashed around restlessly and their nostrils flared.

Would monsters secretly try and approach Dsôn? But where would they be coming from? Try as he might, Daitolór couldn't explain his misgivings.

Firûsha reined in her frisky stallion. 'Look at them! They want to sink their teeth into barbarians,' she cried out, laughing and getting guffaws of approval in return. 'We're better off riding out before they get so wild that they . . .'

A powerful gust of wind made a low-pitched whirring sound as it swept through the group of älfar, churning up dust and earth. In the blink of an eye, the steeds disappeared along with the troops behind the grey-brown clouds of dirt.

The rapidly fluctuating sounds from the artwork's eight spinning blades drifted over to the benàmoi, but now they didn't seem fascinating or soothing. On the contrary, they seemed to intensify and fan the flames of his anxiety.

The god of wind seems to want to have some fun with us. Daitolór tightened his grip on his spear, tiny granules grinding between his teeth – then he felt the prickling all over his skin.

This time it wasn't a vague premonition, it was the consequence of powerful magic suddenly appearing all around him.

What could . . . Before he could let out a warning cry, a shrill crackle cut through the whirring of the wind. In the middle of the dust, dark green finger-sized runes lit up.

Then death cries rang out.

The night-mares were neighing wildly. Daitolór heard the clicks of their teeth snapping shut, followed by loud, dry cracks. Someone or something was breaking the mighty animals' spines.

Then warm fluid from the haze of dirt sprayed at the benàmoi. The smell told him it was blood.

Älfar blood.

'Aklán!' he shouted, brandishing his spear at the invisible foe attacking under cover of dust. 'Watch out!'

'Get out of here,' Firûsha shouted frantically from somewhere in the sandy haze, profound fear in her voice. '*He* is here!'

He? Daitolór made out the galloping sound of approaching nightmare hooves, mingling with the renewed hissing as magic was unleashed. *Lot-Ionan!*

A beam of emerald light as thick as an arm made a crackling sound as it shot past him and hit the nearest älf, ripping him apart with its force. Blown-off body parts rained down on the benàmoi, and he was sprayed with blood again.

He panted as he knelt down and peered around, his heart racing, his fingers around the now sticky shaft of his weapon.

The loud, discordant sounds of the eight blades wouldn't stop. For the first time, Daitolór wished they would be silent.

The wind toyed with the clouds of dust, gradually dispersing them as if Samusin wanted to reveal the horror confronting the älfar.

The Aklán and four of her companions were riding in the distance. They could not stand up to the superior magic of a Lot-Ionan.

Bloody scraps lay beside and in front of the crouching benàmoi – it was only the pieces of armour that identified them as älfar limbs. Two riderless night-mares were stomping around and snorting, getting their bearings in the dropping wind.

The artwork went silent.

Where is the magus? Daitolór felt he knew what his mission was: he had to make sure the Aklán had time to reach safety so that she could command her surviving people. A spear was not enough to kill the magus, the älf knew that, but it would definitely be enough to distract it. With Inàste's aid, a miracle might happen.

Out of the mist emerged the silhouette of another älf-warrior whom Daitolór didn't know. *He must have been one of the Aklán's guards who had fallen off a night-mare.*

Without looking around or taking any other precaution, the unknown soldier went over to one of the black horses and swung himself into the saddle to follow the queen.

'Where are you going?' came the sound of a sonorous voice from the last of the grey-brown clouds. Then, less than five paces from Daitolór, there appeared a thin, bald figure holding a long staff in his left hand.

The benàmoi ducked even lower, ready to throw his spear. *I might manage it if the magus is distracted.*

The älf on the night-mare spurred his stallion so that the huge beast lunged at the magus and—

Steed and warrior were enveloped in green light mid-leap. They were flung to the ground as though they had been struck by a giant fist. The night-mare's legs broke with a crack and the älf warrior was pinned down by the black horse's heavy body. Because the suffering, raging animal was snapping its jaws shut in all directions, the warrior was forced to kill it with a swift blow to the neck before the lethal teeth could get him.

'That's how quickly an attack can turn to defeat,' the sound of the magus' voice rang out, speaking excellent, almost archaic älfish.

Daitolór stayed still, not letting the enemy out of his sight as he calmly approached the pinned rider.

The last of the dust clouds dispersed – and he saw his error.

Aiphatòn! Although the benàmoi had never set eyes on him before, he knew immediately that the emperor had come to Dsôn.

No other älf looked like him. Most of his chest, stomach and lower abdomen, as well as his shoulders and upper arms, were covered in plates of armour sewn into his flesh. The metal, people said, consisted of a special alloy that absorbed and stored magic energy. That explained his powers, which rivalled those of a magus. He was bald, wore heavy armoured gloves and a black, wraparound skirt-like garment around his hips.

The pinned warrior pointed the sword covered in night-mare blood at Aiphatòn. 'You're a traitor to your own people,' he said, groaning. 'First you bring that scum out of the south, now you want to kill the Aklán. And all the while you are the son of the Inextinguishables!' He clenched his teeth together to suppress a cry of pain. 'Think, Aiphatòn!' he continued. 'Ally yourself with . . .'

The bald älf threw his head back and roared with laughter. 'You're just about to pass into endingness and you're trying to talk *me* into an alliance with the Aklán? I am your *emperor*, älf!' he thundered, pointing the narrow tip of his spear at the prone man. 'You ought to obey me without asking a single question, just like the Aklán should! Instead they carried on with their intrigues, sought to depose me and saw themselves on my throne. Do you think I'll be so kind as to forgive that crime? A crime against me, the son of the Inextinguishables?'

Daitolór didn't dare move.

By now he seriously doubted he would be able to do anything to stop Aiphatòn. Anyone who could simply fling a night-mare to the ground as it galloped would laugh when faced with a conventional spear. He saw his warrior-women and warriors lying around, dashed to pieces, torn apart by magic as if they were battle debris, deemed worthless. *But what will I do?*

'The Inextinguishables abandoned us back then,' snapped the pinned man. 'We were stuck in that hole, in the middle of the Grey Mountains, waiting for news from Tark Draan. But it didn't come. It *never* came! Without the Dsôn Aklán, we would have been wiped out in Phondrasôn.'

Aiphatòn scrutinised him with eyes like dark black holes that gave his narrow, symmetrical face an extremely sinister look.

It was said his eyes never revealed their true colour, not even at night when älfar eyes usually did. As the child of Nagsar and Nagsor Inàste, he was a shintoìt, the highest and purest being. He was invariably recognisable as one, even without the armour woven into his flesh.

'It would have been better for you all,' Aiphatòn declared in a whisper and stabbed the prone warrior in the neck. 'And for Girdlegard. But know this: *I* will make up for my mistake.'

The injured man's breath rattled as he grasped the rune-embellished spear-shaft with one hand and tried to pull it out, his sword bouncing off it ineffectually.

'The Aklán will be the next ones I dispatch into endingness. Then I will return and set your beloved Dsôn alight. I am their emperor and the älfar will meet their downfall at my hands, just like I promised an old friend of mine they would. The realisation came late, but it did come. Your death is named Aiphatòn,' he said solemnly. 'I will take your immortality from you and leave your remains to the carrion-feeders. Isn't it funny that you have that in common with the common *barbarians*? Thus the differences end.'

Gurgling, the älf died beneath the night-mare, blood running from the open wound at the corner of his mouth and dripping onto the ground. His body went limp.

Daitolór didn't move. *He must not see me.* Having heard what he had, the benàmoi had reached a decision.

Motionless, he watched as Aiphatòn pulled the narrow spear-tip out of the warrior's flesh and cleaned it on the man's clothing. Then the emperor ran off, apparently hard on Firûsha's heels.

Daitolór, whose whole unit had been taken from him in the blink of an eye by this älf, saw that the shintoìt was not wearing boots, but had taken up the pursuit barefoot.

Only once the enemy had moved further away did he stand up and throw his spear carelessly to the ground. With an adversary like Aiphatòn, wood and steel were no use.

He thought his people were fully capable of getting rid of a magus, but when the son of the Inextinguishables was against them, they were in great danger. And they would remain so until the last älf was wiped out as he had promised.

I've got to warn the Aklán. She and her brothers will find a way to stop him.

Daitolór went over to the remaining night-mare and grabbed hold of the harness, soothing the animal with a few murmured words and swinging himself into the saddle. There was no special art to reading the tracks, the hooves left clear imprints in the earth. Unfortunately, Aiphatòn had seen them just as easily.

From the black horse's back, he cast an eye over the mound of corpses, then glanced at the rim of the crater a mile away where the town and the palace towered up into the air. *Hold your ground, black heart, and every time you beat, bring endingness to our enemies.*

He had to abandon Dsôn against the wishes of the Aklán because that was the only way for him to protect Firûsha from entering endingness. The warrior-women and warriors holding out in the valley, around fifty of them or so, would be able to defend Dsôn long enough. Even without him.

Samusin, come to our aid. And I beseech you, Inàste, do not allow a shintoìt of all people to be our downfall. Daitolór felt unspeakable hatred for the emperor; the slight twinge in his face immediately told him that anger lines had formed on it.

He turned his head – and saw Aiphatòn standing right next to the night-mare. *Where did you . . . ?* Daitolór's eyes widened in fear. Before he could even move his hand to the hilt of his sword, the narrow tip of the spear was thrusting towards him.

'Why so angry, benàmoi?' said Aiphatòn with an icy cold smile. The blade penetrated through the night-mare's neck and then through the hardened leather into the warrior's chest. 'Go join your unit and let them know *who* dispatched them to endingness.'

The runes on the shaft lit up a dark green; a high-pitched crackling sound rang out, becoming louder and louder until it was the only sound in Daitolór's ears. His last thought was that there was now nobody to warn the Aklán about her deadly pursuer.

Chapter I

I have seen all kinds of characters during my life.

I have seen those who made an effort to achieve something and I have seen those who squandered their talents for nothing.

Worst of all were the ones who didn't behave well and were also unable to do anything of worth. Because they wanted to achieve a lot without putting in the effort, they were capable of the most repugnant things.

Unknown author
collected by Carmondai, master of word and image

Ishím Voróo, Älfar town of Dsôn Elhàtor, 5452nd division of unendingness (6491st solar cycle), early summer

'I couldn't help hearing the last few words you said. Incidentally, I do *not* think that Dsôn Dâkiòn needs to be destroyed.' Modôia was wearing a floor-length black dress with a train two paces long inwrought with silver and she was holding a crimson crystal goblet in her left hand. Her long blonde hair was braided into a crown to stop it getting windswept. 'You're always so quick with the destruction, my dear Ôdaiòn. Please be a little considerate. It did take a while for that town to be built.' From her tone it was clear that she was teasing the älf whose remarks she had just interrupted.

Some of her guests on the enormous terrace of white marble clapped quietly and politely, which caused even more älfar to turn around so that they could follow the unfolding entertainment better.

The sun had long since passed its zenith. The wind had made the temperature more pleasant and the taut white silken cloths protected them from the direct force of the setting daystar.

A sea breeze was coming from the west, carrying the smell of salt and freshness but also quiet, extremely repetitive drumming. This didn't bother Modôia or the nearly forty well-dressed guests in her enormous harbour house.

Ôdaiòn, a young älf in a slim-fitting, dark blue garment gave a slight bow. 'Oh, I'm familiar with your leniency, Modôia, and even I appreciate mercy towards those who are weaker. But you're wrong.' He swept his mid-length brown hair back and placed one hand on his back, standing up straight and looking her directly in the eye.

'Is that right?' Modôia treated him to a scornful smile. *You're angling for a duel?* 'Just so we're talking about the same facts, my dear fellow: when we talk about Dsôn Dâkiòn, are we talking about the town many, many miles away from our island?'

'That's right.'

'The same town that's very far inland?'

'I can't deny that, either.' He smiled a crooked smile.

Modôia took a few steps around the young älf, brandishing her crystal goblet as she did so without letting a drop of wine spill over the rim and drip onto the pale stone; her train rustled softly across the marble. 'So you're calling for the destruction of a town far away that absolutely cannot become a danger to us and is also full to the brim with älfar?' She burst out laughing. 'That would be like smashing a tiny egg because an insignificant little bird could hatch out of it that could potentially fly over one's head some moment of unendingness and . . . well . . . bestow a little grain-sized mess on one's gown.' The älf-woman stopped in front of him. 'And even *if* that were how it turned out: I can wash my gown. Leave the egg in peace.'

The guests laughed and gave another round of applause in support of Modôia. The breeze toyed with the numerous suspended wind chimes made from carved tubes of bone with silver fittings. A randomly generated, delicate melody rang out, reverberating quietly beneath the applause and the drumming.

Ôdaiòn cleared his throat, strolling around her now in his turn. 'What you failed to mention is the river. And I'm not talking about a little trickle,' he elaborated, with a note of haughtiness, 'I'm talking about a full-sized waterway, around sixty to eighty paces wide and deep enough to carry heavy ships.'

'You mean the Tronjor,' an älf-woman chipped in from the edge of the terrace.

'The very same, darling.' Ôdaiòn raised his glass in her direction gratefully. 'This river, this Tronjor, flows into the sea not all that many miles from us.' He looked at Modôia. 'Sorry, but I'm sure you know how far it is better than I do?'

'Twenty-three miles,' she said, precise about the details. She feigned cheerfulness but it was clear from looking at her that she was getting increasingly annoyed. *He is good. I know what he's trying to get at.*

Ôdaiòn smacked his forehead. 'How could I possibly forget? After all, we teach it to the youngest schoolchildren, don't we?' he cried with fake contrition which earned him the guests' laughter this time. 'And have we not had a situation where that town set their allies on us before?'

'That was a misunderstanding,' exclaimed Modôia.

'Of course. A misunderstanding. Like a mistakenly fired arrow that still hits the bullseye, to use a timely analogy,' Ôdaiòn cut in immediately.

Yet more laughter broke out.

'It didn't hit the bullseye, although it may have been flying in our direction when we smashed it to pieces in the air,' she countered.

'I accept that argument.' The älf tilted his head. 'But back to *your* imagery: how do I know that a . . . dragon or . . . the embryo of a horrific monster won't hatch from the tiny egg instead of a little bird?'

'Because we know that Dsôn Dâkiòn is allied with us in a . . . special way . . . in a friendly manner. So the egg would have glass walls. We would know what would be inside,' Modôia shot back. 'And we would be able to see it was harmless.' *That should do it.*

This time she received the applause and toasted the crowd.

'Because we believe the visible embryo wouldn't change. But what about when it came into contact with the air?' Ôdaiòn wasn't giving up, which was making the älf-woman dig her heels in. 'Let's take a tadpole, for example. Who would think a tiny black dot could turn into an animal many times its size that looks completely different?'

Now I've got you. 'By that reasoning, you think the town will turn into a great big ship, hundreds of paces wide and long, that will descend from the mountain, glide into the river and come to wipe us out?' Modôia drank a sip of wine. 'Well, my dear Ôdaiòn, I would go so far as to say that you're drunk. Go home before you fall over the balustrade and plunge into the harbour.'

The guests laughed loudly now, clapping for a long time.

Ôdaiòn smiled and raised his glass. 'I surrender, but only for this splinter of unendingness. My own analogy led me into a trap I couldn't get myself out of.'

Modôia granted him a look of approval. 'You're getting better every time. I've got to be on my guard, otherwise you might find too many supporters in Dsôn Elhàtor after all.'

He nodded gratefully and grinned.

Modôia was about to raise her hand to place it on the young älf's shoulder but a searing pain ran warningly down her spine. The old pain was setting in much too early. *I should use this opportunity and withdraw before . . .*

'It's starting!' came a joyful cry from the balustrade. 'They'll be here very soon.'

And the moment has already passed. Modôia and Ôdaiòn plunged into the stream of festively dressed guests as they moved forward to look out over the white-painted stone handrail at the sea. At first the sculptors had tried to make the handrail using skeletons, but the sun and salty air quickly made the bones porous and fragile. Before any fatal accidents could occur, they had been replaced with painted granite hewn from the walls of the island's extinct volcano.

The sea spread out before Modôia and her guests, barely a wave on its surface and glittering picturesquely. It would be the perfect moment to head to the harbour for a swim – if the onwú fleet wasn't coming towards the mouth of the harbour.

From the terrace high above the surrounding buildings, they had an unimpeded view of what was happening.

'I count twenty-one ships,' Ôdaiòn said by her side and leaned forward, resting his elbows on the railing. His aftershave smelled of pepper, of lilies and nutmeg. 'That must have taken them a lot of time. And gold.'

'The most expensive floating firewood currently at sea,' Modôia remarked, helping herself to one of the canapés being offered by the waiters. Smoked shellfish had been paired with mild gado fruit. The fruit's sweetness and freshness went wonderfully with the taste of the fish. 'You should use less aftershave or you'll attract bees.'

Ôdaiòn smiled, looking straight ahead. 'I only attract what I like.' He gestured discreetly towards a young älf-woman in a white dress. 'Describing *her* as an insect would not do her justice.'

The drumming was drifting up to them more clearly from the decks of the enemy ships. Orders were being barked out, sails reefed and dozens of oars lowered.

While the majority of the onwú fleet fell back, two armoured models were gathering way. They had long, iron, naval rams mounted on the bows, aimed at the big fence in front of the mouth of the harbour.

They are making an effort in terms of strategy. Modôia looked down.

The harbour wall was crawling with älfar. They had gathered to watch the spectacle, as if the onwú were dropping by in battleships for a joint party. There was food and laughter while children sat on the stones between the battlements to get a better view.

Modôia noticed some älfar on the wall and the terrace were placing bets. It wasn't about who would win. The question was how long the enemy would stay afloat or which of the ships would hold out longest. *I wouldn't bet on the two out in front.*

'Would you like to share what it is we're about to see?' asked Ôdaiòn eagerly. 'Will our war fleet swoop out of the secret exits and surround the onwú by any chance?'

Modôia clucked her tongue scornfully, and even this caused her pain. But there was no going back, as so often before. 'Don't be impatient. You're about to see.' She climbed onto a small platform that had been brought out and erected on her orders, then tapped her glass with the tionium signet ring on her middle finger. All attention turned to her. 'My dear guests, could I please ask that you listen for a few minutes. It will fall to me in due course to explain what the renovations in the last few moments of unendingness were for. Please keep watching the harbour to see for yourself.'

Everyone looked back to where the onwú fleet had gathered.

They will be surprised. Modôia forced herself to smile and drank some more of her wine, winking at Ôdaiòn and waiting for her cue as the conversations on the terrace temporarily fell silent. The tension grew. People were desperate to find out what the scholars had come up with.

The blonde älf-woman swallowed her fears as best she could, letting her gaze sweep over all the houses built right the way round the protected bay and stretching as far as the crater cone. *Samusin granted us such luck in reaching this island.*

Very much in the tradition of their people, the designs of the buildings were ornate yet elegant, some straight lines here, some wavy ones there. Awnings broke up the hard edges, while flags and banners fluttered in the wind.

Due to the strength of the sun, the walls and flat roofs were painted white with delicate accents of black curved lines, runes, patterns of spots and paintings. Occasionally the decorations stretched across entire streets and created an enormous image that could only be appreciated from the sea and from very far away.

At night, hundreds of lights flickered on the terraces and flat roofs as if the town were a mirror of the stars.

The very steep streets, as well as the steps and arched bridges, were inlaid with little tiles of bone; the roughened surface prevented people slipping and falling when it was wet. As soon as they were too badly damaged by heels, soles, sun and salt, they were replaced.

Roughly ten thousand älfar lived in Dsôn Elhàtor, the älfar realm that, just like Dsôn Dâkiòn, was nothing more than a big town.

A sanctuary after the many divisions of unendingness I lived through in Phondrasôn and Tark Draan. Modôia closed her eyes and tilted her face towards the sun which was now shining past the silk cloths. Ever since surviving her adventures in Tark Draan and the Grey Mountains, she loved intense warmth more than anything else; it also helped with her pain.

I've changed so much in the last twenty divisions. She sighed. *We've all changed so much. Who would have thought that Ishím Voróo might have something good in store for us if we just travelled far enough?*

'The onwú's ram-ships will arrive soon,' she heard Ôdaiòn's voice next to her. 'Isn't it about time something happened?'

'The cîani are ready to step in if necessary,' she replied without opening her eyes. 'But I trust our architects' skill.' Modôia opened her eyes and looked at the harbour. 'My dear guests, pay attention,' she said loudly. 'Keep an eye on the towers on the right and left.'

The two armoured vessels ploughed through the gentle waves, displacing the water with their low-lying bows. Foam sprayed high into the air, hitting the armour-plating that was mounted above the oarsmen to protect them from missiles.

'New iron pipelines were laid from the volcano's extinct crater down to the harbour,' Modôia said. 'The seawater that's sucked up by pumps there and then stored, shoots downhill with great force, which the pipes can now finally withstand.' The blonde älf-woman took a deep breath. *It will start very soon now.*

The naval rams were less than twenty paces from the fence when the thin white jets shot out of the lower third of the towers. Instead of striking the ships from above like stones or arrows, the concentrated water sliced through the ship's side planks at the height of the oars and shot through the slots for the rudder stocks.

Wherever the jets of water hit, the wood caved in and split.

Splinters flew inside the ships and the screams of the injured and dying oarsmen were audible from far away. Clouds of foam sprayed up, glittering and making rainbows.

Meanwhile Modôia was proudly explaining, 'The further the water flows downwards, the more constricted the pipes become. This increases the force with which it shoots out of the swivelling nozzles set into the towers.'

Since the powerful ships couldn't simply be brought to a stop, the hulls were sliced open along their entire lengths. The vessels were being torn apart more and more.

The architects are keeping their promise. Modôia watched as the barbarians plummeted into the churned up waters from the upper deck and the rowing decks.

One jet severed the naval ram on the right-hand ship with perfect precision. Falling to pieces, the wreckages reached the fence and smashed into it.

The älfar on the wall cheered and clapped. Even the guests on the terrace joined in the jubilation, and someone ran away after losing a bet.

'The pipes were laid all over the island,' Modôia cried over the furore. 'We can strike in different places and if necessary, have extra pipelines laid, so that it's even easier to defend our homeland.' She raised her goblet, the sunlight catching it and making the wine glow. 'To Dsôn Elhàtor, the Magnificent! That it may remain undefeated as it has done for the last twenty divisions of unendingness.'

'To Dsôn Elhàtor, the Magnificent,' her guests cried.

'And to Modôia,' said Ôdaiòn and held his glass out to her. 'Remain our guiding star and shine on in well-deserved splendour! Nobody could lead us better.'

Applause rang out once more, full of excitement and confidence this time as it echoed across the terrace and down into the town.

Modôia gave a very small bow. 'No, that's enough. This is too much praise,' she humbly rebuffed the adulation. 'Especially when it's my own son calling for it.'

The crowd laughed.

'He was just quicker than me, monarchess,' an älf called out. 'But you certainly deserve it, Modôia. A thousand times over.'

She climbed down from the platform with a perfect, charming smile, Ôdaiòn offering her a helping hand as she did so. 'I like competing with you,' she murmured, 'but stop demanding admiration for me.'

'Why, Mother?' The brown-haired älf grinned. 'What kind of son would I be if I didn't keep seeing to the status you deserve?'

Modôia sighed again. 'I won't be able to forbid you from doing it.'

'That's right.' Ôdaiòn hadn't let go of her slim hand and was about to guide her back into the crowd, but she stopped. 'What is it?'

'I've done my bit,' she replied gravely. The pain wiped the smile off her face. 'Now it's your turn.' Modôia pointed to the harbour. 'Whatever happens now, it's up to you to give explanations. I want to conduct the transfer of power soon, and the more present you are, the sooner they'll accept you as the future monarch of Dsôn Elhàtor.' She was aware of her influence on the island town's residents, which could practically be described as supernatural. *He will find it difficult, despite his sharp mind.* 'By the way, that shouldn't happen again.' She took her hand away from him.

'What do you mean?' he asked, perplexed.

'You letting me win. It was very obvious that you deliberately let yourself be driven into a corner during our debating contest.' Modôia placed her hand on the back of his neck, drew him towards her and kissed him lightly on the forehead. A blessing-like gesture. 'Rule her well.' Then she turned and withdrew, to the sympathetic applause of her guests. The monarchess had fulfilled her duty.

Nobody had noticed how difficult it was for her to do so; she appeared to be feeling fantastic. But she was fit to burst with the pain.

Modôia returned to the house, holding herself upright as long as she was still within sight of the älfar, but after rounding a bend, she collapsed.

She quickly leaned against the white wall decorated with mosaics and pressed her lips together to stop herself screaming. Her spine burned, sending pain into every corner of her body.

The medicine is wearing off more and more quickly. I should have gone for a higher dosage. She was not the only person in Elhàtor who had had to pay this price for a new homeland, and yet it seemed to her that she was suffering the most from the consequences. No cîani could help her – on the contrary, using magic made her agony worse. The sun helped. The sun and the essences she got from her most trusted confidante, Leïóva.

With some difficulty, she dragged herself into her bedchamber where a concerned face awaited her.

'It's getting stronger,' was Leïóva's assessment. She was wearing a simple white dress, her black hair flowing down over her strong shoulders. She met Modôia and supported her as she guided her to the bed.

Leïóva picked up the bottle of elixir that had been set out, holding it to Modôia's chattering lips. 'I warned you about too much exertion.'

'I thought I . . .' The pain robbed Modôia of the power of speech and she sank onto the bed. After just one mouthful, her mind drifted away into soft black cotton wool.

'You have fulfilled your duty. Leave the land to your son. I'll watch over you,' she could still hear Leïóva's soothing words and feel her cooling fingers stroking her temples.

Then Modôia drifted off, floating in pleasant sensations, far from all pain.

Tark Draan, Human kingdom of Gauragar, in the foothills of the Grey Mountains, 5452nd division of unendingness (6491st solar cycle), early summer

Aiphatòn stopped at the crossroads and let his gaze wander over the stony paths. *Where did you make a turn off?* As he couldn't tell anything from a quick glance, he crouched down, leaning on his spear.

The unique älf had dashed through a flourishing Girdlegard, jogging steadily, and followed the tracks that Firûsha and her little entourage had left in the ground. The night-mares' shoes and the slight scorch marks stood out unmistakably in the soil.

Hurrying along, he ran through sprouting fields of grain and across meadows with gnarled old fruit trees. He raced down roads and paths, rushed through thick woods and soon he was back in great expanses of grassy plain.

His legs constantly rose and fell. He leaped over obstacles, hurrying through sunshine, rain and storms. He took food from people's pantries along the way without asking, or picked ripe fruit. He kept breaks to a minimum.

The hem of his long black trouser garment, which went from his hips to his toes, was tattered, the fabric extremely dirty by now, but he didn't care. His wiry torso had tanned in the unrelenting sunshine.

The spur that drove him onwards was hunting down the dangerous älf-woman.

He had also already dispatched the southern älfar – who had made it to Girdlegard because of him – to certain death using insidious poison. That didn't mean he could wash away the guilt he had incurred in the previous cycles, but he could eliminate any more threats to Girdlegard.

Meanwhile Ireheart and the armies of the dwarves and humans in conjunction with the maga Coïra would triumph over Tirîgon, Sisaroth and Lot-Ionan. Aiphatòn had no doubt about that – and for that very reason he needed to catch the Aklán, who had a very specific goal when she fled. There was a reason why Firûsha wanted to get to the north and enter the Grey Mountains. He was sure of it.

Nothing to be found. No matter how hard he tried, he couldn't make out any tracks this time. It seemed like the rock was in league with the Aklán. He straightened up. *How can that be?*

The night-mares moved with incredible speed. Even on a reliable horse Aiphatòn would not have caught up with the flesh-eating creatures. He hadn't passed a farmstead with outstanding steeds yet, so he had kept on running. It gave him greater agility.

Aiphatòn turned his black-eyed gaze to the mountain slopes that soared into the air up ahead, an increasingly leaden grey.

He saw steep, sharp-edged rock faces that would hurt you as soon as you touched them, as well as cloud-wreathed peaks in strange shapes that the dwarves had given appropriate names. Shadowy ditches miles long and filled with snow and ice ran along the sides, making climbing extremely dangerous. There were also porous ledges and fragile overhangs, narrow treacherous paths and storms that picked up quickly and spelled death to any inexperienced hiker.

What can they be doing there? There's no way out. There was nothing for it but to follow each of the four paths for quite a few paces, perhaps even for miles, until he found reliable tracks. Once again, that would mean him losing time, which was lucky for Firûsha.

All right then. Aiphatòn chose the northern road, which was wide enough to allow two carts to pass each other.

He shouldered the rune spear and balanced it so that the spear didn't slip or tilt to one side as he jogged along. The älf liked to have his hands free.

His thoughts wandered, but he kept his gaze riveted on the rock underneath him.

This hunt shouldn't actually have been taking place, because Firûsha ought to have been dead. During an attempted attack, she had been struck by Coïra's magical charge and had plunged many paces deep into the sea.

He still couldn't understand how the älf-woman had managed to return from the bottom of the ocean. *Ireheart sounded so convinced when he had spoken of her death.*

But as Aiphatòn was all too aware, almost anything was possible when an Aklán was involved.

She and her brothers had led many älfar out of Phondrasôn and into Girdlegard, conquering mile after mile using cunning, magic and phenomenal combat skills, before he and his älfar invaded from the south. *She won't evade endingness a second time.*

Aiphatòn's guilt was constantly on his mind, with every step he took, from the moment he woke up till the moment he fell asleep. And even in sleep it didn't spare him – the memories and images pursued him into his dreams: the vanquishing of Girdlegard, his merciless troops, the enslavement of the tribes, his title of the 'emperor of the älfar' and the ruthless hunt for elves.

But with Tungdil's return came the realisation – no, the *awakening* – that he had become the monster he had never wanted to be.

What demonic frenzy did I succumb to, that I acted in the past as if I were depraved like my parents? Besides, he had once sworn to the dwarf never to become like that.

Evil dwelt in him and occasionally it was able to gain the upper hand.

That must never happen again. Henceforth, no älf in Girdlegard can be allowed to live. His own death was a foregone conclusion. His death, and before that, the death of every last älf.

The road climbed sharply upwards and was leading him towards a town with two guards standing in front of its gate, as he could make out after a few bends in the path. Carts rattled along ahead of him carrying barrels and wooden beams.

To avoid drawing attention to himself, he hid in the shadow of the rock face. And there, in some dried lichen close to the edge of the path, he saw half a horseshoe print that matched the night-mares' shoes.

They rode along here. Aiphatòn looked at the unfamiliar town.

He dismissed the idea that the group surrounding Firûsha had dispersed. They hadn't separated before now, why would they start now?

Is this ordinary town their destination? What could be of interest to the triplets there?

He couldn't let anybody notice his arrival; he wanted to avoid a commotion. He could forget disguising himself as a beggar in rags – the perpetually black eyes that he had inherited as a shintoìt and his slightly pointy ears gave him away as an älf. The news of his arrival would spread swiftly and reach Firûsha and then the element of surprise would be lost.

But I could get inside if I was in one of the barrels. Aiphatòn took the spear off his shoulder and silently caught up to the nearest cart, jumped onto the loading area and crouched down to check what was inside the containers.

From the bung holes on the tops and sides it was clear that a liquid was inside, and judging by the faint smell, it was wine.

He quickly tapped the side opening of one barrel and let a considerable amount of liquid run out. The pale wine flowed onto the street behind the wagon, the splashing sound lost in the creaking and clattering of the wheels. He stopped up the hole with dirt and resin he had scraped from the slats of the carriage.

Aiphatòn hid his spear underneath one of the rolled-up tarpaulins, hoping that would be enough to escape the guards' notice. *Otherwise I'll draw a lot of attention when I invade the town.*

It took some skill for him to get the top open so that he could ease himself into the fermented grape juice and pull the lid back over the opening.

He didn't find the wine's aroma all that pleasant, and with every pebble the cart jolted over, the swill sloshed over his face and bald head. He refrained from taking a mouthful of it.

Aiphatòn couldn't help grinning. *No doubt Ireheart would have lapped it up until he could stand up in it without drowning.*

The wagon jolted onwards before slowing and coming to a stop. It seemed they had reached the gate.

'I'm bringing the wine for the mayor,' he heard the cart-driver's voice, muffled by the wood.

'We know that. We've been notified about you,' came the bored reply. 'You can . . .'

'Hey, what's this here? One of these barrels is leaking,' a second guard interrupted him, his voice coming from the rear of the cart and therefore very close to Aiphatòn. 'The side bunghole doesn't seem to have been sealed properly.'

The driver cursed. 'They'll take that out of my wages. And I told them they should check the stoppers. That bloody jolting!' Judging by the rumblings that ensued, the driver was preparing to climb up onto the loading area.

'Get going, you old sod,' the other guard ordered him, laughing. 'You're blocking the gate on us and I can see the extra-long wagon with the timber down there.'

Something scratched at Aiphatòn's barrel, followed by a firm smack. 'There, the cork fits nice and snug,' called the guard. 'This way, at least you'll get as far as the mayor's wine cellar without losing any more.'

Aiphatòn exhaled as the cart rolled on.

It would have been easy for him to leap out of his hiding place, overpower the watchmen and violently force his way into the town, but he would rather be discreet. If the Aklán and her entourage were still here, he wanted to ambush them.

I have no idea what this town is called. He hadn't spotted any signposts along the way. It was either insignificant and small or so big that everyone knew how to get there. *In any case, the boss likes wine. A lot of wine.*

It was a long time before the wagon stopped again.

Then the driver ran around the loading area, murmured something, hummed a song and hit the sides of the barrels, probably with a hammer, so that he could tell from the sound whether he had lost any more grape juice. His checks complete, he jumped down off the cart and called out that the delivery for the mayor had arrived.

There was silence.

Aiphatòn pressed cautiously against the lid – and nothing happened.

Just as he was starting to assume the wood had become stuck, he heard a soft laugh outside.

'We know you're in there,' he heard a man's voice. 'You're surrounded by my best crossbow archers.'

Aiphatòn summoned up his magic powers, but waited.

'My name is Kerjan Münzler and I'm the mayor of Güldenwand.' He heard the man again. 'In the name of the Dsôn Aklán, I'm arresting you, Aiphatòn, self-proclaimed emperor of the älfar. If you don't come out, the bolts will penetrate through the wood. We can shoot you dead even in your hiding place.'

This just gets better and better. He toyed with the thought of tasting some of the wine after all. 'In case you didn't hear,' he answered loudly, 'the triplets' reign is over. Girdlegard is making every effort to defend itself from them. You no longer have to prove any loyalty to Firûsha, unless she's standing next to you with a sword.'

'She's not. And she has informed us about the uprisings against the Dsôn Aklán,' replied the mayor. 'But Güldenwand remains loyal to the triplets. My family swore loyalty to Firûsha once and I am abiding by that oath. We owe her too much to abandon her now.'

Ah. Well, well, well. That explains them making their way to Gülden-wand. A safe area. Aiphatòn took some deep breaths and had to suppress a cough. The fumes from the wine were tickling his throat and making him feel slightly light-headed. *Firûsha is, or was, here: so I can learn more from Münzler.* But first Aiphatòn needed to get out of the barrel. *I'll act submissive and lull him into a false sense of security.* 'Can I come out?'

'Yes. But if you look for your spear, you're not going to find it. *I* have it.' Kerjan laughed. 'Come on, get out so that we can put you in chains.'

Aiphatòn thumped the barrel walls to his left and right at the same time and it broke open; the rings hit the loading area with a rattle and the pale wine slopped out of the cart and onto the ground.

'Here I am.' Slowly, he stood up and looked around.

The cart-driver had brought the wagon into a huge barn that could withstand the heavy mountain storms and protected everything stored inside. A vaulted ceiling stretched over the älf's head as well as some rafters with hooks, ropes and pulleys dangling from them. The windows were too small to escape through.

Just as Münzler had claimed, the men stood in a circle around the cart. Aiphatòn counted a dozen archers and two dozen armoured guards armed with spears, shields and swords. The pairs of eyes looking up at him from behind their helmets were mostly extremely alert, although some also looked anxious. It was clear they were afraid of what he was going to do next. He spotted some grain scattered in the corners. So the barn was mainly used as a granary.

He recognised the mayor straight away. The brown-haired man stood out with his sumptuous clothes, his ostentatious wealth resplendent on his fingers and around his neck. He had commissioned rings and necklaces in every kind of precious metal in existence.

Aiphatòn's lip curled. *He must weigh ten pounds less without his jewellery.* 'I surrender.'

Münzler, who couldn't have been all that old, laughed as he brandished the iron chains and shackles in his right hand; in his left hand he was holding the rune spear which looked hopelessly incongruous in his fingers. 'That's more sensible than the Aklán predicted. She warned us you would double-cross us.' He threw the chains to one of the guards. 'Put them on him.'

The man caught the metal shackles and walked slowly towards the älf.

'What's going to happen to me?' Aiphatòn remained calm and jumped down off the wagon, landing right in front of the armed guard who flinched and tentatively lifted the handcuffs to put them on the prisoner.

Münzler stroked the forlorn, thin, dark beard on his chin. 'The Aklán wants us to detain you here and keep you in our dungeon until she and her brothers secure peace. The rumour is that the älfar from the south have been wiped out. Or rather: that you poisoned them, you traitor.' He ran one finger along the shaft of the spear, pressing a fingernail into the runes. 'Your fate is to be decided later, although I would be more than happy to execute you on the spot.'

'All right,' Aiphatòn held his fists out to the guard in resignation. 'Where was the Aklán headed?'

Münzler laughed, a gold molar glinting. 'That's not your concern. You're going to stew in our jail and wait.' He scrutinised the confiscated weapon. 'I like this spear. The runes are exquisitely crafted and . . . Is it made entirely of metal? It seems very light to me if so.'

'It's the same alloy my plates of armour are made from,' the älf explained calmly. 'It could be mistaken for tionium but it's more than that.'

The soldier placed the iron rings around the prisoner's wrists and realised they didn't fit securely. 'His arms are too thin, sir,' he informed the mayor, out of his depth. 'He could just take his hands out.' He slid the pointless handcuffs off to demonstrate.

Münzler sent one of the guards to get chains and padlocks to tie the prisoner up with. He gripped the spear and lifted it up, examining the shaft. 'An alloy harder than steel?'

Aiphatòn nodded. 'You've acquired a one-of-a-kind trophy there.'

The mayor tried to swing and twirl the weapon, then did a playful stab in the älf's direction, his ostentatious necklaces jangling. It looked very clumsy. Münzler obviously did not often find himself in the embarrassing position of using a weapon himself.

The älf suppressed a laugh and looked at the soldier who was still standing hesitantly in front of him with the handcuffs, unsure what to do.

'It feels very well balanced,' Münzler said, claiming to appreciate the mastery of the spear and put the blunt end back on the ground.

Aiphatòn decided to turn the tables. He had hoped that the mayor would blab, but he didn't seem willing to share any more information about Firûsha. *At least not voluntarily.* 'And another thing I don't want to keep from you,' he began. 'You can make the runes light up.'

'Because of that alloy you talked about?' Münzler peered at the weapon. 'Do you have to leave the spear in the sun for that, so that it stores up its power?' He looked thoughtfully at Aiphatòn. 'No, with you people I'm sure it's the moon that makes the runes light up. Am I right?'

'It's magic, actually.' Aiphatòn made a small gesture and leaped vertically upwards as quick as a flash, hiding among the rafters from the impending crossbow bolts; cries of surprise came from his captors' mouths. At the same time, he stretched his hand out.

The symbols on the shaft and the blade gleamed and the spear slipped out of Münzler's fingers to fly to its true master. As it did so, the weapon ran through the guardsman who was meant to put the shackles on the älf and snatched him up into the air with it. The handcuffs fell to the ground with a clanking sound as the archers finally recovered from their stupor and shot at the escapee.

The thick metal tips studded their own man all over, but his screams of pain stopped abruptly.

Aiphatòn twisted the spear shaft, making the corpse slide off. It fell down and hit the loading area and the wine barrels with a bang.

He jumped down after it into the midst of the guards while the crossbows weren't yet ready with fresh rounds. The archers died first, killed by swift stabs and slashes.

Then the älf threw himself at the guards who attacked him with their swords. But they couldn't find a way to hurt an enemy who wouldn't keep still: he ducked, dodged and jumped relentlessly, whipping around, launching himself off bystanders' shields to wield his bloody spear with double the force.

You've had so much time to study my people's tactics and you've learned nothing. Aiphatòn didn't even need his magic, or darkness or fear, to hold his own against a superior force that just surrendered. *Nothing at all.* With one blow from the blunt end to the neck, he floored the last of the soldiers, who fell face first into a pool of blood.

Münzler was already at the exit about to escape.

'Wait.' Aiphatòn hurled the spear after the man. 'I have another question for you.'

The blade penetrated his forearm and nailed the mayor firmly to the door. Shrieking, he tried to pull the blade out, but it was stuck fast in the wood. 'There was nothing I could do,' he whimpered, tears in his eyes.

Aiphatòn went over and fixed his black eyes on him. For the man, it must have been like being observed by pitch-black precious stones shimmering weakly in the light. 'What exactly does your family owe the Aklán?' he asked quietly.

'*What?* That's what you want to know?' Münzler screamed at him and spat. He bit his lips until they bled. The pain must have been severe, the spear had definitely gone through the bone. 'Is that . . .'

'I'm trying to understand why you are *so* grateful that you would willingly rush towards death for her. Because of gold maybe?' Aiphatòn interrupted softly. 'Were you really so stupid as to think that you and your guards would arrest me?'

Münzler gulped and looked away from him, staring blankly at his arm where the expensive fabric was turning red as it became drenched in his blood. 'The Aklán told us you had as good as lost your power,' he whispered. 'My ancestors . . . she made one of my forefathers on the council into the mayor and since then our family has . . .'

'So you'd give up your life for a job?' Aiphatòn ran a hand over the jewellery around the man's neck. '*And* for wealth.' He pointed one outstretched finger of his armoured right hand at the dead guards. 'They died for you. For a fool.'

'Please, I . . . I can tell you where she was headed.' Münzler seemed to have grasped, despite the pain and shock, that the situation had changed and that he depended on the emperor's mercy. 'She wants to go up to the Jagged Crown.'

'And she told you that?'

'No. But I'd bet my life on it.'

'Which is in my hands anyway,' the älf added, laughing. 'What is the Jagged Crown?'

'A mountain half a mile to the north of Güldenwand,' spluttered the brown-haired man, his face contorting in pain. His blood was trickling gently out of the fabric and splashing onto the floor. 'Apparently the Aklán sent a troop of her best veterans up there many cycles ago. But they never came back.'

'How long ago might that have been?'

'Around . . . two hundred cycles ago,' he stammered.

'What's up there?'

Münzler was breathing faster, the colour visibly draining from his face. It wouldn't be much longer till he lost consciousness. 'I don't know. But there's a persistent rumour that there was a passage. Out of Girdlegard.' He slumped, but was kept upright by the spear which made him gasp out.

She wants to flee and leave her brothers behind? Aiphatòn couldn't believe this outrageous theory. 'A mountain pass?'

'I don't know!'

No. There must be something else more valuable to the Aklán up there. An artefact perhaps? Brought from the depths of Phondrasôn and too unpredictable to use under normal circumstances. Just like the demon who helped Sinthoras and Caphalor in the conquest some time ago. Aiphatòn needed certainty. 'How do I get there?'

In just a few whispered words Münzler described where the way up to the path was located. 'But you'll never manage it. The Aklán won't either,' he groaned. 'Nobody comes back.'

Aiphatòn placed a hand against the spear and the runes lit up, then he pulled the blade out of the wood and flesh as easily as if it had been stuck in butter. The mayor fell at his feet. 'Then Girdlegard can consider itself lucky that the Aklán and I will both go missing there.' He gave the man a disgusted look. 'You, on the other hand, will not get anything out of it.' Aiphatòn raised his foot and kicked.

The outer edge of the braced sole hit Münzler in the back of the neck and cracked the vertebrae in half.

Nobody who supports the älfar should remain alive. People like you enabled them to wield their power. Aiphatòn took two cloaks from the dead guards and threw them round his shoulders, then grabbed himself a pair of boots before leaving the stone barn by a side door.

More soldiers approached him, but nobody stopped him because he was wearing the guards' cloaks and masking his real build from view. Besides, because of his dip in the barrel, he stank of wine like a terrible drunkard. Nobody suspected he was an älf, let alone the former emperor, underneath.

Aiphatòn wanted to stay in the town long enough to steal all the equipment he'd need for the climb, and then he wanted to hunt down the Aklán.

He was sure Münzler had not lied to him and Firûsha really had ridden up into the mountains. *But what is she looking for up there?*

Chapter II

It is better to feign ignorance than to announce dangerous knowledge.

Wise saying of the Älfar
Collected by Carmondai, master of word and image

Ishím Voróo, Älfar town of Dsôn Dâkiòn, 5452nd division of unendingness (6491st solar cycle), early summer

Iriïanora stepped onto the north tower's wraparound observation deck. Three paces wide, it ran around the upper third of the outer wall like a horizontal collar. It was the second highest point of a town built entirely on a wide mountain in the middle of a rolling plain. *What an awful summer. Not even a breath of air here.*

The pale clouds looked like they were glued to the sky, not budging an inch. The building that towered up behind the young älf-woman did cast some shade but there was no escape from the stifling heat. Even though she had thrown on just a thin, blue linen dress, sweat was running down her slim body.

An älf with short red hair was standing with his back to her, using the gap between two battlements as a table and spreading a map out on it. His pale torso was bare – he was wearing nothing but knee breeches and wide, flat, leather shoes. More scrolls peeked out of his shoulder bag.

The great Bethòras. Punctual and exemplary. Irïanora smoothed her long blonde hair back and approached him. 'Sorry I'm late, but my uncle wanted to discuss a few pressing matters.'

He nodded before turning around. 'I was enjoying the view and I took the opportunity to check the accuracy of the map.'

They gave each other a lingering hug in greeting.

Irïanora noticed his fresh aftershave and took a deep breath in to smell as much of it as possible. She saw compasses, a ruler and optical instruments lying on top of the drawing. Next to that lay a coal-dust pencil and a sheet of paper with notes all over it. 'Revisions need to be made?' She let him go.

Bethòras smiled. 'Nothing major. A few trees were added and the riverbed over there' – he lifted his arm to point towards it – 'extended eastwards. If we were to rely on judging by eye, we would be no better than the barbarians and monsters and, like them, we'd be surprised when something got trapped or stuck.'

'My uncle knows why he made you the master architect and cartographer.' Irïanora looked around to check if they were still alone.

'Nobody was following me,' the älf said, taking a folded drawing out of his pocket, opening it up and placing it on top of the map of the town's surrounding areas.

They didn't waste any time admiring the beauty of Dâkiòn, which they were very familiar with.

It became clear to newcomers that the town had already existed in a different form before the älfar arrived, but it had been derelict and unfinished. It was built on a mountain, but a ravine separated the upper and lower parts of the town – there was just one wide stonework bridge stretching across it. Nobody knew whether the original builders had created the chasm on purpose to protect the upper town more easily in case of attack; the footbridge could simply be demolished.

Legend had it the original inhabitants and architects were enormous creatures. This was evident from the fact that the floor plans of all the houses, palaces, streets and other buildings looked four times too big. The average home had ceilings twelve paces high or more, and the sovereign's palace looked as if it had been constructed so that giants could do gymnastics in it.

The älfar had completed the buildings, all of which were made of black stone, and added elaborate extensions to the massive structures; they had decorated them with the artistic attributes of their tribe, from bone carvings to specific types of stone, ornaments, precious gems, paintings and runes.

Its scale gave the town its epithet: the Majestic. The roofs, the towers, the supporting arches and pillars reached far into the sky, making it clear that it was unconquerable. There was only one footbridge to the upper town. Nobody in their right mind would dare to attack – but there was a legend that some day, the giants would return at dawn to demand their town back.

The two young älfar had other demands on their minds: preparations for war.

Bethòras pointed to the lines that represented a ship, with details of the length, width, draught, mast height and much more. 'I made a start on a little draft.'

Irïanora pored over the blueprint, her heart beating loudly in her chest with excitement and joy. 'How many warriors can that take?'

'It depends what equipment they're carrying,' said Bethòras, avoiding the question. 'In the light armour that I recommend for this kind of mission, it would be around fifty. On top of that, there would be smaller catapults on deck and the necessary cargo, as well as the crew.' He pointed at the corresponding parts on the sketch each time he explained something.

Her brow furrowed. 'How much time and money would it take?'

'As soon as we have the wood, it will take sixty moments. Our carpenters are good enough and quick enough to implement the plans I give them.' Bethòras pointed to the wide river two miles away that flowed past the town. 'There are two spots where the shipyard could be built without having to clear soil away. I've studied the frekoriers' sketches which had exact descriptions of how . . .'

'Aren't we having some wonderful weather today?' came the sound of a cheery old voice from the doorway. 'But I do hope a storm will relieve us of this mugginess. You barely take a step or two and your clothes are soaked through with sweat.'

Irïanora and Bethòras did not turn around straight away because they knew who had come to pay them a visit, unasked and unannounced.

'Not a word,' the blonde älf-woman whispered to the cartographer and picked up the drawing of the boat, folding it with calm but swift movements and sticking it underneath her dress. In the space of a heartbeat, she had plastered a winning smile on her face. 'Uncle,' she said loudly and turned round to him.

'Are you enjoying the view?' Shôtoràs walked towards them, his right hand leaning on a walking stick made from silver, tionium and bone inlay. He was the sovereign of Dsôn Dâkiòn and undoubtedly the oldest älf living in Ishím Voróo.

There was a distinct clack every time the end of his stick touched the stone flags, as if the älf was trying to awaken something living in the ground beneath their feet.

Like most älfar, he wore a black robe wrapped around his broadly built body. His right leg dragged slightly, as it had done ever since blood poisoning had nearly cost him his limb. In terms of physical strength, he was still a match for every warrior in the town's army, but as Irïanora knew, he was not as quick as he once was.

His most powerful weapon, which he knew how to deploy so well, was his mind. And that was the very thing she feared.

'Not only are we enjoying the view, we're working. I asked him to check the map of the surrounding area,' she lied and gave a small bow. Bethòras followed suit.

'What did you find out?' Shôtoràs had reached them and was smoothing back the thick, light grey hair that reached the nape of his neck. A thin beard glinted around his chin.

'There were minor details to be corrected,' the young älf explained, clearing his throat. He turned to the side, revealing the papers; he briefly outlined what had been going on two miles from the mountain.

'Trees. How they grow and stretch upwards,' mused Shôtoràs and looked over at the river Tronjor, 'as if there was something for them to capture or prop up in the clouds.' He smiled contentedly. 'Wasn't it lucky our Creating Spirit brought us to this place?'

'*You* brought the survivors here, Uncle,' Irïanora corrected him kindly. 'And for that, Dsôn Dâkiòn owes you its thanks above and beyond death.'

The sovereign burst out laughing. 'My *mortality*. How little I think of it. And yet I probably should. I've been alive for so many divisions of unendingness.' His expression grew more solemn, his gaze pensive. 'How painful it was for me to see Dsôn Faïmon fall. And how much it hurt to lose so many of my tribe's little towns to the barbarians and monsters after we thought we were safe from the nomadic towers. And why did we lose? Because we didn't have unity.'

Not again. Irïanora knew what was about to come next: a discourse on what had been experienced and endured, which she herself knew only from stories. The banishment by the Dorón Ashont; the lengthy trials and tribulations through Ishím Voróo; how the numbers of älfar kept dwindling and finally Shôtoràs had led a small band far into the north to settle on this mountain in the enormous ruins of the fortress and consolidate a realm of their own. *He's too old.*

Shôtoràs stamped his stick on the ground, making a banging and rattling sound all at once. 'From the black ruins, left for us by long-departed giants, we created our new homeland, entirely free of the Inextinguishables. Now we live undisturbed and safe. Because we are of *one* mind, united. The other town states remained susceptible to attacks by the beasts because of their own disputes.' He laughed bitterly. 'Wars between the älfar. *Wars!* Just imagine it, the chaotic and horrible times we used to live in.'

Irïanora groaned with boredom. 'We know about the sensitivities and long-standing hostilities between the families and their political opponents,' she said with a long-suffering undertone. 'Uncle, you've told me so many stories about . . .'

'Only two towns survived that chaotic bloodbath. Us – Dsôn Dâkiòn, the Majestic – and Dsôn Elhàtor, the Magnificent,' the old älf went on, ignoring her objection.

Bethòras leaned against a battlement, listening to the sovereign's remarks out of politeness.

'Neither of these towns has ever been conquered. Although I don't trust Modôia and her son, I do respect her,' Shôtoràs was speaking to himself. 'Despite her young age and the fact that she comes from Tark Draan.'

'People say she's from Dsôn Sòmran, actually, which was once located in the Grey Mountains,' Irïanora interjected and dropped her smile. He had interrupted their meeting to babble away, because he clearly felt lonely in his palace. *An incredible test of patience.*

'Apologies.' Shôtoràs finally seemed to notice that he was boring them with his monologues. He lifted his stick and tapped the handle, which was modelled on a bird of prey's beak, against his bearded chin. 'How did I get onto that?'

'The trees,' said Bethòras, eagerly coming to his aid.

'Ah yes. The trees.' The grey-haired sovereign sighed. 'That reminds me of life in the old Dsôn, when I was still a member of the Constellations – one of the älfar with power over the Inextinguishables –' he told the red-haired cartographer as if he needed to explain it to him, 'who were against expanding the kingdom. Unlike the Comets.' He turned his black eyes to the treetops. 'Now that I really think about it, we could equally have called ourselves *Trees*: with deep roots, powerful and strong, braving and surviving the storm in order to preserve the land where we were born.'

Irïanora gave a slight but deliberate cough. The heat and twaddle were making her impatient and assertive. 'Uncle, don't be cross with me, but Bethòras and I would like to continue our walk and check the map.'

Shôtoràs clucked his tongue. 'Of course. I've started telling stories yet again.' He turned on his heel; as he did so, the hem of his billowing robe caused a slight draught, enough to lift up the map.

The thin paper slipped off the stone and threatened to glide into the abyss.

'Watch out!' Bethòras rushed forward and reached for a corner of the drawing to stop it sailing down into Dsôn Dâkiòn's streets where he'd have to painstakingly search for it.

Meanwhile Shôtoràs continued pivoting on the spot. The curved handle of his stick hit the young älf out of nowhere between his bare shoulder blades, shoving him over the wall with some force. As Bethòras disappeared, screaming, into the abyss, the metallic beak swooped down and pinned the map to the spot.

'Take it,' he commanded Irïanora harshly. She was staring at him in horror.

'You ... you've ...' Trembling with fear and fury, she took the paper out of harm's way.

Shôtoràs used the handle to thrust directly into the fold of her blue dress where she had hidden the drawing of the ship. The sharp, curved beak made of tionium pierced the paper and scratched her skin. One jerk and the sovereign had got his hands on it. He ignored the gash in the älf-woman's skin and the tear in her robe.

Bastard! Irïanora took a breath in, the scratch burning. She was familiar with that cold expression on her uncle's face so she remained silent as a precaution.

The first distant screams of the älfar who had discovered Bethòras' body dashed to pieces in the street rang through the quiet air.

'Unity,' repeated Shôtoràs and held up the folded drawing to underscore his words, her blood spattered on it. 'That goes for our town too. I cannot tolerate my own niece pursuing plans that run counter to what I consider right and what is necessary for our survival.'

'I just wanted to build a boat to travel along the Tronjor and . . .' Her voice quivered and she balled her hands into fists.

'You,' he interrupted, hissing at her, 'would like to build a *fleet* to travel down the river and the coast as far as Elhàtor and attack the island.'

'It's just a small *ship*,' she protested.

'It's a *start*,' Shôtoràs snapped at her. 'A start that will end in war and lead to the downfall of both towns. Look around you: what happened to the other settlements? They quarrelled with each other and fell. Do you think' – he took a limping stride towards her – 'that I can allow that?'

'And what if I had a plan to bring Modôia and her followers to their knees?' Irïanora jutted her chin out.

'You haven't got a plan. If you're alluding to your childish attempts to incite the onwú and other maritime tribes against Elhàtor, I'm telling you now: let it go, niece.'

'Think of the power we'd have if Elhàtor was under tribute to us. Their fleet is undefeated and unrivalled.' She gulped, excited. 'And we could finally have our revenge for Modôia enticing so many of our residents away from us . . . on the way to the sea when she . . .'

As quick as a flash, Shôtoràs grasped his stick and hit her hard in the side so that she crumpled with a cry of pain and slid down the wall to the ground. 'Don't you dare try it again,' he threatened her. 'Next time, I'll hit you with the beak. Two towns, bound by respect and cautious regard. There will be nothing more than that.'

He tore the sketch of the ship into tiny scraps in front of her and threw them over the wall. The little pieces spread like snow and spun away, scattering as they flew through the air and seeming to melt like flakes in the heat.

'There, they're following their creator. Now I'm going to find a new cartographer. This one wasn't as careful about integrity as his job required.' The sovereign limped back to the doorway and disappeared through it. 'Anyone who succumbs to your way of thinking will suffer the endingness,' his voice echoed hollowly from the tower.

Miserable, old, repulsive . . . Irïanora breathed in and out several times then let out a short, piercing cry filled with her fury, her sense of powerlessness and her disappointment. The anger lines flashed across her face, her skin warmed up and an ache masked the pain in her side for two or three heartbeats.

Finally she got up, groaning, and looked down over the battlements.

A hundred paces away she saw Bethòras' mangled body lying on the street between the black stone houses, älfar crowding around it. The unmistakeable red stains and smears on two roofs told her that the cartographer had hit their sturdy surfaces during his fall, before his body ended up on the road. *A hideous death. And undeserved.*

Two watchmen hurried over and attended to the fallen man. One man raised his head and looked up at the tower.

Irïanora automatically drew back.

They couldn't have recognised her. Besides, the sovereign would attest that it was an accident caused by carelessness while they were checking the maps.

I must never underestimate him again. The young älf-woman walked over to the steps that led down from the tower. She didn't use the lift, even though it was quicker. She wanted – or rather, needed – to stretch her legs.

As Irïanora hurried down step after step, her defiance returned: she would send a boat down the river. *Or at least a handful of scouts, and then I'll get my war – and it will end in Dâkiòn's triumph.*

Her hands instinctively balled themselves into fists once more.

Yes, her uncle was old.

Very old.

And ready for endingness.

Then she would see what Dsôn Dâkiòn said about a war against Elhàtor.

Tark Draan, Älfar realm of Dsôn Bhará, formerly the elf realm Lesinteïl, 5452nd division of unendingness (6491st solar cycle), early summer

. . . I assume, based on the aforementioned reasons, that the battle of T versus G took a different course than has been claimed and no shapeshifter was involved. Carmondai put down the quill he had written these last lines with.

His back hurt but he was trying to ignore it. The aching in his finger joints was either from the chilly damp in his accommodation or the meagre rations he was allowed.

Carmondai read through his notes again in the greenish-yellow light from the phosphorescent moss. They contained his theories on the events that took place during the exile of the Dsôn Aklán. The duel that Tirîgon supposedly fought single-handedly against a shapeshifter was, in his telling, overflowing with discrepancies.

Carmondai did not believe everything the triplets had told him without doing his own research.

For that *very* reason, he had been stuck in this spartan room – probably underneath the siblings' palace – for what felt like a hundred divisions of unendingness.

The aged älf with long, brown hair had experienced and endured a lot, from the thick of battle and the lightning-swift cûithones, to sea voyages, a long stay in Phondrasôn and dangerous journeys through Tark Draan during the period of the Inextinguishables.

Rarely had he found himself in the predicament of having to sit around waiting.

But on returning to Tark Draan with the triplets, fate had turned against him – or else Samusin was suddenly demanding a sacrifice in return for everything good that the älf had been granted: Carmondai had spent the last cycles, or more specifically, tenths of divisions of unendingness, under lock and key.

He constantly had to turn over the hourglass standing on his desk because it was the only means he had of telling whether it was night or day above ground.

He seemed to be ageing fast down here, as if radiation was hastening his physical decay. *I cannot remember my eyes ever burning or feeling tired before.*

Treated kindly by the Aklán at first, they later arrested him because of the unrelenting, probing questions he was asking the northern älfar. They had him thrown into an almost forgotten, dusty room, with his books, writings, notes and sketches thrown in after him. The respect for his words was too great to just destroy them, but nobody was going to see them again.

Obscurity – that is the fate in store for writers and writing. Carmondai sighed and looked at the window he had painted for himself on the thinly plastered wall. *Even Phondrasôn was nicer than this.* The motifs that looked like they were beyond the window pane were ones he sketched out on paper and changed according to his mood.

His eyes flitted over the old Dsôn Balsur that he had built for the Inextinguishables. He had committed every detail to paper, from the Bone Tower to the palaces and temples; at the bottom of the page stood Caphalor and his lover.

That was so long ago. Carmondai rubbed the back of his aching neck. *They're long dead, and I ought to be too.*

He was supplied with rations, ink and paint, occasionally with clean clothes, but the Aklán did not allow him anything else. He was not allowed to see the sun or take little excursions under guard. He lived and wrote by the light of phosphorescent moss. The brown linen robes the guards left for him were cut simply; they scratched his skin and still had stains from their previous wearers that wouldn't wash out.

I'm too old to starve in here. Carmondai put aside his notes, which he had written in a secret language so that his thoughts could remain private for the time being. He really hoped his stories were still being recounted.

They probably spread a rumour that I had died. He stood up and walked his usual route between his desk, door, wardrobe and bed, eight paces in between each one. *I won't give them the satisfaction.* His writing was stacked up on the shelves and new work was constantly being added.

Carmondai threw off his rough shirt because he was starting to sweat, then changed direction; after a few more laps, he did some quick jumps, press-ups and chin-ups. The warrior blood in him refused to lapse into complete physical inactivity. It also wouldn't accept the excuse of a cell or the occasional pain in his old joints.

He may not have had any weapons, but he used two long rulers to practise dagger combat for at least a splinter of unendingness every day. He wanted to be prepared for anything.

He wasn't going to contemplate escape until he could figure out how to take his writings with him, but he would defend himself if the Aklán ever made an attempt on his life.

I used to be quicker. Panting, he put the rulers away and wiped off his torso with a cloth, unable to help smiling as he looked down at his skin. *I've got wrinkly. The young älf-women gave me more pity than attention.* He looked at the washbowl with the near-empty carafe next to it. Food hadn't appeared for two turns of the hourglass either.

Carmondai went to the door and kicked it several times to draw attention to himself but there was no response. The slide on the little hatch stayed shut.

Has the time come? Am I going to die of starvation and thirst? He took one look at the carafe and decided to save the rest of the water. He sat down at the table again and started to write. But his precarious situation was visibly troubling him.

They'll hardly have forgotten me, Carmondai reflected.

The door couldn't be forced open, not even if he were to put the wooden shelves together and use them as a battering ram. There were three horizontal iron bars on the outside holding the door securely in place.

His minders had brought him here blindfolded, but he remembered the three hundred and eleven steps down. So he was underground, surrounded by solid rock. *Before I could dig my way out, I'd die of thirst.*

Another idea occurred to him.

Carmondai looked at the blank pages. *That would be an option. But it's dangerous. Both for me and everything that I've created in this cell.*

He got to his feet and picked up a pile of papers, went over to the closed door and tried to slide a page through the gap between the wood and the stone floor.

It worked.

If the Aklán force my hand, I'm going to risk it. Carmondai slid more pages underneath the door and tore additional sheets into tiny little scraps and piled them loosely on top until they formed a little mound; on top of this he crumbled his pencils made of compressed coal dust. Using a metal quill and a piece of stone he had broken off the wall, he struck sparks onto the thing until tendrils of smoke were curling upwards.

Now then. The älf blew carefully until little flames flared up and spread along the door.

The sheets of paper pushed halfway under the door caught fire and he hoped they would spread the blaze to the other side.

Carmondai kept adding paper, crumpling up blank pages and throwing them onto the gentle flames, then he smashed some shelves into wood splinters and put them on too, wedging them under the frame where possible.

Come on! He couldn't help inhaling the smoke and it was making him cough. It was accumulating on the ceiling of his cell. It wouldn't be long till the älf suffocated.

The lower section of the door was turning black, smouldering and toying with the flames, but still the wood would not burn properly.

Carmondai fanned it, keeping an eye on the rising sparks so that fire wouldn't break out anywhere it wasn't useful to him.

Finally the little flames danced along the bottom edge of the door and slowly started to eat their way upwards.

Carmondai held a cloth over his nose and mouth and looked at the ceiling where the gathering smoke was gradually darkening. *I have my own storm cloud*, the thought flashed across his mind, and he couldn't help smiling. *A flash of lightning would be genuinely helpful.*

The fire climbed upwards, but as it did so, it gave off more smoke than he had expected. The älf had to lie on the floor to avoid the swirling blackness.

Where exactly were the three iron bars positioned? Carmondai looked at the carafe then poured the remaining water into the bowl. He tipped in every non-flammable paint and ink he could find after it. He soaked his housecoat in the liquid, wrapped it around himself and took a run at the door.

After ten or eleven short, quick strides, he threw himself flat on the stone floor, sliding feet first.

The soles of his feet crashed into the blazing wood in the lower section of the door – and broke through it in a hail of sparks.

Carmondai had enough momentum to get into the hallway up to his chest, then he turned over and used his arms and feet to crawl commando-style backward out of the room.

His face was glowing and there was a smell of scorched hair, but he managed to get through the gap into the adjoining hallway.

A fat orc would not have been capable of that. Carmondai got to his feet and took a step away from the burning, crackling door.

The hallway was lit by oil lamps and the smoke was drifting through it in pale-coloured, grey streaks. Nobody came to check on the cause of the fire.

What is going on here? Carmondai took his damp coat, which had stained his linen clothes a strange colour, and threw it at the flames, but they wouldn't go out. *I need water.* Hoping against hope, he hurried on.

He passed empty cells until he reached the passage to the guards' common room. Two chairs stood neatly at the empty table. The logbook was open, the names of every inmate crossed out without comment. *Apart from mine.*

They must have needed the imprisoned älfar, Carmondai speculated. *If they were merely killing them, they could just as easily have done it down here.*

He went through a second door and up the three hundred and eleven steps and found himself in a second guards' room.

There were pieces of armour strewn about the floor as if they had been cast aside, and swords and daggers of various sizes lay on the tables.

The other älfar were taken upstairs and prepared for the battle, he deduced and to be on the safe side he slipped on some plain armour.

Next, he wanted to bring the fire in front of his cell under control before everything inside was lost. *How desperate must they be if they're pardoning criminals and sending them into battle?*

To his right stood an orc-sized water amphora with a tap in it. Next to that were three buckets and he filled them with water one by one.

Carmondai was just about to hurry downstairs with them when he heard a quiet, steady rumbling like a prolonged rockfall in the distance.

Torn, he paused.

With some effort, he chose a sword and two wide daggers with bent-up crossguards before peering cautiously out the door. He had to make sure that he would not be in immediate danger while putting out the flames downstairs.

The palace's enormous reception hall, made of dark grey marble, stretched out in front of him, and there were white statues towering up on all sides covered in little tiles of white bone.

Nobody in sight and not a sound to be heard. Carmondai crossed the hall quickly and found himself in a high-ceilinged dark passage with walls covered in lengths of crimson fabric.

The constant rumbling and banging sounds could no longer be ignored. And they were coming from *inside* the crater.

After walking the length of the corridor, he went out and stood in front of the huge building and looked down the mountain. He was in the open air a mile above ground and was briefly dazzled by the evening sun. A staircase stretched out in front of him leading downwards and at its foot was Dsôn Bhará – but it no longer looked the way he remembered.

The countless sculptures that used to line the streets and the squares in the black caldera no longer existed – and the majority of the elaborate buildings lay in ruins. More than two hundred houses had once been built, in black and white, with pointed and sloping roofs, some with straight walls, some plain or even adorned with little hexagonal towers.

Someone or something had violently torn them all down.

Catapults made of blackwood taken from the beams of the destroyed roofs rose up out of the rubble as well as from the landings on the staircase. The slingshots – at least a hundred paces high – and their ammunition were trained on the tower behind the palace.

Carmondai ducked his head as the shells shot almost vertically upwards and flew over him, hitting the towering building. *Not one defender in sight? The Aklán must have been defeated!*

He couldn't tell if the attackers were Aiphatòn and his southern älfar, or troops from Girdlegard or even another army entirely. He was too far away.

The round crater wall was about five miles away, but he could see that the edges were being tampered with, broken off to try and fill the three-mile deep hole with rubble. That was where the elf realm of Lesinteïl had once had its Moon Pond.

That will take them cycles, if it's even possible in the first place.

A catapulted stone went astray and whirred on.

The impact, in the middle of one of the many landings on the staircase below where Carmondai was standing, pulverised one of the fountains – red water burbled up out of it. It was made of the same grey marble as the steps.

The shell bounced upwards, levelling the extraordinary polished stairs encrusted with crystals and diamonds. The cut jewels flew, glittering, through the air along with the red droplets. Finally, it rumbled on to the right and came to rest in the gushing blood-coloured stream.

The sound of a horn rang out from the catapults. Figures of

different sizes were gathering among them and looking up the broad staircase at Carmondai. His appearance was clearly not unexpected.

Those are groundlings, he gaped. *Groundlings and barbarians and . . .* An armed woman who seemed to be dressed entirely in white towered over the rest of them. *An elf-woman?*

Even he, who was used to coming up with the most fitting of words, couldn't think of any way to describe his shock. In his busiest times as emperor of the älfar, Aiphatòn had savagely hunted down his sworn mortal enemy and wiped out the last of the tribe.

That's what everyone had believed.

Either they had entered Girdlegard from outside or they were able to hide from the emperor and the Aklán. Carmondai could scarcely believe it but at the same time he knew what it meant for him. *And thus I've become game for a hate-filled huntress.*

Fittingly for what he was thinking, the fair-haired elf-woman and some soldiers swung themselves onto their horses and rode up the steps.

Carmondai slowly shrank back, but didn't know where to flee. The only thing on the whole two-mile wide mountain was the oblong palace made from dark grey marble.

He turned round and looked up at the large tower that rose hundreds of paces in the air behind the palace. The awning wires that had stretched taut from the top of it across the town as far as the edge of the crater were nowhere to be seen. The destruction of Dsôn Bhará was well underway. *Only idiots would flee up there.*

The black glass dome that had once arched over the centre of the palace had been destroyed by a boulder.

Carmondai's gaze flitted over the marble façade – all kinds of skeletons had been affixed to the walls. *No barbarians, elves or groundlings will have any sense of the beauty in that.* Or the beauty of the bone-segment-adorned portal, the rounded fronts of skulls belonging to all the races and monsters of Girdlegard jutting through the gaps. *All the races apart from älfar.* He looked over his shoulder at the long stair-case; the enemy was still climbing up it towards him. *They'd probably like to stick my head up there too.*

The catapults kept on firing, not letting up. The stones in the lower section of the tower and the palace were cracking. Something that had taken countless slaves four divisions of unendingness to create, and which they had given their lives to, was gone in no time, turning into ruins and threatening to vanish.

Carmondai weighed up his remaining options.

He could forget about a battle; he would be no match for the stronger side. Fleeing into the tower, which was being shaken by renewed rounds, or into the dungeons, didn't make any sense.

I ought to get out of the crater and fight my way to . . . probably to Ishím Voróo. The thought of the writings he had to leave behind was unspeakably painful to him. *How can I save them? I can hardly take them with me.*

The elf-woman and the soldiers had covered two-thirds of the distance. They stopped and went the last few paces on foot; they left their steeds on the landing of the staircase.

I need a horse. With a horse I'd have a slim chance of getting away.

'Hey, you cowards!' Carmondai brandished his sword at the attackers. 'I'm going to nail your skulls to the wall where you belong.' He burst into peals of laughter and ran back to the palace. *That should provoke them into chasing me as fast as they can.*

A heavy shell crashed into the façade, crushing numerous bones into a fine powder that fell to the ground along with the marble that was blasted off.

He hurried inside the building through the haze of white dust. Cracks had formed all over the walls and they reminded him of anger lines. They looked like they were revealing their hatred of intruders before they shattered and crumbled.

After going down the dark corridor, he turned off into the reception hall and hid behind a statue to let his pursuers pass by; he threw one of his daggers across the room so that it landed in front of a door to lay a fake trail.

He silently congratulated himself on keeping physically fit in the dungeon. He didn't have the heart for battle, so escaping the enemy – who had every right to try and kill an älf – would be a question of speed.

The soldiers ran through the corridor as though out of their minds, before stopping and standing indecisively in the hall – until one of them spotted the dagger and the troop raced off towards it. In the blink of an eye, they dashed through the doorway and disappeared.

They must all have been barbarians. Carmondai waited impatiently. The elf-woman didn't appear.

Shell after shell rained down on the palace, the first clouds of dust wafting into the hall now too. Sections of the ceiling panels came loose from their fixtures and the slabs of bone smashed onto the marble. The missiles had blown the roof off, wreaking more and more havoc every time they struck.

Carmondai didn't want to wait any longer; it was getting dangerous inside and the soldiers were sure to come back soon. He darted off down the corridor, sword and dagger ready to defend himself. He tried to stop thinking about the books he'd had to abandon.

He ran outside, ducking as he sprinted across the small forecourt and down the steps. The elf-woman had obviously taken a different turning in the palace; she was nowhere to be seen.

The horses were on the landing, waiting patiently for their riders to come back. The troops on the ground didn't see the älf as they continued the constant reloading and firing of the catapults.

Carmondai reached the animals and approached the elf-woman's chestnut horse, who lifted his head and snorted suspiciously. 'Easy, I'm not going to hurt you,' he soothed the animal.

'But I will hurt you.' The white-armoured woman emerged from behind the fountain. She was pointing two long swords at him. 'I thought you'd run away,' she said with satisfaction, her gaze taking in his spotless blades. Her voice was laced with a slight elven lilt which lent even the common language of Tark Draan a certain melodiousness. 'The soldiers are still alive?'

'I didn't lay a finger on them.' Carmondai's thoughts were racing. 'What has happened in Dsôn Bhará and what happened to the triplets?'

The elf-woman raised her delicate eyebrows. 'What do you mean by asking such an absurd question?'

Carmondai listened out for potential footsteps ringing out behind him, alerting him to the arrival of the warriors who'd been led astray. 'I was a prisoner. I've been locked in a dungeon underneath the palace for many orbits. I escaped and . . .'

The elf-woman laughed as the sun bounced off her white palandium armour. 'A pretty story to wash your hands of any responsibility.' She swung the swords. 'But there are no innocent älfar!' She stabbed the sword in her right hand forward and slashed horizontally from right to left at head height. 'You are the spawn of the devil!'

Carmondai parried the high strike with his dagger, catching the enemy sword in the massive crossguard; he dodged her stab with a swift turn of his body, then rammed his elbows at the elf-woman's face. But his opponent ducked and headbutted him with her helmet.

I used to be much quicker. Stars flashed before Carmondai's eyes and blood spurted out of the cut on his forehead so that he couldn't see anything.

Blinded, he staggered backwards into the agitated, snorting horse, wresting one of the elf-woman's swords away from her with his dagger by chance; it clattered to the ground. Using quick, short slashes, without being able to see his opponent, he kept her attacks at bay and rubbed at his face with his upper arm so that he could see again.

Then he was flung backwards by a remarkably powerful kick to his middle.

He tried to regain his balance but failed and tumbled down the stairs.

The armour protected him from broken ribs but Carmondai was forced to let go of his weapon to make sure he didn't injure himself with it. With every somersault, he wondered again how many steps the stairs had.

When he finally came to a stop, he could feel the tip of the sword at his throat before he could even move. Dizziness raged through his head, and his right arm and leg were throbbing alarmingly like they were broken.

'You are one of the last älfar in Girdlegard. Anyone who escapes me and my fellow warriors will be hunted by the dwarves,' he heard the elf-woman's voice. 'To put it in your own terms: your death is called Fiëa.'

Carmondai was too dazed to sweep the sword aside with a desperate shove at the broad edge, particularly as the blade had already penetrated the skin. *At least I'm not dying in the dungeon, I'm dying in the open air*, he thought cynically.

'Stop!' came the sound of a loud cry from a powerful, throaty voice. The point dug deeper into his throat.

'Why?' the elf-woman called back, perplexed. 'He's an älf, the . . .'

'*That* is Carmondai,' the man interrupted her. 'The writer who penned all those stories.' Heavy, brisk steps were approaching from above him.

'Ah, the one who celebrated the supposedly heroic feats of his people,' Fiëa retorted scornfully. 'Then it will give me great pleasure to chop off his hands before I behead him.'

Carmondai's dizziness was subsiding, the spinning world coming to a stop.

The elf-woman was standing over him, the sword pressed underneath his chin.

'Just wait, I'm telling you!' A smaller figure appeared next to her. Its body was encased in black leather armour fortified with tionium plates, but the runes had been scratched off them. A skirt-like garment made of little tiles of blackened iron covered the legs, and a black leather close helmet decorated with numerous rivets and silver wire hid the head.

Gloved fingers pushed up the visor and a blackened face with a cropped beard came into view. 'Yes,' said the dwarf, nodding. 'That's Carmondai.'

The älf was not yet sure if it was a good thing to have been recognised. It was possible someone might enjoy torturing him even more than they would a normal warrior.

Judging by the groundling's appearance, he was a zhadár, one of the Invisibles who formed an elite unit from the ranks of the Thirdlings. Transformed by Sisaroth's potions and trained in älfar magic, they were a powerful weapon against the triplets' enemies.

They've switched sides. Carmondai slowly raised his painful arms.

'So what?' Fiëa shot back. 'What reason could there be to spare his life?'

'We could force him to write down *our* history this time. How *we* hunted the älfar and what atrocities *they* carried out and that kind of thing.' He placed his left hand on the hilt of his sword-like weapon. The lower part of it was wide to parry powerful blows but the upper part was shaped into a long thin point so that it could penetrate through gaps in armour. 'The victors determine what will be written from this point onwards. And he is good. I read a lot of his stuff before he vanished all of a sudden.'

'I was the triplets' prisoner,' Carmondai said. 'You'll have found my cell.' He remembered the fire, which was surely still raging. 'Would it be possible to save my writing, the papers I wrote while I was locked up?'

Fiëa upped the pressure and Carmondai's face distorted in pain. 'And he thinks he's going to be spared.'

'At least until he's done some writing.' The groundling scrutinised him. 'Think about it: he's very useful, Fiëa. He was there when Dsôn Balsur began and knows many of the Akláns' secrets.'

'Well then, we should interrogate him.'

Carmondai could already see himself being tortured and was still nervous about his hands. 'I promise to tell you everything and answer all your questions.'

The groundling crouched down next to him and grinned. 'That you *will*, black-eye.' He pushed the elven sword tip away. 'That you *absolutely* will.'

The sudden, powerful punch to the chin dispatched the älf into darkness.

Tark Draan, Human kingdom of Gauragar, Grey Mountains, 5452nd division of unendingness (6491st solar cycle), early summer

Aiphatòn had to abandon the steady jog that had got him through Girdlegard and into the north so quickly.

In all kinds of ways, the Grey Mountains put him in his place: treacherous ground, very thin air and extremely unsettled weather.

Coming up against these kinds of barriers was a new experience for him.

Mayor Münzler had been telling him the truth. Aiphatòn had little trouble finding the steep path. What he noticed immediately were the muddy rivulets coming towards him and softening the trail wherever it didn't consist of solid bedrock. The intensifying sun was also thawing ice and snow in the upper regions.

At least the Jagged Crown is unmistakeable. Aiphatòn looked at the faraway, oddly shaped peak that looked like it was formed of upright obelisks. *It's bound to take eight orbits to get there. Or even more.*

The white stretches on his route worried him. He had read about the mountains' countless pitfalls. Besides the thin mountain air, in the upper regions there was also permanent frost and several fathomless ravines in the bedrock, hidden under thin firn, which he might smash through thanks to the heavy equipment in his rucksack.

Aiphatòn looked ahead, keeping an eye on his surroundings. He hoped that Firûsha had just as little experience of the climb as he did.

He might encounter her soon – or an ambush by one of her warriors. Four veterans had been accompanying her since he deliberately let her get away in Dsôn Bhará. He wanted her to reveal her secrets to him or maybe even lead him to her brothers.

From what he knew of the Aklán, he thought she would very likely have had two of her warriors lie in wait to kill him while she herself kept moving.

Aiphatòn didn't believe there was a mountain pass or tunnel leading away to Tark Draan. A secret like that could never have lasted so long.

And yet he was inwardly worried there might be a kernel of truth to it.

He was more willing to accept the existence of a magical artefact than a passageway. But ever since it had become common knowledge that the foothills of Phondrasôn reached underneath Girdlegard, the utmost vigilance was necessary. Because a passageway or a sunken lane would be perfect for avoiding the existing five entrances. The dwarf tribes usually stood watch at them for anyone coming in or out.

Anyone who snuck past the fierce, short-statured, brave defenders via a different path through the mountains could smuggle in an army – or a worse threat – unnoticed and attack the country. It would take place in secret and probably be just as successful as Sinthoras and Caphalor had been in the past with their conquest of the Stone Gateway. It ranked as one of the dwarves' greatest defeats and it had led to the extermination of the Fifthlings tribe.

But Balyndis and huge numbers of volunteers had resettled the dwarf kingdom since then and Aiphatòn knew they kept watch. Once again, the stony mountain ranges surrounding the people's, elves' and dwarves' kingdoms were considered impassable for hikers, carts or any kind of carriage. Even the expeditions dispatched by the Smith's children either turned back or were presumed missing in the sea of basalt and granite.

Aiphatòn's instinct had not let him down when he had held off on shooting Firûsha among the artworks in Dsôn. It seemed she and her brothers had worked out a plan to stave off the älfar's impending defeat. To achieve it, she needed to get to the Jagged Crown.

Whatever the reason: I'll find out. Leading Girdlegard and even Aiphatòn to believe the Aklán had died turned out to be an extraordinarily good move. An enemy everyone thought was dead could strike all the more cruelly and savagely.

That way, they surprise us. He walked on, the spear balanced freely on his shoulder. *It's Samusin's providence that I encountered them.*

Aiphatòn had no doubt Ireheart and the band of heroes were

defeating Lot-Ionan and the älfar already. He would help them as soon as he had killed Firûsha.

The time is ripe to break free of the shackles of all foreign powers. Soon the inhabitants will rule over their own homeland, free from the influence of a vile magician or the dragon-worshippers of Lohasbrand and most definitely free from the tyranny of the älfar.

He stopped and took a deep breath to get some air into his shrivelled-feeling lungs. *And free of me.*

Aiphatòn remembered the conversation he'd had with Tungdil on the ship some time ago. *Never strive to be like the Inextinguishables.* Still, despite every good intention, his self-control had slipped away. *My past words will finally be followed by actions.*

His gaze swept across the countryside that stretched out in the valley to the south of him.

Little white clouds drifted across the blue sky, some dancing around the smaller peaks as if they wanted to stroke the rock and make it slightly less harsh. The sun shone, bringing the plains the warmth they desperately needed to allow the summer crops to ripen.

It seemed to Aiphatòn as if he had woken from a dream in which evil, hunger for power and unhappiness prevailed.

He had let himself get carried away, hunting the elves even more successfully than the Inextinguishables before him. He almost wiped them out, despite the fact he once named himself after their life star.

What a mockery. His ever-black eyes turned to the blueness high above him. *So many things I'll never forgive myself for doing.*

It was still too early to see the first stars twinkling.

His gaze kept returning to the same place, but at night only a dark mark was visible there. The elves' life star could no longer be made out. With every death of a member of their tribe, it had darkened further. *I really hope I see it shine again one day.*

Aiphatòn resumed his slow march and recalled the promise he had made to Tungdil the last time they met. *I swear I will never return to Girdlegard unless someone invites me.* That's what he'd said, and he'd meant once the battles were over. After the great, deadly slaughter.

But, in fact, he hoped he would pass into endingness with the last of the northern älfar. Until then, his hunt would continue, his next five opponents awaiting him.

Aiphatòn knew he was superior to them in terms of fighting skills. Besides, he had magic within him, stored in the rune-inscribed plates stitched fast into his skin. He used this energy intuitively, without reciting any spells. Five älfar warrior-women and warriors represented at most a *minor* challenge. He was thoroughly justified in this hint of arrogance.

He reached a plain that was practically designed to enjoy the view to the north.

He didn't know the names of all the peaks and mountain ranges that had towered up since time immemorial as if to prove his own insignificance, and which would continue to do so after he'd gone. Ireheart or one of the new Fifthlings would surely have been able to tell a story about every single mountain.

No particular imagination was required to pick out specific shapes, like a sword or a dragon's head. On closer inspection, a wall with a ridge jutting out of it became the back of an enormous monster disappearing into the rock, its last vertebrae just visible as it vanished.

If Vraccas really did create these mountains then he has shown a flair for variety. Aiphatòn smiled and shielded his eyes from the daystar in order to observe the beauty without the glare.

He didn't feel any kind of urge to translate the view into a painting, sculpture or ballad. Even this proved to him how much he differed from his people.

During his years as emperor, the idea of sitting down at a canvas because of a whim or emotion had never even crossed his mind. Although he had tried his hand at it many times out of a sense of duty, it didn't do anything for him.

He valued art without being an artist. And sometimes he valued it when things stayed as they were, and kept their own uniqueness.

To his astonishment, Aiphatòn didn't miss anything. He didn't miss his palace or servants or anything else that came with his title of emperor and his once-powerful kingdom.

Things in Girdlegard ought to go back to how they were before Caphalor and Sinthoras' invasion, he mused. *And then that's how they should stay.* He felt a duty to the inhabitants and would do anything to protect them. Sighing, he looked out over the mountains. *I should never have got carried away like that but that's behind me now.*

The hiss of the arrow and the soft sound of the string snapping back into place were unmistakeable in the silence.

It told Aiphatòn where the archer was.

He grabbed the spear resting on his shoulder, turning round as he did so and flinging it in one fluid movement.

The blade made a whirring sound and hit the tip of the black arrow whizzing towards it, breaking it and destroying its shaft.

Continuing its flight, the spear plunged through the hardened leather armour and into the chest of the warrior who had taken up a good shooting position on an overhang thirty paces above.

He dropped his bow, sank to his knees and stared in bafflement at the shining runes filling with his blood. The stricken älf tilted backwards and came to rest on his back, the projectile sticking out of him like a thin flagpole.

Tiny fragments of the arrow clinked harmlessly onto the stony ground, one dark feather floating slowly towards the earth.

A warrior-woman stepped out of a dark niche in the rock and came towards Aiphatòn, holding one long sword and one short one with a serrated blade.

'Your journey ends here,' she announced firmly. She was wearing the black armour too, dark blonde hair peeking out from underneath her helmet. She lifted the hand holding the smaller weapon and pointed it at his solar plexus. 'Know this: you were *never* our emperor. And the moment we send you into endingness is long awaited.'

'That moment has not yet arrived, however. Not for me. But your own end might put a stop to your agonising wait.' Aiphatòn scrutinised her. 'You ought to know that I'm in full possession of my powers, in case the Aklán told you something different to reassure you.' He lowered his head a little so that a shadow fell across his finely chiselled features. 'I'll give you the chance to walk past me and jump into the abyss. With no pain, no injuries. A small step, a fall during which you can curse the Aklán or pray to a god and then there'll be nothing more to worry about.' With a jerky movement, he threw off his cloaks along with his pack and revealed his bare torso with the stitched-in rune plates; the symbols shimmered, green and menacing, as if they were waiting for an opportunity to be allowed to prove their power. 'Anything else will cause you pain. I will show no mercy.'

'Your death is called Tanóra and I . . .' the älf-woman began.

'*My* death does not have a name yet,' Aiphatòn interrupted her and closed his armour-encased hands. He felt the magic within him as a gentle warmth flowing through his body. 'And if it does come my way, it will have a nicer sounding name than yours.'

Tanóra launched her attack, lashing out with swiftly alternating kicks and punches, which he dodged with expert twists. When he needed to, he used the large metal fittings on his armoured gloves to block the blades; metal sang as it clashed with metal.

Through careful observation, Aiphatòn saw his opponent's weak spot: just before the attack with the long sword, she lifted her shoulder slightly, giving herself away.

When Tanóra, panting with exertion, went to deliver another horizontal blow, he took a swift step towards her, knocking the attacking short blade aside and punching the älf-woman in the upper lip and nose.

A loud crack rang out as bone and tooth shattered.

Blood spurted out of Tanóra's cracked lip and smashed nose, the redness running down her chin and dripping steadily onto her armour.

She staggered backwards to put some space between them again so that she could use her blades.

But Aiphatòn stayed an arm's length away and rained down punch after punch on her face, the runes on his armoured knuckles glowing more and more with every hit. Five blows landed on target in the space of a heartbeat. Then he wound his arms right back and launched a double attack on the dazed woman, using both fists on her armour.

A dazzling explosion discharged.

His knuckles smashed through the hardened, reinforced leather and undergarment, where they met vulnerable flesh. There was a loud hissing sound and Aiphatòn knew that her pale skin had gone black.

Tanóra shrieked and was simultaneously flung upwards, her swords clanking down onto the stony ground.

The magical-physical attack flung her straight out over the edge of the mountain until the momentum subsided and she plunged downwards, still screaming. As she fell she suddenly started to burn, a dark cloud of smoke drifting out behind her.

You could have made it less excruciating for yourself. Aiphatòn watched her descent until Tanóra finally got too close to the mountainside and was torn to pieces, pulverised on the rugged surface. Only once almost nothing was left of her did the flames go out.

'Your death is called Aiphatòn,' he murmured as he picked up her weapons and threw them into the abyss. 'As I predicted.'

He raised his hand and his spear extricated itself from the corpse of the first slain älf and flew to its master, landing neatly in his open hand.

He quickly looked for the two veterans' equipment but couldn't find any.

That meant that they had fully expected to kill him and return to their group. At this altitude, running fast was exhausting so he reasoned that Firûsha could not be far away.

He put his cloaks and pack on again, placing the blood-spattered spear on his shoulder as before. With no regard for himself or his well-being, he started jogging. His body would just have to endure the strain.

Aiphatòn caught up with the group towards evening.

They may have decided against a fire, but he could hear their quiet conversation coming from a small, sheltered recess.

He threw off his rucksack and cloaks again so that he could move more easily. He crept cautiously towards the recess and noticed at once that it was just *one* älf, who was disguising his voice as he spoke, quickly switching between voices.

So at least one of them must be lying in wait out here for me. Aiphatòn presumed that the Aklán was sacrificing the last two veterans to stop him. He could not ignore them and leave them on his heels. He knew that, and Firûsha did too.

He looked around, searching for positions where an archer could easily hide.

Up there perhaps? There was a groove four paces above the ground, as if a giant troll had cut a notch into the rock with an axe.

He took the spear and threw it on the off-chance, making the runes at the front of the shaft light up as well as the runes on the blade.

The greenish light from the symbols dragged an astonished älf-woman partially out of the darkness. She had been waiting at her post with a bow at the ready, wedged inside the rock face.

There she is. Aiphatòn cut his weapon's flight through the air short and made it hover menacingly in front of the warrior-woman. The tip was pointed at her face, the shimmering reflected off the gleaming blade, casting the light onto the rock even more intensely.

'Climb down,' he called. 'And you, sitting in the recess: show yourself.'

The älf-woman in her raised hide stood up, casting her bow and arrow aside, and jumped out of the crevice, landing elegantly on the rock. A warrior came out of the entrance to the little cave, a spear in his right hand and a square shield in his left.

Aiphatòn let his weapon float downwards, bringing it between himself and his opponents. 'You think you'll make it out of this alive, but you're mistaken. I'm giving you just one chance to choose a swift death instead of agony.' He drew himself up. 'Tanóra did not make a wise choice. You may have heard her screams? The mountains carry echoes quite some way.'

The two älfar watched him over the spear, their eyes brimming with hatred.

You're not going to surrender either. 'A swift death is yours if you go to the edge and –'

The älf-woman went to stand behind the shield-carrier who immediately held the shield in front of him, hurled his weapon at Aiphatòn and then charged forwards; as he did so, he ducked so low he almost disappeared completely behind the shield, so as not to offer Aiphatòn a target.

It wasn't difficult for the shintoìt to dodge the missile. At the same time, he forced his own hovering spear to attack magically.

The blade penetrated the shield's thin metal coating and the wood underneath, then penetrated the älf's arm along with his helmet and skull.

Before the warrior-woman could even realise the enemy weapon was unstoppable, the tip bored into her shoulder and flung her to the ground, along with the dead älf; she was sprayed with the blood of her companion. Skewered, she lay underneath the motionless warrior, moaning with pain. Every attempt she made to free herself from the spear failed and ended in an agonised, furious cry.

As I thought: they didn't want to surrender. Aiphatòn approached her slowly, stopping two paces away from her. 'What's your . . .'

She reached for her belt, drew a throwing knife and tossed it at him.

Aiphatòn turned so that the blade hit one of the sewn-in plates of armour on his torso. It shattered against it with a dull clatter. 'What's your name?'

She spat.

'I left it up to you to decide,' he said, 'what kind of death you wanted. And look: you're in agony.' Aiphatòn cast a glance at the dead body. 'He was lucky he kept his head ducked right down.' He crouched next to her. 'The Aklán let you and your veteran friends pass into end-ingness. Did she tell you I had no power left too?'

The warrior-woman's eyes flicked right and left. 'You are the worst thing that could have happened to our tribe,' she shot back, groaning. 'You brought the scum to us.'

'*Every* älf is scum. Dangerous scum that threaten the unity and harmony of a peaceful world,' he said thoughtfully. 'Where would Girdlegard be if it hadn't been for all of you? If *I* hadn't existed? The people, elves and dwarves . . .'

The älf-woman laughed scornfully. 'You think they'd be living in peace? We were what first enabled them to unite. We throw them into the dust, give them the enemy they need in order to stick together. They were too foolish to pool their forces and skills of their own accord.' She groaned, then fixed her gaze firmly on him. 'End it now, *scum*,' she said, grinning maliciously. 'I can call you names now, and what's more, I'm entitled to do it.'

It's not going to be that simple. Aiphatòn placed his index finger on the shaft of the spear and the runes lit up.

Slowly but surely, the metal warmed up as magic flowed into it.

Smoke was rising from the warrior-woman's shoulder and she clenched first her lips and then her teeth together hard.

'You still owe me your name.'

The älf-woman was sweating, droplets glinting on her forehead and rolling into the blood spatter. She lowered her head and gave a loud shriek, anger lines forming across her face.

'I promised you pain. And I don't think we'll be done any time soon.' Aiphatòn placed his hand on his weapon and lifted it up slowly, bit by bit.

The dead body slipped down the shaft onto the female veteran, pinning her with its weight. She wailed and tried to sit up without making the pain worse.

'Vonòria,' she gasped. 'My name is Vonòria.'

'Now tell me: what does Firûsha want on the Jagged Crown?'

The älf-woman's breathing was jerky and she seemed determined not to say anything more.

'*What* does the Aklán want on the summit, Vonòria?' he repeated his question, making more energy flow into the spear.

The smoke thickened, and there was a smell of roasting flesh. Burn blisters appeared around the edges of the wounds.

'The Ten. She wants to get to the Ten,' she said in a high-pitched gasp, imploring him with one arm outstretched. 'Stop!'

Aiphatòn dimly remembered the story but couldn't recall it fully. He let go of the spear so that the pain wasn't being unleashed for the moment. 'Who are the Ten? Do they live up there?'

Vonòria gulped; she needed to take several breaths before she could go on. 'The Ten were a unit of female and male veterans dispatched by the Aklán to search for the mountain pass reputed to run from the Jagged Crown to Ishím Voróo. Apparently elves were fleeing from the Dsôn Aklán via this route, unnoticed at first.'

Elves? 'When was this?'

'Soon after the beginning of their reign in Tark Draan.' She sneered at him. 'You didn't know everything, you wretch. There was a *lot* you didn't know about what the rulers were doing and setting in motion, from the zhadár to . . .'

Could this be true? Aiphatòn hit the spear and she fell silent with a groan. 'What are the Ten doing at the summit?'

Vonòria was gasping for breath. 'I don't know,' she panted. 'We were to accompany the Aklán but she didn't let us in on her plans.'

A passageway and apparently it leads away from here. Aiphatòn placed a foot against the warrior's corpse and pulled the spear out of a moaning Vonòria and then out of the dead man, before pushing his body off her. Using some magic, he warmed up the weapon and made the blood on it evaporate.

He pointed the spotless, gleaming tip at the älf-woman, blood oozing out of her shoulder. 'Do you at least know what she was planning to do *after* she'd visited the Ten?'

Vonòria lay still on her back, her eyes closed, seeming to be waiting for the pain to subside. She shook her head feebly.

'Then I don't need you anymore. Your death is called—'

A pebble skittered across the ground behind Aiphatòn but the warning wasn't enough.

A powerful blow hit him in the back, the blade of a heavy sword striking the plates as well as his bare skin.

The älf was thrown forwards by the force of it and, without meaning to, he rammed his blade through the front of Vonòria's neck and right up into her skull. *You'll pass into endingness before me.* He ducked instinctively.

The sword hissed as it sliced over his head and an älf-woman cursed loudly.

Aiphatòn did a foot sweep to take his opponent's legs out from under her, turning as he did so – and saw the black tionium armour of the Aklán in front of him.

Firûsha staggered but kept her balance. She immediately started hacking at him, the long blade coming down like a guillotine.

Aiphatòn whipped his arms up into the air and crossed his armoured fists to block the sword before it could plunge into his head and cleave him in two. There was an unpleasant ache in his back and he could feel his own warm blood running over his skin from a cut.

The two-handed, powerful blow flung him to his knees and the soles of Firûsha's boots were already poised to kick him in the face.

Fiery smoke flashed before Aiphatòn's eyes. He flopped backwards, grasping her blade with his armoured fingers as he did so and trying to pull his opponent with him.

But the Aklán let go of the hilt and immediately took two polished discuses out of the holders on her forearms and hurled them at Aiphatòn, who with some difficulty managed to deflect the missiles with the sword he had seized. He had no time to summon his own spear.

'You're going to die, you self-proclaimed emperor,' she cried and lifted the dead warrior's spear to stab him. 'Here, in the wasteland!'

I'll be okay, even without a spear. Aiphatòn rolled aside and escaped her attack, getting up on one knee and swinging the long sword by the blade like a heavy hammer; the hilt was aimed at the älf-woman's skull.

Surprised by the unexpected attack, she was still trying to pull her head away when the polished sword guard slid through her helmet at the height of her ears.

Firûsha's strength suddenly deserted her. She collapsed in a heap in front of Aiphatòn. Writhing, she panted and opened her eyes wide.

'I . . . can't feel my body anymore,' she murmured in abject terror. Her blue eyes darted around searchingly. 'What . . . where am I?'

She won't reveal anything to me voluntarily. But if her mind is sufficiently disoriented by the injury, she might reveal something after all. He knelt down next to her. The visor on her helmet wouldn't open so he leaned close to her to ensure she could hear and understand him. 'You're here, with us. With the Ten.'

'With the Ten?' Firûsha was breathing so hard that she had to pronounce each word separately.

'At the summit of the Jagged Crown, yes.'

The älf-woman must have been smiling, judging by the crow's feet he could see, although fear radiated from her pupils. 'I can't see the settlement. Is it as beautiful as I heard it was?'

A settlement? Aiphatòn had to check himself to make sure he didn't give away the trick he was playing on her with a careless word. 'Yes, it is. Now that you've found us, Aklán: what should we do?'

'The älfar need you,' she murmured. Firûsha looked relieved for a heartbeat. 'You . . . you must rally the resistance against the scum from Tark Draan. Look for our far-flung people!' Her eyelids fluttered. 'We mustn't give up. The settlement is our new cradle and in one division of unendingness, I'll lead you back so that we . . .'

Her ribcage suddenly stopped moving and her pupils clouded over. The blue of her eyes dulled and became streaked with endingness.

Aiphatòn watched the transition from life to death. 'Thus you pass on without fame, without fuss, without becoming a legend,' he whispered to the Aklán who could no longer hear him. 'You wanted to execute me in the wasteland of the Grey Mountains, but instead you're passing into endingness.'

He pulled the sword's crossguard out of her head, blood and slimy grey brain matter clinging to it, then peered closer.

Horrified, he recoiled at the sight of her face. *That's not her! The features are similar, but that's not her.*

He quickly released the chin-strap and tore the helmet off her mop of hair. He smelled a strand of it and noticed the scent of pnia root, which was used to dye fair hair black.

Astonished, he sat down, his gaze fixed on the älf-woman.

I've been taken in by an imposter. Along with everyone else who believed her. Then Aiphatòn burst out laughing. *What a con! This warrior-woman passed herself off as an Aklán to rally as many warriors and warrior-women as possible to her command.* He could feel the pain in his back but was ignoring it as much as he could. *In any case, she did delay her death.*

He lifted his head and looked at the Jagged Crown, glowing in the light of the stars in the night sky.

If the con woman had stayed silent and passed away without

uttering those mysterious words about the settlement, he would undoubtedly have travelled back to Girdlegard immediately and would have helped to raze Dsôn Bhará to the ground or hunt dispersed älfar-units.

But now I've learnt too much not to look into it more closely. Aiphatòn believed there really was a secret surrounding the strangely shaped peak.

And he would find out what it was.

Chapter III

Ishím Voróo, Älfar town of Dsôn Elhàtor, 5452nd division of unendingness (6491st solar cycle), early summer

A steady rustling woke Modôia from her slumber.

She opened her eyes and looked out the open, floor-length window at the rough sea; thin white curtains fluttered in the warm wind, dancing for the monarchess.

But it wasn't the waves making the soothing sound.

Dark veils of mist hung from the low-lying grey clouds, covering the sea and the island with rain.

The fat drops pelted down on the balcony, the cane chair and the little table, bursting on them and slowly running off. The first big puddles had formed on the floor outside the room.

As if the sea needed watering. Modôia smiled and slid one arm underneath her head and used the other hand to sweep her long blonde hair back. *Who would guess what's hidden from us in there, growing and sprouting?*

She knew a whole moment of unendingness had gone past. The elixir that Leïóva mixed put her to sleep for a long time and helped her recover. Meanwhile, Dsôn Elhàtor had to manage without her and rely on her son's judgement.

For a little while longer, Modôia enjoyed the sight of the rain and the clean smell that was streaming inside.

Far in the distance the cloud cover was already scattering and the sun was forging its way through, its rays glittering on the waves.

Amid the gently rising and falling waters, many black silhouettes appeared under full sail.

Modôia narrowed her eyes and sat up. *Sails!*

All of a sudden she realised that the First Fleet was expected today. It meant there was a huge amount to be done at the marketplace.

Eagerly anticipating all the goods and new sights, she got out of the bed with its embellished frame made of polished basalt and glass, making sure not to move too fast. Her body was still shattered. Incurably so.

Modôia threw a dark red brocade coat with black and gold embroidery over her white nightdress and opened the double doors from the bed chamber into her study.

She wasn't surprised to find Ôdaiòn at the carved whale-bone table. Surrounded by balled up sheets of paper, he was just writing something down only to cross it out immediately with a despairing groan. The dark blue robe suited him very well and he had sandals on his feet. The whiteness of the floor-to-ceiling bone shelves made the room look bright and welcoming. The papers relating to decrees, laws and events lay in stacks on the floor.

She looked at her son with a smile – he hadn't noticed her coming in. *He is really working hard.* 'What are you working on?'

Ôdaiòn looked up at her, seeming embarrassed that she had caught him trying unsuccessfully to do some writing. He was using the tincture that stopped the white of the eye clouding over in daylight, so the radiance of the deep-sea blue was clear; it went very well with his clothing. This invention would have been invaluable in Tark Draan around the time of Sinthoras' and Caphalor's invasion. Modôia herself didn't think much of it.

Ôdaiòn shuffled the balls of paper together with his foot, to make it seem like there were fewer of them. 'I'm trying my hand at writing to the sovereign of Dâkiòn. It's time for a few more little white lies,' he explained. Breathing heavily, he put the silver ink-pencil he had been writing with to one side and tore up the latest draft. 'How do you manage it, Mother?' He threw the scraps onto the bone tabletop with a flourish.

'I'm older than you and have more experience. That helps a great deal,' she replied. 'And Leïóva's elixirs make me very calm.'

They both laughed.

Modôia went over to him and leaned against the edge of the table. 'So has someone written us a letter?'

The älf, who looked remarkably like his father, nodded. 'It came at dawn. It's the usual, the pleasantries we're used to.' He gestured towards the blank page. 'And even though I'm just as familiar with the niceties, I can't seem to arrange them in a way that still sounds genuinely friendly, despite their triviality.' He ran a hand through his shoulder-length hair, brushing the unruly brown strands out of his face.

Modôia picked up the letter from Dâkiòn.

The sovereign, Shôtoràs, was a seasoned politician to his core, as well as a vehement advocate of the Constellations. He was undoubtedly one of the oldest in his tribe and he came from the days when Dsôn Faïmon was a strong and feared kingdom, when the radial arms were at the height of their powers and nobody could beat the älfar.

Under no circumstances would Modôia underestimate him. While *she* spoke about experience in comparison with her son, Shôtoràs was unassailably superior to *her*.

She knew the old älf hated her. Profoundly and irreconcilably. Her emergence from Tark Draan as if out of nowhere was reason enough. But on top of this was the fact that back then, she had convinced hundreds of älfar to follow her further north, where the sea awaited them.

The monarchess firmly believed that these inhabitants of the Majestic who had been enticed away were the reason why Shôtoràs refrained from attacking Elhàtor: the sovereign dreamed of getting his lost älfar and their grandchildren back. The fragile peace was founded upon it, the peace that was about as buoyant as a plank floating in water: it would founder at the slightest pressure.

Modôia skimmed the message overflowing with friendliness. *And Shôtoràs has been aiming for restraint until now.* 'These are the usual pleasantries,' she confirmed her son's impressions. 'We should reply in a similar way.'

'Just out of curiosity: how would it go if you wrote it?' Ôdaiòn tried to sound somewhat nonchalant.

'My dear Shôtoràs,' she dictated with a self-satisfied smile because he wanted to make her do the work again. 'I was delighted to read your letter. I too assure you as ever of my friendship and goodwill. The town and its residents are well. One of our fleets has just returned from a trading voyage, and there are such delicacies coming up out of the holds.' Modôia looked out the window at the rapidly approaching sails. There were two enormous ships and five smaller auxiliary boats, just like they had learned from the frekoriers. With them, any unit was unbeatable. She cleared her throat and looked at her son. 'At that point you could put in everything that you'll see down at the marketplace.' She put the letter from Dâkiòn back down and stood up. 'Just like that or along those lines, is how it would go if I wrote it.'

'What about the question in his brief second message, Mother?' Ôdaiòn picked up a small piece of paper and passed it to her.

The blonde älf-woman took the piece of paper and her brow furrowed. The lines in her smooth skin deepened as she read aloud:

> 'My dear Modôia,
>
> We once agreed that no ship from Dâkiòn would travel more than four miles downriver. However, how would you feel if we at least permitted our fishermen to go as far as the estuary and within a mile's radius of it? The fishing grounds upstream have been exhausted and you wouldn't want our residents to starve, would you? Plenty of their relatives live in your town.
>
> It's time this permission was granted as a gesture of solidarity and mutual respect.
>
> Please use the bird which brought this message when you answer. He is more reliable than all the others.'

Extremely odd. Modôia lowered the sheet of paper, thought it over, then picked up the first message and held one on top of the other to compare them.

Ôdaiòn laughed softly. 'I had the same thought. And I think the writer went about imitating Shôtoràs' handwriting extremely skilfully. It must be someone who has access to his papers.'

'And the instruction to use the same bird too,' murmured Modôia. 'No doubt the message was never supposed to get to Shôtoràs.' Her stomach grumbled – it was about time she ate something. She couldn't make any decisions before breakfast. 'We won't answer this for now. Since it wasn't written by the sovereign, it can wait.' She handed the sheets of paper back to her son. 'Keep them both safe. Leïóva will be waiting for me with the food. She gets angry if I don't eat.'

Ôdaiòn nodded. 'May I also say that you did well against the onwú, in case Shôtoràs has changed his mind about the peaceful coexistence of the towns?'

'Are you referring to the letters?'

'I was thinking and it occurred to me: isn't it also possible that Shôtoràs did actually write both?'

Modôia was taken aback. *What a strange thought.* 'You think the sovereign wants us to believe there's someone double-crossing him, but in reality he's behind the message?'

'Wouldn't that be an obvious strategy? He could safely gauge our reaction to the request and then easily talk his way out of it by blaming treacherous älfar in his circle.' He leaned back in his chair and pondered to himself, gesticulating, his eyes fixed on the white bone shelf in front of him. 'And if we *were* to allow it, he could use the fishing boats for espionage. It wouldn't be long until one of them happened to get lost along our coast. Badly damaged by a storm, of course, so that it seemed credible.'

She smiled mischievously. 'That would be like Shôtoràs. And kudos to you: you're already thinking like someone who had to operate in the snake pit of the old Dsôn among Constellations and Comets.'

Ôdaiòn looked at his mother. 'Ah, what a great compliment.' He bowed slightly.

'Don't get too full of yourself. And don't forget to go to the market. Our ships should have come into port just this splinter of unendingness.' Modôia left the study and entered the short corridor adorned with mosaics – it had three other doors off it made from opaque, very thin sheets of rock.

At the end of the corridor, she entered a very spacious, bright room which, with its extremely broad glass façade, offered an unimpeded view of the sea at its far end. The delicious hot and cold dishes arranged on the table were giving off delightful aromas.

Chandeliers made from delicate fish bones hung from the ceiling and gave off a lovely light in the evenings. Gold and silver splashes and streaks clung to the whitewashed walls as if the precious metals had been thrown at the walls in a liquid state before hardening.

The rain had subsided and the sun seemed unrestrained, casting its rays on Dsôn Elhàtor and forcing the grey clouds apart.

Modôia noticed the slight twinge as her eyes turned black. Her confidante's essences meant it often took longer, and sometimes the clouding over didn't happen at all on overcast days. That didn't have anything to do with the tincture that her son used but was a side-effect of her own remedies. That's probably why she hated that trendy elixir.

Leïóva was standing at the window with her back to her, dressed in a floor-length silvery white skirt and a chest wrap in the same colour that revealed her willowy physique and brown skin. The sun couldn't bleach the black hair that reached down to her behind. 'I hear the First Fleet is returning from its voyage,' she said in greeting. 'We really need to check what they've brought with them.'

'We will.'

'After some refreshments,' Leïóva added pointedly, without raising her voice. She radiated gentleness and elegance in all that she did. Even when she was killing someone. 'You need your strength and something in your stomach, otherwise my remedies will eat away at your insides.'

Modôia sat down at the table. 'I know,' she responded with a sigh.

Leïóva stayed by the window and crossed her arms underneath her bosom, the muscles across her back and powerful shoulders glistening in the sunlight as she did so. 'I was in the grotto earlier. Work on the ships is coming along well. The only difficulty that may arise is the ships' draught. If the catapults we plan for the upper decks are too heavy, we could run aground.'

'I'm aware of that.' The sovereign helped herself to some of the thin milk soup, scattered some dried fruit into it and then stirred in little pieces of twice-baked spice bread. She always forced herself to eat.

Her spine was sending out a weak pain impulse, which was making its way into the furthest corners of her body. Modôia stopped moving briefly. *The remedy is wearing off again already. Oh, Inàste, what I wouldn't give if it would only stop getting worse.*

Leïóva didn't seem to have noticed. 'Sailing upstream will be a challenge for the helmsmen,' she said quietly.

'It's possible that we'll be putting out to sea earlier than we thought a few moments of unendingness ago.' She ate spoonful after spoonful, barely enjoying the taste that spread across her palate. The frekorian and älfar cuisines complemented one another extremely well, the art of meticulous spicing crossed with careful preparation.

'What do you mean?' Leïóva was still standing serenely at the window.

Modôia told her about the two messages and the suspicion her son had mentioned. 'Either way, it seems like someone doesn't want to stick to the agreement that the Majestic and the Magnificent's spheres of influence remain separate,' she finished, scraping the remaining food in her bowl together. 'Besides, the onwú didn't come up with the idea of sailing in our direction by themselves.'

'So our preparations have turned out to be spot on.' Leïóva laughed drily. 'I knew it! Till his dying breath, the old älf will not be able to get over the fact you took residents away from him and that you transformed Elhàtor into a strong naval power within the space of just a few cycles.'

'We achieved it *together*,' the blonde älf-woman corrected her.

'As far as the outside world is concerned, it was *you* and that's how it's going to stay,' Leïóva insisted and took a deep breath. 'So after our meal, I'll go back to the grotto and tell the architects to come up with a way to reduce the draught.' She turned to the side so that Modôia could see her beautiful, regular profile. Her hair looked like it was made of silken black threads. 'We need something to make the ships lighter and increase the buoyancy.'

'Maybe a specific kind of wood with air pockets?' Modôia offered and beckoned her over. 'Keep me company. We see each other rarely enough without being interrupted.'

Leïóva walked across to her, every step looking easy. Easy and pain-free. She sat down and helped herself to a slice of the dark bread; she sliced some cheese and poured tea, adding milk and ground spices to it. 'That's true. But hasn't it always been that way?' She gave Modôia a warm, affectionate smile and placed one hand on hers. Her eyes were clear and white, not a trace of discolouration visible; there was an amber glow around the pupils, although the colour turned greenish depending on how the light fell.

'Your tinctures to block the colour change are incredible,' the sovereign remarked and winked.

'Aren't they? They're selling very well, although not everyone responds to it equally well. Anyone island-born can tolerate it much better than newcomers descended from the old älfar realms.' Leïóva laughed. 'You could mistake half of the townspeople for elves. Shô-toràs would die at the sight of them.'

Modôia joined in the fun and also ate some bread and cheese, with greater relish this time. The presence of her confidante gave her a lift.

They told each other the latest gossip, none of which had anything to do with politics or disputes. Town life in Elhàtor always had some-thing new in store, bringing couples together and separating them again. Sometimes this happened spectacularly, sometimes quietly and with barely any fuss.

From time to time, Modôia's friend put a drop of elixir in her tea. Without the dose of reddish-brown medicine, she could barely get through the day without screaming.

After a good splinter of unendingness, Leïóva got up. 'Now, if you'll excuse me. The fleet must have sailed into the outer harbour by now.'

'Say hello to your daughter from me.' Modôia nodded to her and drank the rest of the tea in one go under the watchful eye of her friend. 'And Ôdaiòn sends his very best too.'

The slim woman smiled knowingly. 'You and your son would be so pleased if our friendship was carried on into the next generation through their marriage.'

'My son likes her. As far as I know, he's already told her as much.'

'And as far as I know, she informed him that she holds him in high regard. But as commander of the First Fleet, she isn't looking for a long-term relationship.' Leïóva nodded to Modôia and walked towards the door. 'I'll give her your best.'

'Thank you very much.' Modôia propped her elbows on the table and clasped her hands together; she watched her friend leave, then turned her head towards the window.

Her thoughts returned to Shôtoràs and the two messages as she watched the waves and their foaming crests. *The mystery will be solved.*

Tark Draan, Älfar realm of Dsôn Bhará, formerly the elf realm Lesinteïl, 5452nd division of unendingness (6491st solar cycle), early summer

Carmondai woke to find his wrists in iron handcuffs. *A prisoner yet again.* He sat up.

All of his armour and clothes had been removed apart from his loincloth. From one ankle shackle there was a chain tethering him to a ruined sculpture in the middle of the crater. The sun beat down on him, the skin on his face felt tight and he was hot. His overriding feeling was thirst.

It's the simplest form of torture.

'Black eyes and red skin. That looks funny.' In the shadow of a tent, holding a bottle of water in his hand, sat the black-armoured groundling who had saved his life. 'You really haven't been outdoors in a long time, judging by how quickly you burnt.'

'Cheers,' Carmondai replied, scraping dried blood out of the corners of his eyes.

'For letting you roast in the sun?'

'For saving my life.' No matter what position he was in, he couldn't escape the scorching rays. What little remained of the artwork was no use.

'Well, you've heard what I expect in exchange.' The mysterious dwarf took a mouthful of water and the älf's mouth suddenly went drier at the sight. 'Will you do it?'

'You're a zhadár who has switched sides,' Carmondai realised and shielded his eyes with one hand. Dust crunched between his teeth. 'Did you all do that?'

'We never served the triplets with our hearts. Even the admirers were waiting for the orbit when they could drop their masks like all Thirdlings and wipe out the älfar.' He drank some more. 'Until recently I was called Balodil. And yes, I'm the last zhadár created by the älfar. And it's specifically *your kind* that I'm going to hunt until I've driven the last one out of hiding. I know all the secrets you thought were safe.'

'What are you called now?'

The groundling laughed wickedly. 'What would you call me?'

'It would probably be an älfar name.'

'That would probably be appropriate, especially as' – he looked down at himself – 'I'm still wearing my old armour, although without the Aklán's runes.' He poured some water over his furrowed, black face. The drops trickled down off his thick beard and onto his armour. 'Think it over, writer. In the meantime, I'll tell you what you missed when you were locked up down there and time moved on without you.'

'Have you saved my papers?'

'Quite a lot of them, yes. The fire had already spread. The sparks were to blame, I'm afraid. But escaping from the cell like that was a good idea.' The groundling looked up at the palace, a loud explosion audible from it. Shortly afterwards the earth shook slightly beneath them. 'That was the tower,' he explained. 'Caved in, right in the middle. That was it.'

Carmondai swallowed, feeling like his tongue was swelling in his mouth. 'What are you planning?'

The zhadár made a soothing gesture. 'One thing at a time. In broad brushstrokes, the situation is that Girdlegard is free of every insidious threat, from you lot right through to Lot-Ionan, the kordrion and the dragon Lohasbrand. All crushed and stamped out.' He stamped his foot on the ground once. 'When the uprisings against the älfar broke out, Ilahín and his wife Fiëa turned up, having been deep in the woods, hiding from Aiphatòn's hunt. Under their command, an army of humans, dwarves and magicians marched, destroying huge swathes of Dsôn Bhará, and they didn't leave Phôseon Dwhamant unscathed either, or Âlandur, to give it its ancient elven name again. The people in these areas ensure that nothing remains as a reminder of the älfar's existence.' The groundling shook the water bottle enticingly, and there was a splashing sound. 'Have I forgotten anything?'

Sweat ran down Carmondai's brow and trickled into the cut which instantly started to sting. 'Quite a lot has been going on,' he murmured, trying to take in everything that had happened.

'Oh yes! The elves will return. Ilahín and Fiëa started preparing the Golden Plain for resettlement by their people. For some reason, they're convinced the elves will settle down in Girdlegard again.'

A plague on them. Carmondai laughed nastily. 'Whatever they've promised you, if I were in your position, I would make sure that no pointy-eared creature sets foot in it. They cannot be trusted.'

'An *älf* certainly cannot trust them,' the groundling retorted. 'The rest of us can, though.'

Carmondai sighed heavily. 'And *that* is coming from a *dwarf.* These really are new times.'

'And that's coming from a zhadár.' He threw the water bottle to him and watched the älf snatching for it. 'As far as the two of us are concerned: I'm going to go hunting, and you are going to come with me. I've read some of your stories and I liked them.'

Carmondai didn't ask what would happen if he refused. *Better than boiling and roasting.* 'And the elves have agreed to this?'

'Yes. They know your death has not been called off completely and that instead you've been given a postponement before endingness.' He grinned. 'You'll have the chance to clear your name.'

'Of what? I didn't spread any lies.'

'You described the älfar as your people saw themselves. But now you'll see what they did to Girdlegard.' The zhadár watched as the älf greedily sucked the last drops out of the bottle. 'I know three places where the Aklán constructed secret hide-outs. Aiphatòn is travelling through Girdlegard with the same objective as me. But I know he won't find all of you. You'll be a witness to those I track down in the hide-outs.'

Carmondai slowly lowered the bottle, looking astonished. 'Why was the emperor, of all people, spared?'

'Because he helped to defeat Lot-Ionan in the Blue Mountains and led his southern älfar to their doom without causing any casualties on our side.' He pointed into the crater. 'This hole is going to disappear. The catapults are razing the palace to the ground and when the last few threats to the tribes in Girdlegard have been eliminated, the magicians will come and use spells to fill the crater in. A wood will grow over it and its roots will hold prisoner something that will never again be allowed back to the surface: the last few remnants of your race.'

'I see.' Carmondai realised that so many things had happened during his imprisonment that he could have filled countless books with it all. *The most important thing is my survival. Everything else will become clear on the journey.* 'I will go with you and I'm excited, genuinely so, about what I'll see on the way.'

'So be it.' The groundling placed a hand on the hilt of his unusual sword. 'If you don't follow my instructions, I will kill you. If you try to escape, I will kill you. If you try to kill me, I will kill you. If you write anything but the truth, I will kill you,' he rattled off calmly. 'Those are the conditions for our journey together.'

'They are very simple and consistent,' Carmondai commented wryly, wishing he had ten more bottles of water to quench his thirst. *I won't make it that easy for you.* 'Know this: I'm putting my life in your hands.'

'What do you mean by that?'

'Since you won't allow me any weapons, I presume, you will have to protect me. The humans are vengeful.' Carmondai tossed the empty container to him. 'And without me, there are no beautifully written stories about the end, only second-class attempts by humans and groundlings that don't captivate anyone and come across as clumsy. You need me, my dearest new friend.'

The zhadár laughed. 'You're a true älf, just with a bit more subtlety. I'm putting you in chains, which will allow you a certain freedom of movement to dodge pitchforks and projectiles. If the people attack you, I'll stop them slaughtering you. We'll make sure you look sufficiently worse for wear, which will keep their anger at bay.'

'You're too kind.' Carmondai gave a cheerless laugh. *From the master of word and image to a clerk of the decline.* 'When do we set off?'

'As soon as the palace has fallen.' He looked at the älf. 'So what about my name?'

Carmondai was silent, his gaze fixed on the once-imposing building.

The entire tall marble façade tipped slowly forwards, raising clouds of dust as some parts crashed onto the mountain and some parts onto the stairs, wreathing the mountain in grey clouds. Some rubble tumbled down the staircase, destroying the steps and tearing down the fountains on the landings. The red water in the streams and ponds splashed into the air and turned a dirty brown.

All those beautiful skulls and skeletons. Orcs couldn't wreak worse havoc. 'Carâhnios,' he muttered. 'That's what I'd call you: the exterminator.'

'Sounds good.' The zhadár nodded, pleased. 'See you tomorrow morning.' He got up and left the shadow of the tent to make his way to the catapults.

'Are you going to let me roast? I'll lose my head!' Carmondai blinked in the bright daylight.

'See it as preparation for your journey with me. You're going to have to get used to all kinds of headaches.' Carâhnios walked away, laughing. 'Especially when my constant teasing starts to do your head in.'

Groundling humour. The älf turned his attention to the Dsôn

Aklán's collapsing stately home, just a few of its walls still standing. *A symbol of what is happening to us.*

An entire side wall several hundred paces long began to sway, and after a shell struck, it slid down the mountain. Disintegrating, it crashed to the ground and set off a fresh round of quaking through the earth. Clouds of dirt rose up and spread across the surrounding area.

But this time the ground didn't stop shaking.

What have they started? Carmondai heard the first agitated cries coming from the siege equipment and saw an extremely heavy, enormous catapult tilt to one side and disappear downwards. The troops ran in the opposite direction.

That's when he realised: the bombardment was not going to plan.

Tark Draan, Human kingdom of Gauragar, Grey Mountains, 5452nd division of unendingness (6491st solar cycle), early summer

This beats all of my expectations! Aiphatòn was standing at the upper edge of the valley, looking down at the lush greenery surrounded by craggy rock faces, thick sheets of ice and permanent snow. *You could mistake it for a magical illusion.*

But as he didn't feel a twinge or prickle warning him of magic, it had to be real.

Aiphatòn reckoned it was two miles long and half a mile across. Terraces had been built and the trees growing on them bore fruit that did not look ripe enough to eat yet. Amid the tree trunks different types of grain grew wild, as if either their seeds had been mingled when they were being sown or the fields had long since been left to their own devices. A wide, babbling waterfall came gushing out of the mountain at the far end of the valley and plunged into a small lake.

On the ground, he could make out the ruins of stone buildings. Their charred walls and rock faces made it clear that a fire must have raged here a long time ago. Just two buildings seemed to have been built more recently.

Aiphatòn walked cautiously down the steps towards the abandoned basin-shaped valley; he was holding his spear in his right hand.

On one point, in any case, Firûsha's doppelgänger had not lied to him: there *was* a settlement – or at least the remains of one.

He had reached the Jagged Crown several orbits ago and from the summit he had noticed this idyll a few miles below and to the north, eye-catching with its vivid colours in the midst of white and grey.

It would be an ideal place to rally the resistance, just like the älf-woman said. It wouldn't occur to anyone to look here. A warm draught of air was blowing at him, streaming steadily out of the many holes, large and small, in the rock face. That was why the ice couldn't damage the plants and the inhabitants. Aiphatòn noticed a mild sulphurous smell.

He stayed on his guard, but the further he went down the stairs, past the overgrown fields and trees, the more certain he became that nobody lived in this safe, secluded spot anymore.

Least of all any älfar warriors. Aiphatòn reached the ground. Once he had taken off his cloaks and rucksack, he jogged over to the two houses that had been built from the remains of other homes. He could see traces of the fire that must have ravaged the valley on the stones and beams that had been used.

Around the lake, and also to the right and left of the waterfall, he could see metal suspension systems that must once have supported something heavy, something big.

Mill wheels, perhaps? From the durable foundations and last iron remains, he figured there must have been equipment there and it had succumbed to the flames. The former settlers might have had mechanical systems far superior to Girdlegard's from a technical point of view.

Who used to live in this valley? Aiphatòn walked around the first building and after straining his ears briefly, went inside. Whatever had happened here, it was a long time ago.

The furniture seemed very sparse to him and was reminiscent of the elves' tastes. Even the decor had elements that could be traced back to the älfar's mortal enemies; however, he recognised utensils here and there with dwarf runes emblazoned on them. From the different sizes of the mugs, knives and handles on containers, it was clear that dwarves as well as humans and elves had used them.

That's odd. It's as if they were all here at the same time.

In the middle of the only room was a table that also had scorch marks on it. A series of wooden boards lay stacked in a pile on the table.

Aiphatòn picked up the top one and cast a glance over it: the characters carved into it were älfar.

His confusion knew no bounds. *Elves, älfar and dwarves in one place – did they live here together? Did one of them invade the others?*

Aiphatòn sat down on the floor and focused his attention on the letter that had been left prominently enough that a visitor couldn't help but find it. And someone had been absolutely certain that the visitor would be an älf.

My name is Modôia,

I serve Dsôn Aklán Firûsha and came here on her orders to pursue the elves who fled Tark Draan because of us.

When we set out there were ten of us, but the elves were lying in wait and attacked us deviously. The elements and other imponderables also whittled down the size of our party.

In the end I was the only one left and I made it to this settlement.

According to my investigations, groundlings and elves once lived here together, whatever their reasons for deciding to do this might have been.

I'm not staying here long – I'm going to continue the Dsôn Aklán's mission to locate a route past the groundlings' kingdom and stronghold west of here. It's called the Stone Gateway.

I will find a way to Ishím Voróo so that I can look for more älfar there, unbeknownst to anyone else, and lead them back to Tark Draan as reinforcements. If needs be, common beasts who follow my orders will do.

One way or another, the arrival of new troops will surprise everyone and lead the Aklán to victory.

Last but not least, I'm pursuing the last elf-woman. Northwards.

I will leave markings along the way that will be impossible for älfar eyes to miss.

If whoever finds my letter can only read and understand the language of my tribe, it will not be of any use to them.

If the finder is not an älf but an ally of my people, then here are your orders: bring the boards to the Aklán or their successors. You will be rewarded for it.

I don't know whether I will find a path through these wretched mountains.

I desperately hope and wish to catch up with the elf-woman and dispatch her into endingness.

Thus I place my fate in the hands of Samusin. The god of balance has the power to decide what I experience and endure along the way.

Whoever follows me and walks in my footsteps, pay attention to the ground and forge ahead with courage!

Aiphatòn placed the boards to one side and stared at the fireplace where cooled ash had lain for so long. *After me, nobody will find this message again.*

He swept the ashes aside, building a small tinder pile out of wood chips lying around and placed the thin little wooden boards on top, one by one. With flint he got out of his rucksack and a few powerful blows, he set the thing alight. The little flames crackled as they engulfed the dry wood.

Whoever you were, Modôia, your self-sacrifice was for nothing. Aiphatòn waited until there was nothing left of the message. It was possible there were rumours in Dsôn Bhará of the existence of this place full of promise high in the Grey Mountains. *If that is the case, they will not find anything to help them sow terror throughout Girdlegard again.*

He took the rucksack and spear, stepped out of the hut and surveyed the slopes surrounding the valley. He dismissed the idea of setting the fields and trees on fire too. The smoke might attract more attention than was necessary.

Then Aiphatòn turned northwards.

It was possible the veteran hadn't got more than a mile away.

Perhaps she had frozen to death after twenty minutes.

Or she had caught up to the elf-woman and they had both died in the struggle.

One possibility after another occurred to him.

But *one* possibility made Aiphatòn particularly uneasy: with a lot of help from Samusin, through luck or some such, she might have managed to walk to Ishím Voróo. *And left telltale markings behind.*

In his mind's eye he saw Modôia, whom he didn't know at all, recruiting new armies, training them and leading the troops on a narrow path through valleys and along mountain passes towards them.

A fresh stream of starving, revenge-seeking älfar could pour into

Girdlegard, which still had a long way to go to recover from the impact of the oppression and battles.

She set out two hundred cycles ago. What could have happened to her? Aiphatòn contemplated the sky and the glowing sunset bathing the rocks in a warm golden light he had never seen on the plains before. He put it down to the air being thinner up this high.

The moon was out, clear against the night sky, and the most valiant stars were twinkling, almost winking at him.

His gaze wandered to the spot that always remained dark and empty.

Then a shiver of pleasure ran down his spine, despite the warm gusts still flowing out of the holes. *That's the elves' life star! I can make it out again!*

That could only mean one thing – that the battered people were slowly recovering and even announcing births.

Aiphatòn gave a small smile. *I'll sleep better tonight than I have in a very long time.*

He knew what he needed to do at dawn: this twist of fate had changed his mission and might lead him back to his parents' homeland to look for älfar there – they were a greater danger than the Aklán's remaining troops. He would look for them and the path that the last of the Ten may have discovered.

Truly, the mountains are full of wonder.

Ishím Voróo, Forty miles north of the älfar town Dsôn Dâkiòn, 5452nd division of unendingness (6491st solar cycle), summer

'You know the old man will kill us for this?' Gathalor kept looking around as he pulled up the cord with the coloured markings.

Miserable ditherer. 'The depth?' Saitôra replied, unfazed.

'Eight fathoms,' he grumbled, ready to do another measurement right away.

Sitting an arm's length away from him in the bow of the fishing boat, Saitôra noted down the number. 'Only if he finds out what we're up to – and how would he do that?' She remained the picture of calm and glanced over at Iophâlor who was in charge of the steering, keeping them in the middle of the river the whole time. 'Width?'

'The heaving line measurement hasn't changed. For the last two miles it has maintained twenty-eight paces,' he reported, and the älf-woman wrote it down.

The river Tronjor drifted along with the three of them, at its most calm. Their little boat had already weathered two rapids – the most dangerous points of their reconnaissance trip so far.

The young älfar were wearing Dâkiòn fishermen outfits as disguise: brown shorts and sleeveless white shirts. They had brought nets as well as mooring lines with hooks on them. If they met people from Elhàtor, their excuse would be that their boat broke adrift and that they found themselves fleeing swamp creatures using a damaged oar.

Their armour and weapons were stashed in the bow compartment under a pile of empty sacks. These were only there in case someone wanted to harm them. After all, they could run into monsters living in the nearby swamp.

I wouldn't have brought Gathalor with me, but Iriänora insisted. I know all too well why. Saitôra was a good friend of the älf-woman whom many considered the future successor to Shôtoràs. As Saitôra was always game for an adventure, she had taken Iriänora up on her suggestion to measure the river as far as the estuary in secret. The up-to-date map was intended as a gift for the eccentric sovereign's new architect and cartographer. The last exploratory trip had taken place quite a few divisions of unendingness ago and the Tronjor had changed.

Saitôra grinned. *I'm having an adventure.* The black-haired älf-woman had to make numerous notes on the old sketch. The river was the only link to the sea – to its right and left stretched miles and miles of moorland and marsh. The Tronjor was the safest route through it.

The reedy embankments gave way to dizzyingly sheer rock faces, then the terrain became open again and practically boundless until woods and thickets loomed into view. Now their boat was gliding past stony banks with a lush green, grass border rising up beyond them. The blades of grass infused the air with the pungent smell of leeks.

Gathalor fed the string into the water again. 'Eight fathoms,' he announced, sounding like he was about to burst into tears.

White-haired moaner. He's only doing this to impress Iriänora. She nodded and made a note.

According to her calculations, they were at most just one moment from the estuary. As soon as they reached the sea, they would set sail, travelling back upstream to Dsôn Dâkiòn.

It sounded easy when they had discussed it, but the rapids and shallows they had passed through worried her. Iophâlor knew how to sail, and in the places where it was sixty to eighty paces wide he would be able to tack against the current. But they didn't have a reliable plan if there was no wind in the narrow points or the gorges that hadn't been sketched in yet. Disembarking, abandoning the boat and walking didn't seem like a good idea.

Saitôra looked down at the box beside her containing the half dozen pigeons she'd brought. She could use them to send messages to the town in case anything happened to them on the journey or she had important discoveries to share that couldn't wait.

Her favourite was the bird with the golden yellow feathers. A pre-prepared message was on his foot, only intended to end up in Dsôn Dâkiòn in case of extreme emergency: their three wills, succinctly and clearly written.

The pigeons cooed, waggling their heads and looking startled.

This isn't the right way for you to travel. Saitôra slid into a more comfortable sitting position.

'Will we make it through the rapids?' Gathalor asked uncertainly and wound up the cord as if he had heard her thoughts.

'No,' replied Iophâlor from the stern, steering the boat around a piece of driftwood and adjusting their course so that they were back in the middle of the river once again. 'We'd be better off swimming back.' He gave a broad smile.

'What?' Gathalor went pale.

'He was making a joke. It depends on the wind,' Saitôra chipped in. 'Let's pray to Samusin not to forget us.' She looked down the Tronjor and saw the narrow point that was also marked on the map. It didn't seem to have got any wider.

The riverbed narrowed to barely eight paces here. The flat, pleasant banks were gone and rock faces loomed up menacingly. There was no escape now. The water sloshed, foaming, against the obstacle in its path and eddies formed on its surface – a warning sign of a whirlpool.

The boat was gathering speed.

Worried, Saitôra looked at the towering walls either side of the Tronjor. *Our boat is going to wreck against them if Iophâlor doesn't hold his course.* She gulped and couldn't help looking over to the helmsman again.

The dark-haired älf behind her laughed. 'I'm not about to let us crash into them,' he reassured her.

'Twelve fathoms,' Gathalor reported in astonishment. 'It's getting deeper?'

'Because of the current. The eddies wash the sand away.' Saitôra made a corresponding note. 'Keep measuring.'

The rushing water got louder and the hull began to bob in the waves. Droplets sprayed up and sprinkled the passengers.

Saitôra cursed. She needed to be careful that the map didn't suffer any water damage.

Iophâlor's expression had closed off. He had both his hands on the helm now to make sure the boat didn't veer off course.

'Twenty fathoms,' Gathalor cried anxiously. 'And ... here, there isn't enough string anymore.' He turned to the älf-woman, looking horrified. 'The bottom is more than twenty fathoms below us. And the Tronjor is powerful. It's literally yanking at the line like there's a heavy fish hanging off it.'

'Calm down,' she snapped at him, barely managing to make legible entries anymore. The boat swung from right to left, then suddenly the bow dipped down, scooping up a deluge of water that swept over the deck.

This inadvertent braking made the stern swing round and their course changed. They weren't heading towards the gap between the boulders anymore.

Saitôra jumped up in horror and held the map close to protect it. 'Iophâlor!'

'I see it,' he replied in a choked voice and braced his feet against the side of the boat to swing the helm around with all his might.

But the Tronjor defied him.

Gurgling and burbling, the water surged around them, the bow making straight for the wet, black wall.

Saitôra could only guess how fast they were going. *It would definitely rival a swallow in flight.*

'Gathalor, come here,' Iophâlor shouted and leaned his upper body right out over the side of the boat. 'I can't do this alone.'

'I knew it! I knew it!' The white-haired älf staggered awkwardly towards the back and threw his body weight against the thick handle now moving slowly but surely to portside.

'If we drown, you'll have no need to be afraid of Shôtoràs anymore,' Saitôra remarked. *Iriänora will have to explain to me why I have him with me. He's useless.* 'Go on, put some effort into it! This is taking too long.'

Both älfar were screaming with the strain, their muscles bulging. The wood of the helm groaned and creaked under the stress but they managed to make the boat turn back into the current so that they were speeding towards the gap.

Saitôra was taking deep breaths, wiping the spray off her face. 'Well done,' she praised them loudly over the roaring of the Tronjor.

The boat headed for the gap between the boulders and the bow was racing through it when there was a deadly jolt and their journey ended abruptly.

Saitôra toppled forwards and lost her balance. She fell flat on her face on the deck.

The impact as she hit the planks was very painful, but the älf-woman didn't let go of the map. The deck was bucking and rocking beneath her so that she struggled to get to her feet.

Huge amounts of water washed over the stubborn boat as it turned very slowly and began to present its broadside to the current more and more. A loud cracking and splintering sound underneath the soles of their feet made it clear that the timbers were breaking and being torn apart.

Wrecked on a bloody rock! Saitôra was furious and only just about managing to keep her balance. She shoved the map into the waistband of her shorts. If Gathalor hadn't been needed for maintaining their course, the accident could have been prevented with just one glance.

But then the älf-woman heard, amid the roaring of the river, a soft rattle mingled with the cracking of wood.

Is that . . . Her gaze flicked right and left. She could make out rusty iron rings in the rock fitted with a chain that ran underneath the surface – that's what they had crashed into. *What on earth . . .*

At the same moment, the Tronjor hurled itself at the boat and pushed one end down.

The capsizing hull was pushed against the chain along its entire length and split against it, breaking into separate pieces.

Saitôra fell into the torrential river, got caught by the current and was pulled downwards.

It got suddenly colder; the water was like liquid ice. The älf-woman lost track of which way was up and which way was down in the gushing water.

The Tronjor pushed her forwards and her head and face were dragged along the rock, making her cry out in pain – and swallow water that tasted metallic and coppery from her blood.

All at once everything brightened.

Hands grabbed her by her black hair and shoulder; two voices were shouting over each other, then Saitôra was pulled roughly out of the water and across soft sand as she retched and vomited.

Rescued. She propped herself up on all fours. She vomited surges of river water several times, and she was trembling and coughing. Her right cheek burned and she could feel the blood running down it. The wound must have been deep.

When there was no more water to come out of her lungs and stomach, Saitôra knelt back on her heels. She had grazes all over her arms and legs, redness oozing out of them. The map was gone from her waistband.

She had expected to see Iophâlor or Gathalor, but found herself instead facing four älfar wearing green, light leather armour that made them difficult to spot among woods and grassland. Even though Saitôra was still gasping and could barely think straight, she grasped that her rescuers were not warriors from Dsôn Dâkiòn.

She brushed her dark, wet hair out of her face so that she could see better. 'Who are you? How dare you string up a chain and . . . we're fishermen who . . .' She retched again but didn't vomit. 'Where are my friends?'

The unfamiliar älfar silently exchanged looks. Then one of them raised his hand and pointed at the map he held with her blurred notes on it. 'Simple fishermen would hardly have something like this with them,' he replied frostily.

'You're forbidden to travel more than four miles down the Tronjor,' another of them chipped in. 'You would have avoided the shipwreck if you'd adhered to our pact.'

Saitôra tried to pull herself together. *They're scouts from Elhàtor.* 'You have just as little right to be here,' she said, trying defiance and accusation. 'It's more than four miles from here to the mouth of the river.'

'I could claim that we didn't use a boat,' retorted the warrior who had spoken first, splitting hairs. 'Hence we're not breaching the agreement. We're just safeguarding what we and the monarchess are entitled to: protection from Dsôn Dâkiòn. Who would deny us that? How do I know what you've had installed further upstream as protection from us?' He took a step to one side.

The älf-woman saw Gathalor and Iophâlor lying further up the beach. Their eyes were closed, but her friends were breathing. *At least there was that. Nobody was hurt.*

'You're spies!' The unfamiliar älfar tapped the map. 'You've measured the river again to find out which ships you could sail down it as far as the sea, to attack us.' He nodded to his people, at which signal they grabbed Saitôra and dragged her to her feet. 'You're coming with us to Elhàtor. The monarchess should interrogate you herself.'

'No!' she cried indignantly. *That* was too much of an adventure for her. 'No, it's not like that!'

'The monarchess will be the judge of that.' The commander looked at Gathalor and Iophâlor. 'Bash in their heads and throw them back in the river. We only need the girl.'

Struck dumb with horror, Saitôra watched as two of the soldiers picked up huge boulders and dropped the stones multiple times on her companions' skulls and backs of their necks. The twitching bodies of the young älfar were shoved into the gurgling, swirling waters with boot-clad kicks, and then were washed away.

Saitôra had her arms bound behind her back, then two warriors set off with her while the others stayed behind at the bottleneck.

Listless, she let them do as they pleased.

Chapter IV

A timid hand on the bowstring violently jerks the simplest shot.

Wise saying of the Älfar
Collected by Carmondai, master of word and image

**Ishím Voróo, Älfar town of Dsôn Elhàtor, 5452nd division of
unendingness (6491st solar cycle), summer**

Modôia entered the gallery. From it, you could look down into the
large, austere basalt hall. The only embellishments were the runes
chiselled into the walls. The monarchess was followed by Khônatá,
the top cîanai of the fine art, who wore her hair tucked underneath a
coil of colourful cloth. The monarchess felt the painful prickling on
her skin. *It smells of blood, and the air is charged like it is before a storm.*

Below them, half a dozen älfar were practising combat, being
instructed by both warriors and cîani at the same time, in order to combine their skills to become invincible in battle; the shooting pains from
the constant release of invisible energies reached them where they stood.

There were no flags or pennants hanging down or anything that
could go up in flames or get entangled – just pure, fireproof basalt
which could withstand very high temperatures.

Who would have thought it? Fascinated, Modôia watched as the students combined the sword and spear attacks with magic in a supremely confident way.

A house-sized cloud of the blackest darkness formed in one corner of the hall despite it being broad daylight. Modôia just caught a glimpse of the attacker hiding inside it. The edges of the cloud rippled like mist and expanded, edging its way forward.

'So you can spread them out?' the monarchess asked, wearing a deep red, floor-length silk robe with black and silver embroidery on it.

'The girl is capable of plunging the whole building into darkness,' Khônatá explained. 'Her sister is able to create mirages and apparently move everything: walls, doors, windows.'

One young älf got ready to jump and then shot far up into the air, covering a distance of fifteen paces without visibly making any effort. He pulled off the landing as easily as if he had just done a little hop. As he landed, he used a short sword to split a tree trunk as tall as a man in two, right down to where it was clamped to the floor.

Then there was an älf-woman sitting on the floor, rotating five short swords around herself so quickly that no blades or arrowheads could get near her.

A shield made of dancing blades. Modôia nodded almost imperceptibly. 'And they were all born on Elhàtor?'

Khônatá came and stood next to her. She had chosen a high-necked, brown robe that allowed enough air onto her skin through slits. 'The youngest generation, monarchess, and yet the strongest that I've ever trained. They have all absorbed the magic of the island without suffering from it.' Her sympathetic glances did not go unnoticed by Modôia. 'They even manage the spells more easily than anyone else to date. I've never seen our tribe produce anyone like them.'

Only a hundred of them and all of Tark Draan would have fallen to us. 'How strong are they?'

'The real question is this: how strong are they capable of becoming?' Khônatá placed her ringed hands on the railing, black ink stains on the fingers of her right hand. 'And if you *were* to ask me that question, I couldn't answer it for you. The älfar have not had cîani of this quality before.'

That was for sure. Modôia pursed her lips and reflected. 'So we need magical spells to develop their skills further.'

Khônatá bowed. 'And the necessary teachers. Our older cîani may have been exploring our powers and possibilities in Dsôn, but very few of them managed to go beyond the innate skills.' She pointed at an older cîanoi with a brisk gesture. 'Take Olòndôras, for example. He's able to influence the weather if he concentrates hard. But afterwards he has to lie down for ten moments, on the brink of death.'

'The old guard from Dsôn?'

'Correct. Like me, he is able to use the magic of the island but it causes us pain. Or rather, the energy field is not very pleasant.' Khônatá turned her face towards her. 'I heard that you were doing worse, although you're not weaving shadow around yourself or . . .'

Modôia raised a hand to deter her. 'My troubles have not worsened here. And you can save your sympathy too. Elhàtor has become my home and I'll gladly pay the price for us all living here in safety.' She smiled down at the students. 'They've got it better than we do already. Can you imagine how life will be for their descendants one day? What power they will possess and how confidently they'll use it?' The monarchess sighed happily. 'This island, Khônatá, will never be conquered.' *My people are protected from all harm.*

'That is my firm assumption.' The cîanai drew a folder out of her white shoulder bag. 'I took the liberty of writing down some remarkable new advances in detail, so that you can study them at your leisure in your chambers. Soon we'll be able to deploy two cîani on each of our ships instead of one.'

'And that's not counting the magic-wielding warriors and warrior-women in this hall?'

'I'm only talking about cîani of Olòndôras' ilk. Soon the fleet will no longer be dependent on temperamental winds and treacherous ocean currents in order to . . .' Khônatá broke off and stopped herself saying any more.

So you're one of them. Modôia knew that the chief cîanai had come within an inch of mentioning an attack on Dsôn Dâkiòn.

Quite a few of the islanders agreed with her; they wanted to get rid of the latent threat and focus on new goals. Before starting a new war, end the old one, so the saying went.

But war hasn't even broken out. At most, we have a war of words and we're sinking ships belonging to tribes who are deceived or stirred up. There had not yet been any proof that the sovereign Shôtoràs was involved in these attacks in the past. Modôia was relieved by this, because she really would have to start a war if he was.

'Well, that puts paid to the last of our worries, doesn't it? What can stop us in the future if we command the winds?' Modôia chattered away coolly, clapping her hands once before taking the folder. 'Thank you for your thoughtfulness and your time.' She rested her left hand on the cover. 'I am going to read this thoroughly and let you know what magic I want to see improved.'

Modôia turned around, sighing softly as her spine sent scorching heat into all of her bones. She swallowed and moved more slowly, but still steadily, towards the exit of the gallery and the basalt building. She wouldn't have been able to endure it any longer without fainting.

Being in a place where the magic was concentrated caused her a huge amount of pain, which she had tried to combat by taking a double dose of elixir in advance. *Leïóva needs to change the formula of the concoction or soon I'll barely be able to leave the house.*

Khônatá saw her out and the älf-women said their goodbyes.

Her gait stiff, Modôia went down to the harbour to enjoy the wind and look at the wares the merchants had on display.

The further she got from the academy, the more the pain subsided.

Khônatá once tried to explain the discomfort with an analogy. The magical field, palpable across the whole island, affected the älfar from Ishím Voróo like a thin spike. For some, a poison flowed out of the spike, for others it was an invigorating substance.

Khônatá attributed the fact that Modôia suffered more than anyone else to the fact that the monarchess had been in Tark Draan, where a different kind of magical energy prevailed. Her body had grown accustomed to one kind and was rejecting the new kind. The youngest generation, however, was born with none of the foreign magic at all, and enjoyed the advantages of the island's version.

I wonder if they would be in as much pain as I am if they were to go to Tark Draan? Modôia walked stiffly on, as if she were in the cold winds of the Grey Mountains, her limbs and muscles nearly frozen solid.

The cries of the locals rang out ahead. The merchant fleet had brought an array of goods to be given away and bartered. No coins were used on Dsôn Elhàtor; the locals bartered for things they needed.

Along the coasts and on some of the islands in the area, the älfar did use gold as a currency, because the inhabitants liked to hear it clinking in their purses, but the abundance of wealth on Elhàtor made all currency redundant.

Modôia strolled through the narrow alleyways, enjoying the shade, the wind and the hubbub of voices growing louder. Children raced along the cobbled streets and played tag. *The young generation that no longer needs to put up with any disadvantages.* She waved to the boys and girls and they returned her greeting cheerfully and effusively. *Innocent and perhaps more powerful than the Inextinguishables ever were.*

There was no cult surrounding Modôia and nobody worshipped her as they did Nagsor and Nagsar Inàste. She was the monarchess and nothing more. If her death came, the people expected her son to follow her into office. Her clever Ôdaiòn was very well suited to it, he was good-looking and aware of how things worked despite not being island-born. *He's still finding it difficult, but he's learning.*

Modôia had reached the harbour, which was protected by an enormous wall and the fence.

The remains of the ships that had attempted the ramming attack and been smashed to pieces by the concentrated jets of water had left sculptures on the quay and turned them into works of art; the dead body parts in them served as food for small crabs. They plucked the flesh meticulously off the bones.

A work of art that constantly evolves. Modôia nodded approvingly as she strolled past the artworks, admiring and marvelling at them like some other locals.

Her thoughts turned to Leïóva, who was overseeing the construction of special ships that could be used to travel the eighty miles up the Tronjor and disembark outside her hometown.

Dsôn Dâkiòn would be surprised by their arrival and their cîani's skills would shock old Shôtoràs and his guards even more. The river may be two miles from the Majestic but that could be factored into their plans. Magic was swifter than any arrow or night-mare.

But there was as yet no well-thought-out plan incorporating the exact sequences of events in their military campaign.

Modôia thought about the two messages she had received, one from Shôtoràs and the shorter one from an unknown hand. Unlike Elhàtor, other places seemed to be preparing.

Was it a mistake not to be making these kinds of invasion plans? Modôia stopped in front of a sculpture without really taking it in. *How quickly could the sovereign drive his troops downstream?*

She placed one hand against the rotting wood which was held in place with gold, silver and tionium wire. She could clearly feel the warmth radiating from its porous, rough surface.

A new thought occurred to her: had Shôtoràs already sought out allies? Would some coastal towns potentially make their boats available so that Dâkiòn did not even have to come down the river, but could just walk to the coast?

But the moorland between the town and the coastline was considered impassable. An eighty-mile strip of land inhabited by monsters, diseases and mosquitoes that attacked hikers in swarms and killed them. Even marching along the riverbank was too risky – there were quite a few areas of swampland and quicksand.

Modôia sighed again. *I just wanted to stretch my legs and get away from the pain. Instead I'm brooding over what I should do.*

If Leïóva had her way, the grotto would already be full of the long, narrow boats that fit through the narrowest parts of the river.

They could glide up the river with their diamond-shaped sails. The lack of woods around Dâkiòn would not prevent a conquest: straight after landing, the ships could be dismantled according to a detailed blueprint so that ladders and catapults could be built from them. The fixing bolts were prefabricated, the parts carefully marked. The scholars had thought of everything.

And yet I don't want that. There have been too many wars. Modôia was looking ahead to the marketplace with its spices, the barrels full of goods and fabrics, and the news the sailors had to report. *One more alley and I . . .* Then she noticed the shadow falling next to her own.

As if out of nowhere, the black-haired Leïóva was standing next to her looking very solemnly at her. 'You've got to come with me.' She was wearing the white skirt and matching chest wrap. She didn't seem bothered by the heat; there wasn't a drop of sweat on her tanned skin.

'Did I miss a meeting?' She looked around in astonishment. 'I was with Khônatá and . . .'

'We've taken a prisoner,' the slim woman interrupted her. 'In the area around the estuary, at the bottleneck our scouts are safeguarding.'

'Why have the warriors brought them to Elhàtor?' Modôia's thoughts were struggling to keep up. First, she had to shake off what she had just been thinking, which fit unfortunately well with this news.

'For interrogation. She's a spy,' Leïóva replied brusquely.

That got Modôia's attention. 'Proof?'

Her confidante handed her a crumpled, tattered map with the river sketched on it. The paper must have been in the water, but it was clear amendments and annotations had been made to it.

Now I've got the proof I never wanted. Modôia put the map away and motioned for Leïóva to walk on ahead of her.

They crossed various bridges and smaller footbridges before reaching one of the closely guarded and secured entrances to the grotto.

The lightly armed guards let them pass and soon they were descending a wide staircase into the cavern hidden below the surface of the island.

The air temperature was noticeably cooler and felt damp. It smelled of wet stone, algae and mussels.

The sea cave they entered was a mile wide and had four entrances; the ceiling was high enough to accommodate the fleet despite the height of the masts.

Modôia had had the heavy stalactites cut down and made into missiles for catapults to prevent any harm to ships and crews. If the large and small vessels weren't in the harbour to unload goods, they were steered into the grotto. The commanders were able to set sail at any time and in any direction via the tunnels.

Leïóva led Modôia past the long harbour wall – from which long footbridges led to the waiting ships in the grotto – and towards the empty prisoner wing.

Anyone who did something wrong in Elhàtor – and that happened extremely rarely – ended up here after a good beating. If they didn't learn their lesson, they would be put out to sea in a boat with no oars. If they found their way back to the town, they were pardoned.

But with spies from Dâkiòn, Modôia would show less mercy.

They entered the large space that had been hewn out of the rock, the place where the punishments were meted out; at the sight of the älf-women, the two warriors waiting there wearing the green armour of scouts rose to their feet and greeted them respectfully.

The prisoner had been stripped and was standing with her arms forced above her head in the middle of the room. Her wrists were in iron handcuffs bound to the ceiling via chains. They had refrained from tying her to one of the upright wooden stakes where the beatings took place.

'Monarchess, we detained the boat at the strait we were guarding,' one of the two scouts began their brief report. 'This one survived. She wouldn't tell us her name.'

Modôia dismissed the scouts with a nod and walked slowly up to the black-haired prisoner; she took the creased map out as she did so.

'You measured the river,' she said pleasantly. 'Give me *one* good reason why I should *not* assume that your intentions were related to war.'

The naked älf-woman looked past her at Leïóva and remained silent.

'Do you want to tell us your name, little girl? It'll be easier to speak then,' the monarchess suggested, taking in the side of her face that had cracked open as well as the raw skin on her scalp. 'That looks bad. I've got good healers who will take care of you. Afterwards too, once I've finished your interrogation. But only –' she rolled up the sheet of paper and forced the prisoner's chin upwards with it – 'if you tell me what you were trying to do.'

'An attack, what else,' grumbled Leïóva in the background. 'Width and depth are marked, and in the most minute detail too. I . . .'

Modôia raised her other hand and her friend fell quiet. 'Would you bring me my whip?'

'Of course.' Leïóva hurried out.

'I'd like to warn you that the pain I inflict on you will not be out of malice, little girl,' she said apologetically. 'You could spare yourself all this by speaking to me.'

The unfamiliar älf-woman gave her a searching look, then raised her pale grey eyes to the ceiling and acted indifferent.

'Ah, you're a warrior, of course, and you think I can't scare you.' Modôia put the map away and turned to the door just as Leïóva was returning with the coiled whip. 'After the first blow, you'll see that you overestimate yourself.' She removed the protective caps and jerked her arm to unfurl the weapon.

The three straps slid to the floor and looked like they were creeping forwards like snakes; there was a soft clanking sound. At the end of each strap was a blade sharpened on both sides; a thick wad of wire wrapped around the leather protected it from the sharp edges.

'My son and I are only ones who know how to use this without cutting ourselves to pieces.' Modôia enjoyed the sight of the blades twitching as if they were alive. 'I don't use it often. I used to be able to slice the limbs off a full-grown barbarian and cut his throat in just one blow. Since you're not wearing any armour or even any clothes as protection, you're making it very easy for me.'

The prisoner swallowed. Goosebumps formed on her bare skin.

'It takes skill and a good eye to swing this vicious weapon in such a way that you hover between death and agony.' The älf-woman lifted the whip and cracked it gently.

The straps hissed straight at the terrified prisoner – and changed direction at the last moment. The blades shaved three long strips off the wooden stake right next to the trembling captive.

'You haven't lost the knack,' Leïóva remarked and laughed quietly.

Modôia nodded approvingly and ignored the pain in her shoulder, her spine warming up. 'That ought to give you an idea of what is about to happen to your flesh. I will slice out little sections all over your body. Then I'll continue with the bones,' she explained politely. 'My healers will stop you dying on me and then . . .'

'Saitôra,' she blurted out. 'My name is Saitôra.' She strained furiously at the chains.

Leïóva emitted a disappointed sound. 'Now we'll both miss out on our fun, monarchess.'

'Be patient.' Modôia moved her arm, flicking the three straps at the ground in front of her feet with a jingling sound. 'Now, Saitôra. You measured the river . . .'

'Your warriors murdered my friends Gathalor and Iophâlor,' she shouted, enraged. 'They bashed their heads in to make it look like an accident.'

'It was an *accident* that you encountered my scouts. Because you and your friends were not allowed to be there in the first place. Let's leave it at that. And you ought to be glad you escaped the *accident*. It could just as easily have been you getting eaten by crabs and fish.' Modôia spoke like a scolding mother. 'Did Shôtoràs dispatch you to the *accident*, to use your term?' she asked, condescending now. 'How far did the preparations for the attack get?'

'I don't know anything about an attack.'

'So you measure the river as a way of killing time, make notes on the map out of boredom and breach the agreements between our two towns on a whim?' Modôia made the leather lashes twitch, the blades sliding towards Saitôra's bare feet. 'One more time: who sent you?'

The älf-woman stared at the blades, petrified. 'Iriänora. My friend and Shôtoràs' niece.'

'Ah, so it is true!'

'No, nothing to do with a war. She wanted to give the map to the new architect as a gift!'

Leïóva laughed in disbelief. 'Somebody thinks you're more stupid than she is herself.'

We'll see. Modôia struck as quick as a flash.

The straps with the blades whistled as they darted forwards and Saitôra screamed in fear of her life. Her courage vanished as quickly as it had come.

But the monarchess had planned the blow in such a way that the leather wrapped itself around the upper arms and torso of the prisoner without the tips piercing the skin. 'One last warning, Saitôra. My next blow' – she undid the straps which left dark blue welts on the älf-woman's grazed skin – 'will go deep and it's going to be bloody.'

Saitôra was panting hard. 'I swear I don't know anything else,' she said, weeping. Modôia simply gave the whip a crack and the prisoner screamed as though out of her mind. 'I swear! Please, I just wanted to have an adventure.'

Leïóva came forward, approaching Modôia, who was looking indecisively at Saitôra. 'I get the feeling,' she murmured, 'we have the wrong person in chains.'

'So do I. Your friend Irïanora should have a taste of my whip.' *If she was ever truly a friend.* Sending this young älf-woman down the Tronjor without even hinting at the danger it put her in showed an extreme ruthlessness on Shôtoràs' niece's part. Modôia turned to Leïóva. 'Might Irïanora have written the second message, do you think?'

'We could let Saitôra have a look at it. She may recognise the handwriting.' She left the room at a signal from the monarchess.

'Tell me about your friends,' Modôia said on the spur of the moment.

'They're dead,' Saitôra spat.

'Yes, slain in an *accident* that Irïanora is responsible for.' She relaxed her painful shoulders and this alone was enough of a threat to make the prisoner start whimpering. 'Who were they?'

'I didn't know Gathalor, but Iophâlor . . . he was a good warrior and swimmer. He served in . . .'

'Did they come from prominent families?'

Saitôra looked at her in astonishment. 'I . . . don't know. I doubt Iophâlor did.'

'Think!' Modôia lifted her arm and thrashed the whip in one fluid movement, despite her own pain.

The blades leaped into the air, whirring away and burying themselves in the post in a vertical line; the tips sank deep into the wood and wouldn't come out again when she tried to pull them out with a jerk.

This was always its flaw. Modôia swore inwardly. *Luckily Ôdaiòn has mastered another method.* She went to the large stake and, with some effort, pulled the blades out one by one.

'Did you see how easily . . .' She turned to Saitôra who was hanging limply from the chain beside her. Modôia couldn't help laughing: the young prisoner had fainted in fear.

Tark Draan, Älfar realm of Dsôn Bhará, formerly the elf realm Lesinteïl, 5452nd division of unendingness (6491st solar cycle), early summer

Cracks formed in the earth beneath Carmondai's bare feet as the ground continued to shake unrelentingly. He couldn't crawl away; the chains were holding him in place near the remains of the statues with steely indifference. *I mustn't stay here.*

'Carâhnios!' he shouted.

Next to the mountain, the crater was subsiding even further. The sides of the banked-up mound collapsed and slid into the opening. The edge of the opening was coming closer to the älf with every heartbeat. The catapults vanished into the hole one after another.

The shaking under Carmondai's feet was not letting up. There was still no sign of the groundling.

'Zhadár!' Unlike the others, he guessed – or rather he *knew* – what was happening. They were standing in the oldest part of Dsôn Bhará, where the Moon Pond had been – it was through here that the triplets had led the älfar out of Phondrasôn. After the Aklán arrived, the marshy pool had run dry and caved in.

Nobody had ever reckoned on this phenomenon happening again. *There was too much heavy siege equipment in one place. Along with the palace's land collapsing, the weakened crater floor gave way.* At

Carmondai's feet the earth sank by two or three hands' widths, but it didn't cave in altogether.

The quaking ended.

Then the groundling appeared by his side. 'Ah, you haven't left yet,' he cried, grinning. 'Just stay there then.'

Never. 'Untie me!' Carmondai demanded fiercely, noticing more fissures forming beneath him. He suspected the destruction could start again at any moment. 'I'm meant to be recording the decline. This event is part of it.'

'Not in the way I had intended, but all right, fine,' Carâhnios agreed. He took a key out of his pocket and detached the foot shackle fixture from the chain. 'Your hands stay in the cuffs. You'll have to remember what you see. We've got nothing to write with here.'

Carmondai followed the zhadár. His skin was noticeably tight, the sunburn making itself felt despite his agitation. He tried to ignore the fact he was wearing nothing but a loincloth so as not to feel too ridiculous.

Right next to the palace mountain, which had lost a whole chunk out of one side, a hole had formed with a diameter of a hundred paces. Terrible clouds of dust were rising up out the hole, as if rainclouds and thunderclouds were being created in the abyss and making their way towards the heavens.

The people and the elf-woman stood at the edge and looked cautiously downwards. From time to time they leaped backwards when smaller pieces broke off.

Carmondai reached the edge with the zhadár, and both of them looked into the darkness.

It looked like a wide well shaft had opened up. Along with the catapults – whose remains could be seen at the bottom of the abyss – the palace and mountain debris had smashed through multiple layers of rock.

Near the bottom there were clearly discernible holes and signs of cave entrances in the walls, which suggested there were passageways down there and that beasts could appear through them at any moment.

'An entrance to Phondrasôn,' Carmondai murmured. *Just as I thought.*

'What do you think?' Carâhnios looked at him.

'The Moon Pond was once in this spot, and beneath it were the foothills of Phondrasôn, the place of exile. I escaped from there with the Aklán more than two hundred cycles ago,' he summarised. 'The elf-woman may still remember the Moon Pond.' He felt a shooting pain at the back of his neck, partly because of his old bones and partly because of his burnt skin. And he was still parched. 'Pray to your god Vraccas that the collapse didn't create any openings that will allow monsters to escape.'

'That's all we need,' Carâhnios grumbled. 'Vraccas, hurl glowing coals into this hole and burn it out.'

Fiëa spat into it. 'The älfar's gift to us. We defeated them and in return they fling open the gateway to Tion's kingdom.'

'Blame the advisor who had the catapults built,' Carmondai said. 'There was no earthquake while the Aklán lived and ruled here.' He looked at the elf-woman. 'In my dungeon, I would have noticed it immediately.'

'What do we do now?' asked one of the soldiers, at a loss.

'Scrape the loose earth away from the crater and push it inside,' Fiëa replied anxiously. 'Ideally before the monsters realise they have a path to freedom.'

'You should be quick about it,' Carâhnios remarked. 'And until the passageways that we can make out down there are blocked off again, we should also have pots of boiling pitch and tar lined up so that we can tip them out over any attackers climbing up.'

'Hear hear,' Carmondai agreed in an undertone.

'You ought to be pushed in, black-eye!' a soldier said menacingly. 'As a sacrificial offering.'

'The dwarf is right.' Fiëa looked out over the ranks of her volunteers to the right and left. 'Prepare cauldrons and then send for more workers from the surrounding kingdoms.' She turned around, fixing her gaze on the mountain. 'Chip away at the sides more and push the ruins of the palace downwards. That will get us part of the way there anyway.'

The captains passed on the instructions and Carmondai was silent so as not to draw any more attention to himself.

'Four good men have fallen in. We should climb down and look for them,' one warrior said.

Fiëa shook her head, her fair hair bouncing. 'Nobody is setting foot into it.'

'But they . . .'

'They are dead or so severely injured that they will be dead by the time you've risked your life and made it down,' she cut across him unsympathetically. 'We will remember them but it's more important that everyone helps stoke the fires underneath the cauldrons and fill in this hole.' Fiëa waved her arms over the pit in a blessing. 'May Sitalia receive their souls and take care of them. Our responsibility is to the living.' She pointed one hand at Carmondai, her index finger extended in accusation. 'Get rid of him, zhadár. I can't bear him near me so long as one spark of life remains in him.'

Carâhnios turned to the älf, snarling. 'All right then. Our trip is going to start a little earlier than planned.' He set off, making straight for the only house in the crater still standing. 'Let me pack up my gear while you count your lucky stars, because you're going to travel through Girdlegard with me killing älfar.'

Better than lingering in the vicinity of the elf-woman. Carmondai followed him, holding his cuffed hands loosely in front of his stomach. 'Something to write with would be a good idea. And clothes. But water is even more important.'

'We will get our hands on that. Stay out here.' Carâhnios disappeared through the doorway.

Carmondai couldn't wait anymore; he saw a horse trough and stuck his head into it. The water tasted stagnant and he saw little bits of straw floating in it, but he lapped it up anyway. Warm yet exquisite, it sloshed around inside him. He swallowed and swallowed until he emerged spluttering and gasping for breath. *Better, much better.*

He looked at the mountain again, a hundred troops scaling it via the remains of the badly damaged staircase.

Despite the sunburn he suddenly felt ice cold: there was a gaping hole where his dungeon used to be. You could see inside the prison like it was a crushed ants' nest.

If I hadn't escaped, I would be dead and my notes would have been lost in the hole. He thanked Samusin for his mercy.

Carmondai didn't for a moment wish the appearance of monsters upon Tark Draan, or at least not as long as he was in the crater. *After that, whatever happens, happens.* He leaned back against the wall of the house. His face burned even though he was standing in the shade. With a cupped hand, he scooped more water from the trough and poured it over himself.

Carâhnios did not reappear for quite some time.

When he did, he was carrying a large bag which he fastened to a white pony, as well as four saddlebags which he tied to a horse. A soldier brought out some shabby clothes and Carmondai put them on awkwardly. His handcuffs were taken off briefly so that he could do so.

He was getting even hotter now; his skin felt like it was glowing and the fabric about to burn. To add insult to injury, the trousers and shirt were too short and the boots were too wide. *I look like an idiot.* The humiliations continued.

'I'm bringing rations and some sheets of paper as well as quills and ink,' the zhadár announced and shooed the älf towards the horse. 'Mount.'

Ink. It will fade and run and leave blots. Carmondai thought wistfully of his smashed, burnt pencils made from coal dust. 'Was nothing saved from my dungeon?' He swung himself into the saddle and every one of his joints hurt. The daystar seemed to have penetrated right through to his bones.

'Some stuff was. But I didn't manage to get my hands on anything else just now.' Carâhnios put the handcuffs on him and attached them to a chain that he passed underneath the horse's belly and secured with a padlock. 'For your sake, I hope you can ride. Because jumping off is not going to work for you.' Laughing, he strode over to his pony and mounted it. 'If you start to slip, let me know straight away.'

'So that you don't miss it, I take it?'

'Absolutely! It's going to be hilarious to see.' Carâhnios howled with laughter.

Carmondai cursed inwardly. He used to be extremely skilled at riding, racing into battle at a gallop brandishing his lance. *Nobody forgets how to do it, but it will take a while for me and the nag to get to know each other.* Disappointed, he inspected the horse. 'Is there a nightmare that I could use, maybe?'

'No. Most of them have been killed.' Carâhnios set his pony trotting. 'If we see unicorns along the way, you can make yourself one. But something tells me you'd die in the attempt.'

Sighing, Carmondai followed him to the winding paths that led out of the basin-shaped valley and up to the plains. *This is going to be the hardest journey I've ever undertaken.*

Quite apart from becoming a witness to a zhadár killing one älf after another, the spectre of his own death hung over him constantly. Either in the form of angry locals who wanted to take revenge for oppression and abuse, or at Carâhnios' hand when his mission was complete and there was nothing left to hunt or for Carmondai to record. What's more, he doubted whether the elves could restrain themselves from demanding his life much longer.

I'll need to have a plan by then.

Escape or become indispensable, those were the options.

He didn't have much faith in an escape.

What could I offer them to avoid endingness? Carmondai rode after the groundling. *Knowledge. That's the advantage I have.*

Now he needed the people and the groundlings to ask the right questions about his knowledge – then he would be allowed to keep living.

Only the living get options.

Ishím Voróo, Älfar town of Dsôn Dâkiòn, 5452nd division of unendingness (6491st solar cycle), summer

Irïanora was looking anxiously at the two bedraggled pigeons that had turned up in the pigeon loft just a few moments before.

Pecking and cooing, they walked back and forth on the landing board, their heads bobbing as they went over to the water bowl and drank in small sips.

No message for me. The älf-woman left the cramped coop on the roof of her house and looked at the river. She traced its course until the trees got too high and she could no longer make out even a flash of it.

Irïanora could vividly imagine why there was no scrap of paper, but she didn't dwell on the explanation for how the pigeons had got away: the boat carrying Gathalor, Saitôra and Iophâlor had had an accident, either in the rapids or because of driftwood, or another unfortunate series of events. The cage had smashed in the accident and these birds had found their way home; the rest of the carrier pigeons had probably sunk to the bottom of the river.

She didn't dare speculate whether her friend Saitôra was still alive.

And Irïanora was equally unsure whether she ought to wish the gods came to the aid of the trio and that they found a path back through moorland and swamp teeming with vermin and snakes. Not even monsters ventured into the woods either side of the river.

Even our best scouts don't get more than half a mile in before having to retreat. Not one of the three of them is capable of fighting their way through that terrain. So many thoughts were racing through her mind, and none of them good ones.

Assuming they managed it nevertheless, Saitôra, Gathalor and Iophâlor's return would obviously be noticed straight away, no matter what state they were in. Plenty of questions would be asked if inhabitants of Dsôn Dâkiòn disappeared and then suddenly turned up outside the gates.

They will not be able to wriggle out of it with talk of getting lost. Irïanora felt like having a large glass of wine.

The trail would inevitably lead to her, the niece of the sovereign, and that meant she would be in huge trouble with her uncle. But all she had wanted was to have a map of the river, an up-to-date one, so that she could discuss her ideas with like-minded people, of which there were quite a few in Dâkiòn.

I should have allowed for an accident in my plans. She walked over to the narrow staircase down to her living quarters.

She quickly swapped the grey shawl she always put on before she went up to the pigeons for a bright red dress. A few feathers came loose and floated through the room with its ten-paces-high ceiling.

Irïanora took a pitcher of wine out of the cabinet, poured herself some and diluted it with water. The alcohol ought to do the trick somewhat. Maybe then she could come up with a plan for how to explain the whereabouts of the missing trio.

But short of sending out a second group, she was stumped.

Would that be wise? Hesitant, she poured herself a second glass and this time didn't add the water. *No, I can't do that. It will attract even more attention.*

On her third glass of wine, Irïanora decided that the pigeons had simply escaped. An accident hadn't necessarily happened, and the little group might be on their way back already. In complete secrecy so that nobody found out anything about it.

If the three didn't turn up within seven moments of unendingness, their families would send out a search party. And as soon as that happened, an expedition could potentially be sent down the Tronjor after all.

I'll just say that they wanted to go fishing. Irïanora took a deep breath, and another sip. *It will work out. I'll get my map. And maybe more. I didn't send that idiot Gathalor along for nothing.*

There was a knock on the door downstairs and her maid, Zelája, answered it. After a loud argument that came closer and closer to the room, the door to her chamber opened.

An armed man stood on the threshold wearing the insignia of her uncle's bodyguards.

This seems like perfect timing for bad news. Irïanora sipped her wine. 'I didn't invite you to come inside.' Offence was the best form of defence and it suited the sovereign's niece very well.

'I request that you follow me.' His eyes were alert and fixed on her, his expression hard. He would not stand for any arguments or excuses. 'I have been sent by Shôtoràs.'

'On what business?' She made an effort to look nonchalant although she was rattled.

'My task is to accompany you to the sovereign. I don't need to know any more than that.' He unblocked the doorway, which was a clear command.

Iriänora decided against playing any more games and walked to the warrior's side; she polished off the wine as she did so and handed the empty glass to the waiting Zelája.

'Have dinner ready just after sunset,' she ordered as she passed by. She appeared unfazed.

They left the house, walking through the neatly laid out streets and over the bridge into the second, larger part of Dsôn Dâkiòn. The majority of the residents lived there.

In Iriänora's district, some buildings had stood empty ever since so many älfar moved to Elhàtor with Modôia. The generations that followed were too small to fill the gaps and bring back the old hustle and bustle.

Iriänora used this walk, which she was trying to make last as long as possible, to examine her hometown in the radiant sunlight.

Due to Dâkiòn's position, perched on top of the mountain with its impassable, steep slopes, the Majestic was impregnable. This was what Iriänora firmly believed as she walked over the ravine between the upper and lower towns and looked down into the abyss.

Nobody knew what had happened to the giants who had built their fortress on this spot in earlier times. A few bones had been found and they stood in the squares as works of art, reminders that the älfar owed their sanctuary to the transience of their predecessors.

They must have been wiped out by an epidemic. A fever from the moor, Irïanora thought and after the bridge, she turned onto the path that led to her uncle's palace.

The warrior escorted her in silence, not revealing what he was thinking.

Soon they were standing in the Hall of Entreaties, as the locals had taken to calling this auditorium with cross vaulting and a ceiling thirty paces high. Artists had decorated the walls, and the ceiling was panelled with slivers of bone while the arrises were plated with silver. Multiple chandeliers hung low to provide light.

Ah, I'm to lend the old man a hand. Irïanora moved towards the chair to the right of where her uncle sat whenever he heard suggestions, entreaties and complaints every forty moments of unendingness. She had been present at the last session, bringing him wine and correcting the scribe if he made a mistake when recording the cases.

'Stop.' The warrior held her by the arm. 'You're to wait here.'

With a mixture of disbelief and bewilderment, she stood still.

Now I'm the one who's to be heard? Anything was possible. Maybe it was repercussions from the onwú or maybe it was probing questions about the boat she had had designed. *For the first time, I'm on this side of the hall.* The älf-woman had a bitter smile on her face.

The side door swung open and Shôtoràs entered without deigning to look at her; for once he was tapping the end of his walking stick down softly.

He ascended the platform and took a seat behind the balcony-like desk. He shooed the guard out with an impatient gesture.

The door banged shut behind the älf, setting off an echoing rumble like a thunderstorm.

The sovereign rubbed the back of his neck with one hand and tossed back his thick, pale grey hair. One hand rested on the metal crow's beak, the other lay on the little desk. His eyes were fixed on the dark wood for now, his mouth pressed into a very thin line.

Iriänora sensed it was smarter to wait, although it took some effort.

Suddenly Shôtoràs tapped the desktop quickly with the tip of his index finger, drew breath and emitted nothing but a loud exhalation. He seemed to feel the words that occurred to him were inadequate.

Without warning he reached into the pocket of his robe, took something out and threw it at her. Pale feathers twirled across the room.

Iriänora was hit by a dead golden pigeon that must have fallen into the clutches of a bird of prey.

The animal fell at her feet with a muffled rustling sound, one of its wings splayed out; red spatters were clearly visible on it.

Iriänora understood within half a heartbeat and she started to feel hot. Beads of sweat formed on her back and forehead. She needed to come up with something right now. Neither of her plans had foreseen that her uncle would receive news first.

'I, Gathalor, declare that my worldly goods should go to Iriänora,' he quoted from memory, reciting the words as if they were a poem. 'As she already possesses my heart, may she also, in the case of my death, be given my assets.'

The sentences echoed across the high ceiling and took a long time to fade away.

You mustn't make any mistakes now, Iriänora warned herself and conjured up an expression of shock on her face. 'Gathalor is dead? How terrible!' She looked at the battered pigeon. 'Why does the news come to us like this?'

Shôtoràs leaped up and banged the walking stick on the desk; the bone inlay rattled as it shattered and then skipped along the stone floor. 'Try again,' he thundered.

Irïanora tried to work out from his furious expression what he already knew and what he was still figuring out. She admired his composure. If he were any other älf, the black lines on his face would long since have become visible.

'So he has put into action what he used to tell me about so often,' she began cautiously. 'He dreamed of travelling down the river.'

Shôtoràs sat down very slowly and didn't say a word.

'He, Saitôra and Iophâlor had made firm plans. They wanted to explore the Tronjor and see what adventures there were to be had along the way. Life in Dsôn was too boring for them and didn't offer any excitement,' she said, concocting an explanation in which she was ultimately the least to blame. 'I tried to dissuade them. Our last conversation about ships was still fresh in my mind. Poor Bethòras.'

Shôtoràs shifted his probing gaze away from her and stared at the high ceiling with its little tiles of bone; his right hand remained on the handle of his stick. The reflection of a beam of light from one of the silver arrises fell right across his face, as if he had a glowing scar.

'Since absolutely anything can happen on a trip like that, I asked Gathalor to take some of my carrier pigeons with him so that they could summon help in case of an emergency,' Irïanora continued, feeling slightly more sure of herself. *He knows less than I feared, otherwise he would have interrupted me long since.* 'I gave them an old map to take with them so that they could get their bearings and not be at the mercy of every set of rapids.'

'When did they set sail?' he demanded in a husky voice.

'I couldn't say exactly. They just wanted to take a simple fishing boat and . . .'

Shôtoràs' head jolted to face her, his pale grey hair slipping forwards. 'Why did you keep it secret from me?'

'Because it's not my expedition,' she dared to protest slightly. 'If

Gathalor and his friends are prepared to take the risk, why should I stop them? I'm not allowed to, but at least they can try.' Irïanora cupped a hand over her mouth and cleared her throat. 'Uncle, I bear no responsibility for their deaths.'

The sovereign took his time before answering. 'Yes, you do. And I cannot absolve you of it. Because if I had heard about it, they wouldn't even have boarded the boat in the first place.' Shôtoràs lifted his stick, the tip pointing towards the domed ceiling. 'We are able to imagine who built these enormous halls. Who stacked the ashlars one on top of the other, the ashlars that are twice as thick as an älf is tall, and yet they were defeated by something. An illness, a plague, magic – who knows?' Suddenly the tip was aimed at her. 'And what I *very much* suspect is this: you had a hand in their *adventure*.'

'Uncle, I . . .'

'*You* sent them out, *you* gave them the map and *you* sent them to their deaths!' he shouted at her, getting to his feet. The anger lines shot across his face now. The stick shook and his knuckles stood out, white. Shôtoràs clasped the handle with unbridled strength. 'And all that you're giving me is this made-up story?' He leaped down from the platform and rushed at her, the tip still pointed at her chest like he was going to bore a hole through it at top speed. 'I warned you!'

Irïanora shrank back in fear. 'I didn't lie to you,' she cried. Then the stick whizzed downwards and caught her in the hollow of her knee so that she collapsed in front of him. 'No, please, I . . .'

Shôtoràs beat her, battering her shoulders, her back, the nape of her neck, head and arms until the skin changed colour and cracked in several places. Blood oozed through her clothes, dripping onto the floor of the hall in multiple places.

Panting, the sovereign at last let her be, tossing his dishevelled hair back. 'Stand up.'

Irïanora struggled against the dizziness. The pain overwhelmed her, and with every heartbeat another stabbing pain went through her body. She tried to rise but her legs wouldn't obey her.

'Stand up!' Then the sharp crow's beak was hovering in front of her eyes. 'Or I'll help you up with *this*.'

The älf-woman struggled first to her knees and then to her feet but couldn't keep upright.

'I have received a message from Dsôn Elhàtor,' she could hear her uncle was keeping his voice in check with some difficulty; it cracked from the restraint. 'They wrote to me asking how I could explain that a boat had been captured with three spies from Dâkiòn on board. And why equipment for accurately measuring the Tronjor had been found?' He grabbed her by the throat. 'And they would like to speak to an älf-woman called Irïanora who was accused by the spy Saitôra of being the instigator of the plot!' Shôtoràs shook and choked her at the same time.

'She's lying,' gasped Irïanora, 'or they forced her into it.'

His laughter echoed. 'They forced her to give *your* name? How would that happen? Does the monarchess just know you from hearsay because you've performed so many glorious deeds and she's dying to get to know you?' he sneered and tossed her across the room. 'Or because the onwú mentioned your name?'

Irïanora flew a good distance across the hall before crashing into a pillar and sliding down it, moaning. None of her thoughts could be pinned down, the excuses slipped through her hands.

'You stupid idiot! With your lust for war you've already ensured that poor Bethòras didn't survive a fall from the highest tower. How much further does your destructive impulse go?' Shôtoràs planted himself in front of her again, then slowly crouched down and grasped her by her mop of fair hair so that she was forced to look at him. 'You knew how fond I was of Gathalor. So I'm sending *you* to Elhàtor so that you can explain to the monarchess how this could have happened. You will apologise and accept any punishment that this älf-woman metes out to you so that this does not end in war between the towns.' He let go of her hair. 'Bring me back Saitôra, Gathalor and Iophâlor. Don't you dare show your face to me again with excuses.'

Iriänora was too weak to reply so she just nodded. Blonde strands of hair covered her face.

Shôtoràs limped over to the platform and returned with a sealed casket which he threw into her lap. 'You're to hand that over to Modôia. Nobody else is allowed to accept it or open it. My personal apology to her is inside. I can only hope that it satisfies her.'

'Yes,' groaned Iriänora, wiping away the blood running into her right eye from a wound on the top of her head. *I must not underestimate the old bastard anymore. That was my last mistake.*

'The healers will tend to your wounds, but not too much, so that the monarchess can see that I've disciplined you,' Shôtoràs informed her. 'Oh yes: and I keep my word.'

Before Iriänora could ask what he meant by that, she felt a blow to the ribs followed by a diabolical stabbing pain and rupturing.

Without any input from her, she was lifted up like a doll, feeling like she was hanging on a hook.

She looked to her side, screaming, and realised that her uncle had rammed the tip of the beak into her side and pulled her to her feet by it.

'I told you I was going to choose the *other* end next time,' she heard his chilling words. 'Bring me back my three älfar. Alive! I've lost too many to Modôia already.' He pulled the metal out of her and Iriänora fell to the floor again, whimpering.

She saw the sovereign's broad back limping away from her. So the älf-woman dared, despite the pain, to grin furtively as the blood gushed down over her eyebrow and her side burned like fire. *Sending me to Elhàtor will be your downfall.*

Ignoring the excruciating agony for a moment, her plan was far from doomed.

Chapter V

One can hang a barbarian even on the most crooked tree.

Wise saying of the Älfar
Collected by Carmondai, master of word and image

Tark Draan, Human kingdom of Gauragar, Grey Mountains, 5452nd division of unendingness (6491st solar cycle), summer

There's another one. Aiphatòn was climbing the adjacent rock face, his movements feeling clumsy and slow. Although he had walked several orbits at altitude, his body couldn't seem to acclimatise to the conditions. He still needed to pause and get his breath back every fifty paces.

Good thing this kind of pursuit doesn't depend on speed and my targets are fixed in the rock.

The gusts were tearing at his cloaks as if the wind was trying to strip him, but his armoured gloves dug too firmly and securely into the small number of crevices for him to be in any danger. *It's getting even colder. Without sunshine I'm going to freeze as soon as I stop walking. I'll need to give up the night search completely soon and make a stop by a fire.*

The markings the unknown älf-woman had left behind for him had been done in a colour that an älf could only see if his eyes were clouded over by the daystar. She must have got the extract from the plants in the valley. No other creature would have been able to identify them.

Aiphatòn's unusual feature as a shintoìt was the fact that, due to the permanent pigmentation in his eyes, he was identifiable as an älf even after sundown. *Finally there's a perk to being the son of the Inextinguishables.*

He had reached the marking about five paces from the ground and two arms' lengths wide. It was in the shelter of an overhang so that it couldn't get covered up by swirling snowflakes.

Petrol had turned out to be the most effective antidote. He had brought some from the hollow in a leather pouch to kindle fires on his journey. But the fluid had run low two orbits ago so Aiphatòn had to scratch the surface carefully with his spear or gloves. If he pressed too hard, the runes would be immortalised as an engraving, visible to all eyes.

He wasn't using his magic anymore either because he didn't know how much of a supply the alloy armour had stored in it. There were no signs of a magical source in the Grey Mountains.

The stone is soft, he noted to his relief, gripping tightly with one hand. *This will be quick.* He carefully rubbed one hand across the rock.

He looked around casually to see if anyone was watching, which was of course highly unlikely. But carelessness had sent more lives into endingness than the most hideous diseases.

Once the sun had set and its indirect, blood-red light reflected off the slopes, he finished his task.

Another one down. Aiphatòn looked to the ground and let himself drop. The thick snow muffled the impact. *Tomorrow, the work continues.*

He picked up his rucksack and the holder he'd built to carry his spear on his back when he climbed.

What he didn't have was somewhere to spend the night.

By now he could tell from the cloud formations what was in store for him and the small, seemingly harmless scraps in the sky signalled an advancing storm front he did not want to face out in the open.

A recess in the rock would be more than enough for me. Aiphatòn adjusted his cloaks and cursed the fact he didn't prepare for his adventure properly. It had been impossible to say in advance how long it would last. *A fake Firûsha, a mysterious settlement and a search for runes.* He ran a hand over his skull where black hairs were sprouting. *Still too short to keep me warm.*

He set off, paying close attention to the rock face further ahead. The älf-woman, whose name he'd already forgotten, generally left her markings at one-mile intervals and was careful that they caught the eye without needing to look for them too hard.

The light was fading, which was not a problem for Aiphatòn – however, the swiftly descending cold was, despite the double layer of cloak fabric and magic.

Hoping to find shelter, he marched onwards.

He walked along a narrow, ice-covered path, not knowing if there was a ravine or solid rock under it. As the ground got steeper and steeper, he needed to use his spear on it to stop himself slipping and falling.

Suddenly the next rune glowed on a cliff two hundred paces away. Something was written underneath it.

That's new. Aiphatòn was still too far away to make out the sentences but his curiosity compelled him to run to the marking despite the pain in his legs and heart. There was no cave or niche anyway.

The path suddenly fell steeply away and turned into a channel of ice. The glittery coating evenly lined the sides of the narrow pass.

Aiphatòn stopped and looked ahead. *Fate seems to decree that I slide down.* He took off one of his cloaks and laid it with the rough side face down so that he didn't hurtle too quickly down the sheer ice. *At least it'll be easier for me to breathe down there.*

He sat on the pelt and pushed himself off, using the spear so that he at least had the illusion of being able to steer as he slid.

Aiphatòn flew downwards, faster and faster.

The rune was clearly visible and the writing underneath it said . . .

The cold wind brought tears to the älf's eyes and it was difficult for him to make out the small symbols.

I've got to stop, one way or another. He drove the tip of the spear into the ice behind him, and with a loud scraping sound, tiny ice chips sprayed up in a shimmering white fountain.

But he wasn't slowing down.

Soon I'll have gone past it. Aiphatòn infused his weapon with a pinch of magic.

The runes shimmered green, and now the blade plunged into the layer of ice as far as the beginning of its shaft, creaking as it carved through it. Cracks darted out from the groove in every direction and streaked to the edges of the iced-covered pass.

Aiphatòn came to a stop directly beneath the rune.

Now for a spot of acrobatics. He worked the spear free without taking the magic out of it and threw it into the sheet of ice right underneath the markings.

Straight away, he leaped after it and landed on the shaft. He skilfully kept his balance and read.

Here ends
what I have left for the älfar.

That could
be for many reasons.

You must discover
the truth
for yourself.

But I doubt
you will
find it
and still be alive.

Endingness
is more free from fear
than you think.

What does this mean? Aiphatòn read the lines over and over again. *This must be a riddle. Or there used to be more here.*

He rubbed a hand carefully over the wall, but he couldn't make out any traces of paint.

With a loud crack, a large chunk of the icy path cracked and sank downwards, as the älf saw at a glance over his shoulder. More fragments were following suit and hurtling into a chasm so deep that no explosion or crash signalled their impact.

Stunned, Aiphatòn sat on the spear and watched the disintegration progress. It must have been caused by the long cut he had made. The path was turning into a gaping abyss. The ground was literally being taken out from under him. *Along with my second cloak.*

Then he saw lights approaching from higher up the slope, where he had just come from.

He strained his eyes.

A troop of armed figures draped in pelts and carrying torches and lamps in their gloved hands were on the upper section of the slope – which wasn't too steep – when it was suddenly struck by the growing cracks in the ice. They were pulling a sled in their midst with a modest wooden sarcophagus three paces long lying across it.

Things are going to turn out badly if they don't go back the way they came in time. 'Hey,' called Aiphatòn to attract their attention, although he didn't think they could see him in the darkness.

'Get back!' he shouted in various human dialects. 'Get away if you don't want to lose your lives.'

Not that he cared about the fate of these strangers especially, but he thought that they deserved to be warned about the impending disaster he had caused.

The troop stopped and the fissures darted beneath their feet. There were loud shouts when they realised what was happening.

Two of them tried to push the sarcophagus back, while five masked figures raced up the crackling path and tried to outrun the destruction; four others thought they could cling to the edges of the walls.

The collapse continued at top speed.

In the upper section, however, the ravine underneath the ice sheet was only just beginning, so that the pieces only fell one pace and shattered on the rocks underneath.

As a result, the sarcophagus fell, then shot downhill almost vertically, rumbling over the heap of broken ice.

Some of the figures couldn't keep clinging to the rock face and fell into the depths where the abyss lurked; two of their comrades rolled down after the wooden casket screaming but soon fell silent.

They must have broken their necks.

Only four of the masked figures were in the safe area, which had only caved in by half a pace. They were holding the torches and lanterns down to shine the light into the ravine and look for the survivors as well as their cargo. Their muffled voices drifted over to Aiphatòn.

Quite interesting, what you come across in the mountains. The älf was looking for a way to climb down and look at the sarcophagus and the bodies. It didn't solve the puzzle the älf-woman had left for him, but the clothing down there was better than what he had. *And there were rations.* And besides, he could light a warming fire using the wood of the casket.

With his armoured fingers, he found purchase in the rock, then took the spear out of the ice and slid it into the holder on his back. The runes went dark and he became an invisible shadow.

Aiphatòn climbed down, hanging by his hands, the exertion warming his muscles and hence his whole body. As he descended he mused that he could give up the search for more runes.

The älf-woman had started her journey into the Outer Lands a long, long time ago along the ice path. Since it no longer existed thanks to Aiphatòn, every other traveller who came from Girdlegard from this orbit onwards would have to take a different route. Nobody could stumble across any other potential signs anymore.

The torches and lamps were quickly approaching the ground too. The armed troops had to jump down between the lumps of ice despite their heavy furs and weapons. The fact that they were taking this risk meant they were trying to get to the sarcophagus quickly because it had some special value to them. They didn't even stop to call or look for the injured.

Maybe they stole the coffin from the dwarves? That would be brazen and very courageous. Aiphatòn started to descend more quickly.

But the strangers reached the floor of the ravine before him. There were large and small mounds of ice lying around.

They hadn't noticed him so he was able to get closer using the milky, opaque blocks as cover without revealing his presence.

The strangers weren't worried about their own casualties. They wore scarves over their mouths and noses because of the cold and the only thing they seemed to be worrying about was the casket they were examining from all sides with their lamps. The weapons hanging from their belts and on their backs looked heavy and bulky. One of them held a shield in his right hand.

Aiphatòn could hear their voices better now. *What are you going to do now that you have it back again?*

The troop spoke a human dialect, and one of them stank of orc. That could be because he had seized a monster's armour and buckled it on – or because he actually was one of the green-skinned beasts. They were all broadly built and their clothes would be too big for the älf.

You are an unusual bunch. When he focused, he could understand what they were discussing, so he stayed in the shadow of a lump of ice the size of a cottage to concentrate on their words.

'A big fat sacrifice to every fucking demon: the thing is still intact,' one of them cried out in relief.

'Gricks and Tratshka aren't,' interjected the smallest one, who was still probably as tall as Aiphatòn, with a bleating laugh. 'Man, did they go flying! Squealing the whole time!' He did an exaggerated impression of his comrades' dying screams.

'Did any of you see who called out to us before the path caved in?' the stoutest one interrupted, running a hand over the sarcophagus. 'Ah, the wood has cracked here, but the charm rune wasn't damaged at all.'

'It was like that already. And so what? He's in shackles.' The smaller one bent double with laughter, the sight of his dead comrades seeming to delight him. 'Now that's a box! I should have sat on it and used it as a sled! I would never have thought I'd start sweating in an ice chamber. It's this stupid jumping around.' He wiped the sweat off his brow. 'How do we get him out of the ravine, my friends?'

'The first sensible thing you've said,' the stout one praised him, before turning to the tallest member of the group. 'What do you think, Cushròk?'

A figure more than two-and-a-half paces tall turned aside slightly and pulled his scarf down, showing Aiphatòn his hulking great face, which bore orc and troll characteristics in equal measure.

It hardly gets uglier than that. The älf did not want to imagine how the creature had come to be.

'Let's get him out of this,' Cushròk ordered in a deep, grating voice. He revealed pointy, stained teeth when he spoke. 'Then we'll take it in turns to carry him.'

With those molars he could crush nuts in their shells, Aiphatòn supposed.

'But we're carrying the sarcophagus with us specifically to prevent him moving and to keep him safe,' the smaller one countered.

'We've put steel clasps around him. What could he do to us?' Cushròk placed his enormous hand on the edge of the sarcophagus, underneath the lid. 'Are you afraid of an opponent who weighs barely a quarter of what you do and whose muscles are nowhere to be seen?'

The other masked figures laughed softly and nastily.

Aiphatòn still could not work out the exact races of the figures hidden beneath the thick clothes and the scarves. *Could they possibly be monster and human half-breeds?* He was familiar with the south side of Ishím Voróo, where he had found älfar who had turned out differently. He knew that creatures and things existed that were beyond the imagination of anyone in Girdlegard. *Even after the events of the last three hundred cycles.* The same went for peculiarities in the north.

Cushròk tensed his muscles, which were big enough to rival the hind leg of a night-mare, and grasped the top of the coffin.

But instead of the lid coming off, the entire sarcophagus lifted up.

His companions burst out into guffaws of laughter, enjoying his failure. This made the ringleader yank all the more furiously on the sarcophagus – to no avail.

Eventually he lifted the casket and roared as he tossed it at the rock face.

It crashed into it, bounced off and flipped over as it landed among the creatures who puffed and panted as they jumped out of its way.

'What a piece of demonic shit!' shouted Cushròk and stared at them all, eyes wide and angry. 'Keep your big mouths shut! All of you!' He pointed to one of them. 'Nrashq, you try it.'

Nrashq, who beneath his scarf looked like the ugly brother of the ringleader, gazed at the sarcophagus. 'Not a single new crack or a scratch.' He passed a hand across the runes. 'I think we can save ourselves any more attempts. This is powerful protective magic.'

'So we drag it after all? You're so good at that, of course,' joked the smallest one to Cushròk, who simply grunted and panted with exhaustion.

The stout one shoved Nrashq aside and placed both hands on top of the lid. His lips moved swiftly and silently while the älfar symbols on it glowed brighter and brighter.

Keep what's in here hidden, Aiphatòn read what the letters said. *Freed, it spells great trouble. Destroy what escapes. It will kill as long as it breathes.* He couldn't help an icy shiver running down his spine. *They should take this warning seriously. Too bad they don't understand it.*

He took off his one remaining cloak. Since he didn't want the ignorant beasts dragging him to his doom with them, he had to take action. He was also curious about where they came from and *what* they were transporting.

Aiphatòn stepped out from behind the block of ice, holding his spear in his left hand. 'Whatever you're doing,' he said to the stout one, 'you should stop. Immediately.'

Cushròk turned his head with a grunt, already holding his morningstar in his right hand. Apart from the stout one, his companions all drew their weapons and pointed the ends of them at the newcomer. 'The voice in the night,' snarled Cushròk.

'He deliberately made the path collapse; I bet he wanted to rob us,' the smallest one said to stir things up, the largest sword in his hand.

'He's a black-eye,' Nrashq observed, wielding a lance as long as a leg. He held his shield protectively in front of both the casket and his stout comrade, who had not allowed the challenge to distract him from conjuring spells over the sarcophagus.

'And an odd one at that. Since when do they sew the armour into the skin and since when do their eyes look like *that* when the sun has long set?' Cushròk added, scrutinising Aiphatòn from head to toe. 'Why should Obko stop what he's doing?'

'Because the runes warn against it. I can read them, unlike you.' He had been standing still since the ringleader had pointed at him. 'The contents will kill us.' He didn't reveal that he had been observing the group earlier. *One of them will blab.*

'The contents are harmless,' Cushròk contradicted him calmly, but his glittering eyes the size of hands glinted with suspicion. 'What exactly do the runes mean?'

The älf revealed what they said.

'And how do I know that what you're saying is true?'

The warning didn't seem to have made much of an impression on any of his fellows, although they must have known what was in the sarcophagus.

Aiphatòn took his spear in both hands and wrapped his armoured fingers around the metal shaft with a click. 'I will stop your comrade, and if I have to kill you to do it, then that's how it'll have to be. Is my determination proof enough?'

Cushròk contemplated Aiphatòn, maintaining eye contact as his eyes narrowed more and more, gradually becoming slits – then he let out a sound; his breath shot out of his lips in a white jet and expanded into a cloud.

Nrashq immediately launched an attack.

He took a step towards Aiphatòn and dealt an arching blow with the edge of his shield; Aiphatòn drew his head back, dodging the shield. At the same time, Nrashq's other arm thrust the long lance diagonally upwards from below, directly at Aiphatòn's throat. The attack with the shield had just been a diversion.

For a creature this size, he is surprisingly quick. With one judicious arm movement, Aiphatòn jerked the spear around so that his opponent's weapon was knocked aside. His armoured right hand jolted forwards over Nrashq's shield as swiftly as a snakebite, gripped his throat and crushed it with a cartilaginous crack.

Groaning, his enemy sank to the ground, clutching at his disfigured neck, but he could not stop the suffocation.

'It would be easier,' Aiphatòn said, 'if you stopped setting your people on me. Otherwise you'll end up having to carry the sarcophagus yourself.'

Cushròk remained angry but called a halt to any more attacks. 'Leave it, Obko.'

'I – I can't,' the stout one replied, clearly trying to take his hands off the lid. The runes' glow was spreading over the entire coffin. 'It's got me.' Obko looked from one companion to the next in desperation. 'It won't stop anymore! It's draining me!'

Cushròk's broad, high brow furrowed and he nodded to his smallest mate.

But the underling didn't dare get any closer to the shimmering sarcophagus. 'Oh no, I'm giving *that* one a miss,' he said, refusing to obey. '*I* didn't tell Obko to cast a charm. And besides, we were forbidden to.'

Aiphatòn could feel the magical radiation as a tingle on his skin. *This is . . . like nothing I've ever felt before!* He had opposed Lot-Ionan and found out what it meant to get into a fight with a magus. The armour and his own powers had protected him from the might of the old magician. But this radiation signified something else: it was both familiar and alien, powerful and uncontrollable.

Aiphatòn automatically took a step backwards, away from the sarcophagus. *The runes are right!* 'He's got to stop or I'll kill him,' he murmured absently.

'What?' Cushròk's lips retracted, showing his teeth and puckering the bridge of his nose.

'Leave it,' the älf commanded Obko, raising his spear to throw it.

'I can't! I . . . But you're a black-eye. Help . . . me!' stammered the stout one, squirming. 'It – it hurts!'

It can't be helped. Aiphatòn hurled the spear.

Obko couldn't raise his hands to defend himself or dodge the missile. The blade came whizzing towards him and he screamed out in terror – until the tip plunged through pelt, armour and clothing, through skin and bone and into his heart. The runes on the shaft of the spear flashed.

The stout one immediately fell silent and collapsed next to the casket. As his life stopped, the symbols on the sarcophagus stopped glowing too.

Aiphatòn could clearly feel that the magical radiation had lessened in strength. *But it's still there.* 'You should be grateful to me,' he said to Cushròk. 'I saved your life.' He extended his arm to summon the spear back. The weapon flew out of the corpse and landed in his metal hand. 'Now tell me: what's in that casket that cannot be taken out?'

'This is truly the first time I've seen a black-eye like you.' The ringleader could not be rushed, even though he had just witnessed the death of his comrade. He still seemed convinced he could hold his own against this opponent. 'You read the runes, you're an expert in magic and you're capable of tricks with your spear that I'd like to be able to do too.'

The first time? This phrase did not bode well. 'How many älfar do you know?' Aiphatòn suspected there must be more of his people in the north. He had heard the stories about the downfall of the älfar realms Dsôn Faïmon and Dsôn Sòmran, but he had always feared there were survivors. *No matter how many there are: I must find them and exterminate them.* 'Did you steal the sarcophagus from them?'

The other masked figure laughed. 'This black-eye is not from here. Or he was trapped in the ice and then thawed out. We should take him with us too.' He pointed at the casket with his sword. 'Preferably in there. Then he won't cause any trouble.'

Aiphatòn found it admirable that they were both ignoring how effortlessly he had picked off two of their team. He leaned on his spear. 'Yes. Take me with you. I'm looking for my tribe.'

Cushròk's laugh boomed out and he clapped a hand against his thigh. 'It just gets better and better with you, black-eye.' He wiped tears of laughter from the corners of his eyes.

'Take me with you,' the smaller one imitated him and copied his posture. 'I'm looking for my tribe.'

Cushròk's cheerfulness evaporated swiftly and all of a sudden he was holding another morningstar in his other fist, and it seemed weightless to him. He attacked the älf with both weapons and the smaller one set upon him from the side.

Only an inexperienced warrior would have let themselves be fooled by their trick of good humour and let their guard down. Aiphatòn leaped over the smaller one and past the whirring, spiky iron balls, landed on the sarcophagus and used his spear to stab Cushròk from behind between the dorsal vertebra.

The thick pelts acted like a cushion to stop the blade plunging deep enough to kill the monster.

Cushròk bellowed and turned around, the balls whizzing closer. The smaller fighter swung his extra-long weapon down vertically.

Aiphatòn let the short chains of the morningstar wrap around the shaft of the spear, then yanked it and intercepted the blade slicing towards him with the taut iron links.

The heavy sword bounced back and hit the small one on the forehead, who staggered aside, dazed, and fell. 'Dirty black-eye!' he howled.

'Come over here!' Cushròk tugged on the morning star handles and pulled Aiphatòn towards him.

'You want my weapon? Here, I'll give it to you.' The älf let go of the spear and tried to throw himself at the ringleader to get at his broad back and floor him with blows to the skull.

But it didn't go as planned.

The jolt made the spear turn slightly and the blade inadvertently sank into the wooden lid of the sarcophagus – directly into a rune.

All of the symbols on the spear and the casket gave off a blazing light and there was a loud clap of thunder. Aiphatòn had to close his eyes.

The warm air suddenly smelled of burning fields and ripe cherries, of tobacco and a westerly wind carrying the smell of iron and earth.

Then Aiphatòn was struck by a violent blow that hurled him onto the sarcophagus.

Ishím Voróo, Forty miles outside the älfar town Dsôn Dâkiòn, 5452nd division of unendingness (6491st solar cycle), summer

Having an uncle like him is such a pain. Irïanora watched from the bank as the älfar pulled ashore the boat in which they had travelled down the Tronjor as far as the strait. *The old bastard should have killed me. I would have preferred that to grovelling in front of the scum.*

She had disembarked via a plank with her servant Zelája and one of her uncle's warriors and had sat down in the shade of a weeping willow that functioned as a parasol with its low-hanging branches and dense foliage. The tree got its name from the translucent petals that closed once they'd withered and lay on the ground like tangible tears; but the willow was still in bloom.

The warrior kept watch while the servant gave loud instructions to the crew about which pile to leave which piece of luggage on. An impressive, varied wardrobe was important on a mission like this.

Irïanora watched the crew at work as if through a billowing curtain and rearranged her black and yellow dress.

They had stopped on the grass-green bank before the bottleneck where Gathalor, Iophâlor and Saitôra had presumably come a cropper. Rushing and frothing, the river hurled itself furiously against the large rocks further down, gurgling as it squeezed between the boulders, only calming again several paces downstream.

How could Saitôra have survived this? Irïanora looked around and spotted an älf on top of the boulder on the right-hand side, wearing a pale green wrap over his armour. His helmet was covered in the same coloured fabric, while the trousers made from light brown leather and the rest of his camouflage clothing meant he as good as disappeared in front of the trees.

And there they are, the watchful eyes of Elhàtor. If the älf hadn't moved, Irïanora would not have noticed him. She took a deep breath and instantly groaned; her side hurt where the spike had bored into her ribs. *Who would have guessed they'd conceal scouts at this spot?*

Since the measuring expedition had failed, she would have to make the best of the scraps that providence threw her. *There's nothing else I can do.* The young älf-woman couldn't find a way to sit to avoid more pain. Her whole body had been beaten black and blue and the healers had refrained from using healing magic on her. The monarchess was supposed to see what Shôtoràs had done to her in his fury and cunning.

By now, the boat had been pulled up the slope and the crew were throwing themselves into the tall grass and relaxing. Bread, sausage and cold meat was shared around, there was wine; they scooped water out of the river.

Nobody saw the enemy scout still standing above them – apart from Irïanora.

But instead of pointing him out to her companions, she picked up the casket entrusted to her by Shôtoràs which she had placed in direct sunlight. His wax seal was resplendent on it, keeping the lid shut.

Jewellery to make amends, maybe? She shook the box back and forth but couldn't hear anything. *Or an insulting letter?*

She didn't like the thought of carrying something around that might put her in a difficult position with her enemies. There were stories of messengers carrying a note saying that the recipient was to kill the bearer immediately. That would not fit in with any of her plans.

Irïanora tested various places on the piece of wax that had warmed up in the heat of the daystar. *That should be enough.*

She pulled her small knife out of a fold in her dress and carefully eased the thin blade underneath the edge of the seal and pushed cautiously until the whole disc of wax came away from the lid and the front of the box with a sticky sound.

The älf-woman carefully opened the box. It would be child's play to glue the supposed safeguard back on before she got to Elhàtor then pretend she knew nothing about the contents.

Irïanora was smiling as she lifted the lid – and found herself looking at a message fixed to the inside.

Her good mood evaporated.

I guessed you would try and gain access to the contents.

   See it as another test you have not passed.

   One of your companions is carrying my message to the monarchess. They would have taken the box away from you before reaching the town.

What can I say about your attempt to circumvent my orders?

   Inàste must hate me that YOU have to be my flesh and blood.

   As your uncle, I must confess you are an unparalleled disappointment. Your mother was so much better than you and departed from us far too soon.

   Be a worthy successor to her at long last!

   For her sake, I desperately hope you will be successful.

   Otherwise I don't know what to do with you on your return.

Irïanora shut the lid, her face getting warm.

She could quite clearly feel a rage line forming above her right eyebrow and then creeping across her face in jagged strokes. It moved gradually and tentatively, as if exploring the älf-woman's skin and facial features.

I will be successful if I achieve MY goal, not yours! She raised her arm and flung the casket in a high arc through the branches of the willow and into the river. Green leaves snapped off and fell onto the grass, while blossoms came loose and floated down far too slowly.

The current swept the light wooden container away.

Iriïanora watched as it collided with a boulder and smashed into several pieces; some fragments were sucked downwards, some drifted away in the Tronjor.

What a pointless test, she thought. *What did he mean by it? That he thinks he knows me?* The blonde älf-woman felt the wax seal with her uncle's symbol on it in her fingers. *He's in for a surprise.*

She pocketed the little disc, making sure not to break it or put too much pressure on it. It could come in handy to blame an action or gift on Shôtoràs and put him in a tricky position.

Iriïanora smiled coldly but even that caused her pain. *He underestimates me, as I do him.*

And yet she would have been so glad to know he was on her side, although his past as a Constellation seemed to make this impossible. But a war and conquering the satellite town meant everything to the blonde älf-woman and her supporters.

Her mother had not passed into endingness as her uncle's wording implied – she had been one of the ones who moved to Elhàtor, leaving everything behind to risk a new start.

Since then she had been dead to Shôtoràs. Iriïanora had the same profound hatred for her mother that she did for the älf-woman who had taken her mother from her. Her father had raised her alone before succumbing to a fever. Some people even thought he never got over being separated from his wife and perished because of it.

On his deathbed, Iriïanora had promised him she would do everything she could to defeat Elhàtor and its monarchess because they had unleashed misery on Dâkiòn a hundredfold, and even worse on her family.

Iriïanora looked at the river. *I will not ask after my mother. I couldn't care less about her now, just like she couldn't care less about me when she left me.* Maybe her traitor of a mother would give her a hug and pretend she was delighted to see her. *If that happens, I'll stab her, Father.*

Shouts started to ring out – the boat crew had noticed the scout.

The älf from Elhàtor climbed down to them and two more approached from the adjacent forest. Although they had been hiding right next to the group, nobody had noticed the scouts till now.

They are dangerously good. Irïanora wrenched herself away from her musings about her past and wondered how many of these spies were dotted across the land surrounding Dâkiòn with a view of the town at all times.

That would put her plans at risk too.

I can occasionally get away from my uncle but what if they're watching me and my preparations? The älf-woman lapsed into unpleasant brooding once more. *I will have to take countermeasures.*

The warrior from her uncle's bodyguard, whose name she kept forgetting, pushed the branches aside with his spear and came to her underneath the weeping willow. 'The delegation from Elhàtor is here. They're going to take us in their boat from here,' he reported.

'Is it big enough for all of us then?'

'They're only taking you, your servant and me with them,' he replied and prompted her with a nod. 'Our crew will wait here. If the trip drags on, I'll send a message to Dâkiòn to have the crew turn back.'

Irïanora got up carefully with his help, clenching her teeth and suppressing any cry of pain. She didn't want to give the bodyguard any opportunity to laugh mockingly at her. 'It's a miracle anyone can camp here at all.'

'It's the only place for a radius of forty miles,' the scout said. 'The creatures and animals who live in the swamp don't dare approach as long as there's a fire burning.' The warrior glanced around, looking for something. 'Where's your little box?'

'The river knows where it is,' she responded nonchalantly, picking one of the translucent blossoms off her dress.

He looked at her, aghast. 'The present for the monarchess of . . .'

'Save yourself and me the farce,' she countered acidly. 'Show me to the boat taking us to Elhàtor.'

His brow was furrowed, which she could only just make out because of the helmet, but he was silent.

Irïanora strode towards the three enemy scouts as best as the ground and the pain throughout her body would allow, making an effort to look as arrogant as she could.

She had actually planned not to come face to face with any of the seaside town's älf-women or älfar until their conquest was complete and she was receiving the surrender from the survivors. *I'll regard this as practice for the big moment.*

The Elhàtor soldiers' annoyed expressions made her certain: she had passed this test.

Tark Draan, Blue Mountains, Kingdom of the Secondling dwarves, 5452nd division of unendingness (6491st solar cycle), summer

'King Boïndil: I said, we've removed the last of the corpses.' The dwarf in a coat of chainmail and leather trousers waited in vain for the monarch to turn to him. In the end he bowed and left the room. The room's only function was to serve as a reminder.

He was my scholar. Wistful, Boïndil Doubleblade from the clan of the Axe Swingers was still looking at the little box made of pure vraccasium that held some of the ashes of Tungdil Goldhand.

The preliminary sketches etched onto the walls of the room showed the intricacy of the reliefs the stonemasons were due to carve to honour the memory of the dwarf people's great hero. Various episodes from the recent past appeared as well as the first time Goldhand met the twins.

But there was still plenty of other work to be done in the Blue Mountains, apart from carving images in stone, applying gold leaf and encrusting ornaments with precious gems. Decorating the memorial chamber would have to wait.

The powerful fingers on Ireheart's right hand played with his black beard, silvery grey hairs shimmering in it. His advanced age had brought them on, and they appeared in the long, black plait that dangled down to his belt too; he wore the sides shaved so that the coronet-like crown sat a little looser.

In his mind, he found himself in the assembly hall in the fortress at the Black Abyss, where he had received the little box with his share of the remains. Contrary to tradition, every tribe and the freemen and freewomen had kept a part of the best, the most heroic and simultaneously most controversial high king, in the form of ashes.

Ireheart sighed and rearranged the thick belt he wore on top of his coat of chainmail.

The container should really be placed in a statue but there had not been time to arrange it yet. He preferred the idea of this room, where you could come to think and remember anyway. *It would have appealed to him more than a likeness that wouldn't have done him justice, no matter how large and magnificent it was.*

After the death of the magician Lot-Ionan and the liberation of the Blue Mountains, the home of the Secondlings, the surviving dwarves had to deal with disposing of the corpses of the southern älfar poisoned by Aiphatòn. The cadavers lay decaying in the passageways, polluting the otherwise fresh mountain air.

Ireheart contemplated the little box. *Or are the sceptics right after all?*

He turned his head towards the door and started to respond to the dwarf until he realised there was nobody there anymore.

Sighing, he left the memorial chamber to make his way through his kingdom which lay in the south of Girdlegard overlooking the Stone Gateway. Aiphatòn had once got through the gate with his älfar, and it was from here that the magus directed his reign of terror.

That was over, the clearing up had begun.

Ireheart placed his free hand on the stone wall and ran his calloused fingers over it. *It belongs to us again now. This time, nothing will drive us away from here.*

He strolled on, smelling the faint scent of decay. The dead bodies of the black-eyes had lain here for too long. It would be some time before the stone could be purged of the decomposition fluids. Despite cleaning and scouring, the smell remained as if it was the final rebellion of the villains and an attempt to remain from beyond the grave.

Deep in the south, the fortress had to be completely rebuilt. All the equipment and retractable bridges had been destroyed. The good thing was that during this time, beasts couldn't cross the ravine anymore either.

This cursed restlessness is back. Ireheart shouldered his weapon with its long shaft. At one end it was double-sided, with both a heavy, flat head and a hooked spur the size of a forearm. His brother, Boëndal Hookhand, used to carry it into battle and now Boïndil owned it. Nothing could withstand the crow's beak – every target was either drilled through or smashed to pieces.

Ireheart walked and walked.

He saw all the destroyed dwarf runes on the walls of the halls and corridors, damaged indiscriminately by the magus and his famuli during their training. The runes had been target practice for their evil magic. *A disgrace.*

The dreaded restlessness was accompanied by an unquenchable thirst that frightened the dwarf. Ever since he had been forced to drink the secret zhadár elixir to escape death, he had sensed his addiction to it.

Distilled elf blood and all kinds of strange substances. Ireheart felt nauseous. *But without the potion I would have died of the scorpion bite.*

He was glad he had consigned the last mouthful to the flames and thus destroyed it. He was nonetheless tormented by the fear of becoming a zhadár himself and losing his dwarfness by gaining älfar powers. He had drunk the concoction more than once.

Vraccas, protect me.

Ireheart went through a small portal into a beautifully laid out ravine garden where squat trees grew and sheep and goats grazed on the meadow. It smelled of honey as bees buzzed and flew the pollen to the plants for the sweet, liquid gold. Exquisite mead could be made from the honey. *Perhaps I'll find some peace here.*

He sat on a wall, leaned back against the gnarled old tree behind him and closed his eyes; he put the crow's beak down next to him.

The rustling of the leaves and the tranquil buzzing made his heart beat more slowly. He dozed off into a half-waking, half-sleeping dream filled with chaos.

In this dream, he even saw the dwarf who had supposedly been the real Balodil. He watched him attacking the älfar.

Balodil. Apparently, Tungdil had dropped his son into the river while drunk. A current had carried the little dwarf to humans who kept him as a slave until he ran away when the älfar invaded. After spending some time in Toboribor, where he had allegedly lived a life of pillaging, it was said he ended up in a zhadár's house and that's how he had joined up with that strange unit.

Ireheart didn't believe that was how things had happened. The zhadár had been having some fun with his well-crafted story.

But when the king woke up, he did so with the crazy idea of setting out to look for Tungdil's only legitimate son, the truly missing one.

Because the scholar isn't here, it would be all the more important to have the son of this great hero for support. The King of the Secondlings looked at the sun through the ceiling of green foliage. *It's pure fantasy. I wouldn't even know where to begin looking. He could easily be dead.*

Ireheart cursed the daydream that had got his hopes up that there was a part of his dear friend he had not lost after all. He was overwhelmed by despair. *Ashes in a vraccasium box. What am I meant to do with them? What should the dwarf tribe do with them? We need him. Alive.*

'King Boïndil?'

He turned his head. A dwarf in a simple brown and white leather robe was walking around the large garden, looking for him; the animals were running away from him, bleating, as if he were a walking affront on two legs.

'Over here.' Ireheart reached for the crow's beak and waved it. 'What is it?'

The red-haired dwarf came towards him with two documents in his hand. It was Baromir Goldenstein and his job was to collect all messages in the newly rebuilt Secondling Kingdom and pass them on to the relevant people. 'There's been some news.' The three braided parts of his beard shook as he spoke, the tiny silver hair clips knocking against each other.

The pages changed hands and inquisitive bees buzzed over the words, as if they could suck sweetness out of them.

Ireheart read the message written by the elf Ilahín which described in detail how the demolition work in Dsôn Bhará was going – and it said that by a stroke of bad luck, a hole had appeared in the crater.

It seemed that a passage to Phondrasôn had been opened up. Ilahín's wife had taken some precautionary safety measures, so that nothing escaped from the hole into the weakened Girdlegard. However, he was requesting a small division of Secondlings to keep guard.

'That's all we need.' Ireheart groaned as he sat up straight. His exhaustion, thirst and despair were forgotten for now. 'We barely have enough warrior-women and warriors to clear up and guard the Blue Mountains.'

'That's what I was thinking.' Baromir frowned. 'Shall we decline?'

'With a heavy heart, yes.' Ireheart reckoned that at best the Thirdlings would have enough soldiers and hoped Hargorin would send some.

His gaze scanned the next lines without taking in what they said. He was still preoccupied by the opening to Phondrasôn, as the älfar called the place.

It crossed his mind that many people assumed that the Tungdil Goldhand who had returned and died was a doppelgänger, created by dark forces and the älfar. Was something like that possible?

Ireheart was breathing faster. *If the scholar was still down there, how would we find him? People say it forks endlessly.* He dismissed the notion as too obscure and far-fetched. *We could travel for a thousand cycles and not find even a trace of Tungdil.*

Only now did he grasp the rest of the message.

Ilahín wrote about an älf who had supposedly been locked in a dungeon in the triplets' palace but was overlooked during the initial search because they thought all the cells were empty.

The älf in question was Carmondai who had previously helped to build Dsôn Balsur and had returned from exile with the Aklán.

The letter said he was currently travelling through the country with Balodil, who was now calling himself Carâhnios, to document the deaths of the last älfar. The zhadár was interrogating him from time to time and sending all the information to the royal courts of the humans, elves and dwarves.

'Hurrah!' Ireheart exclaimed, jumping to his feet in excitement and heaving the crow's beak onto his shoulder with a flourish. *So I do have an älf who has been there before!* 'That's the solution.'

'The solution?' echoed Baromir in bewilderment.

'We'll take the black-eyed braggart as a guide who will lead us through Phondrasôn to the place where he last saw Tungdil before leaving,' he spoke swiftly, placing one hand on his forehead as if needing to stop his ideas bubbling out. 'A troop of fifty dwarves from across all of the clans.'

Baromir blinked in surprise. 'Tungdil is dead.'

'The creature we thought was him is dead.'

'But didn't you say yourself you were convinced he was the real deal?'

Ireheart hesitated. *Am I giving in to an illusion? Is this illusion caused by withdrawal from the black remedy of . . .*

The next brainwave was already coming to him.

This Carmondai used to live with the Aklán. Maybe he knows the potion's formula and how to counteract the withdrawal symptoms! Ireheart started running. He would never have dared to dream that a black-eye could be the key to two big puzzles at the same time. 'Come with me,' he commanded the dwarf, barely able to keep his excitement in check. 'Send the message to Dsôn Bhará and Ilahín at once.'

'What message, King Boïndil?'

'They must stop filling in the hole immediately. We need a way in,' he said as he ran. *They'll all think I'm crazy, even Goda and my children.* 'They are to get the black-eye to me in the Blue Mountains.'

Baromir looked sideways at him in astonishment and clasped all of the silver clips in his beard in one swift movement. 'King, I can put it like that in the message, but many questions will be asked.' The way the dwarf spoke, it was clear he was among those who doubted the king's sanity.

Ireheart smiled at him. 'On the contrary. *I* have many questions. And this Carmondai needs to answer them all for me.'

Chapter VI

Dance and combat are fuelled by the same fire.
Hence bad dancers fall first in a duel.

Wise saying of the Älfar
Collected by Carmondai, master of word and image

Ishím Voróo, 5452nd division of unendingness (6491st solar cycle), summer

Aiphatòn crashed into the sarcophagus just as everything around him lit up a blazing white and blinded him. *What kind of magic is this?*

He was buffeted by wind that tore at his trouser garment, then he fell to the ground and pressed his body flat against it to stop himself getting wrenched away by the violent gusts; his metal fingers clung to the rough stone.

As abruptly as it had come, the storm died down again.

Bit by bit, Aiphatòn started to be able to see again, but the world was just a blur. *Is it over?* He opened his hand and summoned the spear.

It took a little longer than usual, but the weapon obeyed his wordless command. He had been afraid the accidental magical discharge had damaged it.

He felt the prickling straight away. The spear must have been in contact with enormous energy stores in the sarcophagus runes. He felt barely capable of conjuring up those kinds of effects. *The alloy must have discharged during the encounter.*

Aiphatòn got to his feet, blinking as he looked around, holding his weapon loosely at the ready.

The mighty slopes, the steep, craggy rock faces and the peaks of the Grey Mountains were – gone.

The älf found himself in a flat landscape that smelled of sewage gas and moist earth. Trees towered up out of the dark brown earth at irregular intervals and marshy pools with brackish water gleamed in between them, slick and menacing.

Far into the distance, several white towers rose up with smooth, white walls. Most of them seemed to be in ruins; two of them were ablaze, as if they were mainly made of wood and not stone. Clouds of dense smoke rolled lethargically and languidly towards the heavens, the smoke seeming sluggish and heavy.

Is that a mirage? Aiphatòn took a breath and felt sweat break out all over his body.

The weather was muggy and swarms of midges were flitting by in whirring black clouds, looking for fresh blood.

Or I'm dead and . . .

He turned around and saw the sarcophagus lying in ruins less than two paces behind him.

Underneath the broken fragments was a figure that could certainly have been an älf.

Inàste had made Aiphatòn's race particularly skinny, but there was barely any weight to this specimen. He was sheer bone with thin parchment skin and just a hint of musculature. He was pure white from head to toe.

His emaciated rib cage slowly rose and sank, the prominent deep blue veins on his neck and stomach pulsating in time with his heartbeat. Old scraps of material had been wrapped around his stomach, but otherwise he wore no clothing.

The steel clasps the monsters had spoken about lay around the stranger, smashed to pieces; just one clamp was still tight around the upper body, keeping his arms pressed firmly against his body.

Cushròk was right about the prisoner's condition. Aiphatòn pushed the pieces of the wooden coffin aside with his spear to get a look at the älf's face.

A black-metal mask covered the lower half of the face, from the chin to the cheekbones. Level with where the mouth would be was a thin hole with a slide in front of it – at most a narrow straw could fit through it. His eyes remained closed, and his curly hair was a messy jumble on his head.

Aiphatòn found it difficult to identify the colour of his hair. *It's like glass.*

He carefully examined the runes on the metal shackles. When he reached his hand out towards them to wipe away the dust so he could read them more easily, he felt magic within them too. *What kind of älf are you, that you are so feared?*

He was familiar with these types of half and full masks, used on the mentally disturbed so that they didn't spit, bite or assault anyone around them. The shackles also indicated an immense danger that Aiphatòn could not fathom at first glance. This was why he didn't immediately stab the masked figure to death. There was a mystery to investigate, and it might prove useful.

And where have we ended up? He straightened up and looked around again.

No matter how hard he tried, he couldn't even see the foothills of the Grey Mountains.

He presumed he had been brought to this deserted place by a magic spell. So Aiphatòn looked through the rubble, searching for the rune that had been pierced by the tip of the spear to unleash this charm.

After a lengthy rummage, he found what he was looking for.

That is the älfar symbol for swift return, he realised in surprise. Soldiers used these signs to give each other rapid instructions on the battlefield by brandishing flags and some explorers carried them in coin form as talismans for longer journeys. *A return to this place? Or did my spear make the spell go awry?*

Aiphatòn couldn't come to a clear-cut conclusion, but there was one hypothesis left and it might be correct or as far from the truth as he was from the Grey Mountains.

On the other hand, did I not want this? Did I not want to get away? In any case he had taken the markings away and made the ice path collapse. Ireheart and his friends could deal with the rest in Girdlegard themselves.

His black eyes swept around, finally coming to rest on the burning towers. He might find someone there who could explain to him where he was.

It doesn't look like things are peaceful over there. Aiphatòn shouldered the spear. *But who should I be afraid of?* he thought, looking down at the unconscious figure. *What shall I do with you?*

Until he had solved the mystery of the unknown madman, he would hold off on killing him.

Maybe he can tell me if there are any more älfar in Ishím Voróo that I need to kill to eliminate another swathe of the villains from the face of the earth. He picked up the unconscious figure and was astonished at how light he was. He couldn't have been more than eighty pounds and that was while still wearing the clasp and the half-mask.

A miracle that he didn't pass into endingness from exhaustion. It's possible the magic of the sarcophagus protected him from that till now. With the spear on his right shoulder and the älf over his left, Aiphatòn set off through the flat landscape towards the towers.

The ground beneath his boots was springy and squelchy, and the stink of excrement and sewage gases worsened.

Here and there, the rotting bones and corpses of monsters and humans jutted out of the earth, and in between lay filthy, trampled standards and flags. Rats and carrion birds hopped around the remnants, insects and maggots crawling over the mortal remains. He couldn't make out any älfar among the victims.

A battlefield that has already seen much conflict. Aiphatòn walked down into a shallow dip and the ruined, burning towers disappeared from view; the only sign of their presence was the smoke.

It's not a good idea to go any closer. He glanced at the overcast sky. Through the haze and thick smoke he glimpsed the sun – a small, dim disc shining dully and feebly.

It must be around noon. So the south is approximately that way, he decided and pivoted to the west. *They can fight without me. It's not my business. I'll make my enquiries elsewhere.*

The dip, which might once have been an anchor trench, screened Aiphatòn from view and he advanced a few miles undetected. The ground was still strewn with the remains of bones, twisted armour parts and shreds of banners; the odd barely legible symbol on fabric and chainmail meant nothing to him.

Then he passed the ruins of homes that must have been in bad condition even when they were still inhabited.

Whoever had produced them did not seem to have a sense of craftsmanship – they looked haphazardly nailed together, piled up lumps of rock quickly encased in clay and held together by prayer.

Disintegrating, rotten planks broke beneath his feet. The decayed wood seemed to have been used in place of a road.

The recess in the ground ran straight through the middle of the abandoned settlement. The scorch marks on several walls told the älf that the residents had not left voluntarily.

Who settles down in a swamp like this . . . or . . . did it form in the first place because they were here? Aiphatòn didn't feel any fear, but a sense of unease had become his constant companion.

The area didn't resemble anything he'd seen in Girdlegard or the southern wasteland. It was full of repulsiveness, unleashing wave after wave of disgust in him.

Could it have been the work of demons?

The dip got shallower and shallower. Soon he could peer over the edge and see what was on the other side of the former embankment.

The towers were now diagonally behind Aiphatòn and looked like finger-high chimneys spewing out smoke. Directly in front of him, at the edge of the dip, the remains of another tower soared three paces into the air. It must have been destroyed a long time ago.

The white paint was flaking off the outer walls and creepers twisted around the ruins, as though trying to pull the charred scaffolding, beams and cladding into the earth, to obliterate every reminder of it.

The towers are not solidly built. Aiphatòn suspected that the buildings only partly consisted of the precisely hewn stone blocks that were strewn about. The rest were support structures made of wood, false ceilings and painted outer walls with metal fittings. *They were not made to withstand a siege.*

A shot from a small catapult could make a hole in it. Three shots and the tower would collapse. This led him to conclude that the towers could be assembled and disassembled for transport. A more comfortable, showy alternative to a tent.

If he had ever had any doubts he was in Ishím Voróo, they were now gone. These things didn't exist in Girdlegard with all of the upheavals and catastrophes it had experienced in recent cycles: he would have known about it.

And yet it seems familiar. Have I read about it?

His prisoner suddenly groaned and started to stir.

Aiphatòn quickly laid him on the ground and crouched down next to him as the prisoner's veiny, parchment-like eyelids flicked open. The black eyes stared at Aiphatòn and he could see astonishment in them.

'My name is Aiphatòn,' he said. 'I am an älf like you and I freed you from the clutches of thieves whose ringleader was called Cushròk. They were carrying you through the Grey Mountains in a sarcophagus with älfar runes on it.' He placed an armoured glove on the clamp that was radiating magic just like the half-mask. 'Can you let me know who you are and how I can release you from your shackles?' *It would mean he'd be even more in my debt and would reveal information more willingly.* He was mentally preparing a story he could tell to win the prisoner's trust.

The stranger lay still, examining Aiphatòn's face. Then he turned his head frantically right and left as if he wanted to make sure that they were alone and his captors were gone.

'Do you understand me?'

The moon-pale älf nodded slowly and relaxed slightly. It seemed he was only just starting to believe what his rescuer was saying.

Aiphatòn reached out a hand to the little slider in front of the prisoner's mouth. 'It's best if I take this mask off you, so that we can speak . . .'

The älf shook his head in fear and uttered some muffled sounds, pressing his heels into the soft ground and trying to creep away from Aiphatòn.

'All right, I'll leave it then,' he reassured him. 'What about the clamp? It's magical, I felt it. Is there . . .'

Calm now, the älf nodded and angled onto his side so that he could reach the earth with one finger. He sketched runes in the soil with his fingertip, then scooted aside and kept drawing.

'Is that the order I need to touch the runes in?' Aiphatòn attempted to make sense of them.

The stranger bowed his head in agreement.

Aiphatòn didn't feel completely at ease as he reached out his right hand and tapped one symbol after another in the given sequence with one armoured index finger. Anything might happen next – the älf could even attack him. *But otherwise, I'll never find out who I'm carrying round with me and what he knows.*

The runes he touched glimmered and didn't extinguish again. On the last one, there was a distinct click and the link rattled as it came away. The clamp opened a crack.

Aiphatòn got up and held his spear at the ready. 'Break free. But don't you dare try to attack me or try any other tricks.'

The wan älf pulled his thin arms out of the clamp and held them out, although this took visible effort; his muscles were trembling like they were at the limits of their endurance already.

He sat up carefully, panting hard through his mouth and nose, the half-mask turning it into a sinister, hollow sound. Condensation dripped onto the ground from underneath the metal on his chin. Nevertheless, he wrote on the ground again with one dirty finger, then pointed to himself.

'You are Nodûcor.' Aiphatòn pointed at the mask. 'How do we get that off you?'

Nodûcor shook his head once more and his glassy hair whipped around but didn't break. He drew the words in the earth again.

A tedious way of communicating. 'There's no way. There are safeguards, both magical and mechanical,' Aiphatòn read in bewilderment. *Why go to so much effort?*

A soft crack made both älfar look over at the ruins of the closest tower at the same time: someone had stepped on a shard of glass or a roof tile.

'Might be an animal just scavenging for carrion,' Aiphatòn murmured. He took the spear and crept towards the ruins, noticing out of the corner of one eye that Nodûcor was burrowing in the ground for a rusty old dagger. *If it's not, he'll be food for them.*

Crouching down, Aiphatòn started to work his way silently around the ruined building – and spotted two lightly armed beasts sitting on a rock in the shade on the far side of the tower's ruins, sharing a piece of rotten meat.

They looked like orcs but without the greenish or black skin. They cut off slice after slice of meat, stuffed them into their gobs, devouring them without enjoying them; their movements looked jerky. Cloudy juice ran over their lips and trickled down their cracked, scabbed skin.

Aiphatòn thought their gazes strangely vacant and fixed, as if they were sleeping with their eyes open. They didn't exchange a word during their revolting meal, and they didn't behave in that rowdy, showily loud way he was used to beasts behaving.

Have they taken a drug that's clouding their senses? White runes stood out on their armour but they weren't älfar in origin and seemed too curly and ornate to have come from an ungainly clawed hand. *Or could those runes be charm runes?*

All of a sudden, another figure emerged from inside the ruins, moving just as silently as Aiphatòn. He approached the two monsters and they ignored him. His filthy armour was made up entirely of replacement parts and was loose on his slim body; his straggly brown hair with grey mud clinging to it came down to his shoulders, and a sword dangled at his side. His gait was swaying and unsteady.

Aiphatòn only realised he was an älf once he turned around. The same white runes glowed on his forehead.

Is he the commander? But then why is he wearing that dreadful armour? Even the sword wasn't right for an älf.

Breathing heavily, the unidentified man sat down next to the beasts and stared in revulsion at the putrid meat – then raised his hand.

He rested his fingers on the hilt of a dagger stuck into his entrails. After it had been thrust into him, someone had wrenched it up to the base of his ribcage. With a tug and a scream, he pulled it out of the wound and, reaching over to the beasts, he used it to cut himself off a chunk from their meat, gagging as he stuffed it into his mouth and chewed.

Aiphatòn couldn't grasp what was happening before his very eyes. The blood was gushing out of the älf's wound as he tearfully chewed; the beasts didn't even glance at him – they kept on eating just as silently as before.

I'll need to ask questions if I want to understand. He stepped out from his hiding place. 'Who are you and whose symbols are you wearing?' he demanded in a firm voice.

The monsters may have been moving sluggishly until now, but suddenly they lost all their ungainliness and got to their feet quick as a flash, whipped out their weapons and launched themselves at their enemy without a sound.

Aiphatòn brandished his spear. The tip plunged through the knee of the attacker on the right and severed the joint from all the muscles and tendons. He fell down mutely.

The other beast came at Aiphatòn with a sickle-shaped sword and a light cudgel with spikes, and he was extremely skilled.

You're quicker than a human. He dodged and parried the attacks, the blade and metal spikes clinking as they glanced off the shaft of the spear. There was considerable force behind the blows.

The unkempt älf in the cobbled-together armour was still sitting on the rock, chewing and bleeding, his black eyes riveted on the fight.

Could they be zombies? Aiphatòn rammed the bottom of his weapon into his opponent's face, and his enemy snapped at it as if that might stop it. When the älf yanked the shaft back in one tug, shattering and wrenching the beast's teeth out of its mouth, it wasn't bothered. *It seemed that way.*

The blade of his forcefully wielded spear cut the attacking monster's right throwing arm in two at the elbow.

The sickle sword fell and was sprayed with blood – but the enemy was undaunted, continuing to attack him with the cudgel until Aiphatòn penetrated his eye socket and kept pushing until he had forced the tip through the brain and out the back of the skull.

The beast collapsed and lay still.

Aiphatòn looked over at the chewing älf, who had the black lines on his face now. He walked over to the first, fallen attacker and, with one swift movement, his blade sliced through the cringing, injured beast's back into his heart. He too slumped to the ground and died.

He brandished the bloody spear-tip at the älf. 'Tell me what's going on.'

'Are you from Elhàtor or Dâkiòn?' he groaned, but didn't stop chewing the lump of meat.

'What are they?'

'Our towns, the . . .' He rolled his eyes, writhing. 'You must warn them. About the botoicans.' He panted as he spoke and spat out chunks of meat. 'They – it . . . will attack. We're not protected anymore . . . Surrender . . . Complete surr . . .'

Of course! Aiphatòn remembered why the outline of the building looked familiar. It reminded him of an old story he had read. *It was in Carmondai's writings.* 'I can bandage your wounds and –'

'No,' screamed the horrified älf. 'No, I *must* die! I *want* to die! I did it myself when the control . . .' His upper body shook. 'I'm escaping the madness,' he murmured contentedly. 'Save the towns! Warn them.'

'Where do I find them?'

'Further northwest. Further towards . . .' The injured älf let out a terrible scream and fell forwards, twitching, his feet shuffling in the dirt as if they were trying to run away. 'End it!' he screeched shrilly. 'Put an end to this!'

'I will.' Aiphatòn leaped onto the rock in front of him, forced the unnamed älf into an upright position with his foot and, facing him, stabbed him in the heart with the spear. His body stiffened immediately. 'Your death is called Aiphatòn,' he said. 'I will find the towns – and destroy them *before* the botoicans reach them. Is that a consolation to you?'

The dying älf opened his eyes wide, then he passed away and the blackness disappeared. What remained were cloudy, greenish eyes.

Who would have thought: two towns. Elhàtor and Dâkiòn. He jumped back onto the ground and walked around the ruins to look for Nodûcor. *At least I'll have something to do in Ishím Voróo. And I thought the death of the Dsôn Aklán meant that the evil had been wiped out.*

The emaciated, wan älf had not moved. He held the dagger pressed against his body, as if he had to protect the weapon instead of using it to defend himself.

Aiphatòn smiled at him. *He must come from one of the two towns. I'll take him along for now and ask him about it. Every piece of knowledge is important for me to be able to destroy the towns more easily. I can kill the bag of bones any time.* 'On your feet,' he ordered and held out the armoured fingers of his right hand to him. 'We're moving on.'

Nodûcor nodded hesitantly and grasped the outstretched hand, letting himself be pulled to his feet. He tentatively grasped the dagger and bent down to pick up the clamp.

'Round the corner you'll find clothes better than those rags, at least, and weapons,' Aiphatòn explained to him. 'Then we'll move on and look for a straw you can suck some water through.' *He won't be able to eat anything but gruel.*

Nodûcor hobbled away slowly, and Aiphatòn followed.

When they walked round the ruins of the building, they saw to their surprise that a massive army was approaching from the west less than half a mile away, marching silently across the marsh. They were quite clearly making for the towers.

Just as many warriors were approaching from the towers, however, as was evident from the pennants and lances reaching up into the air.

But Aiphatòn could not make out a formation or even an attempt at battle array in either army.

Is this a merger rather than a battle?

'Choose something for yourself. Quickly,' he urged Nodûcor and climbed the ruins to get a better view from three paces up. He was careful not to be seen by the armies as he did so.

The warm, putrid wind carried the soft sounds of the soldiers' armour and weapons jangling and clinking.

The warriors were marching in silence, trudging through the mud as it splashed up among their bare feet and boots. While the first row was still making good progress, the ground would have turned to thick sludge after the twentieth or thirtieth soldier, which did not seem to slow them down.

Aiphatòn shook his head as he watched.

Monsters from all kinds of races, known and unknown, from orcs to trolls to hybrids, were walking shoulder-to-shoulder with humans. Foot soldiers with long pikes trotted along next to sword-bearers, while bow and crossbow-archers were marching elsewhere in the pack. Among them rode warriors on horses and oxen and there were even ordinary carts trundling along with warriors gathered on them.

The crowd reached as far as the horizon; far away an enormous banner fluttered in the air, probably so the troops could tell where their commander was. Aiphatòn's vantage point was not high enough to have a clear view of everything. *This is an unparalleled mess. This cannot be the build-up to a battle.*

Everyone's heads were facing forward, and not one person in the armies spoke.

Like the beasts during their meal. The älf was astonished. He now vaguely recognised the white runes painted on bare skin, on pelts and on armour. It looked like everyone was wearing them. He could see less armour than might have been expected of an armed force. And the number of weapon-bearers seemed low too – the rest of them would need to fight with their bare hands.

There are thousands upon thousands of them. They could form ramps with their bodies just like crabs and scale walls. If the armies joined forces, Aiphatòn estimated the number of warriors at just under two hundred thousand.

'We should get going,' he called to Nodûcor who had stocked up on clothes without taking his eyes off the crowd trudging along. It seemed this was new to him as well.

When the first rows of the factions came within twenty paces of each other, they suddenly started to rush at each other – without uttering a single scream.

Ishím Voróo, Älfar town of Dsôn Dâkiòn, 5452nd division of unendingness (6491st solar cycle), summer

Shôtoràs walked across the bridge that linked the two parts of Dsôn Dâkiòn and stopped exactly in the middle, then moved to one side so he wouldn't be in anyone's way.

The strong wind whistling constantly through the groove in the mountain tore at his black robe which was embroidered with old Dsôn Faïmon patterns. He made no secret of his origins and was proud of his past.

I've experienced and achieved so much in the last divisions of unendingness. He looked back and forth between the river two miles away and the ravine below. *For so long I've managed to avoid anything that would force us into a dispute with the Elhàtor scum. And now this!* From time to time he turned around and watched the residents crossing the footbridge.

Shôtoràs silently cursed his niece. *She may be cunning, but she is remarkably foolish all the same.* He couldn't comprehend her desire to provoke outright war. *What is she thinking?* Irïanora didn't even have a specific strategy. Surprise alone was not enough against the Magnificent.

The battles would last too long. The monarch shook his head and fixed his gaze on the Tronjor once more as it meandered along steadily, a sparkling blue in the sunshine. *The only ones who would be pleased are the tribes in the surrounding areas. This means they'd either be rid of us or they'd attack us because they knew we were weakened.*

Shôtoràs shut his eyes and listened to the rushing of the air; he could feel his beard and hair fluttering.

The past came rushing at him, conjuring up certain images.

They had gathered near the Black Heart, which had been corroded by acid. They had seen the land caving in and knew that the nomadic towers were prowling through the area and the Inextinguishables had fled rather than coming to their aid.

Fled. Shôtoràs snorted in disdain. *Traitors to those who had been loyal to them for so long.* He of all people, a glowing Constellation, was among those who led the survivors northwards to find a new home.

But the harmony didn't last long. The älfar scattered and that's when the defeats started. The dying. The endingness.

But not in my town. In his mind's eye he saw Dsôn Dâkiòn being built under his leadership and guidance. Thousands of älfar daring to enter the enormous ruins, searching and securing them, always vigilant about the return of their most recent inhabitants; marvelling at the gigantic towers and buildings and wondering what race of beings had erected this monument; building on the old foundations, constructing new buildings from the ruins and upholding traditions.

Even though there were quite a few older residents like Shôtoràs, time could not be stopped. New generations brought new ideas and thoughts.

This didn't make things worse, although it often required a lot of effort on the monarch's part to accept and agree to these changes. There were no slaves anymore, älfar served älfar now. Different classes had arisen out of the different professions and it took a huge amount of energy to make sure none of them looked down on any other class.

Anyone who rejects the pressure to change will crumble. Shôtoràs placed his hands on the sun-warmed stones of the parapet.

Ishím Voróo changed so many things. Even the älfar themselves.

At first, nobody noticed; it was accompanied by mysterious deaths that were put down to fevers and other illnesses of the wasteland – until the cîanai and cîanoi among them suddenly grew stronger.

It might be because of the stones. Shôtoràs thought about how the basalt ashlars apparently came from the island where the Magnificent was. A considerable number of cîani had left Dsôn Dâkiòn with Modôia long ago. *May Tion devour the soul of that blonde villain!*

He hated the monarchess. From the bottom of his heart, desperately and with a real passion. She had come from Tark Draan down at heel and over the hill, accompanied by dishevelled älfar she had picked up along the way like cattle. Then she claimed to have previously lived in a town called Dsôn Sòmran in the Grey Mountains. And she had supposedly been in service in an älfar realm in Tark Draan.

Ridiculous!

Hundreds followed her flattering words and her promises of a better town. They had once owed their existence to Shôtoràs.

To me! He breathed deeply and opened his eyes.

He didn't think Irïanora was capable of – to use a coastal town metaphor – calming the troubled waters. It was possible Modôia herself was waiting for the chance to start a war.

The king looked back at the river, the greatest danger facing his town. At the same time, it supplied plenty of fish, the necessary water for the surrounding fields and enabled trade with the areas upstream.

There were reports that the monarchess was secretly having a fleet built with the sole purpose of sailing up the Tronjor. Boats with minimal draught, very well-balanced but with capacity for huge quantities of military equipment and soldiers. Apparently dozens of these boats already lay at anchor inland on the island.

Oh, my foolish niece. It looks as if you're in agreement with her and you're trying to provide her with a pretext for having the ships put out to sea. Shôtoràs smoothed down his pale, tousled hair. He had been brooding long enough. He had made a decision now and he wanted to put it to his two closest confidants.

They would not be able to talk him out of it, but they could help by fleshing it out.

Because his word was law in Dsôn Dâkiòn, undiminished despite the innovations and changes. Anyone who opposed his word crumbled.

'This is the starting position.' Shôtoràs had summoned Pasôlor and Horgôra to the hall where Iriänora had recently been given a taste of his stick. They were two of his best friends and were able to say things to the sovereign that other residents would receive severe punishments for.

The älfar were standing around the big desk with the map spread out showing the town and a surrounding area of just under forty miles. That was as far as the area claimed by the Majestic extended. Anyone who wanted to cross this land or settle down on it had to pay a fee. The marsh was exempted from that, but nobody tried to build a settlement there.

Shôtoràs pointed to the Tronjor. 'The river has barely changed in our region, the riverbed just got slightly wider. So Elhàtor's ships would come within two miles of us, as before.'

'Reminds me of my last game of Tharc,' Horgôra replied, bouncing up and down on her tiptoes. 'I'll take the blue army.' The black-haired robe-maker, who was generally good-humoured and fond of jokes but also had a very sharp and agile mind, turned aside and poured grape juice from the carafe into three glasses. Her bright flame-coloured coat with its sophisticated cut showed her expertise in handicraft.

'If we could be a little more serious, please,' Shôtoràs chided her. 'So?'

'We've heard the rumours about the fleet,' Pasôlor murmured and placed his hands on his back. He had had his hair shaved off and now wore caps that he changed as often as other people changed their underwear. The bald älf had conceived of the bridges that led into the town and was considered a prudent strategist. 'There are only two places where we could lie in wait to ambush the ships.'

'Probably,' Horgôra agreed, pensive, 'but they'll send scouts on ahead to secure the bank as much as possible.'

'They would suffer huge casualties because of the quicksand, insects and monsters,' Pasôlor shot back immediately and placed one hand on the woven silver-wire belt fastened around his dark green robe at hip height.

'Better than losing the fleet. *I* would do it like that and discover the ambush.' She held one hand to her chin and reflected. 'Tell me: what makes you so sure Modôia is going to attack us?'

Shôtoràs leaned on his walking stick to relieve his painful leg. 'She comes from Tark Draan – the älfar there had to be hell-bent on conquest to survive in that prison and they became scum themselves. You don't just shake off a trait like that.'

'Might it not be the case that *you* would like her to attack?' Pasôlor ventured to remark.

If it were any other älf, Shôtoràs would have knocked him to the floor immediately with one blow, but he allowed his closest friends to speak openly at all times. 'How could I wish for an attack?' he answered. 'Älfar would die. Our tribe has been decimated enough already and we certainly do not need a war with our own kind.'

'But you hate them. Because they cost us some of our residents,' Pasôlor persevered with his suggestions undaunted. 'It would suit you very . . .'

'A war will cost us even more residents. I would immediately set a zhartài on her to dispatch her into endingness if the infamous assassins were still around,' admitted Shôtoràs, grumbling. 'And if he were to ask for all of my riches, my artworks . . .'

'. . . even if he demanded your high office?' Horgôra added, challenging him.

'Yes,' he exclaimed and clenched his teeth. 'But we're not here because of my darkest desires.' He shifted his weight and used the stick as a pointer; the silver tip was directed at a valley eleven miles west of Dâkiòn. '*That* is my solution.'

Pasôlor exhaled contemptuously, 'A parade?'

The sovereign grinned wickedly which was a clear *no*.

'This valley is half a mile from the river.' Horgôra tilted her head slightly, her black hair flowing like ink over her shoulders and hanging down as far as the table. 'Crazy, the thought that just crossed my mind – but perhaps it's the same thought that occurs to you?'

It took Pasôlor less than half a heartbeat to catch up with what they were thinking. 'That is just *too* crazy. And besides . . .'

Shôtoràs held up his free hand in his defence. 'The fact that barbarians live there is not important. We'll have the little men dig the canal. The brats and womenfolk will have enough time to get away. If they don't do that, then that's their lookout. I'll warn them and nothing more.' He nodded to his friends and smiled. 'I see you agree with me?'

'You know that we don't need to give our opinions,' Pasôlor said.

'Or that you don't need to have them anyway,' Horgôra corrected him in a mocking voice. 'And yet he wants to listen to us. I think he is unfailingly noble. The power hasn't gone to his head.' She took her hand away from her chin. 'We divert the river into the valley, fill it up and the old riverbed dries out. So Elhàtor's ships – provided they have some – don't reach us because the water needed to travel the remaining miles upstream is missing.' Her eyes narrowed. 'I see one significant danger in this: it would mean an army and all manner of monsters could reach us on foot.'

'We could flood the old riverbed at regular intervals,' Pasôlor suggested and pointed to various points on the map. 'We make the barbarians build a second, narrow canal fitted with a large dam. Open the sluice gate, the trash is washed away and swept into the sea to be devoured by fish.'

Shôtoràs hammered his applause on the little desk with his cane, the rumbling echoing for a long time. 'You've grasped my plan quickly.'

'Because it makes sense. I think it's elaborate and grandiose,' Horgôra added, 'but it's good.'

'I'll take it even further.' The sovereign pressed down so hard on the map at several points along the riverbed downstream that he left marks. 'We'll station warrior-women and warriors here, in troops of ten. We'll give each post a hundred barrels of petrol which we can also use to flood the dried-out riverbed.' The tip of the cane traced the bends in the Tronjor. 'It's not enough to produce a sustained surge, but it is enough to set monsters and Elhàtor's army alight. It only needs to roar towards them ablaze at ankle height and we'll be rid of them.'

'It could be mixed with the water, if needs be,' said Pasôlor and nodded approvingly. 'If this were a game of Tharc, our opponent would give up before we had even started because they would be forced to acknowledge our superiority.' He looked delightedly at Horgôra. 'Is that not right?'

'Exactly: that is *not* right.' The älf-woman placed her right hand on the extensive swampland in one delicate movement. 'Doing that would mean we also dry *this* out. *Therefore* the most dangerous section – the quicksand, moorland and swamp – becomes passable much too soon. *Therefore* the monsters can escape in all directions. Not to mention: Elhàtor could launch its troops at us on a broad front. Eighty miles – a quick-moving army could cover that in two or three moments.'

Pasôlor laughed. 'We're talking about ten or twenty divisions of unendingness, that's how long it would take to dry out the moor. If not more.'

'No. Canals run along there, water seeps into them and gets diverted. Our initial scouts told us about them – in case anyone at the table has forgotten,' she countered, enjoying being able to make a significant contribution. 'Within forty or fifty moments, you could march through the natural barrier using certain pathways.' Horgôra looked back and forth between them. 'What's the point of winning a battle if it doesn't settle the war?'

Shôtoràs' expression darkened. 'You're ruining my plan. I still liked you until just now.'

'I'm pointing out the weakness to you, before monsters and Modôia do it. Be grateful to me, sovereign.' She laughed cheerfully. 'Don't look so bitter. Think further ahead, like I've already done.'

'A continuous supply line,' he replied after a brief reflection.

'A trickle that keeps the swamp wet enough. Superb!' Pasôlor shook his head, baffled. 'Sometimes the simplest solutions remain out of reach.'

'I'm happy to help,' she said, laughing, and drank some of her juice. 'Not bad for a robe-maker, eh?'

Pasôlor bowed to her. 'I will never play Tharc against you.'

'I knew there was a reason I listened to you two.' Shôtoràs pulled his stick back to lean on it again. His confidence and satisfaction had returned. 'Let's do it exactly according to this plan then.'

'*You'll* do it that way, monarch. We are simply honoured to have been allowed to help you and our homeland.' Horgôra bowed to him and Pasôlor followed suit.

Shôtoràs accepted the obeisance because he knew it was purely intended to tease him. 'Yes, yes,' he mumbled. 'Make fun of me.'

'I would never dare do that.' The älf-woman winked at him. 'And as your chief robe-maker, I can tell you: you've lost weight, sovereign. Drop by and have your clothes taken in. You could do with it.'

Pasôlor was still looking at the map, lost in thought as he retraced the waterways. 'I agree, there's no other plausible possibility.'

There probably were some. But the monarch didn't like to consider those.

I would not like to send our budding cîani out into the wasteland to fight against the monarches' ships. Shôtoràs was aware that the town was educating around a hundred talented pupils.

Thirty of them were advanced enough to be deployed in battle because they had a good enough command of their spells to cast them under great stress. But in the face of a hail of arrows or brandished swords, the beginners would lapse into stammering or lose focus. *No, they're staying put. They will back us up in case the Elhàtorians do manage to get right up to the steep cliffs.*

'Some may take this remark badly, but there's still *one* thing I'm hoping for above all else,' Pasôlor interrupted Shôtoràs' thoughts. The two other älfar looked expectantly at him. 'That we take every possible precaution and don't need them.' He pursed his lips and looked back at the map with a steady gaze. 'May the gods give Irïanora enough sense to placate Modôia and convince her to forgive Irïanora for her absurd idea.'

Shôtoràs didn't know what to say in response, though his first thought was: *Then bring me a zhartài who will finish off the scum.* He truly did not want a war with the Magnificent, just the death of the monarchess. But who could carry out that assassination?

I would need a warrior, an älf, who is not from this town. A hitman. Shôtoràs was sorry the zhartài were no longer around. They would have come in useful on occasion, and nobody would have been able to trace anything back to him.

'May the gods see to it,' Horgôra agreed.

'And if they don't hear our prayers – no matter if it's Inàste or Tion or all of the rest of them, for all I care – then we will be prepared and settle this dispute for ourselves,' Shôtoràs said absent-mindedly; a part of his brain was still occupied with other thoughts. 'I swear to you, friends, that I will eliminate Modôia and only Modôia. Afterwards the Magnificent and the Majestic can live in unity and peace.' His fingers clicked as they closed tightly around the handle of his stick, and he was breathing faster. 'Her dead body will lie before me and I will have it disembowelled by my best artists. It will be scattered in tiny pieces all over Dâkiòn so that everyone understands we can never trust the scum from Tark Draan.'

'Strictly speaking, she's from Ishím Voróo like we are,' Horgôra interjected. 'Her town was located . . .'

'Regardless! She divided a powerful town and brought us discord.' Shôtoràs was panting as if he had just done a long, strenuous jog. He quickly wiped the sweat back off his brow and into his pale grey hair. 'You understand me, don't you?'

Pasôlor and Horgôra looked at the old älf.

'We do,' the robe craftswoman answered sympathetically for both of them. 'You are our sovereign. And our friend.'

Shôtoràs stretched his broad back and then stretched the rest of his body. 'I will order the relevant decrees then. As early as tomorrow, our warriors will travel into the valley and set the barbarians to work.' He felt incredibly thirsty and simultaneously exhausted. *I've got to rest.* 'Let's believe in the gods and trust ourselves most of all.' That's how he had achieved his greatest successes so far.

He turned around and limped away from the balcony-like platform and into the hallway.

Chapter VII

Garnish a rumour that revolves around you with obvious lies. The lies will be detected and the rumour will no longer be given any credence. Even if it was true.

Wise saying of the Älfar
Collected by Carmondai, master of word and image

Ishím Voróo, Älfar town of Dsôn Elhàtor, 5452nd division of unendingness (6491st solar cycle), summer

Irïanora wiped away the water that was intermittently hitting her in the face in thin veils and tasted the drops. *Saltier than tears.* She hoped the foam wouldn't leave any white ring marks on her yellow and black dress, but the place she was standing was just too tempting.

They were travelling towards the Magnificent in a three-masted ship and the young älf-woman was standing at the bow.

The sea was practically still, not one sail was hoisted and the oars were pulled into the belly of the craft. But the little waves were being carved in two by the hull as it glided along, without any magic coming into play.

Irïanora could see the thick, taut cables that ran through a narrow opening next to the anchor chain then disappeared beneath the surface ten paces from the front of the ship.

Her bodyguard was approaching, wearing the leather armour with the insignia of the bodyguards to Dâkiòn's sovereign. He was walking so defiantly across the deck it was as if he wanted to challenge the men from Elhàtor to a fight.

Or he's not capable of moving normally on board ship. Irïanora smiled disdainfully at him. 'And what were you able to find out about how our journey seems to progress as if by magic?' *Arthâras, that was his name.* She was forgetting it less often, but it gave her fiendish pleasure to ask him his name constantly, to show him how utterly insignificant he was to her.

The bodyguard, a veteran of eleven divisions of unendingness, came and stood next to her. He wore his fair hair short and the air couldn't mess it up. 'With this calm weather, the crew is using an undersea current so that they don't have to row in this heat and work themselves into exhaustion,' he explained. 'Lazy bunch!'

'I call that *clever*. I think they're doing it to try and impress us.' Irïanora looked towards the island where the white town rose up into the sky. Patterns were becoming visible on the roofs and, taken together, they formed images yet to become fully clear.

She knew the monarchess had received help from the frekorian soldiers: boat-building methods, navigation and the various ways of travelling at sea. All of that knowledge had been passed on to the älfar. 'How does it work?'

'If there isn't enough wind and you don't have any oars or you want to spare the crew, you lower weighted objects shaped like fishing pots to a precisely calculated depth,' Arthâras explained. 'The currents seize them and pull them forwards. That's how we're making headway.'

Clearly there's a particularly strong current between the coast and

Elhàtor. Irïanora was still experiencing pain throughout her body, which meant her hatred for the sovereign was as strong as ever. 'My calculating, oh-so-cunning uncle,' she muttered contemptuously and thought of the casket he had used to play a nasty trick on her. *Why does he have to go on living?*

'What about the sovereign?' Arthâras asked.

'I was just mentally admiring his foresight,' she said aloud.

The bodyguard laughed softly. 'Yes, he's well capable of that. That's why our homeland still exists and wasn't destroyed like all the other älfar towns. By scum, by barbarians or by beasts.' He followed her gaze, his hand moving to the hilt of the long dagger he wore strapped to his thigh. 'A very large town. I can barely see any defensive fortifications. There are just the two towers at the harbour.' He pointed at the ship. 'But I see why their fleet is considered invincible. The hull of this main ship that we're travelling on is eighty paces long and around twenty across, but the draught is very low.'

'They won't get through the bottleneck on it.'

'Not on this. They'll have other boats built for that type of plan.' Arthâras couldn't hide his admiration despite his dislike. 'These are made for living at sea. Multi-storeyed, with fish ponds and crops growing during the voyage; they even have hen coops,' he reeled off. 'It's a warrior settlement on the sea.'

'That someone could sink,' the blonde älf-woman cut in.

'That would be difficult. I couldn't see much, because they won't let me get into every corner, but I think there are compartments in the hull that could be separated by bulkheads. If there were a leak, this ship won't go down straight away, it will continue to deliver lethal strikes.'

Irïanora looked at the three large masts and the two narrower ones close by on the foredeck. The enormous ship was accompanied by four smaller, easily manoeuvrable sailboats that served as extra back-up. They had also joined forces with the undersea currents via the fishing pots and were being towed along.

Arthâras placed one hand on the railing. 'The frekoriers knew how to remain undefeated and Elhàtor has perfected it. We could do with this fleet.'

'You'd like to go into battle against Elhàtor,' Irïanora said in astonishment, when she recognised the expression on his face. *The pride of a veteran.*

'Possibly.'

A kindred spirit. She lowered her voice. 'But my uncle will never allow it. He wants to keep the peace.'

'That's why I'm bringing you to the monarchess,' he said. 'It's his will. As you said yourself: he has foresight and he made sure that Dâkiòn grew strong and survived. *My* thoughts are irrelevant here.' He laughed suddenly.

'What's so funny?'

'That you're genuinely trying to work out whether I'd come over to your side. First me, then maybe the guards and then, some moment of unendingness in the future, you'll consider a rebellion against your uncle,' he guessed what she was thinking. 'Don't you think he has already considered *that* too?' Arthâras pointed to the emblem on his armour. 'I'm as loyal as they come. Sticking together makes us strong. Without him the Majestic is lost.'

Irïanora felt her damp blonde hair, which was slowly going frizzy from the effects of the saltwater and the sun. She was annoyed about the insolent bodyguard as well as the fact that her uncle was at the head of another battalion. 'Oh, you've got it all wrong. I wasn't thinking that,' she lied – and had a brainwave. 'I was thinking about the casket.'

'Oh?' He smirked as he turned towards her. 'What about it?'

'My uncle wrote a note in it that one of you two was carrying the real message for the monarchess.'

The hull jolted forwards slightly; the undersea sail must have been caught by a powerful current. The bow rose up a little and then sank down deeper.

The commanding officer was giving loud orders and from the lower deck came the sound of the windlass rattling. It was clear the length of the ropes was being audibly adjusted.

Irïanora raised one hand to protect herself from the glittering droplets flying up from the hull. Some of the spray hit her anyway. 'He knew I'd open it.'

'He probably did, yes.' Arthâras laughed gently. 'Now you're wondering which of the two of us is carrying this message: me or your maid, Zelája?'

Irïanora joined in the laughter and hit him lightly across the right shoulder. 'Of course not, Arthâras. Quite the opposite.' She left her hand on his armour and traced the inlaid work in the leather.

The bodyguard was confused now. '*The opposite* means what exactly? That you don't care either way?'

'No. It would make the situation simpler if I knew.'

Arthâras looked astonished now, but he was still laughing. 'You're talking nonsense, Irïanora. You do care, and yet . . .'

The rattling underneath their feet stopped. The ropes slackened and the bow rose slightly.

The älf-woman had been expecting the upward movement. While Arthâras was still shifting his weight to counterbalance the rocking, Irïanora suddenly pushed him hard in the shoulder so that her shove and the movement of the ship coincided.

The bodyguard's hip struck the railing and he was catapulted over it; meanwhile Irïanora acted fast and stole the falling man's dagger.

Arthâras had the physical control of a warrior and he rotated as he fell. He grabbed hold of one of the fishing pot ropes with his right hand.

Irïanora cursed and looked around quickly.

Nobody had noticed anything.

She bent down and drew her own knife. She needed to save the bodyguard's weapon.

'Your uncle will never forgive you for this. An *attempted murder*!' Arthâras was staring up at her and was about to get a firmer grip to pull himself up the cable.

'You're wrong: this is a *murder* he will know nothing about,' she countered and hurled the knife.

In the position he was in, the älf couldn't dodge it. The blade plunged through the hand he was clinging to the rope with. The tendons were severed and his fingers were forced open. He couldn't regain his grip quickly enough.

Arthâras fell into the sea in front of the bow and with a dull sound its planks smashed into his forehead. The water turned red instantly but momentarily.

I'm rid of him. Irïanora straightened up and hurried across the deck. She tucked the stolen dagger away in a fold in her clothes as she did so. 'When do we arrive in Elhàtor?' she called to the commanding officer who, like his crew, was wearing a simple linen shirt and calf-length trousers. His rank was clear only from the insignia on his right breast and his red headscarf. 'I want to freshen up a little and I need to start in good time.'

The crew laughed.

'In a splinter, I'd say,' he answered.

She nodded. 'Thank you. Then I'd probably better get started.' Irïanora ran down the broad staircase and hurried into the small cabin she had been assigned. *My dear uncle, you don't understand me as well as you think you do.*

When she entered the compartment her maid Zelája was just picking out different dresses and hanging them in a row. She was putting them on wire hangers, then hanging them from the hooks jutting out of the ceiling intended for lamps or hammocks. 'Which would you rather wear: dark blue, dark red or dark green?'

Irïanora took the dagger out of the fold of material, went over to the unsuspecting woman and drove the long, thin blade up through her neck, pressing Zelája against the wall of the cabin with her own weight. 'As I just told the late Arthâras: I don't care *which* of you two has the message for the monarchess,' she whispered icily. 'Because neither you nor he will reach Elhàtor.'

She wrenched the dagger out, avoiding the blood spurt and stabbing the älf-woman in the heart straight away to make absolutely certain she killed her.

Zelája slumped.

Irïanora let go and the body slid down the wood, landing at her feet. *From this splinter on, I am the message, the slight difference being that I can now invent what my uncle would no doubt have wanted to be communicated.*

Breathing hard, she took a quick look around, then searched the body as it bled out. But she didn't find a message to the monarchess.

As I said: I don't care. She heaved Zelája's corpse into a chest along with Arthâras' dagger and covered them with a dark green dress. The fabric was thick and absorbent enough to soak up the blood. *I never could stand that design.*

Irïanora pushed the chest over the large stain on the wooden floor and waited a while before going back on deck and complaining loudly that her servant was missing.

*

'Is this her?' The commanding officer was on the upper deck, standing over the open chest with the blood-stained dress and maid inside.

When there was still no sign of Arthâras and the maid after they docked, he had ordered a search of the ship. They found the traces of blood in the cabin during the investigation and shortly after that the corpse of the unfortunate älf-woman with the bodyguard's weapon in her heart.

Irïanora was suitably shocked. 'Oh, how horrific! That's Arthâras' dagger!' She spoke haltingly about a supposed relationship between the maid and bodyguard and how they had argued many times on the voyage. 'Now he's gone and killed her.' She shook her head in dismay. 'I'm sure he'll try and swim ashore to get to Dâkiòn or at least to the strait.'

'He won't manage it.' The commanding officer ordered the chest to be closed and brought ashore. 'The predatory fish are quicker than he is.'

This couldn't be going better. 'Predatory fish!' Irïanora was delighted to hear this. 'In that case, the murderer will get the punishment he deserves.' She pretended to pull herself together and placed one foot on the ramp that led to solid ground.

The dark blue silk and velvet dress was a good choice – she wasn't sweating in it, but she wasn't too cold either. She wasn't wearing jewellery and she couldn't get her blonde hair under control without a maid so she had simply put it in a triply braided plait.

They had put up towering canvas screens everywhere and they blocked Irïanora's view of the town and its fortifications. All she glimpsed was a brief flash of the mouth of the harbour and she didn't glean much from that.

A detachment of armed warriors on night-mares was waiting at the harbour wall with a carriage and a servant showed Irïanora into it. The windows were completely covered on the outside to prevent any light getting in, so that she was shielded, sitting in the dark.

It didn't surprise her to see the black horses with glowing eyes on the island. *They come from Dâkiòn,* she thought angrily. *Good animals, that these scoundrels also wrenched away from us in the old days. What good are they on an island? We need them much more urgently.*

The journey began. Irïanora could only imagine what her surroundings looked like. At least the carriage had good suspension and was comfortable to sit in. She had expected to have a stinking sack pulled over her head and to be driven through the streets while the locals mocked her. This kind of travel suited her better.

The wheels rattled uphill, then crunched through gravel or what she took to be little pellets of bone.

Finally the carriage stopped and the door was opened.

A ghostly hand helpfully reached inside, and soft rays of sun fell on the interior of the carriage.

'If you would like to come out, Irïanora?' came the voice of an älf.

She was too dazzled to be able to make out anything clearly. She grabbed the soft but strong fingers and climbed out of the carriage.

'Welcome to Elhàtor,' the älf greeted her. He was wearing an incredibly elaborate blue and silver outfit, with an upturned collar and cuffs. 'And I am pleased to see: colour-wise we complement each other very well.'

Irïanora could see again properly now.

She was under an awning to shelter guests from the weather when they arrived. Directly behind the young älf were four steps up to a double door with four armoured warriors on guard in front of it.

Their armour is much lighter than ours. 'Thank you so much . . .'

'*Sir,*' the älf with the mid-length, brown hair interrupted her in a friendly, instructive way. 'I've heard that one cultivates less of a sense of politeness and manners in Dâkiòn, but on Elhàtor, I request, *madam,* that you observe the etiquette.' He bowed slightly. 'My name is Ôdaiòn.'

The son of the monarchess. Irïanora kept her composure and inclined her blonde head. 'I will make an effort to please you and your mother, sir.' She was absolutely amazed he didn't have black eyes despite the sunlight. *How does that happen? A freak of nature?*

'You please *me* already, madam.' The young älf gave her a mischievous grin, the interest in his eyes unmistakeable. He escorted her to the portal which opened for her as soon as she had climbed the steps. 'I was very curious about you, Irïanora. The niece of the monarch pays us her respects.'

'What could have triggered this curiosity?'

'Apart from your insubordination and plans to incite a war?' Ôdaiòn sounded extremely amused. 'People say you're very pretty.'

Irïanora was taken aback by his frankness. 'I don't quite understand . . .'

'Your friend told us about you, madam. And based on what I heard, it wasn't difficult to work out your true intentions when you sent those poor souls down the Tronjor to make them measure it.' He laughed and gently kissed the back of her hand. 'Measuring, absolutely priceless! You are genuinely gifted. You should come over to our side.'

Irïanora didn't know what to think. Here she was on her way to report to the monarchess of the Magnificent, and at the same time her son was trying to make her turn her back on her homeland. *A test, I presume.*

'Should I? Not a bad idea at all. But only if the rumours about your fleet are true. Apparently it's hidden somewhere on the island,' she shot back sweetly. 'I'm used to being on the victorious side.'

Ôdaiòn stopped walking, let go of her hand and gave a slight bow, clapping silently. 'You're enchanting,' he conceded. 'Shrewd, attractive *and* quick-witted. And that business with the two murders on board the ship – unbelievable.'

Irïanora grew hot and felt disconcerted. She remained silent as he grasped her fingers again and continued walking. *He . . . cannot know.* She gave him a quick sidelong glance. *He's still testing me.* 'I thought it was appalling,' she replied.

'Is that so?' And he left it at that.

She breathed a sigh of relief. *He wanted to frighten me like you might frighten a flock of birds at a hunt.* Irïanora smiled in relief. *Not on my watch.*

They entered a hall where enormous fish bones served as pillars and turned into a passageway that had been modelled on an open clam.

'Before I forget: your mother has asked me to say hello from her.'

Irïanora flinched. 'My uncle says my mother is dead.'

'She's not. I met her just yesterday in the market square. You look very similar, did you know that?'

She breathed in, unable to quash the various feelings that rose up within her and formed a chaotic mass she couldn't deal with.

Ôdaiòn waited several heartbeats. 'Please excuse my joke, madam. Of course I didn't meet her. But you can do the joke on anyone who comes here from Dâkiòn – it works every time. It's fascinating to watch the reactions.'

Another test. Before Irïanora could even deliver a slick retort, they strode through a black curtain made to look like a tapestry of algae and seagrass and into a small room where a cosy suite of white leather armchairs stood by a fireplace. Waterlilies looked like they were growing out of the walls, and it smelled of flowers and the sea. Small, black birds hummed through the air and sucked nectar out of the roses.

It looks so different from home. Irïanora noticed that the plaster was made of very fine fragments of bone and sharp teeth that must once have belonged to predatory fish. Here and there, tiny tiles of gold and silver gleamed in the plaster.

The monarchess was on her feet and waiting for them, having pinned up her long, blonde hair and adorned it with shimmering strings of pearl and amber. The white dress suited her extremely well and she wore sandals on her feet.

At the arrival of the two newcomers, servants brought out dishes of fruit and carafes filled with various juices and wines, setting them down on the table.

'Keep in mind the correct form of address,' Ôdaiòn murmured to her again. 'Mother,' he cried cheerfully. 'Look who I've brought you. Our guest has just arrived.' He let go of her hand so that she walked the remaining paces by herself.

Irïanora didn't let her unease show. *It feels like they're indulging in a game with me.* She approached Modôia and dropped a deep curtsey. 'I stand before you, monarchess, at the command of my uncle, Shôtoràs, sovereign of Dâkiòn, to speak with you about the incident at the strait and to beg for my friends' freedom.'

Modôia laid both her hands against her flat stomach and nodded to Irïanora. 'I'm delighted to hear that our towns are seeking a solution that does not end in war.' She gestured with an elegant motion to the armchair opposite her. 'Sit down, Irïanora.' She herself sat down on the chaise longue and put her feet up. Her son chose the seat next to her. 'Pick out whatever you'd like and point to it,' she said, indicating the table. 'My servants are swift.'

Irïanora smiled and sat down.

The monarchess' black eyes, which looked surreal in the midst of the otherwise white room, rested intently on her, scrutinising her and seeming to penetrate her thoughts. 'I hear you had a murder to deal with?'

'Yes, it turned out there was an unfortunate death.' Iriänora briefly explained and asked for bite-size pieces of cut fruit to be handed to her on a bone saucer. The spine of the creature they'd used to make the plate must have been wider than three älfar. *What creature living in this sea has bones like that?* 'But I was surprised by my maid's killing.'

Modôia nodded and was sympathetic. '*Surprise*, that's the key word for me.' She had a glass of water handed to her. 'Because *you* in turn surprised me – to put it mildly – rather a lot. Sending your friends to certain death, that is . . . extraordinarily calculating. You are a strategist and a gambler.'

'And you overplayed your hand,' Ôdaiòn added with a chuckle.

Iriänora found this exchange annoying. Even more annoying, however, was their unwavering politeness combined with their bluntness. *My uncle would have been shouting long before now.* She gave a little cough. 'I did not intend to kill my friends. All that was planned was a measuring expedition for the new cartographer because, as you know, the courses of bodies of water change. So there was nothing malicious about it, it was just meant to prevent any unpleasant surprises,' she said, without pausing to draw breath. 'The monsters could have made use of the time to build a fortress on the Tronjor – how else would we have been able to spot it? And the river isn't part of the sea . . .'

'But we have an agreement that you are not allowed to go there,' the monarchess interrupted her. 'It was much more than the four miles downstream.'

'Hence the chain at the bottleneck too,' her son agreed. 'A precaution we took because we expected someone from Dâkiòn to hit upon the idea of breaching the treaty at some point.'

'Even your best excuses won't protect you from punishment.'

Modôia took a little sip of her drink. 'A breach of a treaty is still a breach, regardless of the reason. Even if you'd been trying to save hundreds of lives: I couldn't care less.' The blonde älf-woman asked for a crystallised red fruit to be handed to her. 'You won't be able to tell, but I am incensed.' She smiled as kindly as if she and Irïanora were the best of friends, just chatting about old times.

'You can tell I'm ... astonished,' she replied. 'Again, I merely wanted to have a map made.'

'Those are *your* words, my dearest Irïanora.' Ôdaiòn leaned forward eagerly. 'Now let's hear what message your uncle gave you for the monarchess. I'm expecting an apology from the sovereign and an offer of reparations.'

'Possibly seeds or ...' Modôia shrugged her shoulders. 'Well, there's no limit to your uncle's imagination, is there?' She laughed and reached behind the chaise longue. Suddenly there was a rolled-up triple-strapped whip in her hands, its ends fitted with blades. She removed the safety sheaths from the blades without uncoiling the weapon.

Irïanora gulped. At the sight of the gleaming blades, she could feel fear wrapping its claws around her heart. 'Don't blame *me* if my uncle's words aren't to your liking,' she pleaded. Metal clashed against metal with a soft jangling sound, reflecting the sunlight.

She had heard tell of the weapon capable of causing excruciating pain. Some detached part of her couldn't help but wonder what her red blood would look like on the white leather. Drops, smears, pools, long spatters. She could see there was something very artistic to the idea, despite what it would ultimately mean for her.

'No, we won't blame you at all.' Ôdaiòn pulled a small piece of paper out of his sleeve. 'Look, *this* message from your uncle reached us three moments ago.' He smiled coolly. 'You weren't to know that there are carrier pigeons that can fly back and forth between the Magnificent and the Majestic when a matter is urgent.'

Iriänora drank her wine, her hand trembling slightly. *That old bastard! What else will I need to come up with to outsmart him?*

Meanwhile Modôia got up and let the three straps slide to the floor, the blades clinking as they hit the marble. They hung from the blonde älf-woman's hand like thin, black snakes.

'You get three chances to tell us exactly what your uncle's message to us says,' Ôdaiòn continued. 'Since you have it in your head, as you say, you just need to say it out loud. For every mistake, you'll feel how creatively my mother' – he reached down the side of the armchair and also picked up a whip – 'and I are able to handle these.'

Two of them? Iriänora felt sick; she was fighting the urge to vomit. If she didn't guess the words right, it would not matter. Three blows with those weapons was tantamount to a death sentence. *The first blow alone could tear me to shreds.*

With a conspicuous lack of haste, Ôdaiòn held up the little scrap of paper. 'We're on tenterhooks, sweet Iriänora.'

Tark Draan, Human kingdom of Idoslane, 5452nd division of unendingness (6491st solar cycle), summer

Carmondai was perched on the horse in a slumped position. The shackles didn't allow him to move his hands much. It was not really riding, but he could hold the reins himself; the steel rings clinked softly every time the animal took a step.

Carâhnios, on the other hand, sat upright on the white pony, its colour particularly accentuated by his black leather and tionium armour. One hand resting on his hip, he was humming a sombre song to himself that sounded like a traditional dwarf tune. Apart from the luggage, he was carrying enough weapons for them to go into battle against a thousand orcs.

Carmondai looked up at the swallows performing their breathtaking, zigzagging flying manoeuvres high in the sky. *That is freedom.*

It was inevitable that he was now mulling over an escape plan, though he wouldn't try and escape from the zhadár any time soon. He understood the level of transformation and training the extremely skilled warriors of the Thirdling kingdom had received from Sisaroth.

I would be no match for him in my condition. Plus there were the magical powers the zhadár possessed. *The last one of them left, and I've got to accompany him.*

Besides, he wouldn't know where to turn even if he did manage it. The whole of Girdlegard hated älfar and the passageways were manned by dwarves – there was no escaping. *But living a never-ending life in hiding?*

Time and Samusin would tell how things would go and perhaps his immortality worked in his favour. He hadn't escaped the Aklán dungeon only to launch himself into one last, desperate battle that would prove his downfall out of some false sense of pride. *Only the living get options.*

'Where are we riding to?' Carmondai might have had paper and ink, but on the horse's lurching back it was impossible to write a sentence or start a sketch.

Carâhnios kept humming.

'Did you hear . . .'

The groundling raised one hand, uttering some final notes and holding the last one for a particularly long time before sniggering. '*Now* you can talk to me. And if you speak during my song again' – he looked menacingly over his shoulder, the short, black beard scraping bristle-like over the leather armour and tionium reinforcement – 'you'll be sorry.'

Carmondai made an apologetic gesture. 'Our destination?'

'Where are we?'

'In Girdlegard.'

'Shrewd, black-eye. More specifically?'

'If I've got my bearings right, we ought to be in Idoslane.'

'Aha. Despite being locked up in a dungeon, you've still got the knack.' Carâhnios clapped far too quickly and far too loudly.

'I know Girdlegard very well,' the älf replied, not without a trace of wistfulness. 'And I've known it *longer* than you have.'

'Ah yes. I keep forgetting that you founded Dsôn Balsur.' He stroked the pony between its ears. 'Tsk, tsk, you black-eye. The human women are jealous of you all. You age but nobody can tell how many cycles there really are on your face.'

Carmondai knew that his age was very obvious. 'Inàste was kind to me.'

'That makes one of her then!' Carâhnios guffawed with laughter at his own joke.

Once he had settled down again, he pointed through a thicket at a ruin that must once have been a temple. About eleven miles away from them, it clung to the little hill it was on as if for support.

It was overgrown with creepers and the toppled pillars lay piled up on top of each other, which made them dangerous traps. Even if they had held up for a hundred cycles, one gentle nudge and they could still tumble downhill and bury an unsuspecting visitor.

'*That* is our destination?' Carmondai couldn't imagine an älf living there.

'You'll see, it only looks like an old shrine. The runes inside it refer to gods who have not been worshipped in Girdlegard for a long time.

Nobody is going to go inside.' Carâhnios pulled up the pony. 'We'll camp behind the bushes and go in once night falls.' He dismounted, the small blackened iron tiles of his skirt-like robe rubbing together silently.

Carmondai brought his horse to a halt and slid out of the saddle, looking as clumsy as a drunk while doing so thanks to his shackles. He was desperate for a bath, clean clothes, a mirror to shave with and a meal. A good meal.

Carâhnios chuckled and detached the chain from the iron handcuffs so the älf could move away from his steed.

Carmondai looked through the undergrowth at the hill and the ruins. *The hideaway is inside the hill.*

The groundling tied the horse and pony to a tree and sank down into the grass, then put his arms behind his head and looked at the clouds.

'We zhadár know every castle and every fortress in this kingdom. We spied on all the dwarves, on all the people, invisible as shadows in the darkness,' he said solemnly but grinned as he did so. 'And since our hearts were never in it when we served the älfar, we collected *their* secrets too. Sisaroth made the mistake of believing his concoction made us stupid and submissive.' He looked at Carmondai expectantly. 'How come you're not writing?'

'Just a minute.' As the handcuffs allowed only minimal movement, he dragged paper, an ink bottle and a quill out of his saddlebag with his hands bound. He settled down next to the groundling and scribbled a few notes on what he'd heard. On a second sheet of paper he made a sketch of the landscape including the ruins.

Carâhnios waited a while, plucking a stalk of grass out of the meadow and putting it in the right-hand corner of his mouth. Grass seeds sprinkled into his clipped black beard. 'It's terrible to betray your own people and have to incur the hatred of Girdlegard, just to prepare for the orbit when you ambush the enemy. So many cycles, and we've endured so much suffering.' He made the stalk of grass see-saw up and down.

'Was it worth it?'

'Are the älfar still in their palaces?' Carâhnios retorted cheerfully. 'Without us, Girdlegard would never have been freed from the black-eyes so quickly.'

Carmondai noted these words down. *And not just from the black-eyes.*

He remembered passing hanged bodies dangling from the trees during their journey. If anyone had made common cause with the älfar or declared themselves rulers or lords, the humans strung them up on the spot.

It's true that the queens and kings tried to stamp out these unauthorised killings and set up special courts to execute lawful punishments. But the anger of the oppressed could not be stemmed.

No matter how many laws you have posted on bridges and the walls of houses.

It had been dangerous for Carmondai on their trip too. They had ridden past a town with a market taking place outside its walls. When the people saw the älf, they wanted to kill him, but Carâhnios made it clear that only he could touch his prisoner. The incident repeated itself when they met a group of volunteers who were on their way to a garrison to enlist in the army. On this occasion, the groundling actually had to knock one of the strong men to the ground to make sure the others didn't get too brave.

Carmondai was surprised that Carâhnios didn't just order him to use his älfar powers of fear or use his own. *He's bound to have his reasons.*

The seesawing stalk came to an abrupt standstill. 'I don't trust them.'

'Who?'

'The two pointy-ears who came crawling out of the woods recently and wanted to flood the Golden Plain with new pointy-ears.' The zhadár sounded contemptuous. 'I don't know where these new elves are supposed to have come from unless . . .'

'From outside?' Carmondai suggested.

'Smart arse! Of course they came from outside. But then shouldn't they have put in an appearance to save Girdlegard sooner?' Carâhnios pressed his lips together and spat the stalk out in a high arc.

'How could they have? The gates were locked and the bridges were torn down.'

'Pah. As if that would stop them! The pointy-ears are the most cowardly people I know. Popping up once the bloodthirsty, tough part is done, saying a few unctuous words. And everyone looks up to the glowing elf-lets like they're gods. To hell with them and their Creating Spirit.' He spat a gobbet of saliva to his right. 'Write that down! To hell with them.'

'I am.' Carmondai put this abiding hatred of the elves down to the changes caused by the älfar elixir. *Deep-rooted, unrelenting hatred. Sisaroth's remedy still works as well as ever on that front.*

Carâhnios reached a hand to his belt and took a metal vial out of a leather holder. He opened it, put it to his black-stained lips and tipped one drop onto his dark tongue. His face relaxed slightly. He grinned an evil grin, then carefully put the vial away again.

Carmondai presumed this was the remedy made by the triplets which gave the zhadár their unique powers. 'I heard it was distilled elf blood,' he remarked.

'Did you hear that?' The groundling giggled again. 'Well, it *was* once.' He tapped the leather holder with the flat of his hand. 'It will last for some time yet, I hope.'

'And what will serve as a substitute?'

The zhadár's dark eyes turned to focus on him, and his wrinkled face took on a furtive look. 'What do you think?' he murmured menacingly. 'I'll give you a clue: this source is also dwindling more and more in Girdlegard.'

That's why he's hunting the älfar. Carmondai swallowed. 'You're capable of making the same remedy as the Aklán?'

'We had eyes everywhere, even in Sisaroth's laboratories.' Carâhnios smacked his lips. 'I can't say if it's the same, but I hope it'll do the job.' He shut his eyes again. 'You're safe, scribbler.'

Carmondai sensed the zhadár was lying and not even making much of an effort to do so. *I'm not safe from anything or anyone in Girdlegard.*

The älf had rarely felt so alone as he did in that moment. *Not even in Phondrasôn.*

The groundling's slowing breaths were infectiously sleep-inducing.

He's dozing, as if he were in his own safe bed in a tunnel. Carmondai had to hand it to him. *Either he's crazy enough that he doesn't care where he nods off or he's counting on his warrior instincts to warn him of any dangers.*

He decided to get some rest too.

The älf put the paper and ink aside and stretched out in the soft, dark green grass beneath the tree. He had to keep his hands together lengthways because they were bound by the shackles so he lay his head down on top of them.

He felt like he had barely fallen asleep when a kick struck him in the side.

Carmondai winced and sat up with a bolt, only to see a grinning Carâhnios standing in front of him.

Night had fallen during his nap and a delicate mist was rising off the grass.

'Here we go,' the zhadár whispered. 'Let's check if there are any black-eyes holed up inside the hill.'

With extremely mixed feelings, Carmondai got to his feet and walked over to his horse to follow the groundling.

Ishím Voróo, 5452nd division of unendingness (6491st solar cycle), summer

Aiphatòn was just about to jump down from his lookout point to move further north-westwards with Nodûcor when the battle broke out. *I've got to see this.*

With no shouts, no signals from trumpets or pennants, the two crowds suddenly rushed at each other and merged into one. The clash of swords rang out and the first death cries echoed over to him. *They're not mute anyway.*

Aiphatòn watched the deadly skirmish with around a hundred thousand beasts and a hundred thousand people fighting each other. *Who is in command? I can't make out any captains or military signals.*

The draught animals were being driven onwards by coachmen, thundering straight through enemy lines with their carriages to crush as many opponents as possible under their wheels. There was fighting, mutilation and death everywhere. Lances and spears were flying, arrows hissed to and fro.

Aiphatòn realised there was no letting up. The enemies worked their way deeper into each other's armies, hacking and thrashing, as if there were a reward on the other side. Any soldier they encountered along the way was attacked until they succumbed to enemy bites, punches and weapons.

They're tearing each other limb from limb with their bare hands! He could make out an ogre-like creature sweeping through the opposing army with long strides. Its long, hairy arms darted left and right; its claws ripped heads off and shredded armour, while intestines and severed body parts flew through the air. Red and dark-coloured drops of blood glittered.

Soon even the big beast fell to the ground, after two orcs and eight gnomes had clung to its legs. All its rolling about and lashing out was no good: the orcs and gnomes dug their hands into the enormous beast's flesh and stripped it from the bone. Their fallen enemy had hardly lain still when they picked themselves up, drenched in blood, and hurried on towards enemy lines.

All over the battlefield, scenes of unparalleled brutality were playing out.

A lightly armoured warrior with a copper-coloured, close helmet caught Aiphatòn's eye. He was burrowing forwards ruthlessly, tearing apart anything that offered him resistance with powerful movements, like he was cutting through thin material. He was the furthest into the ranks of the enemy.

This is the most appalling battle I've ever seen. Aiphatòn shuddered. 'We're going,' he called down to Nodûcor again, who had helped himself to the corpses' clothes and was wrapping up the body clamp as if it were a talisman. It was vital that they investigate what the dead älf had said about the towns of Dsôn Elhàtor and Dsôn Dâkiòn.

With one last look at the bloodbath, he saw there were älfar fighting on one side too, throwing themselves into battle. They may have been using swords and spears, but they weren't behaving the way he expected his tribe to either.

It must be the power of the botoicans. Aiphatòn leaped back onto the ground and landed next to Nodûcor. They hurried away together.

They couldn't escape the constant screams and shouts, the roars and metallic clashes from the bloodbath.

Aiphatòn reflected on how little he knew about the botoicans. *If only I had remembered Carmondai's stories better. It would come in handy now.* He had a vague recollection that an älf was usually immune to mind-control spells because they themselves possessed magic. *Or am I getting confused?*

Nodûcor just shrugged his shoulders when he asked him about it.

Aiphatòn was not satisfied yet. As soon as they had put enough distance between them and the battlefield, it would be time for him to question his companion more, starting with his own lot in life and covering the towns too.

Aiphatòn had in fact been expecting to find barely any traces of surviving älfar in Ishím Voróo. But the challenge he faced was now expanding many times over.

The älfar in the botoican army didn't worry him. They were already doomed and would die sooner or later.

But the two towns represent a danger to Ireheart and Girdlegard. I swore to wipe out all älfar. He glanced at Nodûcor. *My vow stands, even if it takes me ten solar cycles or more.*

Aiphatòn stopped himself speculating any further about the size of Dsôn Elhàtor and Dâkiòn. He was relying on his magic, his wits and his speed.

If I reveal myself as the son of the Inextinguishables, they will have to look kindly on me, he thought, forming a rough plan. *That kind of audacity will probably get me further than anything else.*

If they were to go so far as to crown him as their ruler due to his lineage and his status as a shintoìt, it would be child's play to lead them to their doom, just like he'd already done with the älfar from the south of Ishím Voróo. *At least then something good would come of my existence.*

Aiphatòn and Nodûcor ventured on north-westwards, slowly but steadily.

Time and time again, they had to rest because the weak, pale älf couldn't walk any further in the scorching sun. He used a reed to drink with, sucking the water out of puddles that looked cleaner than the sludge in the marshy pools. They may have looked deceptively clear, but the acrid stench promised nausea and vomiting.

Their surroundings only started to change towards evening. The flat swamp with its sea of reeds gave way to a grassy landscape they could take in at a glance. The temperature became more pleasant and when the stars shone in the heavens, the wind blew. It carried the scent of fruit, dew and ripening grain to the älfar.

The landscape's atmosphere changed and became peaceful and pleasant, as if it was trying to make up to Aiphatòn and Nodûcor for what they'd seen, and allow their minds to rest.

They pitched camp underneath an old apple tree that spread its foliage over them protectively like a roof. The lights from a small village they were deliberately avoiding glowed nearby.

They didn't need a fire. The night was mild and the ground having retained the heat from the day, now gave off the warmth from the sun.

Aiphatòn picked some fruit and pounded them down into a fine pulp using stones. The extremely feeble Nodûcor was able to suck the pulp up through a straw. When he sensed the sweet flavour on the roof of his mouth, he groaned with pleasure and a tear of joy ran down from the corner of his eye.

He took Aiphatòn's hand and placed his forehead against it, his glassy hair touching Aiphatòn's arm and seeming to crackle softly.

'You don't need to thank me,' Aiphatòn said, not allowing himself to feel any sympathy. *How do I know what crimes he has committed? He's an älf. He must have killed hundreds and he'll kill again if I let him.*

Nodûcor stood up, his gaze falling on Aiphatòn's face – and he froze. Huge shock and immense awe were etched on the masked älf's face, and it wasn't long before he bowed and then stayed there in that humble pose.

'No, that's not necessary.' *He has noticed my black eyes.* No ordinary älf kept this pigmentation once the sun had gone down, so Nodûcor realised he was in the presence of a shintoìt. 'At the most you can be grateful to me for preserving your immortality, but nothing more. I didn't accomplish anything to receive my lineage.'

Nodûcor looked up and nodded hesitantly.

It's time to find out more about him. 'How did you end up in the sarcophagus?'

The ashen-skinned älf picked up a little stick and used it to write in the loose sand. 'I was following the runes I found in the mountains. They guided me.' Every so often he wiped the sentences away after Aiphatòn indicated that he was finished reading. 'I wanted to escape from this wasteland where there is nothing but fear and stupidity. To me, the runes promised älfar who were interested in art. And a new home.'

These must have been the signs that Modôia left behind. 'How long have you been travelling for?' He observed his companion's face carefully to see if he was trying to lie. But his gratitude to him seemed to be coming in handy. Aiphatòn could not detect any signs of dishonesty. *He suspects it would be a death sentence.*

'I wasn't counting the moons. Then I noticed I was being followed and before I knew what was happening, Cushròk and his people grabbed me, put all of that stuff on me and bundled me into the coffin.' He pointed at his scrawny muscles. 'I was too exhausted to fight back.' But believe me, I'll be more than capable of fighting as soon as I get my strength back.' Nodûcor was smiling underneath his half-mask, the smile obvious from the little wrinkles around his eyes, which were the same shimmering colour as his hair.

'Where were they trying to take you?'

'I don't know.'

'Why did they guard you like you were the deadliest warrior in existence?' Aiphatòn could no longer recall the inscription that Cushròk had not been able to translate but great trouble had been mentioned.

'I don't know,' Nodûcor drew in the sand.

Aiphatòn was sorry not to be able to hear his voice. Telling a lie was easier if you were writing it down. 'The sarcophagus had älfar runes and words on it, and it was the same on your shackles. I don't think they were Cushròk's handiwork. So were they trailing you on the orders of an älf?'

Nodûcor underlined his sentence twice.

'Did you live in one of the towns?'

'No. I roamed around looking for a place where I could find beauty. Beauty and peace. Preferably solitude and nothing but the companionship of the wind,' Nodûcor answered. 'In the mountains, I thought, that's where I'm most likely to find all of that. Then I noticed the älfar runes and followed them.' He gave Aiphatòn a scrutinising look. 'How did you get to this side from there?' he wrote in the soft earth.

'I was following the runes too,' Aiphatòn shot back, thus avoiding a lie as well as the truth, and he looked sharply to one side. *There's someone there!* He had made out a movement in the meadow and heard hasty footsteps; a flag was fluttering softly in the wind.

Nodûcor also peered into the darkness – älf eyes could easily see in the dark so long as a star was twinkling.

They both saw a very muscular, extremely large man in dark brown leather armour that looked almost black in the gloom; the white, precisely drawn runes on it gleamed in the starlight.

His boots rose and fell in a steady jog and leather trousers protected his legs from dirt and the elements.

The monsters and the älf we met at the ruins of the tower were wearing those symbols. But I can't make sense of them. Aiphatòn could see the pale banner the lone runner was carrying on a long pole fixed to the back of his armour. The broadly built man's head was hidden underneath a simple, polished helmet with an intense metallic sheen; slits had been made in it, level with his eyes, mouth and nose.

Isn't that the warrior from the battlefield who fought his way to the most advanced position?

The runner was headed straight for the village, his arms swinging forward and back in a steady rhythm.

No. That other warrior wasn't carrying a banner around. And the armour runes were missing.

Suddenly the armoured man stopped and clouds of dust rose up from underneath the soles of his feet.

Very slowly, he turned his head and the eye slits fixed on the älfar under the tree as if the armoured man could see them in the darkness.

Aiphatòn picked up his spear. *What is he doing?* Before he could even decide to throw the spear, the man turned to face forwards again and continued on his way. *Did he spot us?*

Aiphatòn weighed up whether he still needed Nodûcor, given that he didn't come from the towns. But an älf without a family? With no origin? That didn't exist. His companion was still harbouring too many secrets that he needed to get to the bottom of. *He could still be useful to me, and I'm going to exploit his gratitude.*

'We're moving on,' he murmured to Nodûcor and helped him to his feet. 'I think he's a scout or a go-between. I don't want to be here when the army follows.'

Nodûcor nodded and got to his feet. The food and the brief rest seemed to have done him good and he was looking more healthy.

They took a few more pieces of fruit for the journey, left the shelter of the apple tree and walked briskly and silently north-westwards.

After half a mile, Aiphatòn couldn't help but notice they were being followed: when he looked over his shoulder, he could make out ten silhouettes on their heels and they were rapidly catching up to them. At the same time, it looked like a ragged-edged black cloud with a wide front was dragging itself across the grassy plain and drifting towards the village.

The vanguard of the army. He stopped and pushed Nodûcor behind him.

He wished the people in the village all the best. If he had been in Girdlegard, he would have intervened on their behalf, but not in Ishím Voróo. He had just one duty: destroying the älfar towns.

'I'll get the shadows off our backs,' he said quietly and walked towards the silhouettes. This wouldn't take long.

Chapter VIII

Death conquers all. Except art.

Wise saying of the Älfar
Collected by Carmondai, master of word and image

Ishím Voróo, Älfar town of Dsôn Elhàtor, 5452nd division of unendingness (6491st solar cycle), summer

Irïanora sat in her white leather armchair as though rooted to the spot, her arms on the armrests. *The blades are going to carve me up like a sponge cake.*

She stared anxiously at the piece of paper in Ôdaiòn's well-groomed hand. On it was her uncle's message to the monarchess and it needed to match what she said. Otherwise the whips would fly at her.

'Go ahead, my dear.' Modôia towered above the chaise longue, the black whip looking out of place in the hand of the elegant älf-woman in the white dress, surrounded by yet more whiteness in the high-ceilinged room. The little birds flew tirelessly from lily to lily on the walls, making the scene even more surreal with the sound of their swift, droning wingbeats. 'You know the message. Don't keep me in suspense. It's dampening my good mood.' She smiled coldly. 'You would sense that straight away, at my first blow.'

Irïanora's lips were moving but she couldn't think. 'Before you stands my niece,' she said falteringly.

Modôia's left eyebrow shot up. The blow followed so quickly that even an experienced warrior would not have been able to dodge it.

Irïanora saw the blades glinting right in front of her, the tips heading straight for her middle – before they switched direction with a crack. The three straps jerked to the side, then her shoulders and neck started to burn.

The älf-woman screamed first in fear and then, shortly after that, in pain. The whips were pulled back again, the wet, red blades leaving thin lines on the white stone floor. The top half of her dark blue dress slipped down and warm blood trickled over her skin. The monarchess had cut through the fabric and made just a few minor incisions in her skin.

'I've always thought clothing doesn't show off the effect of the whip properly,' she remarked. 'Besides: you are very attractive and have nothing to hide, if you ignore the bruises.'

'She could be the model for a statue of Inàste. Perfection from head to waist, madam, and perhaps we'll see the rest too,' Ôdaiòn agreed with his mother and looked down at the piece of paper. 'You'll have realised that those were *not* the correct words.' He got up and his whip uncoiled as he did so. 'Someone should paint this, the way you're sitting there, surrounded by cleanliness and blood, the immaculateness fading more and more because of your inability to hit upon the correct message.' He moved his whipping hand and the straps jerked. 'Ah yes: *hit*.'

Another barely perceptible movement and the blades were whirring towards her.

Irïanora screamed when they made contact on her right and left sides and again on her neck. Her dress fell open to her navel after this attack, but she didn't move to cover up her nakedness.

She stared Ôdaiòn in the face – and detected desire in his eyes.

When she saw this she realised, quick as a flash, that the älf would never severely injure her because he was still planning to have some fun with her.

Irïanora held his gaze and stayed seated bolt upright, as if she was trying to offer the whip an easy target.

Ôdaiòn lifted the piece of paper again. 'Now, the second attempt,' he commanded her. A ray of light fell so that it hit the thin paper in his fingers and shone through it.

Irïanora saw that there was nothing written on it. *My uncle didn't send a message. They're playing a game with me. They want to frighten me, humiliate me. Is that my punishment?* She slowly got up from her armchair, blood pearling across her skin, tracing red tracks down to her navel and seeping into the fabric.

'The piece of paper you're holding in front of you is blank, sir,' she said in a firm voice. 'My uncle couldn't have sent you a message because he thought it was a better idea to send me to speak with you instead.'

Modôia's gaze became furtive. 'Why did you try to guess the words at first, if you knew the truth?'

'You were making such an effort to frighten me, I didn't want to ruin your fun, monarchess,' replied Irïanora, putting on just as convincing an act of being fearless as she had of being terrified at the sight of her dead maid. She gave a small bow. 'Now, if you'll excuse me? I'd like to put on a different dress.'

Ôdaiòn burst into peals of laughter and Modôia joined in.

'Just go. My maid . . .'

'I'll go with you,' her son said quickly, carelessly tossing the whip onto the armchair. 'You'll love the rooms I've picked for you.'

'You're too kind, sir.' Irïanora bowed again. Small, red drops were pouring off her skin and falling onto the marble with a soft splashing sound.

Modôia seemed to have enjoyed herself. 'Freshen up then, pick out a new outfit and I'll be expecting you at dinner.'

Ôdaiòn took Irïanora by the hand and led her out.

The älf-woman didn't even consider adjusting her ruined dress. The son of the monarchess ought to enjoy the sight of her. She wanted to arouse his desire and make an ally of him as soon as possible. *Who knows what plans his mother has for me.*

Irïanora was led through corridors and galleries decorated in pale blue and white.

The bone art on Elhàtor was confined to working with enormous bones and fish skeletons. There was no sign of the skeletons of barbarians or other beasts. Two jellyfish-like creatures four paces wide had been recreated with the help of fabric and looked like they were floating across one hall – lanterns inside them made it look like they were glowing.

Sea air made the curtains billow constantly and occasionally Irïanora caught a glimpse of the waves off the coast of the island.

After quite a few sets of stairs they entered the tower room where all of her trunks of clothes already stood, apart from the one containing the corpse of the murdered maid. A bath had also been prepared and there was a scent of lavender and citrus fruits from the warm water.

Without asking, Ôdaiòn undressed Irïanora.

In Dâkiòn she would have had the pushy älf thrown out, but luring him in like a big fat fish was part of her plan. So she bit her tongue as her cuts and scratches stung in protest.

Smiling, he helped her into the bathtub and picked up a sponge to wash the blood off her gently. 'Don't worry. Our healers will make the wounds disappear later, along with these bruises which no doubt came from Shôtoràs,' he said, his voice like velvet. He wrung out the sponge at the nape of her neck. Warm water ran down her back and she shuddered with pleasure. 'Forgive my mother for the little game, but she felt you needed to be punished for what you'd done.'

'You didn't?'

'I saw you, madam, and knew I couldn't harm you in any way,' he whispered in her ear and gently kissed her bare shoulder.

Irïanora laughed coldly. 'The words trip off your tongue so easily.'

'I say them to every beautiful woman,' he replied with a smile. 'Because they're true.'

'But your whip struck me anyway.'

'It scratched you,' he corrected her. 'Not one of my blows would have done anything more than scratch you, unlike my mother's lashes.' Ôdaiòn kissed the wounded area on her neck. 'She tends to be cruel. You can tell she lived in Tark Draan for a long time.'

'So I've had my punishment and I can go back?' Irïanora placed a hand on his cheek and it felt soft and well-groomed. *Come, my little fish. Get into my net.* 'Or can I keep you company a while longer?'

'I would be delighted, even though you'll try and spy for your uncle.' He winked at her and ran his wet fingers through his mid-length hair.

'I hate him,' she blurted out too quickly.

Ôdaiòn laughed. 'Then you're doubly welcome to Elhàtor. We gladly accept älfar who renounce the sovereign, which has been something of a rare occurrence lately. They could potentially unleash a wave of emigration.' He kissed the palm of her hand as he wrung out the sponge on her throat so that the water ran down over her breasts. Then Ôdaiòn leaned forwards, his lips gently coming to rest against Irïanora's.

She returned the caress without much desire. *I certainly won't fall in love with him*, Irïanora thought. *Play with him, yes. But not the other way round. He is my fish.*

When the älf got up and left her apartment without turning around, she ducked underneath the surface of the water, hoping it would wash away and drown any potential feelings.

Towards the evening, Ôdaiòn came to fetch her and bring her to the meal. His fondness for dark blue and silver was in evidence again and despite its opulence, his robe was light-weight.

Earlier, two guards at her door had put paid to any attempt to explore the palace when they made it clear that Irïanora was to wait in her chamber.

Most of the windows had been covered with fabric from the outside so that the älf-woman could only see a narrow strip of the coast and the sea. So the splendid Dsôn Elhàtor, the Magnificent, with its streets, houses, the harbour and the fortifications, remained hidden to her for now. There could just as easily have been crooked huts and ugly stone hovels underneath her bedroom, she wouldn't know.

Irïanora had spent her time watching the waves and writing down her impressions. Two healers appeared at intervals and made all of the wounds and marks on her body disappear using magic.

'You look wonderful, madam.' Ôdaiòn kissed her hand. 'How could anyone not fall in love with you?'

'Is that what you're doing right now?' she teased him and bowed slightly. The red dress accentuated her figure particularly well and she had braided her long, blonde hair into a wide plait. Attempting anything else would have been pointless in the damp, salty air.

He placed his free hand on his heart. 'Oh, you don't feel it then? From the splinter of unendingness when I helped you out of the carriage, you entered my heart.' Ôdaiòn flung open the door to the dining room she'd seen earlier. 'Let's enjoy the jolly part of your visit. I really hope' – he stepped to one side to allow her to enter – 'you're pleased to see the familiar face you didn't ask after once. Just like you didn't ask after either of your other two friends.'

Irïanora looked at the dining table where the monarchess was sitting with a brunette älf-woman Irïanora didn't know who was wearing a short, white leather dress, and Saitôra. Her friend from Dâkiòn was wearing a simple robe in various shades of blue, interwoven with silver and white, as if she had married Ôdaiòn in the meantime. She got up when they entered and nodded to Irïanora.

'Saitôra!' cried Irïanora gladly and hurried over to her, not forgetting to bow to the monarchess, who was now wearing a black dress embellished with pale blue. 'I was so worried.'

Ôdaiòn went to his mother's side. 'We're all here now,' he said, giving her a light kiss on the crown of her blonde head. 'Let the meal begin.'

Saitôra leaned over to her friend. 'Gathalor and Iophâlor are dead,' she blurted out quietly. 'They killed them. Back at the strait!'

Irïanora's mouth was drying out more and more with every heartbeat – but not out of anxiety. *It's a pity about Iophâlor, but good thing Gathalor died . . . That is . . . wonderful!* She didn't let on to Saitôra about her sudden good mood, but quickly gripped her hand and pressed it to feign dismay and seeking support. *The murder of Gathalor will upset my uncle so much, he'll fly into a rage. And a peaceful Constellation will turn into a burning Comet hurtling towards Elhàtor. The whole of Dâkiòn must have heard about the murders. Oh, I . . .*

Her plans ground to a halt: the task she had been given was to bring all three of the missing älfar back. Alive.

Her failure meant she was in danger from the old man too.

The servants entered and Modôia gestured to them to begin serving. 'We're starting with a seafood soup,' she explained. 'The broth contains the best marinated crabmeat, unlike anything you'd find anywhere else.' She picked up her spoon and looked around. 'So I hope our guests enjoy it.'

Irïanora tasted it cautiously and found the flavours of fish, herbs and salt very pleasant. And the taste of the crabmeat was very good too. 'The cuisine is more sophisticated than ours,' she remarked loudly and looked at Saitôra who was eating a little more slowly. 'I think it's exquisite.'

Modôia smiled. 'I'll let my chef know.'

Ôdaiòn leaned back suddenly. 'What bad manners,' he cried in surprise and tapped two fingers on the table. 'I completely forgot to introduce the great Leïóva. What a faux pas.'

Irïanora nodded to her.

'She is Mother's closest confidante. She even shares some worries with her that she keeps secret from me.' Ôdaiòn sat up straight again and went on spooning up his soup with a wink. 'Even though I find it hurtful to be belittled like that.'

Irïanora surreptitiously scrutinised the älf-woman and took an instant dislike to her. *Something is off about her.* It wasn't because of her pretty face or her physique or posture. *Her perfume?*

'Leïóva's daughter commands one of our largest merchant ships,' Modôia elaborated. 'She is the best commander we have.' She pointed at her son with her cutlery. 'She and my son . . .'

'. . . are friends, Mother. Nothing more,' he interrupted her with an air of amused light-heartedness. 'But that's an area of my life our guests will find boring.' He looked back and forth between Irïanora and Saitôra. 'How I'd like to tour you around and show you both the beauty of Elhàtor. But so long as we haven't settled on how to proceed from here, I've got to hold fire,' he explained with that friendly arrogance in his voice.

Saitôra looked at her friend. 'What does that mean? I'm allowed to go back to Dâkiòn, right?' The young älf-woman looked at the monarchess. 'I told you everything that I . . .'

'Hush,' Modôia said kindly, putting her spoon aside. 'Don't worry, my dear. That decision will be made by just *one* person at this table.'

The servants cleared the soup away and brought out plates with prised-open crab shells, various kinds of mussels and a piece of crayfish whose insides had been fried until they were crispy. The monarchess refrained from explanations this time.

Irïanora couldn't take her eyes off Leïóva. *What is it about her?* 'Excuse me,' she addressed her, 'don't I know you from Dâkiòn? Do you have family there? Can I pass on any . . .'

Ôdaiòn snorted, Leïóva and Modôia looked amused.

'Did I say something stupid?' Irïanora didn't know what to make of their reactions.

'No,' answered Leïóva simply and kept eating.

'So you're not a former resident of Dâkiòn?'

'No.'

Irïanora felt uneasy and embarrassed by her ignorance. 'So are you a descendant of the älfar who stood their ground in the wasteland after the fall of Dsôn Faïmon and came to the island some time later?'

'I came here after my people were as good as wiped out, yes,' Leïóva agreed coldly. 'Our enemies pursued us relentlessly, murdered women and children and didn't even baulk at hunting down pregnant women who wanted nothing but to live in peace.'

'Oh, so you escaped from Dorón Ashont?' Saitôra was spellbound.

'For me, there are more appalling enemies. The Acronta don't frighten me.' The älf-woman in the white leather dress carved up a crab shell. 'After a very eventful escape, I met Modôia. And although we hated each other from the bottom of our hearts at first, we overcame our dislike.'

'And survived.' The monarchess pointed to her son. 'Without Leïóva he wouldn't be sitting here today.'

'Without Modôia, my daughter would have been doomed.' The black-haired älf-woman's gaze was fixed penetratingly on Irïanora. 'Do you know any friendship like ours, profound enough to be capable of overcoming hatred?' She pointed at Saitôra with her knife and did not shift her gaze, but the muscles in her shoulders started to stand out. 'Are you two linked by a similar bond, given she was ready to die for you?'

These words were followed by a deathly silence.

No, I can't stand her. Irïanora took a drink of water. 'Yes,' she replied and touched Saitôra's foot under the table to show her how serious she was. She turned her attention to the monarchess. 'I beg you: when you make your decision about Saitôra's fate and mine, please consider . . .'

Modôia raised her hand and the älf-woman fell silent. 'There's been a misunderstanding, my dear. When I said earlier that there was just *one* person at this table who would make the decision, I meant *you*, Irïanora.'

Saitôra laughed with relief. 'Oh, then send us home,' she muttered loudly enough for everyone to hear.

Modôia, Leïóva and Ôdaiòn laughed pleasantly.

'It's not that simple,' the monarchess admitted. 'As that first trip down the Tronjor took such an unfortunate turn – not that you, Irïanora, could have predicted how tragically it would end – I thought to myself that it would be a good thing to leave the decision up to you this time.'

'You killed them,' Saitôra hissed in the monarchess' direction.

'We agreed it was—' Modôia looked to her son for help.

'An accident,' he stepped in immediately.

'What decision?' asked Irïanora uncomprehendingly. 'I thought I was allowed to make up my mind?'

'Just as the river and your decision caused an *accident* that claimed victims' lives, there can't fail to be victims this time either.' Modôia had some wine poured out for her and Leïóva took out a vial and tipped three greenish drops into it. '*One* of you is allowed to return to Dâkiòn.' She raised her glass to Irïanora. 'You, as the niece of the sovereign and the higher ranking of you two, will decide who that will be.' She emptied her glass in one go.

'And the other person?' whispered Saitôra.

'Will stay. As a hostage. If even *one* boat from Dâkiòn approaches the strait, my whip will do the talking for as long as it takes. Until there is nothing but little scraps of the hostage left which I will send to Shôtoràs.' Modôia looked at her plate. 'I don't want to let myself be embarrassed or provoked any longer. Not by your uncle, by you or by any other älf who rules Dâkiòn in the future. That's the end of it.' She cleared her throat and clasped her hands together expectantly. 'So, my dear: who will go?'

Thoughts raced through Irïanora's head, from her uncle's threat and her hatred of him, to her hatred of the monarchess and the barely concealed desire of her son, the little fish in her net that she wanted to exploit.

New possibilities were opening up, old ones bowed to the inevitable and were dismissed, all within the space of a few heartbeats.

It all led to a strategy that fit excellently with her plan.

'*Who*' – Modôia could make her voice crack like her whip – 'will go?'

And Irïanora answered.

Tark Draan, Human kingdom of Idoslane, 5452nd division of unendingness (6491st solar cycle), summer

Carmondai placed a hand on the pillar lying diagonally across another pillar and pushed to see if it would hold. When there was no creaking or wobbling, he continued on according to the zhadár's instructions, ending up in the centre of the ruins.

Carâhnios got a kick out of sending Carmondai on ahead. 'So the black-eye will think he's being given some help,' he'd said with a grin when they parted.

So Carmondai was running along in the clothes that were now too small and threadbare. He was upright and easy to see in the moonlight as he moved through the ruins of the temple while the groundling took care of the security, moving furtively and as silently as an älf.

This is not how I pictured the mission. Carmondai's wrists were still shackled, which Carâhnios had thought made his pretence of being an escaped prisoner look more plausible. He also stumbled now and again as he'd been ordered to do, so that he could be heard. He could not work out the purpose of the large glass bottle the zhadár had pressed into his hand. There was a thin layer of silvery fluid along the glass bottom of the bottle.

Eventually, Carmondai was standing in the middle of the temple and behind him were the remains of a wall four paces high, with colourful glass windows decorated with unfamiliar symbols still preserved in it. The panes of glass turned the moonlight different colours and gave his tanned skin an unfamiliar tint. Five pillars as wide as a man and criss-crossed with cracks towered up in front of this, forming a semi-circle.

What now? He had made an effort to be loud and conspicuous.

Carmondai still didn't know what to do if it came to a fight.

Carâhnios had made it very clear what awaited him if he were to go against the groundling's instructions. But if the fortunes in a battle were to tilt and there was a chance of shifting the advantage more in favour of an älf . . . *And then what? I'm more or less in enemy land.*

He forced himself, despite the humiliation, to stick to the agreed plan for the time being and stay close to the zhadár.

There was a quiet click behind him.

Carmondai turned around and stepped backwards to be on the safe side because he thought one of the pillars was collapsing or a piece of rubble had broken off and was falling down on him.

To his astonishment, a door had opened in the column to his right and a black-haired älf in tionium armour was standing inside it holding a long sword. Instead of paying any attention to the interloper, he strained his ears and carefully scanned the ruins. 'Stay where you are,' the warrior murmured to him.

Carmondai waited, taking time to relish his surprise. *Carâhnios was right.* The entrance to the hideaway – which was indeed inside the hill – was through the pillars that looked dangerously dilapidated.

The älfar stranger emerged slowly from the doorway. 'You're alone,' he said in a normal voice and put the sword away. 'Forgive me for the unfriendly welcome, but times have changed for us. The barbarians might have been using a trick to lure me out of the hideaway.'

Carmondai held out a shackled hand to him. 'I get it.'

'Who are you and how did you know about the ruins?'

The truth would be the most convincing. 'I'm Carmondai. The Dsôn Aklán told me about all of the hideaways they built so that they could go to ground.'

'*You* are the master of word and image?' The stunned älf gave a small bow. 'I adore your works! I praise Inàste for sending you to me and that endingness passed you by. My name is Ostòras.'

'I thank you too, for showing yourself. It saves a lot of trouble. It would have taken me a long time to find the opening mechanism,' he replied, feigning friendly solidarity.

'Then come inside with me so that we can take your shackles off.' Ostòras looked genuinely pleased they had met, although the circumstances left a lot to be desired, of course. His dark red eyes were fixed on the glass bottle. 'Is that valuable? Why are you carrying it around with you?'

Suddenly Carâhnios leaped out of the darkness of the shadows, holding the sword in his right hand and pointing it accusingly at Carmondai. 'Don't believe him! He's an elf in disguise – they sent him as bait,' he shouted menacingly and looked around hurriedly as if he were being followed or was expecting an attack. 'You've walked right into the trap!'

Ostòras almost attacked the groundling but he immediately realised he was a zhadár. He turned this way and that, on his guard. 'I knew it,' he shouted. 'You were much too loud to be an älf.'

Carâhnios burst into gales of laughter. 'This is too good! I use one black-eye to trick the other and I pull a fast one on you twice!'

It took Ostòras several heartbeats to realise he had fallen victim to a trick with a deadly ending. 'This is how you both die!' He went to draw a dagger out of the holder on his back.

As soon as the armoured älf's arm moved backwards, the zhadár pounced.

Carmondai couldn't help but admire the agility of his movements. They were beyond the skills of an ordinary dwarf.

Ostòras dodged the blade, whipped his knee upwards to hit Carâhnios in the face then drew his own sword.

But the groundling dodged the attack. He parried his opponent's sword with his own weapon above his head and used his helmet to ram the älf in the solar plexus with all his might.

Suffocating, Ostòras sank to his knees despite his armour. The tip of the zhadár's weapon thrust vertically downwards through his armour into his collarbone. He dropped his sword and dagger with a clatter.

Carâhnios was still clasping the handle undaunted.

The duel lasted less than three heartbeats. He took the warrior completely by surprise. For Carmondai, not even the slightest opportunity to take sides had arisen, although he wouldn't necessarily have considered it.

Groaning, the kneeling Ostòras hung from the weapon like a fish on a harpoon.

'Now you're utterly confused,' Carâhnios guessed and sniggered. 'Yes, I *am* a zhadár, and that *is* Carmondai. We've set out to track down the last of you in the most secretive hideaways. Because I know every last one of them.'

Ostòras cursed him. 'One day you're going to come across one of us who doesn't fall for your trick,' he predicted. 'And then you'll die. Miserably and agonisingly.'

'Not like you anyway. That's for sure.' The zhadár drew his dagger and stabbed the älf in the neck, hitting the artery. 'Carmondai, the bottle.'

The älf handed it to him.

Carâhnios held the mouth of the bottle to the wound to collect the blood that spurted against the transparent walls in time with the heart's rhythm. His other hand rested around the hilt of his sword, fixing Ostòras firmly to the spot on his knees – he was moaning but didn't move so as not to injure himself more severely.

He's taking the blood to distil the essence from it. Carmondai wished he'd brought along something to draw with. *The former allies, joined in a deadly struggle. The älfars' creature triumphs over its masters.*

'Let's play a game, my black-eyed friend,' Carâhnios announced. 'Your wounds are not yet fatal, and I could let you go.'

'A traitor is not going to turn me into a traitor,' Ostòras replied with hatred and contempt. Anger lines flashed across his face and it looked like his face was glowing in multiple colours because the coloured moonlight was falling on it through the panes of glass. 'I'd rather pass into endingness. But know this' – he looked at Carmondai with eyes that were now black – 'we are everywhere and yet nowhere. We will go into hiding, we will strike from the shadows and kill the kings of the barbarians, the pointy-ears and the groundlings. Girdlegard will descend into fear and chaos.' He laughed and coughed. 'And every time a hero rises up to bring unity, we will be there. We are the darkness!'

Ostòras leaped to his feet and drew a rasping, painful breath as Carâhnios' sword plunged down as far as his lungs, carving up his entrails and severing his arteries. Then the älf fell slowly forwards. Surprisingly little blood came from his two wounds, as if it was pooling internally.

The zhadár only just managed to keep hold of the glass bottle of blood in time. 'He almost cost me my yield,' he grumbled and gave the corpse a kick. 'Dumb black-eye.'

Ostòras' threat had made an impact on Carmondai because he knew it would come true if the groundling didn't manage to check all of the älfar's hideaways in time. *And he won't.* The great and the good of Tark Draan were all in danger. *This is the stuff of great dramas.*

Carmondai could see it now: wise kings rising out of the human and dwarf tribes and getting cut down by a black älfar arrow at the peak of their powers, making the country descend into discord. His mind was already beginning to devise an epic.

Carâhnios held the container up to the moonlight to check it. 'Very good. That's at least three units. The best way to collect the blood is when the heart is pumping it out. Once they've been run through with a sword it's no good anymore. There could be impurities and that ruins the elixir.'

Words failed Carmondai; he could barely tear himself away from his thoughts about the epic but at the same time he was fascinated by the groundling's mercilessness, his coldness. *What did the Aklán create when they formed that unit?*

The zhadár calmly put a cork in the bottle and looked around. 'Everything is still quiet. Looks like there was only one of them. Such a pity.' He took a step through the doorway in the pillar. 'Come on. Let's take a look at this.' Then he smacked his forehead. 'I almost forgot: go to the horse quickly, get yourself something to write and draw with, then come back here. Write down your thoughts and record what we find. Hurry up!'

Carmondai nodded and hurried through the ruins to their steeds. *He's letting me go by myself.*

After the lightning-quick defeat of Ostòras, he knew exactly why Carâhnios was not worried about sending his prisoner off: Carmondai wouldn't get far on his horse. His presence as history's memory didn't protect him from the zhadár's anger and sword. *Besides, he needs my blood. He will never let me go.*

Sighing, Carmondai reached the horse, found what he needed in the saddlebag and hurried back through the remains of the temple to where the skirmish had happened.

I'm really, really intrigued about what we're going to see.

He still could not imagine the ritual in which Carâhnios was going to transform the blood into the distillate that truly kept him strong.

He wanted to be a witness to this miracle too.

Ishím Voróo, 5452nd division of unendingness (6491st solar cycle), summer

Aiphatòn saw the white runes gleam on the armour of the ten enemy combatants in the starlight: four orcs, three humans, two gnomes and an unfamiliar beast with an ugly mug like a wolf.

The six familiar specimens of monster were racing purposefully towards him, drawing their weapons as they ran. The wolf-beast and the humans went round him to get to Nodûcor.

Aiphatòn didn't ask himself what they wanted and beat them to the attack: he threw his spear at the two gnomes who were running in a staggered line, one behind the other, and penetrated their upper bodies; they fell to one side screaming and perished.

Aiphatòn launched himself at the closest orcs, smashing his armoured fists into their ugly mugs with such force that their facial bones caved in with a cracking sound. Blood gushed out of their noses, muzzles and eyes.

Squealing and gurgling, the enemies fell backwards onto the next two beasts and knocked them off their feet.

Aiphatòn landed behind the fallen orcs, dodged their whirring blades and summoned the spear which extricated itself from the dead gnomes and flew into his hand. He used all his might to ram the blade horizontally through the neck of one of the orcs who had been knocked down and carved up its blood-spurting throat.

The last orc got to its feet and swung its sword at Aiphatòn's chest with a slanting blow.

The älf blocked the attack and suddenly pulled the blade of the spear downwards and straight through its hideous head, then immediately thrust the tip into the shrieking enemy's belly and shoved him backwards. After his third staggering step he fell over the corpse of one of his own kind and lay still.

You're all so easy to take down. Aiphatòn looked at Nodûcor who was shrinking away from the humans and the wolf-beast. He was brandishing the serrated dagger at them with the courage that comes of desperation. But given his thin arms and his weakened state, he did not present much of a challenge to his opponents.

Now for all of you. Aiphatòn started running and hurled the spear at the armoured wolf-creature's back – he was the enemy he deemed the most dangerous. Its furry ears twitched; they detected the sound of the thrown spear. The monster dodged the missile with a rapid pivot – and made a grab with its right hand: its claws wrapped around the metal shaft of the spear. Enraged, it turned round to face the älf, holding the weapon it had seized at the ready.

By this point, the men were attacking Nodûcor and he was lashing out in every direction, trying to keep his opponents at bay.

Aiphatòn smiled at the slobbering wolf-beast as it bore down on him, holding the spear in both its hands now, planning to run his enemy through with it. *It won't be any use to you.* He moved towards the beast.

A brief jolt of magical energy made the runes on his weapon glow. There was a hissing sound when the symbols heated up so quickly they burned into the creature's skin; howling, it dropped the stolen weapon.

Aiphatòn came over and with his right hand he dealt the creature a direct punch to the centre of its chest, crushing the armour. The runes on his glove lit up and released a flash from the knuckles that blasted the armour open and carved a hole in the flesh underneath. A cloud of blood and bone fragments flew out of the wolf-beast's back as it shot backwards eight paces and took one of the men's feet out from under him. It landed in a smoking heap on the ground and didn't move; the man under it twitched once before going still.

Nodûcor exploited his attackers' confusion and stabbed upwards at one of the men's chins with the dagger.

But his opponent moved his head back and the tip of the dagger slid uselessly over his coat of chainmail. One kick to the stomach sent the pale-skinned älf flying to the ground.

'It's my turn first.' Aiphatòn sprinted towards them, hunched like a beast of prey, as the spear flew into his left hand and the runes went dark.

The first man attacked him with two short swords and the other one drew his double-bladed axe, which must once have belonged to a lumberjack, and waited.

This is taking too long. Aiphatòn swept the swords aside with his armoured right forearm, the symbols gleamed and the massive blades shattered like fragile glass. His left hand jolted forwards, driving the spear at his opponent's heart and killing the man.

By now, the last enemy had put one foot against Nodûcor's throat and the broad, right axe blade was resting at the älf's neck. 'Surrender, älf,' he said, his gaze vacant. 'You and your friend will accompany this warrior to my army.'

It must be the botoican speaking to me. Aiphatòn wished he had Carmondai's knowledge or that the tale-weaver himself would appear – he was so much more than a gifted storyteller. 'So that you can enlist me like those wretches?' He gestured at the corpses. 'Find someone else to hound to death for your collection.'

'That's what I'm doing. I've heard there are towns to conquer, large towns with älfar living in them. I'll see if I feel like it as soon as my preparations are complete,' the warrior replied. 'But you are something unique, I feel. That makes you all the more valuable in the battle against my foes.'

He heaved the blade at Nodûcor's mask and a metallic clang rang out. 'If you refuse, *he* dies first. I can't allow you to fall into someone else's hands.'

Aiphatòn looked around quickly, but couldn't make out any other enemy fighters.

The mob that had reached the sleeping village half a mile behind them thronged the spaces between the houses and huts, storming into every building they found. Screams cut quietly through the night air.

Aiphatòn felt no sympathy. This was Ishím Voróo, not Girdlegard. Aiphatòn did not feel responsible for the lives of these locals. He had no doubt the people would soon be incorporated into the botoican's army against their will. *They'll be hauled in front of him and then . . .* He realised he knew nothing about these magicians' methods. They wove spells so vastly different from that of a Lot-Ionan. *What then?*

Nodûcor groaned, the axe blade cutting into his skin. Blood ran from the superficial wound.

'It's time, älf,' the man said in a hollow voice and drew a throwing knife. 'Turn around and go to the army in the village so that they can tie you up and guard you. Once you're down there, the warrior will follow with your friend.'

A trick will be more useful than speed right now. Aiphatòn nodded, dropped the spear and walked off slowly; his arms dangled loosely at his sides. Now and again, he turned around.

The warrior grabbed Nodûcor and got him to his feet, pushing him on ahead. He had placed the heavy axe head on the älf's shoulder so that one jerk would be enough to sever the prisoner's skull from his torso.

Oh, that makes it easier for me. I was having misgivings. Aiphatòn was ready.

The warrior passed the spot where the spear was lying in the long grass but didn't check for the weapon. He felt safe at a distance of fifty paces.

'Watch out,' Aiphatòn cried in älfar, still facing ahead. He simply opened the fingers of his right hand.

The spear whirred into the air and travelled in a straight line towards its master.

His opponent was struck in the spine and the weapon lodged there. It seemed like the power of the magic and hence the momentum of the spear was waning.

Nodûcor lifted his hands up quickly and held on tight to the blade of the axe; he tilted his shoulder so that the cutting edge didn't slip and accidentally hurt him after all.

Aiphatòn laughed nastily and ran back. 'Are you all right?' he called to the älf.

Nodûcor nodded and took two paces away from the warrior who was standing there leaning sharply backwards. The end of the spear's shaft had bored into the ground and now functioned as an inadvertent prop so that the man didn't fall over.

The dagger and axe handle slipped out of the enemy's hands and his eyes flicked back and forth between the two of them. 'You won't get away from me,' he promised, his voice breaking. 'And you, you strange älf, will reveal your magical secrets to me as soon as I've broken your will.' The man's arms sank limply to his sides, his head tipped back. 'The Nhatais will take what they are entitled to. And I am entitled to *you*, just like I am to all of your tribe, wherever I find them!' the dying man whispered. 'No matter whe—' The threat faded away with one last breath. Death came more quickly than the botoican's message.

Aiphatòn kicked the body onto the ground and pulled the spear out of the vertebra. He looked at the village where some dots were already breaking away from the black mass and racing towards them. 'Let's get going. The botoican will lose interest in us as soon as he has created enough other toys.'

He let Nodûcor link his arm and hurried away, carrying the light älf more than he was supporting him. Aiphatòn marched on relentlessly, leaving the vanguard behind them to fall back.

They walked throughout the night.

He crushed apples for Nodûcor with his glove and had him suck up the pulp so that he stayed relatively strong. From time to time they quenched their thirst with clear, cold water from streams.

They didn't rest until the break of dawn at the foot of a gentle hill covered in trees.

Nodûcor could not take one more step and his eyes closed immediately. Aiphatòn scanned the grassy landscape that lay behind them. *They've given up or were called back by the botoican.*

He too sank into the soft green carpet and closed his eyes. The scent of the grass, the pure soil and the fragrance of apples coming from his glove pervaded his nostrils.

Yet he could barely relax.

He couldn't imagine how powerful a spell needed to be in order to control a hundred thousand warriors at once and make them fight and commit murders in the most gruesome way. He thought about what he'd heard.

Are the botoicans at war with each other and gathering as many soldiers around them as they can?

The fatigue settled into his limbs like lead and finally drove even these thoughts away.

His breathing slowed and Aiphatòn slipped into sleep as the sun came up over the hill.

Chapter IX

The imagination allows some people to travel in the hopes that they come back educated.

Wise saying of the Älfar
Collected by Carmondai, master of word and image

Tark Draan, The Golden Plain, 5452nd division of unendingness (6491st solar cycle), late summer

Barefoot and topless, Ilahín stepped out of the first house in the emerging elf settlement on the Golden Plain in the middle of the night and looked up at the stars.

The life and destiny star of his people was visibly glowing more boldly and cheerfully, which brought a smile to his slender features. *The Firstlings will come soon.*

He and his wife had made the building they were sleeping in with their own hands. They had carved and painted, hauled materials and built walls, put in balconies and layered up materials until the roof could be thatched with reeds and the inside was protected from the elements.

At the appearance of the special star, Ilahín offered up his prayers to the Creating Spirit of his people that Sitalia and Elria received their oblations.

Afterwards the elf wove a rare spell that only becomes truly powerful when the heavenly bodies shine.

I've had to wait a long time for it to be possible.

The charm sent nothing more than an inaudible but palpable signal through the world and it reached elves wherever they were. From then on they would know that there was enough space in Girdlegard to settle down in safety.

Ilahín tied back his long, almost black hair and watched the nearby river that promised so much life. *Many houses will spring up along the bank, like how it used to be. We will bring the people a noble attitude and make sure the älfar are forgotten.*

'What are you doing out here?' Fiëa walked up behind him and leaned her head against the back of his neck. 'You've already said the magic spell.' She was wearing a transparent, white night-gown made of cool silk.

He was pleased she had joined him and not left him alone with his brooding thoughts. She was visiting him here on the Golden Plain but would head back to the crater the next morning. 'I wanted to see whether our star was still visible.'

She wrapped her arms around his waist. 'Were you afraid it would go out again?'

Ilahín took his time in answering. 'So much has happened.'

'And so much of it in our favour. Our worst enemies are as good as wiped out. After so many cycles of hiding and fear, it's we who survived.'

He turned to face her slowly and she didn't relax her embrace. He stroked her long, white hair. 'Even though this crazy zhadár is hunting them, there will always be a few more left,' he told her gravely. 'They too can do what we were capable of doing. There is enough shadow in Girdlegard to make sure they're not seen. It's only their evilness that causes them to refuse to stop their slaughter.' He kissed her on the forehead. 'They will be the black thorn in the flesh of the kingdoms.'

'Why do you think that?'

'I don't think it. It's a certainty.'

'But even Aiphatòn will leave, and the dwarves are guarding the passageways so that no more älfar can get to us.' Fiëa caressed his face. 'Trust our Creating Spirit.'

'I do. With all my heart and soul.' Ilahín smiled weakly. 'What's happening with this hole that opened up in the crater? You didn't say much about it.'

'There's not much to report. We are filling it in as quickly as we can get our hands on soil and debris,' she said, seeing right through his attempt to change the topic before a fight could start. 'The guards are vigilant in carrying out their duties. It's been quiet so far. Not one monster has been sighted.'

But the elf could tell she was worried. 'You're afraid that it can't be filled in fast enough?'

Fiëa drew closer to him, her head resting on his bare chest. 'It's because of the writings.'

'I don't understand.'

'Carmondai's work, which we didn't find in the palace at first.' Her mood changed audibly. 'I should have killed him,' she said softly. 'But that crazy dwarf stopped me.'

'A task has been found for Carmondai that makes him harmless and even useful.'

'No älf is harmless or blameless. And the same goes for his writings. They are more than just easy-to-read events described excellently well.' She lifted her head and looked at him. 'We've got to destroy them, otherwise they could potentially foster affection for the black-eyes.'

'*Affection?*' Ilahín laughed at her. 'After what they did to Girdlegard?'

'I'll put it a different way then: understanding, fascination, an emotion that negates their terror and brutality. He makes heroes of them. But they're demons who plagued us. He twists the truth.' Fiëa was trying to find a justification. 'We've got to tackle it.' She looked pleadingly at him. 'One thing from the writings has already leaked to the humans and dwarves which I would have liked to have avoided.'

He looked at her in astonishment. 'Who was able to translate the älfar?'

'The black-eyes have ruled long enough that their language and script spread to quite a few humans. They wrote their instructions to allies and deserters in their own language sometimes.' Fiëa closed her eyes. 'How I wish,' she murmured angrily, 'that I had killed Carmondai!'

'I'm still waiting for you to give me the bad news.'

She took a deep breath. 'The village in the Grey Mountains, near the Jagged Crown.'

Ilahín knew what she meant straight away. He was silent for a while. 'There has been a rumour ever since Leïóva and her people climbed up there and a group of älfar followed her. It will die down soon.'

The two of them would never have travelled there to escape the älfar. They would sooner have died than go to the place where their tribe's turncoats were trying to befriend the dwarves in the name of working together.

Ilahín had never understood why the elf rulers had allowed this splinter group to exist. Even when they returned from the Grey Mountains and tried to live on the Golden Plain again, in Âlandur and Lesinteïl, they had not been turned away. But after many cycles of denunciation and occasional friction, the splinter group left the community again and stayed in the mountains.

'The difference is this: it has been written down, it's out there in the world. And the news is already spreading like wildfire in Girdlegard.' Fiëa's concerns were far from over. 'One thing leads to another: as soon as the dwarves hear it, they will check how much of it is true. And the more truth there is in the älf's writings, the more status they'll gain.'

'Then someone might assume that the lies in there about our people are true or at least that there's some truth to them,' he finished her thought process. 'You're right. Could you potentially, after the fact . . .'

'Luckily some parts went missing when the palace and its mountains collapsed, but the rest were passed to various scholars who began to translate them.' Fiëa let go of her husband. 'There can only be so many accidental fires.'

'No, that would be too obvious.' Ilahín looked up, staring at the elves' life star. 'Let's try for truth and reason: we'll convince the queens and kings of the danger of the dishonest writings,' he said slowly, formulating his plan as he spoke. 'I'll work on a speech that will ensure they're more afraid of the papers than the black-eyes themselves.'

'You'll have to hurry though. Once anything gets into anyone's head, it can never be removed again.'

'I will.' He kissed her reassuringly. 'By the way, I haven't been able to find out what happened to the former emperor of the älfar.'

'Nobody knows where his hunt took him.' Fiëa walked slowly back to the house. 'He is to be feared just as much as the impact of Carmondai's writings. Will your speech achieve that?' She didn't think Aiphatòn was capable of leaving Girdlegard willingly.

The same was true of Ilahín. Aiphatòn had hunted the elves for almost two hundred cycles before he awoke from his madness and led his own people to their doom.

But that doesn't diminish the guilt he brought upon himself. 'It ought to.' He followed Fiëa back into the house. *Or we'll kill him as soon as he turns up.* That would be a fair punishment.

Ishím Voróo, Several miles outside Dsôn Dâkiòn, 5452nd division of unendingness (6491st solar cycle), summer

'It seems we chose the right route.' After several orbits of Aiphatòn and Nodûcor walking through hilly grassland, a mountain now loomed far in the distance with a town on it. Long walls ran along the precipices and they would be impossible to climb with conventional equipment, which made conquest out of the question.

You would need dragons to attack it from the air. Who knows what Ishím Voróo has to offer in comparison with Girdlegard. Aiphatòn estimated the summit was about five hundred paces high. The densely packed homes stretched around the peak and stopped a hundred paces above the walls. As far as he could make out, two wide bridges were the only ways to access the town. A deep ravine also ran through the mountain, spanned by just one footbridge. *Gigantic structures. The älfar who live there like things big.*

'Is that Dsôn Elhàtor or Dâkiòn?' he asked Nodûcor.

Compelled to remain mute, the älf made a helpless gesture. His skin had not browned or reddened in the sun, as if stubbornly refusing to betray any sign of life; his hair looked the same as before.

Either he's lying or he's less help than I'd hoped. At least he's putting on weight so I don't need to worry that he could die on me before he becomes useful. On the journey, Aiphatòn had fed him porridge with fruit pulp or meat mixed in, often heavily watered down so that Nodûcor could suck it up through the straw. But in the black half-mask he still made a bony, terrifying sight. *Death in älf form.*

As they walked across the plain they spotted a solitary flagpole as wide as a man, with a yellow älf rune on a black silk flag fluttering in the wind.

When they came closer they saw an iron plaque that had been fixed to the pole at chest-height with long nails.

'Well, this is polite,' Aiphatòn remarked and scanned the message that had been engraved into the metal in various languages.

> *Wanderer,*
> *if you're coming to Dâkiòn,*
> *be advised*
> *you will have levies to pay*
> *as decreed by law.*
>
> *Anyone who roams this land*
> *will pay on request*
> *a coin of gold*
> *apiece*
> *or a jewel of the highest quality.*
>
> *Should you not possess either,*
> *make a detour of forty miles.*
> *Or pay*
> *with your*
> *mortal remains.*

'That solves that mystery. Dâkiòn is up ahead.' Aiphatòn looked at the town. 'A forty-mile sovereign territory? The älfar in Ishím Voróo have become modest with the size of their kingdoms, in any case. Unlike the structures they build.' He could make out several villages in the plain, as well as paddocks and cultivated fields and small patches of woodland. 'The yield from those crops would never be enough to feed the residents for a whole cycle. They must do trade or rely on compulsory levies.'

Nodûcor pointed to the words *gold* and *jewel*.

'Yes, they're definitely rich,' Aiphatòn agreed and rested his spear on his shoulder. 'We'll likely have to pay with our mortal remains, if they catch us.' He laughed and set off.

Nodûcor followed hesitantly. He was still carrying around the clamp that had been on his upper body, even though it exhausted him. It was just peeping out of his rucksack.

At first, Aiphatòn had toyed with the idea of tying up the pale älf in a hiding place and leaving him behind so that he could do an initial reconnaissance by himself. But Nodûcor's weakness and the approaching botoicans stopped him doing that. He didn't want Nodûcor killed by a band of orcs out of hunger or hatred before he could solve the puzzle of the half-mask and its origins. And his conviction that the pale älf would somehow be useful to him had taken root.

By the afternoon, they had covered a third of the distance to Dâkiòn and had walked through the first large village. It was not much different from the settlements in Girdlegard in terms of architectural style or local clothing trends. It seemed humans looked the same everywhere. Aiphatòn saw älfar runes painted or engraved on the homes, but no signs of altars to the gods or statues placed in niches in the houses for protection. It was clear whose favour was prioritised around Dâkiòn.

Nobody paid them particular attention. Nodûcor's mask provoked the odd look of surprise but no sustained interest.

'Either they think we're townspeople or they know they're under the protection of Dâkiòn and we cannot harm them,' Aiphatòn said to Nodûcor, glad that there were no glances coming their way: no anxious, shy or hate-filled looks. Life was rather different in north-western Ishím Voróo; it was practically relaxed.

The locals weren't running away from them or following them. If they had seen Aiphatòn's plate-covered body, the encounter might have gone differently. But as he was wearing a robe over them, nobody noticed. *This is unusual. Incredible.*

As night fell, they reached another village, also populated by humans.

The two älfar were walking along the high street. Nodûcor's posture betrayed the stress he was feeling. He didn't trust the tranquillity.

Aiphatòn stopped abruptly in front of a half-timbered building with a tankard dangling over its open door. The smell of cooked food and the hubbub of conversation drifted out to where they stood.

'This'll be a bar. And I feel like a drink that doesn't taste of water.' He grabbed Nodûcor by the arm and dragged him into the pub, his spear lowered.

Aiphatòn was astonished all over again that nobody cared about the newcomers. The men and women's conversations continued uninterrupted; there was no commotion.

The barman, a tubby little man whose beard and hair were unkempt, looked up, nodded to them and pointed to the right where there was a small table free.

The älfar crossed the room and sat down; they put their luggage and spear on the floor.

The balconies inside the building had been painted a dark brown and the walls were white. Candles and lamps burned in various niches and poorly done paintings of the town hung on the walls for decoration, along with several different flags. Two tables away, some men were singing a rowdy tune and a woman was dancing to it. Swathes of tobacco smoke wafted about and irritated the älfar's noses.

'I can hardly believe it.' Aiphatòn remembered Girdlegard. If he and Nodûcor had walked into a village when his tribe was in power, everyone would have thrown themselves to the floor and asked what they wanted, immediately begging for mercy so as not to have their bones removed for artworks.

The barman, whose leather pub apron harboured an overpowering smell of beer and sweat, brought them two earthenware goblets and a carafe of wine. 'I hope you like it,' he told them in älfar with a very human accent and an unfamiliar emphasis.

Aiphatòn laughed in surprise. 'Am I dreaming?'

Nodûcor shook his head, looking equally perplexed, if not more so.

The barman eyed him with a friendly expression on his face. 'Sir, you're not dreaming. I can tell from your clothes that you don't come from Dâkiòn. Therefore you must have completed a long trek to see the sovereign and become new residents of the town.' He pointed to the wine. 'The local älfar are particularly fond of this one. It's light, fruity and it comes without too much sweetness.'

'We don't have any money.'

'A gift. Accept it, sir. You're welcome to eat as well.'

'Well, I'm dreaming after all.' Aiphatòn picked up the goblet and poured some wine for himself, raising his glass to the barman and Nodûcor. 'To you, my good man.'

The barman bowed and put one hand on his chest.

'Yes, yes, the kind-hearted Joako,' came a voice by the door, followed by a chorus of laughter. 'Likes to make friends he might make use of later.'

Aiphatòn looked toward the doorway. *Apparently the money-collectors are here.*

An älf with dark blonde hair was towering over the threshold. He wore black lamellar armour under a white tunic with the familiar yellow rune and another symbol emblazoned on it in green. There was a silver-plated black helmet in his right hand and iron batons in holders on his thighs.

'Greetings to the travellers,' he cried and entered the room. 'You noticed the sign at our border?'

Business carried on as usual in the tavern, the singing just got a little quieter.

Outside the window, Aiphatòn could see three more warriors chatting, not looking worried. They were holding curved bows made of horn, the quivers full to the brim with long, black arrows. *They're like us on that score.* 'Yes, we noticed it.'

'My name is Vailóras,' he introduced himself and sat down opposite them at the table. 'Joako, fetch me a goblet too,' he said, turning to the barman; as he did so the long dagger at his belt became visible. 'What's wrong with your eyes?'

'They take a long time to lose their blackness,' the shintoìt said, playing it down. 'It's bothered me since birth.'

'Ah. Now then: I'm the one you need to settle your debt with,' Vailóras smiled calmly. 'You choose the currency: gold, jewels or your mortal remains?'

'We have neither the first nor the second and we still need the third,' Aiphatòn replied politely. 'I'd like to go to Dâkiòn.'

'And so you can. As soon as you pay.' Vailóras seemed to have these conversations rather frequently. He sounded aloof, but there was a certain menace in his voice. 'If you think you can slip away from me, you'll be asked for the fee – at the latest – at the gate if you can't present the receipt that I issue after payment.'

'Could you advance me two coins then?' Aiphatòn suggested. 'I'll be sure to pay you back double as soon as I've spoken to the sovereign.'

'Me lend you something?' Vailóras raised his eyebrows. 'Nobody has come up with that idea before.' He grinned and in the end couldn't help but laugh. 'But no. And no jewels either.'

'Your mortal remains then?' Aiphatòn followed this with a wink. 'You'd get those back too.'

'Even less likely,' Vailóras replied, amused. 'You're a real joker.' Joako brought the goblet and the warrior drank from it. 'What ruined town do you and your friend come from? And what's with the half-mask?' He drank and waited. 'Does he bite?'

'He tends to be a bit rude. A mask of disgrace,' Aiphatòn lied. 'He even spits if he gets too worked up. He's trying to break the habit at the moment.'

Vailóras pulled a face. 'Ah, I see. Another funny story. And what about your origins then?'

'Girdlegard,' he responded evenly.

'What?' The warrior did not understand.

'You probably call it Tark Draan, if the Dsôn Aklán informed me correctly,' he elaborated and was amused to see Vailóras' jaw falling open in shock. 'That's where I come from anyway. I rescued him from the clutches of a mob on the way.'

Vailóras polished off his wine in rapid gulps. 'Then count yourself lucky you came across me,' he said; the cheerfulness had vanished from his voice and face. 'The sovereign doesn't like älfar from Tark Draan. You can turn back and I'll forget I ever saw you.' The dark blonde älf placed his hands flat on the table to show he meant no threat.

'Why is that?'

'That's just the way it is. And I can't bring you to him to ask him yourself because you don't have the coins.'

'Well, thank you for your candour.' Aiphatòn nodded slowly. 'But if I've absolutely *got* to see the sovereign?'

'Then you and your friend owe me gold coins, jewels or mortal remains, the same as before. We're going in circles,' said Vailóras, not giving in. 'Unless there was a good reason why I *needed* to bring you to Shôtoràs.'

'Like for the good of the town, for instance?'

'A good reason.' Vailóras inclined his head in agreement. 'But how could that be dependent on you?'

Aiphatòn grinned. 'I can only tell the sovereign himself that.' He raised his glass to him. 'Do you want to be responsible for Dâkiòn being in danger, all because you didn't bring me to him?'

A smile played around the corners of Vailóras' mouth. 'You're smart. But I'm still not convinced. Give me more.'

'How about botoicans?'

The warrior wiped dust off his lamellar armour. 'Nobody is afraid of them. We crushed one of their armies.'

'Well then, what about magic?' Aiphatòn made the spear runes light up and the symbols on his armoured gloves glow.

'We've got cîani who can do a lot more. How else could we have crushed one of the botoican armies?' Vailóras remained unimpressed and got to his feet, readjusting the white tunic he wore over the dark armour. 'I'll give you one last chance. Otherwise' – he drew the right-hand baton out of the sheath on his thigh – 'I'll remove the nicest bones from the pair of you.'

Aiphatòn stood up slowly too. Using the armoured glove on his right hand, he slipped off his robe so that the warrior could see the pieces of metal sewn into his body; with his left hand he summoned the spear and made the runes on the weapon, the gloves and the plates glow with a dazzlingly bright light.

Silence fell across the room now. Apparently this was a rare sight even in Ishím Voróo.

'My name is Aiphatòn. I am the son of the Inextinguishables who once ruled Dsôn Faïmon, cradle to us all, and before whom perhaps even the sovereign Shôtoràs once bowed his head,' he said, speaking so loudly that nobody could fail to hear him, even the älfar outside the window. 'What I have to say to the sovereign concerns him and only him.' He pointed at the exit with his glowing blade. 'Now take me to Dâkiòn!'

Vailóras eyed him with a look that betrayed neither awe nor respect, only hostility. 'Hence the eyes.' He turned round. 'Let's go then,' he ordered briskly and rudely as he walked out.

Let's go then – is that it? Aiphatòn was utterly baffled. By now at the latest, he would have expected demonstrations of respect and bended knees. Nodûcor rolled his eyes. *Everything is different in this wasteland. Even the älfar.*

They quickly picked up their luggage and left the bar. The mutterings started as they left.

The archers were already sitting in the night-mares' saddles. Through the medium of extended arms, it was communicated to Nodûcor and Aiphatòn that they were to mount behind. Just a few heartbeats later, they swung themselves up behind the riders.

'Ah yes: it's possible that I'll demand the levy at a later point,' Vailóras informed them, making his black horse trot with a gentle kick to its flanks.

His warriors laughed softly, in anticipation of watching them suffer.

They covered the final miles to the town in the dead of night underneath the starry sky. The trot turned into a breakneck gallop that required utmost concentration from the night-mares. The earth trembled beneath the stamping hooves as they trampled the ground, bolts of lightning flashing around their ankles.

But the real spectacle was happening ahead of them: the moon shone down on Dâkiòn and made the whole town glow.

The bright, painted roofs cast the light far into the countryside, jewels and diamonds glittered and sparkled all over the walls; the large connecting bridge gleamed, golden in colour. All kinds of artworks fixed to the dormer windows and looming up between the houses were moving and drifting in the gentle breeze.

A quiet, barely audible glockenspiel rang out from the town. The melody touched Aiphatòn's soul, although the wind was rushing in his ears and distorting the notes. *What must the original be like, if I could hear it correctly?*

Runes loomed into view on the enormous defensive walls. They praised Inàste and asked for her protection against attackers.

Save us from new enemies and old masters, Aiphatòn read.

It didn't sound to him like they had been longing for the return of the Inextinguishables or one of their offspring.

Ishím Voróo, Älfar town of Dsôn Elhàtor, 5452nd division of unendingness (6491st solar cycle), summer

Standing with Saitôra at the quay wall, Irïanora hugged her friend, then set one foot on the ramp up to the ship. 'I'll pass on your messages,' she said glumly and held up the folder full of letters to emphasise this. Ôdaiòn had checked the contents in advance for any information about their defences. 'We won't forget you.'

Step by step, she climbed backwards up the gangway, nearing the deck.

Irïanora didn't let Saitôra, who despite her luxurious silver-blue dress was an unparalleled heap of misery, out of her sight. The wood gave way slightly under her, rising and falling with the rocking of the ship and the waves. *She's going to break down any moment now.*

The canvases in the enormous frames that had been put up around the little group stretched taut in the wind. The fabric meant she couldn't get a glimpse of her surroundings; however, she had a clear view of the sea, the mouth of the harbour and the large ship.

Ôdaiòn, in his lavish, sophisticated blue clothes as always, was waiting with five lightly armed soldiers a small distance away and watching the departure scene.

The black-haired Saitôra was close to tears. 'Tell your uncle never to give in to those who want war,' she pleaded, her voice choked up. 'And you . . . please don't send anyone else down the Tronjor. Otherwise . . .' She wrapped her arms around herself and lowered her head, her shoulders shrugging. Her composure was gone. 'Irïanora! I don't want to die. Not here. And I don't want to be alone, away from my family,' she sobbed and sank to her knees. 'Think of me,' she cried, weeping. 'Oh, Inàste!'

Irïanora stopped on the ramp, swallowed and quickly came back down. She took her friend in her arms and embraced her. 'I can't do this to you,' she said, deeply moved. '*You* will travel to Dâkiòn and tell everyone why I stayed.'

'What?' Saitôra stared at her with swollen eyes, and her disbelief turned to overwhelming joy. 'No, this cannot be! You're the niece of the sovereign!'

'And hence all the greater an obstacle for the warmongers if they try to incite our town to fight,' Irïanora added loudly so that the monarchess' son could hear and stroked Saitôra's black hair. 'I'm staying. My decision has been made.' Her gaze shifted over Saitôra's head to Ôdaiòn, who was looking intently at her and smiling slightly. Then she hugged her friend again, reaching into the fold of her dark red dress as she did so, secretly taking out two letters and slipping them to her. 'One is for Shôtoràs, the other is for a good friend. His name is Anûras. You'll find him in the Death-dancer,' she whispered hurriedly. 'Go.'

'You . . . planned this?' Saitôra's pale grey eyes opened wide, sparkling and damp. She was also using the tincture to preserve the whiteness during the day.

'It's the only way I could write messages that Ôdaiòn *didn't* check. Tell our people how brutally they murdered Gathalor and Iophâlor. Their deaths must be atoned for,' she whispered. Then she picked Saitôra up off the ground and put her onto the ramp. 'Tell my uncle I love him,' she called loudly, wiping away hastily faked tears.

Saitôra staggered up the slope and laughed in relief while Iriänora threw her friend's now useless messages into the harbour basin. 'I will let everyone know about your heroism! They will sing songs and tell stories about you!' She blew her a kiss and placed one hand over her heart. 'I owe you my life, Iriänora. I will do everything I can to make sure nothing happens to you on Elhàtor.' Waving, she disappeared on deck where the crew immediately met her and led her inside.

The ropes were untied and the ship put out to sea. Two smaller sails unfurled with a flutter, the bow swung around and headed for the mouth of the harbour.

Ôdaiòn came and stood next to Iriänora. 'So we've got ourselves a little heroine,' he said and laughed kindly. 'I have great respect for you. That was noble and selfless.' He took her hand and kissed the knuckles. 'If I were to claim your presence didn't suit me, I'd be lying.'

'To be frank' – Iriänora dropped him a small curtsey to give him a view of her cleavage – 'I *hate* my uncle. And when I saw poor Saitôra, how heavy her heart and soul became, there was nothing else for it. I got her into this situation so it was up to me to get her out of it.' She waved farewell to the ship with her other hand, as if her friend could see her. 'Besides, this way the risk of a war will be ruled out. Nobody wants to put the life of the sovereign's niece at stake.'

'You escape the great Shôtoràs and become the self-sacrificing friend. Well played.' He reached into his pocket and pulled out a black cloth, stepped behind her and put the blindfold on her. 'By the way, my mother is of the opinion that you're nothing more than a spy. A very cunning spy but still one who ought to be killed straight away.'

Irïanora let him have his way. She smelled his aftershave and felt the warmth of his body. 'Or maybe I fell in love with you, which reinforced my decision to stay?' It was time to lure the fish again but more intensely.

Ôdaiòn laughed softly. 'That's flattering. A symbolic marriage between us would create a firm bond between Elhàtor and Dâkiòn.' He took her by the hand and guided her along. 'But you should know that my mother would like to see me in the arms of Leïóva's daughter.'

'The commander of a merchant ship?' Irïanora protested incredulously. 'That's . . . verging on the ridiculous!'

'The two woman are blood sisters, my dear Irïanora. And in order to carry their friendship on into the next generation, this marriage would make sense.' There was a click as he opened a carriage door, then she was guided into the coach where there was a smell of fresh flowers. She heard Ôdaiòn getting in after her. The door closed with a clack and the vehicle jolted forward.

'Can I take the blindfold off?' The blonde älf-woman breathed in the sweet aroma – and suddenly felt his lips on hers.

She didn't hesitate to reciprocate his tender kiss, clasping his face in her hands and pulling him closer. *That worked better than expected.*

As he was such an excellent kisser, she didn't mind returning his caresses. It was a lovely diversion. It was some time before they separated, breathing heavily.

Ôdaiòn removed the cloth and smiled, fascination and desire in his eyes. 'I think the wedding to Ávoleï can wait.' He stroked the älf-woman's lips with his thumb. 'Or be called off entirely. She doesn't like me anyway.'

'And a wedding would make my uncle even more furious. Fantastic!' Irïanora kissed his finger. 'He hates the monarchess. But that's nothing new.'

Ôdaiòn laughed. 'No, that's nothing new. Because of their past in Tark Draan. And because she allegedly stole his residents from Dâkiòn.'

What do you mean allegedly? Irïanora had to bite her tongue to stop herself responding with anything that would startle her fish. Her hatred for the Magnificent had to remain hidden for her plans to flourish. She smiled at him instead. 'That old fool.'

Ôdaiòn threw himself down onto the cushions as the carriage raced along. He gazed at her face for a long time, looking pensive. 'It's not a good idea to develop feelings for someone,' he said in a measured voice.

'Because you can be disappointed,' she took up where he left off.

'Because you become vulnerable,' he added and cocked his head.

'So what shall we do?' Irïanora's chest rose and sank. 'Do we reject our feelings and deny love?' *Was that too much?*

The brown-haired älf looked taken aback. '*Love?* A word for poets. Right now, we feel attracted to one another.' He took both of her hands in his and covered them with tender kisses. 'We will spend plenty of time together to find out what else we have in common. We come from different cultures, although we belong to the same tribe.'

Irïanora nodded. *You are going to fall under my spell even more. I'll make sure of it.*

She saw through his performance very easily because she was better at it. She had learnt Ôdaiòn was well-known as an älf who had numerous affairs – for one thing, he was outwardly handsome and for another, he had an inherent status that made him attractive. He was the future ruler of Elhàtor and her female rivals would be taking up their positions to push her out, the pretty hostage from Dâkiòn. Or take her out.

'It's up to you. But since I'm assuming I won't leave the island again, may I move around a bit more freely?' Irïanora treated him to another smile full of promise. 'I'm so keen to see the beauty of my new home with my own eyes and not just in sketches.'

Ôdaiòn winked at her and pulled back the carriage's curtains.

Sunlight flooded the coach and blossoming trees stretched out all around them. They were driving down a road along the coast.

'Welcome to your first little tour. You'll see our humble woods, fields and vine-covered slopes.' The älf gave instructions to the coach-driver, then pulled out a drawer underneath the bench. Inside were two glasses and a sealed earthenware jug.

'You guessed I would stay after all?' Irïanora was looking at the drink.

'Oh, it was intended for consoling your friend on the pain of being separated. But it's more suitable for this fortunate turn of events.' He opened the jug and poured the fizzy liquid into the receptacles, holding one out to Irïanora. 'As soon as night falls, we'll go back into town.' He clinked glasses with her. 'Ask me anything you'd like to know. You deserve at least *some* answers.'

Irïanora gave him a kiss before she drank. It tasted sweet, prickling on her tongue and going straight to her head. 'What's this called?'

'It's a mixture of fermented apple juice and new wine. Refreshing and it livens the spirits.' Ôdaiòn looked contentedly out the window and pushed the pane down so that the wind rushed in. 'Isn't it splendid on Elhàtor?'

'Indeed.' Irïanora took another sip. *How soon will I be able to change that?*

She was pleased that this was going better than her initial plan.

The chances of war with the hated sea-town had rarely looked so good. Saitôra was carrying the letters with the fiery remarks and would willingly spread news of the murders of Gathalor and Iophâlor far and wide. She had seen the sustained outrage in her friend's eyes. That, combined with Anûras' activities, would provide the sparks to unleash the blaze.

Gathalor, my uncle's darling, slain like vermin. The älf-woman smiled. *The fire of war will break out and be constantly stoked. And I'll make my contribution on this awful island.*

Ôdaiòn looked at her and wrongly believed her good mood was down to him. 'You are wonderful!' He leaned forwards and gave her a long, tender kiss.

Irïanora returned the caress. *That will not protect you from endingness.*

Ishím Voróo, Älfar town of Dsôn Dâkiòn, 5452nd division of unendingness (6491st solar cycle), summer

The place where the sovereign received them looked to Aiphatòn more like a courtroom than a stately residence, as would have been fitting for the son of the Inextinguishables. What's more, the *Hall of Entreaties*, as Vailóras announced it was called, didn't sound quite as hospitable as the barman's behaviour had led him to believe it would be.

It's like they want to condemn us. The inscriptions on the battlements had already made him wary. The balcony-like platform with the desk on it, where those seated looked down from above, reinforced the impression that justice was administered in this immense vaulted hall, and no heartwarming balls or glamorous banquets took place here.

During their swift ride over the bridge and through the streets, the dimensions of the town had looked different. Giants had clearly founded it before being chased away. But he did like the way the älfar had taken the long, enormous buildings made of black basalt blocks and made them their own. *So different from home.* The Majestic was appropriately named and the nobility of this town and people were obvious in the hall too.

Nodûcor stood diagonally behind him. Vailóras and half a dozen warriors in a semi-circle guarded them.

Aiphatòn waited patiently and listened to his own body. Another thing – apart from the nature of the town – had struck him and it only seemed to affect him. His whole body was prickling so much that it was almost painful. He rubbed his arms several times, but it didn't help at all.

The runes on the alloy plates and the spear flashed from time to time without him ordering them to. Either there was a magical field under Dâkiòn or it was linked to the stones. The runes appeared to be invisible whenever he was particularly near the blocks of stone or where they closely surrounded him.

It's no surprise they have cîani in their ranks. He was sure that their spells would cause difficulties even for him. In northern Ishím Voróo, many things were very different but an älf was still an älf and still evil. *This town will fall.*

A side door eight paces high swung open, the wood creaking.

To Aiphatòn, Shôtoràs was simply a limping, broadly built älf using his right hand to lean on a tionium stick with a skeletonised crow's head on it; its tiny inlaid tiles of bone had been damaged and not yet repaired. His black robe had runes and decorations on it that had long since been forgotten in the älfar realms of Girdlegard.

He was followed by a heavily armed warrior with two swords on his weapons belt as well as a young, red-haired älf-woman who was wearing nothing but tight-fitting shorts and a skimpy top; her nail-like daggers were mounted on tionium forearm guards. Intertwining tattoos of runes shimmered all over her skin, mainly done in black and grey. Glittering precious stones had been affixed to her skin in a number of places.

Bringing up the rear was an elderly älf who favoured a pale purple robe and wore a thick curb chain made of silver, bones and diamonds. His head was covered by a helmet-like cap of white leather.

Clearly a welcoming party. 'I would have expected a little more pomp and ceremony when the son of Nagsor and Nagsar Inàste is standing in front of you,' said Aiphatòn boldly. 'You're not even having musicians and singers put in an appearance to praise my name?'

The pale-grey-haired Shôtoràs dropped into the armchair behind the desk and placed his stick on top of it, while his companions spread out onto the chairs around him. Their heads and hands could just about be made out from below. None of their expressions were friendly and in the redhead's gaze he could read the thrill of the chase.

'I take it you're disappointed, from your accusatory greeting,' replied the sovereign haughtily.

'He's a pure shintoìt,' the älf in the robe remarked offhandedly. 'The eyes aren't just dyed.'

'*Dyed?*' Aiphatòn banged the end of his spear once to give weight to his feigned outrage. The inlaid symbols flashed of their own accord, but it suited his gesture. 'You're acting as though the closest descendant of the Inextinguishables stood before you at sunrise every day.'

Apart from the sovereign, the älfar from Dâkiòn all broke into loud laughter.

'No. There haven't been all that many times,' Shôtoràs announced, smoothing his thin grey goatee. 'It's possible, of course, that the Inextinguishables have produced more than one like you. They've had time enough. In their lovely Dsôn-whatever.'

'They passed away. A long time ago,' Aiphatòn informed them.

'We're delighted to hear that again from an authoritative source. I certainly do not extend my sympathies to you. We've already celebrated the happy occasion,' sneered the elderly älf, looking contemptuously at him. 'What do you want? To fall back on your heritage and demand control of the town with a straight face?'

Vailóras and his troops laughed quietly, and the redhead grinned.

That's exactly what I would have done. But I can discard that plan. Aiphatòn thought it smarter to be less arrogant in his choice of words from now on. But he noticed the älf in the robe looking over at Nodûcor from time to time and trying to conceal his curiosity. *That is more than interest. That is badly disguised knowledge. Is he a cîanoi?* 'I thought I would at least have accommodation and a seat of honour bestowed on me.'

'Why so?' snarled Shôtoràs.

'You used to bow your head to the Inextinguishable siblings and follow their orders. I am their offspring . . .' he began.

'As far as I'm concerned, you might as well be Inàste's son. Or Samusin's. Or Tion's,' the powerful sovereign interrupted him harshly and tossed his silvery fair hair back. 'They would *all* have been more welcome than you, Aiphatòn, son of cowards.' Shôtoràs propped his muscular forearms on the desk and leaned forwards. 'Your parents fled to endingness *the* splinter their people needed them most. They abandoned the survivors while they set off into the lovely new world to build a new Dsôn. They forgot us.'

Aiphatòn was silent. He had not expected hatred towards the Inextinguishables. More like a cooling off of veneration – or yes, their longed-for return. But a complete rejection – never.

Shôtoràs snorted disdainfully. 'Do you know what we would do to them if they stood outside our gates?'

'I'm guessing not invite them inside, if I've understood correctly.'

'Rain missiles down on them,' the armoured warrior replied firmly.

'Burn them to ashes with magic,' the robe-wearer added in a low voice, still easily heard due to the way the hall was built.

'So that Samusin blows them away and rids us of them,' the redhead finished smugly.

That was unequivocal. Aiphatòn waited in silence.

Shôtoràs sat up straight. 'In departing for Tark Draan, they became traitors in our eyes. Traitors to those who remained loyal to them.' He pointed to himself. 'I grew up in Dsôn Faïmon, I fought many battles for them – and *that* was how they repaid me? They turned their backs and didn't care. No news, no messenger reached us.' He banged the stick against the surface of the desk. 'For those of us in Dâkiòn, they passed into endingness as soon as they marched through the Grey Mountains. They snuck away, secretly. Just like cowards do, instead of bracing themselves for their fate.'

Aiphatòn took a breath. *What do I do now?* He hadn't formulated a new plan yet, much less could he predict what was going to happen in the hall next.

'You're at a loss now.' Shôtoràs spun the stick, the metal bird of prey's head twirling around. 'You thought we would wrap you up in golden robes or carry you through our town on a sedan and that we'd be under your command from then on.'

His companions and the guards laughed again.

'Why did *you* leave Tark Draan?' the redhead asked sharply. 'Was it cowardice once your parents were no longer alive? Are you looking for a place to hide away, little shintoìt?'

The älf in the heavy armour bent down to Shôtoràs and whispered something to him, upon which the old älf spread his arms; his expression was both pleased and surprised.

'Oh, Tanôtai does you an injustice! You were a ruler *yourself*! That Tark Draan scum that turned up here about twenty divisions ago mentioned your name. My friend has reminded me of it: *Aiphatòn*, the powerful *emperor* of the älfar of *Tark Draan*!' After a dramatic pause he burst into peals of laughter and everyone joined in.

'If that's the case, powerful emperor, did *your* kingdom fall?' Tanôtai said with feigned sympathy amid their amusement. 'Did you want to talk us into moving to the Stone Gateway with you and wiping out the wicked dwarves and the terrible barbarians and the demonic elves?'

'I'm sure you would stab them to death with your sharp tongue.' Aiphatòn gave a small bow. 'I left Tark Draan because the era of the älfar was coming to an end there and . . .'

Shôtoràs leaned back in the armchair. 'Just like his parents,' he told his companions, turning his head right and left. 'His kingdom is falling and instead of going down fighting with it, he flees and wants to get into the ready-built house.' He fixed his eyes on Aiphatòn.

It was on the tip of Aiphatòn's tongue to say that the sovereign had come into a ready-built house himself, but instead he said nothing.

'You will get *nothing* here, neither sympathy nor control over the town. We've learnt from the past. No matter who wants to conquer

Tark Draan, we would not lift a finger. Not even to exterminate elves. Those are all absurd reasons for a war.' Shôtoràs lifted the stick and traced a kind of circular shape with it. 'We're doing fine here. You might find an audience and refuge more easily in Elhàtor.'

They have changed. Completely. Not a hint of desire to conquer. Aiphatòn could tell that every word the sovereign spoke was true. Judging by his mentality, he suspected Shôtoràs had belonged to the Constellations – the älfar who were against the conquest and ultra-expansion of realms. Still – Aiphatòn had taken a vow of destruction.

Shôtoràs gestured out the window. 'Follow the Tronjor downstream as far as the strait. There are scouts there who will no doubt take you to their monarchess. She will be glad to see you. Trash mixing with other trash.' Shôtoràs' gaze grew hard. 'Dâkiòn dismisses you, Aiphatòn.'

'He still owes us the levy,' Vailóras interjected from the back.

'I am exempting him and his companion from it.' The sovereign got up with a suppressed gasp and leaned on his stick. 'Now throw them out!'

Aiphatòn's thoughts were racing. He was thinking above all about the botoicans and the advancing army who wanted to seize Dâkiòn before he could stir up enough unrest in Elhàtor and unleash a war against the sovereign. *I cannot allow them to be conscripted.* 'One thing,' he raised his voice. 'What are you doing about the botoicans?'

'Why would I do anything about them?' Shôtoràs was climbing down from the platform step by step and his companions were getting to their feet.

'Because there are troops on their way to Dâkiòn. Their commander told me he wanted to capture the town.' Aiphatòn was watching the älf with the white leather cap and the pale purple robe who could no longer take his eyes off Nodûcor. He whispered to the scantily clad älf-woman then beckoned the warrior over. *Either Nodûcor is from here and lied to me or they know more than they will ever let on.*

Caution told him they needed to make themselves scarce extremely soon.

Apparently an älf-woman from Girdlegard ruled Elhàtor. *I'll be able to incite her to war more easily.* 'But if you insist we go, we'll look for an audience and safe refuge somewhere else.'

Shôtoràs froze on the steps. 'What is the commander's name?'

'He spoke to me through one of his men. I don't know it,' replied the shintoìt.

Nodûcor touched Aiphatòn's sleeve and drew him letters in the air that everyone could see.

'Nhatai?' the älf in the pale purple robe blurted out, aghast, and placed one hand on his thick chain as if he could to use it to keep himself on his feet. 'Was his name really *Nhatai*?'

'We saw two armies tearing each other to shreds, commanded by botoicans. Then one marched on further northwest and attacked a village,' Aiphatòn reported succinctly. 'And if memory serves, their commander swore to enslave every älf he could get his hands on as soon as he had overpowered his enemies.'

Shôtoràs and his companions were exchanging glances now.

'The botoicans are overestimating themselves as always. The Nhatais are considered to have been exterminated, having perished in family feuds and internal conflicts. And I'm even more surprised that your friend claims to have heard that name, emperor.' The sovereign limped on, reaching the floor of the hall and then making for the exit. 'We will defeat them just like we've done before.'

There it is, that old arrogance of my race. If they hadn't been botoicans, I wouldn't have warned them. 'There are a hundred thousand of them,' Aiphatòn pointed out, 'or maybe even more. There are even some of our tribe serving in their ranks.'

'You're mistaken,' the älf in the robe said in disbelief and walked down the stairs. Behind him came the redhead and the warrior who were laughing quietly and uncomprehendingly. 'They can't break our will. Our magic will protect us.'

'I killed an älf who asked me to kill him, just so that he could escape the enslavement of the Nhatais,' Aiphatòn protested. 'How could I be mistaken?' *Is he a cîanoi or even their commander-in-chief?* On closer inspection, he noticed that most of the runes on the chain resembled the ones on Nodûcor's half-mask. *Did he order the abduction or is that a coincidence?*

Shôtoràs stopped again, his hand resting on the door handle. 'We will check. And if what you say is true, I'm not afraid. We're protected by the precipices, our catapults are loaded and our cîani are extremely well prepared.'

'Darkness and fear won't stop them.' Aiphatòn was angry that he needed to warn Shôtoràs, whom he thought a miserable end would serve right – if the älfar weren't to become a danger to others. *It's one of Samusin's cruel tricks that Inàste's children lost interest in sub-jugating other tribes and precisely because of that, they represent a danger to them.*

The sovereign pushed the door handle down. 'Lethòras, show him why we're not scared. Then throw them out at long last.' Shôtoràs left the Hall of Entreaties.

'Look at this.' The älf in the robe was standing next to the stairs. He did two brisk moves and uttered two syllables, then a flash of light-ning shot out of the palm of his hand and sped towards Aiphatòn.

The intended display of superior magical power happened too quickly for Aiphatòn to be able to call out a warning to the cîanoi. The spell had barely started to fly towards him when his alloy responded with a counter-discharge, redirecting the energy back at the sorcerer with greater force. The dazzling white lightning turned green in the air.

Lethòras was struck by the beam. A frantically invoked defensive charm did glow around the cîanoi, but the spell was not strong enough to stop the impact.

He uttered a terrible scream and was hurled against the wall as if a troll had thrown him. Blood sprayed on the stonework around his head like a halo. He stretched his arms and legs out, then fell on the stairs and lay still. Strands of hair, pieces of bone and brain matter clung to the brickwork.

The armoured warrior stooped down and tended to the cîanoi while the tattooed redhead stared at Aiphatòn in horror.

I won't be able to ask him about Nodûcor's abduction anymore. 'We're going,' Aiphatòn whispered to the ashen älf and dragged him away. 'They don't want us here anyway.'

The guards and Vailóras shrank back from them; the terrifying impression they had made clearly ran deep. It appeared Dâkiòn's magic had met its match.

Only once Aiphatòn and Nodûcor were back outside on the street did a loud cry go up from the hall.

The warriors came running after them. 'Halt!' Vailóras ordered the pair.

'There was nothing I could do,' Aiphatòn shot back and didn't even consider obeying his order. 'That's what will happen to anyone who attacks me using magic.'

'That's not what this is about. Pasôlor wants to speak to you,' cried Vailóras and stopped. 'It's possible the sovereign is wrong and you could actually enrich Dâkiòn.'

'Enrich it? He probably just wants to enrich himself off me.' *First they throw us out, then they want us to stay.* Aiphatòn shook his head, jogging towards the first bridge with Nodûcor. He wanted to take a look at Elhàtor first. *I know what they're worried about. Having seen my power, suddenly they're afraid we could be of use to the other town.* 'We are not wanted here and we ourselves no longer want to seek refuge,' he replied. 'These two things complement each other very well in my opinion. Farewell! And I'll definitely pay next time.'

They ran through Dâkiòn under cover of darkness, taking the broad main road that ran in a straight line eastwards to one of the bridges and out of the town.

Again there was no opportunity to study the artworks, statues and ornaments in detail as they rushed past. Aiphatòn felt smaller than a child, surrounded by the gigantic, imposing houses. The unpleasant prickling was getting worse. *Maybe my alloy reacted more violently than usual because of it?*

There came the sound of hoofbeats, pursuing them and catching up.

Vailóras and his troops had set off on their night-mares and now they continued to escort them but didn't pester them.

'Come on, wait! Pasôlor is one of the sovereign's most trusted advisors. He is very keen that you stay at least till morning so that he can work on Shôtoràs,' the dark blonde älf tried to persuade them, his white tunic shining in the starlight. 'He thinks you're an asset.'

'Oh, I would have been. But I'm taking the sovereign up on his recommendation and I'm going to pay a visit to Elhàtor. If I don't like it there, I'll come back.' Aiphatòn suspected they hadn't been surrounded only because reinforcements were massing in great secrecy. *A hundred of them will probably be waiting at the gate.*

They were racing across the large, bright golden bridge over the wide ravine between the two parts of the town.

Aiphatòn's gaze fell on the sides that fell sharply away. Climbing down would take too long. He gripped his spear more tightly. *It ought to work with this.*

Vailóras urged his night-mare on; snorting, the creature's muzzle and sharp teeth came closer. 'I'll say it one last time: stay tonight, shin-toìt.' His warriors were loading arrows on the strings in their horn bows. 'Or never see another.'

Without warning, Aiphatòn grabbed Nodûcor around the waist and leaped onto the railing of the bridge, fired himself off it and flung the spear diagonally downwards as he did so.

The runes lit up and the tip bored into the stone.

Still holding onto Nodûcor, the älf landed on a narrow ledge on the slope and immediately continued sliding further into the abyss, straight towards the shaft of the weapon that was jutting out.

The landing was successful – but their escape didn't end there.

Aiphatòn used the spear as a springboard so that he and Nodûcor were carried into the air, then he summoned the spear which came away from the slope and whirred into his hand.

He hurled it into the wall below him as they started to fall downwards and landed on it again. In this way they swiftly reached the floor of the ravine while the shimmering gold bridge above them meant they were not easy targets for the archers. *I could hardly have wished for a better shield.*

'To the wall,' Aiphatòn commanded and let go of Nodûcor who immediately broke into a run beside him.

It was a few hundred paces from the ravine to the bulwark. The long allures weren't manned because there was no imminent attack. The lamplight in the watchtowers a long way off was the only sign of guards, who were passing the time reading, playing cards and observing the plain in front of the town.

Nobody was looking inwards. This made it easy for the escapees to scale the nearest narrow staircase and stare down onto the next steep precipice from the battlements.

Approximately a hundred paces below them was solid ground and the river shining like a silver ribbon in the moon's glow.

Aiphatòn was panting. The magical exertion was slowly exhausting him; he barely had any strength left. He looked at the armoured glove he was using to lean against a battlement. The runes flickered of their own accord again. *Was my hunch wrong? Are the black stones leaching energy from me?* He pointed to the Tronjor. 'That's where we need to get to.'

Nodûcor nodded and looked doubtfully into the chasm.

A metallic, glassy sound rang out on the allure, then a faint breeze sprang up and it smelled of red-hot iron.

They turned around and were staring at Tanôtai, the scantily clad red-haired älf-woman with the tattoos.

Her runes shimmered and pulsed, the jewels on her skin sparkling mysteriously. 'My master said that your friend with the glass hair has to stay.' She was holding her needle-thin daggers in her fists.

How did she get to us so quickly? A spell? Aiphatòn stood in front of Nodûcor to protect him. 'Your master is dead. Save yourself from the same fate.' He pointed the tip of his spear at her. 'Magic is no use against me.'

Tanôtai copied his threatening movement with the dagger in her left hand. 'So I've seen. It will be enough if my weapon is magic.' The älf-woman lowered her head slightly and blinding white flames encircled her round blade. 'Let me see how they fight in Tark Draan, little emperor.'

Aiphatòn went on the attack immediately – and swung his spear through nothing but air.

Tanôtai had anticipated his attack and shot upwards right in front of him, wrapping herself around him like a seductive dancer and swinging behind him underneath his arm. The magic she was radiating made the prickling inside him worse; her skin felt red-hot.

Aiphatòn whirled around, lashing out.

But again she was no longer there. His blade sliced through the air with a whistle and Nodûcor leaped back a pace.

'I,' the älf-woman whispered in his right ear, 'am Tanôtai, the death-dancer. Nobody has beaten me before, and you will be no exception.' She laughed mockingly.

Aiphatòn tried to hit her with his elbow, but this attack sliced through empty space too. *I'm quicker than any warrior. How is she pulling this off?* He assumed that the runes drawn on her skin wove a permanent spell around her that made her supernaturally quick.

The red-haired älf-woman appeared in front of him and stabbed at him with the glowing dagger. 'Here I am, emperor!'

He deflected the glowing tip more out of reflex than in a well-thought-out parry.

'I have another one for you, little emperor,' whispered Tanôtai.

Aiphatòn couldn't hold off the second dazzlingly bright blade anymore: it struck one of his plates directly, and orange sparks sprayed up like a volcano exploding in his chest.

The eruption of energies hurled a blinded Aiphatòn through the air.

When he did not hit the flagstones of the allure or the rock face within the next four heartbeats, he knew: *I'm falling down the cliff-face!*

Chapter X

Bear in mind that decisions always entail consequences. Including unintentional ones.

Wise saying of the Älfar
Collected by Carmondai, master of word and image

Tark Draan, Human kingdom of Idoslane, 5452nd division of unendingness (6491st solar cycle), autumn

Intrigued, Carmondai watched as the älf blood – fresh and fluid – ran down the walls of the glass bottle as soon as he shook it. *That must be the silvery substance that had been added. It stops it coagulating.*

He was sitting at the rough table in the kitchen of a deserted farmstead, whose owners had either wanted to start again somewhere new or had been among the triplets' unfortunate victims.

The zhadár stoked the fire in the man-high, dwarf-wide hearth, throwing another four logs on top. 'I need a really high temperature,' he explained.

During a quick search, Carmondai had found clothes that fitted him better than the much-too-tight and by now filthy garments he had been wearing. At this stage he looked more like an älfar farmer than an artist, but his circumstances didn't allow for such sensitivities.

He felt childish to have been so delighted to find the piece of ash soap among the washing utensils. It might not have been as good as a bath in a tub but his next wash would be more thorough than ever.

Due to the wrath of the people, they avoided staying the night in villages and towns. It was impossible to predict whether the inhabitants would suddenly be overcome with anger and daring in equal measure. Carâhnios didn't want to deploy his powers and those of the älf against the innocent.

Carmondai put down the bottle, reached for his quill, dipped it into the ink pot and recorded his thoughts on the waiting paper. *An Ode to the Soap. Oh what times, oh what customs.*

Carâhnios got up and came over to the table where Carmondai was sitting. He had spread out various jars, vials and caskets over the stained wooden tabletop. 'I stole them from their laboratory. In Bhará.' He sat down and giggled as he opened each in turn. 'I secretly watched Sisaroth so many times.'

'Did you *see* the right thing then?'

'You think I can't prepare the remedy?' Carâhnios tapped the small lid of one mother-of-pearl casket against the bottle and it made a low clinking sound. 'I'll admit I don't have any experience with *älf blood* because Sisaroth distilled it from the blood of elves. I am my own test subject as it were.' He looked at the various receptacles, strange smells and aromas streaming out of them from time to time. Here and there, thin wreathes of smoke curled upwards. 'Good. It's all here.'

'And what are these ingredients?' Carmondai was drawing a quick sketch of the kitchen on the piece of paper beside him. The nib scratched softly across the paper, accompanying the crackling of the burning wood. 'Can you tell me their names?'

To his astonishment, Carâhnios shrugged his shoulders. 'I never found out. Sisaroth had a vast supply of ingredients for his drinks and demonic elixirs. I'm pleased I discovered *which* ones he was even using.'

'Aha. Well, that's brave. Daring.' *Not to mention thoughtless. It's just like you.* Carmondai swept the quill along his chin. 'What are you going to do if you run out of these ingredients? How are you going to know what you're missing and how to source more of it?'

'I'll think of something. And anyway, I've stockpiled a small supply. Since there are no zhadár left apart from me, it will last for a while.' He checked on the fireplace where the fire was still blazing high and sending the flames shooting up the chimney. 'It will take a while before the heat is right for distilling, but I can get to work on the mixing now.'

Carmondai was in awe of the nonchalance with which the zhadár fished spatulas and little spoons with different markings out of a pouch and placed them in front of the receptacles, then fitted together the component parts of a pocket-sized set of healer's scales. 'This is not the first time you've done this.'

'No. I've gone over the sequence many times, but today there will be a yield at the end of it for the first time.' Carâhnios balanced the scale pans, nodded and measured out the ingredients precisely, using a different spoon for each one. 'Some of the ingredients react if you combine them in their dry state or even if the tiniest pinch is mixed with something. Then the distillate would be ruined.'

One substance after another passed through the neck of the bottle and into the dark, almost black, blood, its surface a shimmering silver.

A novelty, even for me. Occasionally, Carmondai saw a glow when the zhadár added a new ingredient and carefully tilted the container to mix them; St Elmo's fire swirled over the surface.

Outside, the first severe storm of the autumn howled across Ido-slane, testing the resistance of the stalks in the last unharvested fields. Strong winds shook the farmstead, making the beams groan. The flames in the chimney even dropped occasionally, but the gusts of wind could not extinguish the fire.

Carâhnios closed the jars, vials and caskets, dismantled the scales and meticulously tidied everything up. 'This will go into the fire very soon.' He put a glass stopper fitted with coils into the mouth of the bottle. On the end of this, he put a tapering porcelain tube that had a sharp bend to the right and ended in a thin outlet that could be opened with an adjustable screw.

Carmondai pointed at it with the quill. 'How much yield will there be?'

The zhadár again had to admit he did not know. 'If we could get one small dishful out of approximately four units, I would be happy. It would be enough for me for one cycle.' He took the prepared bottle along with its contents and set it down ready next to the hearth.

Carmondai alternately wrote and drew like a man possessed, so as not to miss anything and to capture the atmosphere in the kitchen as accurately as possible. *Never has anything more unusual been prepared here.*

As he drew, his thoughts wandered to Ostòras' hillside hideaway in the purpose-built ruins.

Disappointingly, it had been empty and there were no indications of any other inhabitants. Their enemy didn't seem to have been living there long. There were just a few barrels and jars of supplies, bandages along with weapons and a small forge for repairing armour and swords.

Carâhnios looked very unhappy about it too. He had been expecting more älfar.

And more blood. Carmondai believed Ostòras when he'd said the remaining älfar would hide away and sow terror in Girdlegard through ambushes.

The zhadár never dreamt of informing Girdlegard, or at least the monarchs and monarchesses, about the threat because he felt it would lead to uncertainty – and hence the älfar would have achieved their goal before the first death.

Carmondai saw it differently, but it might as well have been all the same to him. He was a prisoner only pretending to be docile.

Carâhnios smashed the last charred piece of wood with the poker and it fell apart, glowing and emitting sparks. He put the bottle on the pulsing, dark red embers and crouched down. With his forearms resting on his knees, he watched eagerly.

Carmondai got up and joined him in watching the process that would produce a remedy from the blood of an älf and other ingredients – a remedy containing and conferring incredible powers.

He suppressed his fear that a small disaster might take place, like an explosion or a deflagration that would badly injure the älf and groundling or even cost them their lives. *That would be a belated satisfaction for Ostòras.*

At first, nothing happened apart from the St Elmo's fire, its greenish-blue flames turning dark blue and flitting here and there as if delighted by the heat.

Or it's trying to escape it. Carmondai sat on the uneven stone floor and started drawing again in order to capture the different phases.

'It's still all right,' murmured Carâhnios, fascinated. 'If I say: *run*, black-eye, you're going to run.'

Just as I thought. The älf stayed bravely where he was.

Above the surface, a thin, greenish smoke formed that was iridescent in the glow of the embers, occasionally looking gold.

And from one heartbeat to the next, the blood started simmering and foaming black. The stopper may have stayed firmly inside the glass rim, but the aggressive hissing was unmistakeable, as if the elixir was trying to corrode its way out of its transparent prison and descend on them.

But since Carâhnios didn't move, Carmondai stayed calm and kept drawing.

The smoked turned white and climbed up into the glass coil where it condensed in the lower part as caramel-coloured drops.

The fine webs that made it as far as the bend looked more like a pale black. Just before it percolated into the little porcelain tube, it took on a light, cloudy colour that Carmondai had never seen before in his whole life. *How am I meant to describe that?*

The simmering and boiling continued, the foam climbed higher and blocked their view.

Carmondai noticed the pungent smell. The glass stopper was leaking somewhere. The next time he drew breath, he had an attack of dizziness so he crawled two paces away from the bottle.

'That,' remarked Carâhnios, coughing, 'is not good.' He reached out his gloved right hand to check the fit of the stopper.

When he increased the pressure on the neck of the bottle, the bottom of it shattered. The viscous contents poured all over the bed of glowing coals and the hissing got louder.

Carâhnios removed the little porcelain tube with apparent calm, then turned to Carmondai. 'Run,' he said and dashed out of the room. As he rushed past, he grabbed the bag of ingredients.

Cursing, the älf snatched up his pages, got to his feet and staggered out of the kitchen. The fireplace was getting dazzlingly bright, as though the sun and moon had been able to unite for the first time. As a precaution, he pressed himself against the wall in the adjoining room, hoping the brickwork was thick and would protect him.

There was no bang, no explosion to make the farmstead collapse. Not *one* spectacular sound and yet the light continued to radiate.

Carmondai tried to make out what was going on in the kitchen, but he couldn't look into the light. It was terribly painful to his eyes.

The wall where he had crouched down for protection from the expected blaze was heating up more and more quickly. The alchemical reaction that the zhadár had unleashed was still happening.

Carâhnios was kneeling on the floor a few paces away, pouring the contents of the little tube into a second vial. 'Better than nothing. It got me a few precious drops,' he announced. 'Let's get out of here. Our enemies are waiting for us at the next hideaway.'

'What happened?' Carmondai still had the pungent smell in his nose.

The groundling grinned and jumped up. He slipped his cloak on over his black leather armour. 'No idea. But I think we're lucky it didn't kill us.'

They ran out to the stables where the pony and the horse were tethered and waiting for them. The restless animals were quickly saddled and the journey continued in spite of the howling winds and impending thunderstorm.

One look back at the farmstead told Carmondai that this had been a good idea: behind the window panes there was a dazzlingly white glow and flames were pouring out of the windows and already spreading to the rest of the building.

What weapon has he concocted? Carmondai thought he was seeing things, but in that moment he could have sworn that even the stone building blocks were on fire. *Ostòras would be delighted.* Even after death, an älf remained bent on destruction.

Ishím Voróo, 5452nd division of unendingness (6491st solar cycle), summer

Aiphatòn was woken by the gentle, steady rise and fall of the surface he was lying on.

It evoked memories of a very special encounter.

He opened his eyes and found himself back on the deck of a ship. The stars sparkled in the night sky above and the air was cool and pleasant.

He turned carefully and got his bearings. The sails on the large mast had filled out and they were moving quickly over the waves; from time to time sea spray spattered on the bow but it didn't reach him.

On top of a knee-high rope pulley, he spotted a squat figure sucking on a pipe. Grey smoke drifted across the otherwise deserted deck like mist. 'Ah, my friend has woken up,' he heard the friendly, deep voice of a dwarf.

Aiphatòn hauled himself to his feet and peered over the side of the ship, looking out for land but not finding it anywhere. 'Where am I?'

The dwarf, whose face lay in the shadow of the mast, puffed several times in a row. 'My home,' came the amused answer.

'How did I end up on the ship?' He looked at his arms, his stomach and legs, and they seemed unscathed. 'I was falling down the cliff-face and . . . am I dead?' He knew humans who believed that their souls would be brought to the kingdom of the dead by a ferryman. *Could they be right?*

The dwarf laughed and leaned forwards so that starlight fell on his features. He wore his brown beard cropped very short and there was a mischievous twinkle in his eye. A gold mark glittered on the hand that held his pipe. 'Then I would be too,' he retorted and laughed softly. 'Which I would find very inconvenient, I must admit.' He placed his other fingers on the handle of his axe whose blade was made of diamonds on one side and long, stone spikes on the other. 'I've got a few more things planned.'

Aiphatòn's eyes widened. 'Tungdil?' He walked over to his friend. By now he had recognised the ship whose planks he was standing on: he was aboard the same boat he'd met the dwarf on long ago in order to find out more about himself and the Inextinguishables. 'Are we travelling across Weyurn's lakes?'

'So you might think, yes.' Tungdil sucked on the pipe again. 'Or we are figments of our imagination because I'm actually somewhere else.' He looked around. 'What can it mean?'

Aiphatòn lifted his shoulders slowly. 'Did the gods send us back in time so that we could decide things differently from how we once decided them?'

Tungdil puffed away at his pipe and pointed at him with the mouthpiece in agreement. 'Oh now *that* would be fun all right!'

'It truly would be. I would not bring the älfar to Girdlegard,' he said bitterly. 'I would go back to the Blue Mountains alone and would not waste any time in killing Lot-Ionan. Finally, I would pounce on the Dsôn Aklán and annihilate them.'

'Good plan, my friend!' The dwarf smiled at him. 'I'd come to your aid and I'd be more on my guard against the triplets.'

A large breaker from starboard crashed against the hull and hit them both with a deluge of water.

Aiphatòn was knocked off his feet and slid over the wet planks to the other side. He quickly grabbed at a rope to stop himself plunging into the suddenly rough sea.

'Tungdil!' he cried. 'Where are you?'

Another wave came crashing down on top of him, filling his mouth with salty water. His eyes burned and he had to close them.

'Hey!' screamed Tungdil.

He wanted to answer the dwarf, but a burbling sound was all that came out of his mouth.

'Hey!' came the cry again, but the voice had changed, becoming higher and more girlish.

Aiphatòn coughed and opened his eyes – and was looking into the face of an anxious, black-haired älf-woman.

Bewildered, he noticed that drops of water were rolling off his face and that the ground was rising and falling as before. *I'm on a ship and . . . in the next dream?* The last thing he could remember was falling over the parapet and tumbling down the rock face in Dâkiòn.

She was looking at him with yellowish-green eyes. 'Finally awake?' She straightened up, revealing as she did so her light leather armour with a red symbol and a white shirt underneath. She wore linen trousers and sandals. 'Get yourself ready. We're landing soon. And my advice is: have a good story ready for my godmother, or else you'll fall from the cliffs a second time.' She stepped back.

She was replaced by a bald älf in a pale robe who held out a mug of foul-smelling liquid to him, which Aiphatòn was presumably meant to drink. His eyes were black, as they were meant to be.

'How long have I been sleeping and how did I get on board? Where are we going?' Even more questions flashed through his mind. 'And *who* are *you*?' He sat up carefully in the swinging hammock and almost fell out. He was not accustomed to lying like this.

'I am Ávoleï, commander of the *Mistress of the Sea*. My godmother is Modôia, the monarchess of Elhàtor, which is where we're going to land within this splinter of unendingness, although the sea is stormy. You seem to be churning up the elements.' The älf-woman nodded to the mug. 'You're going to drink that. It will give you your strength back. A magical healing was too dangerous. After you nearly barbecued my cîanoi in your sleep, I didn't allow another recovery spell to be applied.'

'I'd manage it on a second attempt,' the bald älf interjected. 'I could feel where the magical abutment started.' He gestured towards the plates. 'A more than unusual job. Unique.'

He could feel it? 'My apologies, but it's rarely under my control,' Aiphatòn tried to explain.

'We noticed that.' She smiled but it didn't look friendly. 'As soon as you feel able, come on deck.' Ávoleï went to the door. 'Oh, and you were asleep for eleven moments so you missed the whole crossing.'

Modôia? Where have I heard that name before? Aiphatòn took the potion and knocked it back.

The healer and cîanoi watched him as he did so and took the empty mug back. 'The external wounds are mostly healed,' he explained and pointed to the bandages on Aiphatòn's thighs. 'The broken bones, well, you'll have to see for yourself. It's possible those places have knitted together.' He gestured towards Aiphatòn's chest. 'A blacksmith will have to repair that, although I wouldn't know how they'd do it.'

My armour! He lowered his head.

In the place where the death-dancer's dazzling blade had hit him, a hole the width of a finger gaped in the plate. Underneath he saw pink skin that looked freshly healed.

Aiphatòn placed his hand on it. *She could have killed me,* he realised to his shock. *The first opponent to have put me in that kind of danger.* If not for the fall from the battlement, he would have died at her hands, as far-fetched as that sounded.

'Do you know what happened?' he asked the healer quietly.

'Ávoleï will explain it to you,' the älf replied and got up. 'I'm forbidden from exchanging too many words with you because you're a prisoner. But don't worry: Elhàtor will deal with you fairly.'

'And will throw me off the cliffs if necessary, I hear.' Aiphatòn remained silent and moved his toes cautiously, not feeling any pain in his legs. *I'm afraid I'm going to have to quiz the älf-woman.* Very slowly, he placed one foot after the other on the creaky planks that trembled at intervals with the force of crashing waves. 'It seems the potions worked miracles,' he announced to the healer and stood up, only to realise that they had undressed him down to his loincloth.

'You have a remarkable constitution.' The älf was ready to offer him his hand as a support.

'Where are my spear and robe?'

'You didn't have a weapon on you when you were brought on board. And your . . . robe was as good as non-existent.'

Aiphatòn cursed. 'Then Dâkiòn can expect another visit from me,' he muttered grimly. *Preferably with an army from Elhàtor. And if I'm already there, I can thank Shôtoràs for his hospitality. In my own way. Which he will not survive.*

The healer handed him trousers and a shirt that reached down to the knee and Aiphatòn put them both on. 'What is wrong with her eyes?'

'Because they're not black?' The healer grinned. 'We use tinctures to preserve the white. It came into fashion to emphasise the beauty of the eyes. But I dare say it wouldn't be any use to you.'

That's deceitful. There would be no better way to pass yourself off as an elf in Girdlegard. Unsteady on his legs, he walked barefoot across the cabin to the door, went out and climbed the broad staircase whose steps were wet with spray and waves.

Cool, moist wind howled through the hatch and the waves hurled themselves against the deck, crashing dully. Snatches of bellowed orders reached his ears; sails were being reefed.

Aiphatòn stepped into the open air and the wind threatened to knock him over. He was familiar with storms from Girdlegard, he was familiar with seas that you crossed by ship, but a sea in such turmoil was another new experience. He tasted salt on his lips.

Ávoleï was standing tall at the helm and shouting her instructions over the thundering as if she were leading a battle against the elements.

Only one part of the sail was hoisted on the yards; the three main masts looked like dead trees. The wind whistled and screeched in the rigging.

The *Mistress of the Sea* careened to the side and performed a sharp turn that set them on course for the mouth of the harbour.

Aiphatòn saw four smaller escort ships surging over the crests of the waves to their right and left, racing ahead of them into the calmer dip.

The rain pelted steadily down on the crew. The thick haze from the clouds stopped him getting a good view of the town but the island looked bigger than he had imagined it would be.

And we thought there were practically no älfar left in the northern wasteland. Aiphatòn thought about Shôtoràs' remarks. He understood his attitude and his hatred of the Inextinguishables. *They just had no incentive to show off or conquer. Now we want to hear how . . .* Suddenly the penny dropped. *Modôia! The monarchess of the town is the älf-woman whose message I found in the deserted settlement and whose runes I destroyed! The sovereign mentioned that she had come from Girdlegard.*

Aiphatòn walked across the swaying deck to the stairs to the upper deck where Ávoleï stood. She needed to tell him more before he met her godmother.

The *Mistress of the Sea* entered the harbour and the rocking instantly eased off. The waves were significantly smaller than on the open sea, crashing against the harbour wall in clouds of spray.

You could feel the crew's tension easing. The almost-hundred-pace long ship seemed sturdy and reliable but a voyage always remained a risk.

Aiphatòn approached the älf-woman who gave some final instructions to the helmsman and then turned to him. 'Oh, excellent. So your broken bones have healed nicely?'

'Yes, they have.' Aiphatòn held on tight to the railing of the upper deck and noticed how far they were from the ground. *How many storeys has this monstrosity got?* 'Would you please tell me what happened? I can only remember the fall over the battlement.'

Ávoleï laughed. 'I wasn't there when they picked you up, but the warriors report that at first, they thought Shôtoràs had fired a burning sack of petrol at them that wouldn't fly properly.' She examined his body. 'A miracle, truly. And of course we're rather used to sorcery in Elhàtor. You must have shot down the rock face glowing like a comet and kissed the stone several times.' She reached out a hand and ran it over the scratches on his plates of armour. 'Your magic checked your fall, I'd assume. I've been told countless runes on this lit up. You did hit the ground, but you were still alive. The warriors dragged you away before the rockfall that followed. They brought you to the river and so to me. We were just dropping off a hostage from Dâkiòn there in our dinghy and I decided to take you with us.' She winked. 'Anyone who is thrown out of the town like that can only be a friend of ours.'

Aiphatòn had no choice but to believe her explanations as he had no memories. 'Then I owe my life to you,' he said thoughtfully.

'That you do.' Ávoleï seemed pleased by this. 'I'll claim my reward at some point.' Now, her gaze looked different than before. 'And you are a shintoït, as the cîanoi suspects?'

'Yes.' Lying was pointless, his eyes gave him away sooner or later.

'Then you must be Aiphatòn, the emperor of the älfar. My

godmother will be pleased to hear your story and why you turned your back on Tark Draan.' The statement sounded neutral. 'If you've come to seize control . . .'

'No,' he interrupted her immediately. 'And that was also not the reason why I was thrown off the walls.'

'Shôtoràs doesn't need a reason. You come from Tark Draan and to him you're dirt. That's enough for the old fool.' Ávoleï gave some quick orders and the *Mistress of the Sea* came alongside the harbour wall and dropped anchors at the bow and stern before being tethered. 'But did he know who you are?'

Aiphatòn nodded. 'Yes.'

The älf-woman was watching the ship's landing very carefully, looking visibly pleased with how it was progressing; from time to time she wiped the rainwater out of her eyes. A ramp was placed between dry land and the ship's wall to allow everyone to disembark easily. 'Then he must think you're dead.'

'My spear will be a memento he won't be enjoying for very long.'

'You want to go back?' Ávoleï looked at him in surprise and walked towards the steps to the lower deck. 'Come on. They'll have dry clothes for us in the palace. My godmother will be glad to see you.'

'I hope so. I can't rely on surviving falls from cliffs forever,' he replied and followed her. 'My spear is too special and too unique to leave in ignorant hands.'

'Believe me: Shôtoràs will find a warrior who knows how to fight using your weapon.'

They walked down the ramp side by side and stepped onto the harbour wall which was humming with activity. The crews from the escort ships were unloading cargo. The wall of the *Mistress of the Sea* soared up imposingly behind them.

'What is this kind of ship called?' He just had to ask.

'It's a rònke, frekorian in origin,' explained the commander. 'We improved its performance and changed its appearance to suit our tastes better. When it's in formation with the four sailing boats you see over there, it's unbeatable. You don't need to know any more than that.'

A carriage rolled up and they got in.

'To come back to our original topic: the spear obeys nobody but me. It's forged from the same alloy as the plates.' Aiphatòn sat down and touched the armour.

'And yet I see a hole in it that I presume wasn't there before,' Ávoleï countered, no malice in her voice as she took a seat opposite him. She didn't seem concerned that she was wet through to her undergarments. 'You're in a part of Ishím Voróo where magic is incredibly strong. Let that be a warning to you. Our cîani are varied and they are blessed with gifts that would make a magus or maga from Tark Draan look like a schoolchild.'

Aiphatòn pictured the death-dancer with her glowing needle-dagger blades that had burnt through his armour. Just the thought of it was enough, the prickling spread through him again. 'Someone could have told me that earlier,' he murmured to himself. He stuck his little finger through the hole and clenched his teeth when his finger-tip touched the soft, pink flesh. *It must have been a deep wound.*

The carriage started to roll along.

'Let's consider it a merciful act of Samusin that my people were just off Dâkiòn at the instant you literally fell at their feet . . . or should I say: into their hands,' Ávoleï said and threw him a blanket so that he could dry himself off. 'Don't worry: you're my guest and because I saved your life, it belongs to me.'

'And what does that mean?'

The älf-woman took a second blanket and rubbed her head with it. 'It means my godmother can only throw you off the cliff once I've given her my permission.' She laughed to show him she'd been joking.

Aiphatòn joined in, dabbing the water off his face as well as his short, black hair which had grown back during the course of his adventure.

He thought the commander was more attractive than any other älf-woman he had met in the past solar cycles and yet she radiated something undefinable that he found confusing.

Ishím Voróo, Älfar town of Dsôn Dâkiòn, 5452nd division of unendingness (6491st solar cycle), summer

Shôtoràs was awoken in the early hours by a servant standing next to his bed and gently shaking his shoulder.

'What's happened?' he asked and was immediately wide awake. Under ordinary circumstances, nobody dared rouse him from his sleep.

'Saitôra is back from Elhàtor,' answered the underling and bowed apologetically. 'She brings news of your niece.'

'*Only* Saitôra?'

The älf nodded and held out the black housecoat for him which Shôtoràs slipped into as he clumsily got up. 'She came alone. The Elhàtorians dropped her off at the strait and our people brought her up the Tronjor.'

Shôtoràs reached for his walking stick and had his black leather, embroidered shoes put on his feet before limping out of his chambers in a hurry. He entered the Hall of Entreaties where just a few splinters ago he had received that ridiculous emperor of the curs. He swept his silvery grey hair back but didn't waste time combing it. There were more important things to do.

Saitôra was standing forlornly in the middle of the room as he limped up the steps to the platform and sat down at the desk, beckoning her over impatiently as he did so. She was wearing a blue and silver dress with an Elhàtorian pattern woven into it.

She should have been allowed to get changed. 'Come closer,' he said. 'And don't be afraid. I know that Irïanora dispatched you and the other two on a flimsy pretext.'

The young älf-woman nodded in relief. 'I feel so stupid, sovereign.' She took an envelope out of her dress, glanced at it and held it in her right hand.

'And so you should. Letting yourself be exploited by my niece to provoke a war is the most foolish thing I've been forced to witness in recent divisions of unendingness,' he replied. 'What have you got there? And where are the rest of you river sailors?' He extended his hand.

Saitôra passed the envelope up to him. She had to stand on her tiptoes; her fingers trembled. 'Gathalor and Iophâlor are dead. The scouts from Elhàtor killed them after pulling them out of the water unharmed,' she told him, her voice cracking. 'In front of my eyes, they smashed their skulls to pieces.' She swallowed. 'Irïanora stayed on the island in exchange for me. Sovereign, I was never in favour of the war, but the way they . . .'

'Silence,' he ordered quietly and icily.

The colour had drained from his face and he only just managed to stop the anger lines. *Gathalor – dead? Inàste, keep my soul from shattering!*

He opened the sealed message that was addressed to him in his niece's hand.

Dear Uncle,

    I stayed in Elhàtor to allow Saitôra to travel home and so that I could send you these words. This message has been smuggled past the vigilant rulers so that you could learn the truth. Gathalor and Iophâlor are dead, murdered by Modôia's vile scouts.

And my life will end too if an inhabitant of Dâkiòn travels past the strait, downstream to the sea.

In the eyes of the monarchess, I am the supposed guarantor of peace between the towns – but I ask this of you nevertheless: attack! With everything our warriors and our cîani are capable of.

They have built a fleet that they keep hidden in a grotto in the middle of the island. Saitôra has seen it with her own eyes.

Modôia is deceiving you and all inhabitants of Dâkiòn about her true intentions. The pretence of a peaceful co-existence has been exposed. She will attack us!

It can't be much longer now.

I know you never thought my behaviour was good and that you believe enough älfar blood has already been shed. But if you don't spill it, the monarchess will start to, and she will have an answer for everything that you throw at her.

I would gladly give my life for this.

I'm thinking of you and Dâkiòn and extend my condolences to you!

Don't let Gathalor and Iophâlor have died in vain.

Irïanora

Shôtoràs ripped up the letter and placed the scraps in a neat pile, Saitôra watching on wide-eyed. *You're the one who has been exposed, niece. Even with this pain that you inflict on me, you're ultimately hurting yourself.*

'Don't be fooled by her,' he told the young älf-woman. 'Irïanora stayed because she was afraid of what I would do to her. I sent her to bring all three of you back home unharmed. I vowed she would receive the severest punishment if anything happened to just one of you.' That wasn't completely true but it was enough to make his action look reasonable.

'But the fleet!' Saitôra protested.

'Who said you could read the letter?' he thundered, and she flinched. 'Have you seen the fleet?' Shôtoràs knitted his eyebrows. 'Did you stand in this grotto my niece has written about and see the countless ships the monarchess wants to use to come here?'

The young älf-woman hesitated.

Another Iriänora lie. That was enough of an answer for him. 'You can go.' The sovereign looked at the scraps of paper. 'And remember: the scouts from Elhàtor did not kill Gathalor and Iophâlor, it was Iriänora. She sent you out and made you breach the agreement,' he added quietly. 'I will adhere to the peace treaty and I will not fall for this trap from my niece and her warmongering friends. *You* shouldn't either.' His piercing stare embarrassed Saitôra. 'Go back home and be glad that you were allowed to leave the island, but keep quiet about your adventure. That is an order! Iriänora will be very resourceful. She's cunning.' *And if the Elhàtorians kill her, so much the better.*

Saitôra bowed and walked away, striding through the doorway and vanishing.

Shôtoràs shook his head slowly. *As if these whiny, heroic words would hold any sway with me.* He would never embark on open warfare.

He looked at the window. The first strong rays of sunshine were falling through it and his eyes were turning black. *I'm not afraid of the scum from Tark Draan.*

His thoughts revolved around the countermeasures to be taken if this secret fleet really existed.

Work on the canal was coming along well. By the time winter came, the final touches would be complete and the weirs to dam the Tronjor and allow it to flow the way it needed to would be in place.

The soldiers and barrels of petrol were already making their way to selected sites along the bank so that the flammable liquid could be deployed against the attackers' ships if needed.

Besides, we also have our cîani. Elhàtor will never reach our walls. Shôtoràs placed his lame leg on the desk and massaged the thigh. Over the last few moments of unendingness the pain had worsened. For some unknown reason, the nerves were rebelling against every kind of treatment, from compresses to magic.

He thought about the warning from the self-proclaimed emperor about the botoicans' army. *A hundred thousand. That would be vast.*

He wanted to dispatch Vailóras and four of his best warriors to scout out whether there was any truth to the unwelcome guest's claim. He wasn't afraid of the disorganised packs and hordes the mind-meddlers' armies went into battle with. *As long as no botoican has had tactical training superior to mine*, Shôtoràs mused.

The feuds between families and within the inner circles of the magicians were not revealed to any outsiders.

Shôtoràs had heard that over the last few divisions of unendingness there had been unrest in their ranks and that war had been raging for around a hundred moments. But as to who was lining up against whom, he had no idea. They remained a closed unit, split up into families who fought bitterly.

Destroy us? Ridiculous. The Nhatai family is far too small to achieve that. His gaze wandered to the large red stain and spatters on the wall next to the stairs – they had really seeped into the plaster due to the effect of the magical discharge. *My best cîanoi, destroyed by his own spell.*

Shôtoràs pictured the impact of the reflected spell and the älf's horrified face. The heat surged towards the sovereign, followed by the smell of charred flesh and spilt blood.

In spite of the closed windows and doors, a light breeze blew steadily, carrying the scent of red-hot steel.

He smiled and faced straight ahead again. He saw Tanôtai standing in the Hall of Entreaties, her sinewy hands clasped at her belt, her slender but strong arms hanging down loosely. 'Have you found him?'

'Not yet,' answered the red-haired death-dancer. 'The little emperor has been missing since he fell over the battlements. I think he's under the piles of rock.'

Shôtoràs couldn't help grinning because as soon as talk turned to Aiphatòn, everyone referred to him using the most noble title as an insult. 'Can you rule out him having used magic to save himself?'

Tanôtai looked hesitant. 'We've seen what he's capable of. That explosion when my magic met his was unparalleled.'

Shôtoràs remained quiet because he had been expecting the discovery of a body, not this at all. 'It would have been good to get hold of him. I would have been so pleased to cut those pieces of metal off his body and have a weapon forged for you out of them.'

She smiled gratefully. 'You do me too much honour.'

Shôtoràs took his leg off the wooden desktop. 'It was a mistake to try and chase him,' he told her and got up, leaning on his stick. 'We should have allayed his suspicions and sent him to Elhàtor. He could have killed the monarchess and her son for us. We would have been free of all suspicion and could have blamed an old feud between them. The filth from Tark Draan would be history.' He limped slowly down the steps.

'That would still leave Leïóva and her daughter.'

'The elf-woman is still alive only because she is Modôia's confidante. Without her protection, she'd be cast out by the Elhàtorians along with her brat. And then the inhabitants would come to us, to Dâkiòn, looking for help, which I would offer.' Shôtoràs placed one hand on her bare shoulder, the tattoos feeling warmer than the untattooed skin. 'But I've let this opportunity slip through my fingers. I expect the emperor has saved himself with a spell by now.'

Tanôtai pulled a sour face. 'I'm having the cliff searched carefully anyway. The men will abseil down and the cîani will go out looking with floating spells. It's possible he's hanging from a ledge that we couldn't see at night. And there's always the mountain of debris.'

Shôtoràs squeezed her shoulder gently and then drew his hand back. 'Before that happens, go and shadow Saitôra. If she tries to talk to someone about her time on Elhàtor and stir up the inhabitants of my town, silence her.'

'Would she do that?' The very slender, red-haired älf-woman did not look convinced.

'When she gave me the message from my useless niece, I saw she was carrying a second envelope, hidden in a fold of her dress. Since she didn't mention it, I'm afraid Irïanora has come up with a plan to set the residents against me and make loud calls for war. I cannot allow that.'

'I see. The murder should take place secretly, I take it . . . ?'

'In complete secrecy. Throw the body off the large bridge.'

Tanôtai bowed and in the blink of an eye, she had vanished with that quiet sound that the spell made every time. The death-dancer's powers were one-of-a-kind. The breeze she unleashed sprang up suddenly and blew the scraps of paper off the table.

Spinning and whirling, they rained down on the flagstones, some falling with the letters facing up and some face down. They lay at his feet in no discernible pattern. Just two little shreds floated towards the ceiling as if the sunbeam streaming inside was pushing them.

We've got Nodûcor now, but he's no use to us at all. Annoyed, he stepped over the scraps and limped out of the room and down the corridor to the kitchen to have his breakfast. *He falls into our laps like this by Samusin's providence, and shortly afterwards the only cîanoi who could have taken that damned half-mask off him dies!*

Shôtoràs passed through his palace without taking any pleasure in the artworks and interior decoration.

When he had heard from a merchant that there were unpredictable winds raging and howling through the mountains all of a sudden and that they seemed to be blowing from every direction at the same time, Shôtoràs had sat up and taken notice. The legends of the wind-voice had always been his favourite stories and suddenly it sounded as if there might be a grain of truth to them.

So he had his best cîanoi build a transportable container that was impossible to escape from, as well as making shackles and a mask to prevent the wind-voice being able to unleash its power.

The emperor must have freed him, he mused.

But since neither Aiphatòn nor Nodûcor knew who was really behind the abduction, they came to Dâkiòn unsuspectingly. To the people who had ordered it.

Shôtoràs walked slowly down the staircase. *I desperately need him. He would be perfect for literally blowing the arrogant botoicans away. And of course the unworthy Elhàtor with its traitors, the scum, the elf-woman and its frekorian mercenary roots.*

Surely there was more than one half-breed älf among the residents of the island – the sovereign would have staked his life on it.

I'm just a lock, a pinch of magic and a little metal away from my greatest victory – and nobody would ever suspect a thing.

Having reached the ground floor, Shôtoràs was following the smell of toast drizzled with melted lard, topped with a thin layer of egg and a scattering of fresh herbs. There was nothing better for his stomach and his mood of a morning.

He *loved* giving the impression of being the peacekeeper.

Under no circumstances did he want to hand Modôia a reason to steal a march on him with an attack. Although his preparations were going well, he felt uneasy at the same time. A battle could always take a different course from the one the strategists and his dear friend Pasôlor had planned in advance.

It won't be long until I know more.

Shôtoràs entered the kitchen and was greeted warmly by the servants.

He went over to his seat by the window, through which he had an excellent view over Dâkiòn, and his meal was served. He ate with relish.

On his orders, four cîani were looking into a way of neutralising the protective spells on the half-mask.

Assuming Cushròk captured the right älf, he will unleash a storm for me, a hurricane even, that will churn up the sea and tear Elhàtor apart. The sovereign took a bite of the crispy, delicious sandwich as he gazed at the pale roofs of his town. *The waves will rage over the island until nothing is left standing and the rabble have perished. The survivors might find refuge with us but I will be extremely selective.*

One of his cooks served him a tea made from fresh mint and herbs, and Shôtoràs nodded pleasantly to him.

Nobody would be able to tell from his demeanour what thoughts and images were currently going through his mind. He had led the life of a cunning politician too long for that.

The wind-voice represented the solution to every problem.

But if Nodûcor was just an älf with no special gift, he would have him killed and send a new battalion out on the hunt. *Until I've got my wind-voice. It's in Ishím Voróo somewhere.*

Making Nodûcor compliant was possible, he had no worries on that score.

Wave after wave will break over them, whether they're on the river or in Elhàtor. Irïanora can drown, as far as I'm concerned. That's her punishment for Gathalor's death by negligence. Shôtoràs smiled with satisfaction. *Nature can be cruel.*

Especially when someone is commanding it to be.

Saitôra hurried through the ravine-like streets, making her way towards the Death-dancer.

She knew the institute where they taught you how to move to become one of the exceptional warrior-women or warriors.

Her own cautious attempts had not ended in success so she had dropped out before her first magical tattoo was due to be inked. This procedure could be fatal – the energy had to be infused into the poisonous ink very carefully. If the needles pierced too deep, you died an excruciating death.

Saitôra reached the locked door that had been set into the access gate. She was still wearing the dress gifted to her in Elhàtor. She would take it off later; she wanted to be sure she carried out her tasks first. Anûras was apparently one of the experts who gave lessons, although she didn't know him.

'It's probably still too early,' she murmured and took a step backwards to look up at the windows. 'Hey, can anyone hear me? I have a message for Anûras,' she called loudly and clearly.

She waited a while and repeated her words.

Eventually a window opened and a sleepy älf stared down at her; his long, grey-black hair fell onto his bare torso where colourful runes had been etched. 'What do you think you're doing?' he said, irritated. 'The sun is just coming up and if you . . .'

'Are you Anûras?'

'I am, and I'm grumpy too.'

'Prove to me that you're Anûras.'

'I can wake up other älfar who will give you a beating while they confirm to you that I'm me,' he replied.

Saitôra reached underneath her cloak and took out the envelope Iriänora had given her. 'From a mutual friend,' she replied softly. 'Meant for your eyes only.'

'Could this not have waited?'

'Her name is Iriänora,' she cried, hoping he would hurry up. She was angry that the sovereign refused to declare even a small threat against Elhàtor. Two murders were two murders. *Iriänora could never have wanted that.* She looked around before adding conspiratorially: 'It's about Elhàtor and how things are taking a turn for the worse.' She didn't want to imply any more; her heart was beating rapidly.

'I'll throw on some clothes quickly.' The corners of Anûras' mouth clenched, and he disappeared from the window.

Saitôra found the idea of the älf not wearing any clothes thrilling and couldn't help smiling mischievously.

'Did the sovereign not order you to keep your silence?' whispered the silhouette near her. 'You know your punishment.'

A spy! As she turned around, Saitôra drew her dagger and stabbed at her pursuer.

Tanôtai pirouetted around her and dodged the attack with elaborate grace, the needle-dagger gleaming white in her hands, which were covered in tattooed tendrils. 'You've got to be quicker than that to kill me,' she murmured.

She avoided every one of Saitôra's attacks that followed by writhing like a snake, using swift sequences of steps as though she were dancing to a tune; she swung her arms nimbly as she did so and drew shapes in the air with the glowing blades. The gleam of the light was still visible for a few heartbeats before new lines flared, criss-crossing the old ones.

The lock on the small door clicked.

'Dâkiòn ought to know what I've seen,' Saitôra panted with exertion and missed Tanôtai for the umpteenth time. Tanôtai suddenly wrapped a hand around the back of Saitôra's neck as if they were dance partners.

'Perhaps it should.' The red-haired älf-woman suddenly pulled her towards her, looking like she was stealing a kiss. A thin, dazzling blade shot through Saitôra's neck. 'But *you* will not be announcing a thing.'

Tanôtai expertly intercepted her collapsing, gasping opponent, spun underneath one of Saitôra's arms, then heaved her onto her back, picked the envelope up off the ground and vanished into the shadows with the dead body.

Then the door opened.

Anûras, wrapped in a pale-yellow cloak, looked out but couldn't see the messenger. 'Hey!' He stepped into the street and looked around, searching for her. 'Where are you?'

But Saitôra had vanished.

Chapter XI

Anyone who makes the same mistake twice must love pain.

Wise saying of the Älfar
Collected by Carmondai, master of word and image

Tark Draan, Human kingdom of Gauragar, 5452nd division of unendingness (6491st solar cycle), autumn

'As soon as night falls, let's see who's holed up in this hideaway.' Carâhnios gave an evil laugh. 'You know how this goes now, black-eye.'

Carmondai grimaced and brushed his long, brown hair back with his fingers. Every bone in his body hurt; travelling like this did not agree with him. 'I take it I pretend to be the loud, clumsy älf again?' His gaze swept over the picturesquely colourful, autumnal landscape that stretched out in front of them.

There were no more gentle hills here, apart from the one they were standing on, which had an entrenchment-like path leading down from it. The zhadár had guided them to an area where the woods grew more thickly than in any other region. The mixture of different deciduous and evergreen trees created an unparalleled array of colours.

Carmondai was profoundly sorry he was not able to capture this splendour on paper. With ink, it would remain a uniform black or at most grey. 'What have the Aklán come up with this time to make sure their refuge is somewhere nobody would willingly set foot? Another temple?'

'Much more sophisticated than that: a *legend*.' Carâhnios chuckled. 'I can tell you were thrown into that dungeon, otherwise you would have written it down long ago.'

'And what is the legend?'

'I'm not a storyteller like you so I'll avoid showing off with embellished details.' The zhadár pointed to the section of woodland where nothing but black firs grew. 'A creature lived there who devoured the best warriors and warrior-women of the älfar – the ones who set out two hundred cycles ago to destroy the creature. Four charcoal-burning villages fell victim to the creature so they decided to abandon the area.' He set the pony to trotting.

Carmondai sighed. 'That was the legend?'

'Yes. That was it.'

No, he's no storyteller. 'And that deters humans from venturing into the area?'

'Like any legend, it contains certain truths. The charcoal-burning villages were killed by the älfar themselves, the people were butchered, the pieces scattered brutally all over the place. Even along the street,' Carâhnios said, pulling his helmet off. Short, black hair emerged from underneath. He looked like a dwarf shadow brought to life, having snuck away from its master; the fact he was sitting on a white pony reinforced this unusual quality. 'Of course travellers and merchants noticed this and combined with the relevant legend that I've just told you . . .'

'That wasn't a legend. It was a summary,' Carmondai interrupted him, cursing the chains and the rocking and the ink. *I will have to memorise it.* 'How long will the legend last now that there are no älfar left to make it look like the beast is still alive?'

'As soon as just one brave soul goes inside, it won't be long till they are found torn into nice little pieces.'

'So there are mechanical devices then?' Carmondai guessed.

Carâhnios wedged his helmet under his arm, clapping too hard and too long, and chuckling in his crazed way. 'The Aklán have had clever traps laid – they reset themselves after they've been triggered. The last murder by the supposed beast was eighty orbits ago. That time, all that was left of a woodcutter were shavings.'

Carmondai was following the zhadár. 'Where exactly is the hideaway?'

'In the centre of the four villages. The entrance to it is in the trunk of what looks like a dead, old fir tree. But it's made of painted granite and it's protected by even more traps.' He winked at him. 'Are you excited yet?'

'Very.'

In silence, they rode along the path southwest towards Oakenburgh until Carâhnios steered his pony to the right through the undergrowth and away from the road; he put his helmet back on as he did so.

It looks like things are getting dangerous. Carmondai stayed close behind until the zhadár stopped on the bank of a small stream a mile later and dismounted.

'Let's wait here. The first village is half a mile away.' He watered his steed and removed his prisoner's chains.

The älf slid out of the saddle and stretched. The densely packed firs gave the sunlight a greenish tinge, and there was a strong smell of moss, resin and earth. Needles crackled under their feet. The deciduous trees were harder to spot. *As if they wouldn't venture into the darkness.* 'A beautiful wood.'

'If you're an elf.' Carâhnios chuckled. 'But why do you like it? Is it kinship with the pointy-ears that's making you feel that way?'

Carmondai led his horse to the water to let it drink too. 'My way of seeing things is not necessarily the same as everyone else's.' He breathed in the cool air that smelled of mushrooms. He quickly scooped up some of the gushing water and washed his face with the little piece of soap that he guarded like a treasure, then drank plenty of water. *Cold and delicious.* 'A wood is a beautiful thing.'

'Even if it's not on fire?'

Carmondai smiled. 'Is that the zhadár in you speaking or the groundling?'

'Someone who doesn't like woods,' Carâhnios replied pensively and pointed upwards. 'You have to keep an eye on the ground as well as on all the branches above you to spot dangers. *That* is what I don't like about them.'

They unsaddled the animals and then each lay down on a blanket.

While the groundling fell asleep straight away despite still having his helmet on, Carmondai used the opportunity to fill page after page with sketches of his impressions of the wood; his thoughts wandering all the while.

Carâhnios still hadn't told him how many hideaways there were. He was really hoping there were more than a dozen, preferably scattered all over Girdlegard, although he himself thought that was out of the question. That way he would have more time to devise his plan of escape.

Together with the Thirdlings, the älfar had ruled in Idoslane, Urgon and Gauragar. Therefore his tribe's secret refuges were in these realms, where residents were overjoyed by the freedom they'd gained.

After the end of the occupation and foreign rule, the people had elevated a young woman called Mallenia to be their queen. The

warrior-woman of Ido descent had made a name for herself in the previous cycles as a freedom fighter against the Aklán. The reward for her
life-threatening service was the throne.

As far as Carmondai had been able to make out in the last orbits, a
descendant of Rodario the Incredible ruled over Urgon, because even
the actor had taken part in decisive battles and played an important
role.

*Actors as kings. That's what we've come to. Mere barbarians can do it
too. A fool on the throne ensures laughter, but never order.* Carmondai's
gaze darted towards the snoring zhadár. *Unfortunately he's not a source
of more detailed information.*

He took a break from the drawing he'd begun of a withering
leaf caught in a spider's web. He was desperate to know what the
young sovereign Mallenia looked like. Apparently she was blonde,
tall, a true warrior-woman and good-looking – by human standards,
anyway.

Carmondai remembered her ancestor, the hero and prince Mallen
of Idoslane, so he drew a feminine, slightly altered version of his face.

After a while, he looked critically at the result. *I wonder if she looks
like that?*

A stifled scream made Carmondai jump. He only just managed not
to tip the ink pot over his version of Mallenia.

He looked over at Carâhnios – the noise had come from his throat.

The groundling was sitting on the blanket, the vial with the newly
acquired elixir in his right hand. He seemed to have licked a drop of it
off the index finger of his left hand. His gaze was fixed, his eyes were
open wide. His breathing was very irregular, stopping for several
heartbeats only to start again far too fast.

Carmondai looked at him in a calculating way. *If he were to die
now . . . or if I kill him . . .*

Bolts of light flashed underneath the zhadár's black skin, an outright storm brewing on his face. No emotion was discernible on it.

The älf looked at the tempting dagger that Carâhnios carried at his side. *Should I risk it? But what would happen afterwards?*

Then the zhadár uttered a low sound, and at the same time the tension eased and his body relaxed. He gasped for air as though he'd done a strenuous run, staring at his index finger. 'It was just one drop,' he whispered hoarsely. 'Just *one* drop, but . . .' He swallowed and put the vial away with trembling hands.

'So the remedy works?'

Carâhnios ignored him, his Adam's apple bobbing up and down. First he closed the visor, then his eyes, and lay down again.

There it was, my chance. But Carmondai didn't worry for long. Now that he knew what the reaction to taking it was, he was going to be prepared the next time. *We'll see if your next drop is also your last, zhadár.*

He picked up the page with the beginnings of the dying leaf drawing and completed it by the time darkness fell – it descended quickly on the travellers in the wood.

His vast knowledge of the älfar was in fact his greatest treasure and his most valuable asset. *I've got to get rid of him without them throwing me into a dungeon and torturing me.* Carmondai felt more than capable of suitably manipulating a person. *All I need now is the opportunity.*

Mist was rising off the moss and creeping up the tree trunks like the tide of a ghostly sea. The haze rippled and broke, swirling, on the trees; the temperature dropped significantly.

Carmondai wrapped the pages in wax paper before the moisture could get at them. *Pity. I would have loved to draw this scene.* He could feel a thin film of moisture forming on his shabby cloak.

Carâhnios had got up and seemed to be his old self again. 'Let's go.' He found one of the familiar bottles with a dash of the silvery substance in his luggage and pressed it into the älf's hand. 'As I said: you know how this goes. But watch out for traps.'

'How about you warn me?'

'And let the black-eye know there are two of us?' He snorted derisively. 'Plus it makes your escape more convincing if you fear for your life and have to struggle.' He pointed into the wood. 'Onward, my unwilling ally. But woe betide you if you let the bottle break.' The zhadár grinned demonically from inside his helmet. 'If you do, I'll take *your* blood, you know!'

Carmondai didn't doubt that. He set off down the path, picking up his rucksack and a bundle of pages first.

The mist, which was up to his thighs at this point and had looked picturesque until just now, turned out to be treacherous: he couldn't see the ground at all, let alone whether a snare, sword or harmless moss was in store for him. So he moved slowly, feeling his way forwards with the tips of his boots.

He soon reached the village, which was nothing more than a small cluster of dilapidated huts that couldn't have looked much different even when they were inhabited. The wood had already reclaimed large sections of them. Small trees rose up in the middle of the settlement, pushing the buildings sideways as they grew, smashing roofs or forcing them apart. Here and there lay bits of bone that had been bleached by the sun or were overgrown with moss like greyish scabs.

Now what? Keep going straight? Carmondai looked around and couldn't see the zhadár anywhere. With a bit of imagination it was possible to interpret whirls in the haze as clues to where the groundling was sneaking along.

As he was not getting any whispered instructions, he walked cautiously on, through the village and into the steadily rising mist that now enveloped him up to his waist.

Carmondai was feeling increasingly tense and he was sweating. The closer he got to the hideaway, the more likely it was that he would encounter a trap.

Then he spotted a weather-beaten tree trunk just under five paces high that looked like the top had snapped off.

If Carâhnios had not told him it was painted granite, Carmondai would have walked unsuspectingly past.

How loud do I have to be for someone to hear me? He didn't think stamping his feet was a good idea because of the traps, and falling over or fake limping were out of the question too. His thoughts revolved less around his opponent than around the deadly mechanisms. The wood-cutter had been found in *shavings*.

Carmondai stood motionless in the mist.

I could have been just about to reach it. He stooped, groping through the ephemeral whiteness for a branch or stone he could throw.

His fingers caught hold of a piece of wood, he picked it up – and there was a click.

Ishím Voróo, Älfar town of Dsôn Elhàtor, 5452nd division of unendingness (6491st solar cycle), summer

Aiphatòn left the chamber Ávoleï had shown him to. He was wearing a skirt-like robe of pale silk that went from his hips to his feet and reminded him strongly of his own clothes that he had worn in Girdlegard.

It was warm enough for him to skip wearing a shirt so the armoured plates on his skin were visible; he wore open-toed sandals on his feet. He was not used to having to go without his spear – the armoured gloves were the only weapons he had left. A servant had given him a shave and had cut the black hair on the nape of his neck level with his ears.

'Can I appear before your godmother like this?' he asked Ávoleï.

She scrutinised him hard and walked round him once, her yellowish green eyes looking him up and down. She herself was wearing a shirt and trousers underneath the armour with the commander's insignia. Her black hair was pinned up in a clasp. She was pleased with what she saw. 'You can. It may not be the usual fashion in Elhàtor, but she will be able to overlook that in the case of a guest and especially an älf from Tark Draan.' She pointed at his covered fingers. 'You couldn't take off the gloves?'

'They're bonded to me like the metal. Besides, there hasn't been any reason to do so.'

'No reason?' Ávoleï sounded astonished. 'Do the älf-women from your homeland like it when you touch them with iron?'

Aiphatòn did not respond.

'We are expected.' She took the lead through the palace and he looked around as he followed a pace behind.

Although he hadn't seen much of Dâkiòn, he noticed striking differences in the architectural styles and choice of decoration. Bones and bone segments had been used as ornamentation on the walls and ceilings, but they were all animal in origin. The few bones that came from other beings could be counted on one hand.

The palace had been built in a style that allowed light and air to stream through it, so that the sea wind could blow the heat of the orbit from the rooms. The predominant colour was white, while black was used only to pick out window frames, benches or unusual features in a room. He also saw many symbols that were not älfar.

Completely different from the Dsôns in Girdlegard. Aiphatòn did not yet know what he was going to tell Modôia about Girdlegard and the Dsôn Aklán. Ultimately, he feared triggering her desire to take revenge for the triplets' death and starting a war. *She will have plenty of questions for me.*

The prickling he had felt in Dâkiòn earlier had followed him to Elhàtor. His hope that this pain would stop if he moved away from the gigantic town proved false. He glanced at his armoured gloves, the runes on them flickering occasionally. *Could there be one of those fields here too?* He wanted to ask about it at some point.

Ávoleï turned right and led him into a courtyard covered by a vaulted glass ceiling with raindrops falling gently on it. Four bone fountains were gurgling in the corners, and in the middle was a platform and a suite of furniture around a low table. The water gave off a blossom-like, earthy scent.

They were expecting them.

'The älf-woman in the middle wearing the white dress is my godmother,' Ávoleï explained quietly. 'Directly to her right, wearing the blue cloak of a dolled-up dandy, that's Ôdaiòn, her son. The woman next to him, who is already imitating how he dresses, is Irïanora, a hostage from Dâkiòn and the niece of its sovereign. To the left is my mother, Leïóva.'

Aiphatòn tried to memorise the names.

They had reached the platform and were climbing onto it.

Ávoleï gestured towards the unoccupied thick cushion. Once the älf had lowered himself onto it, she made her way to her mother's side. 'I bring you the emperor of the älfar from Tark Draan,' she announced with a smug undertone. 'We picked him up when he was thrown off the highest cliff in the town by Shôtoràs' warriors.'

Laughter rang out, Ôdaiòn laughing loudest of all.

Aiphatòn put up with it. 'I came to Ishím Voróo by following your runes, Modôia,' he explained, not mentioning that he had removed them. 'My route took me straight from the settlement below the Jagged Crown to Dâkiòn where my journey took an . . . unpleasant turn and I lost my spear.'

'And a bit of your pride,' the monarchess' son chipped in.

'I don't need pride,' replied Aiphatòn politely. 'I leave pride to those who require constant reassurance.'

Modôia's gaze had become distant. 'My runes,' she repeated softly. 'I forgot that I'd painted them on the slopes.'

Leïóva, a slightly older version of her daughter, poured him some water. She favoured a delicate, white skirt and a top that emphasised the muscles in her bare shoulders. 'How did you find the settlement? It's well hidden. And nobody knows about it either.'

'That's not quite true. Carmondai wrote an unfinished *Ode to the Ten* – the Ten who had been dispatched by Aklán Firûsha to get to the bottom of the rumours about the village beyond the Jagged Crown,' he contradicted her. 'I followed a few criminals who were hoping for refuge there.' Aiphatòn had decided not to reveal anything about the incidents in Girdlegard for now. 'After I knocked them to the ground, I wanted to find out which parts of it were true.' He looked at the blonde monarchess as he picked up his glass. 'You and Leïóva were among the Ten.'

Ôdaiòn cleared his throat. 'With regard to the form of address, emperor, we prefer to use titles.'

Aiphatòn eyed Ôdaiòn scornfully. 'With regard to *my* address, there are so many titles you would need to mention that I'll permit you to disregard them. Therefore I will stick to my own ways.'

Ôdaiòn's lips thinned, but he did not venture to protest.

Ávoleï laughed and started to speak but was silenced by a gesture from her godmother.

'I was a member of a troop of veterans who accompanied Firûsha and she dispatched us to find runaway elves and their settlement in the Grey Mountains,' Modôia recounted. 'I discovered a village where the elves and dwarves had lived together. Inspired by the ambition of catching the last elf-woman, I went north, followed her tracks and came here.' She placed one hand on her son's back. 'Samusin was merciful in allowing my destiny in Ishím Voróo to turn out well.' She turned her gaze to Aiphatòn. 'The emperor himself followed my runes – what for? You have thousands of älfar at your command.'

'Who is in charge while you're away?' Ôdaiòn cut in inquisitively. 'Do you have enough confidence in them?'

'Everything is in order,' he answered evasively but without lying.

'Well.' Modôia's smile was ambiguous. 'Now, due to your rescue from Dâkiòn's warriors, you owe me your life, emperor.'

'I owe it to Ávoleï. It's already been agreed that she would like to come back to me on that issue.' In thanks, Aiphatòn bowed his head in her direction, looking as mischievous as possible. 'Elhàtor is beautiful, or what I've seen of it so far, at least. So there would be no reason for you to return to Girdlegard?'

Modôia looked astonished. 'Is that meant to be a veiled request? Bear in mind: you're not an emperor on this side of the mountains. You may be the son of the Inextinguishables but as Shôtoràs has made clear to you: their words count for nothing now.' She called the servants over to the table with the food to begin the meal. 'Dâkiòn and Elhàtor are home to the last of our people in Ishím Voróo. Our towns maintain a fragile peace.'

Irïanora lowered her head in shame.

'We simply want to live in harmony, devoting ourselves to art and not to quarrels of any kind between ourselves – or with anyone else, if it can be avoided.' Modôia's face suddenly distorted and she had to lean back into the cushions as if she had become exhausted in the blink of an eye.

Leïóva immediately tended to her, the women talking quietly to each other.

'When my mother came to Shôtoràs, she saw that she never wanted to live under his strict rule. Together with other älfar who felt the same way, she made her way to the sea and agreed a pact with the frekoriers who lived on this island,' her son took over the story. 'The mercenaries gradually died out, but we are carrying on the knowledge we inherited and are even refining it.' He raised his head slightly. 'Nobody from Elhàtor wants to march into Tark Draan and contest your right to the throne, emperor of the Älfar. Go back there and announce to our tribe that we exist. And I advise you to allow anyone who wants to move here to do so. That's all there is to say.'

Aiphatòn could tell that Ôdaiòn was to become the successor and was already enjoying the role. *His mother looks sick.* 'I think I will.' He believed the assurances that neither Dâkiòn's nor Elhàtor's rulers felt like making their way south and invading the weakened country; besides, he was happy to let them keep believing the Aklán were still alive.

All the same, Girdlegard will only be safe once the älfar are wiped out. Who knows what will sprout from the next seed? They might have passed their thirst for conquest on to the next generation. 'I ought to head back soon then,' he said, tasting dish after dish of the food on the table. *Fragile peace. That sounds perfect. I will know how to destroy it.*

Leïóva had got up and taken a small vial out of her pocket, opened it and handed it to the monarchess. 'And don't be tempted to have your army march against us,' she said. 'Perhaps you haven't felt it yet, but Ishím Voróo changed us, those of us who've lived here a long time and those who were born on this soil. Our cîani are strong.'

'I've had a foretaste of the new magical talents, thank you very much,' Aiphatòn replied and looked at Modôia. *That's what it is! A magical field that made anyone from Girdlegard unwell.* He toyed with the thought of getting himself some of the remedy that eased the monarchess' symptoms. But he could still tolerate it for now.

'Oh, our sorcerers know their craft better than the amateurs from Dâkiòn,' Ôdaiòn interjected pompously. 'No offence, Iriänora.' He pointed to the hole in the plate of armour. '*Our* cîani would have done a thorough job. Then there wouldn't *be* an emperor anymore.'

'Possibly.' Aiphatòn let the young älf brag so that he could marshal his own thoughts and find a way of setting the towns against each other. He glanced at Iriänora. *Killing the hostage? Would that be a reason for the sovereign to start a war?* He couldn't come up with anything off the top of his head, but perhaps something would emerge as the conversation went on.

'I've often mused with Mother about whether the Inextinguishables knew that the älfar would gain magical power if they pushed further into the north.' Ôdaiòn helped himself to delicious-smelling meat and sprinkled extra spices over it. 'The magical fields outside the old Dsôn had a transformative effect on us, on our innate gifts and also our magical power. Nearly every young älf in Elhàtor can do small tricks or make things float. *Without* any training.' He dipped each morsel into a dark brown gravy with a nutty aroma. 'I've come to the conclusion that the Inextinguishables were deliberately preventing an expansion of the kingdom. Out of fear for their power, which could certainly have been endangered.' He gave Aiphatòn an appraising look to gauge his opinion. 'Were your parents ultimately just ordinary älfar who had spent long enough in the north and came back strengthened? Hence couldn't *anyone* have become an Inextinguishable?'

Aiphatòn ate some of the flatbread deep-fried in hot, flavoured oil. 'I wouldn't put it past them.' He would not say any more than that. *Could I talk him into an alliance with me? He seems so hungry that he could be made to cast the first stone at Dâkiòn. His mother and Leïóva might want to keep him in check. But once the stone is soaring through the air . . .* He chewed and swallowed. 'Before I go back, I've got to pay Shôtoràs a visit and reclaim my spear that he's withholding,' he said, beginning the cautious process of sounding them out. 'It's an excellently crafted piece and responds to my magical commands. It's a symbol of my power and I wouldn't like to turn up in Girdlegard without it. There would be stigma, you know.'

'I wish you the aid of all the gods in that,' said Modôia, sitting up straight once more. The remedy Leïóva had administered was having its soothing effect.

'Well, I thought you could send a few good cîani along to accompany me. Or warriors. I just need a bit of a diversion to get into the town.' Aiphatòn looked innocent. 'It could be the beginning of a pact with Tark Draan and me. Think about it: more trade, more residents for Elhàtor, more security . . .'

'No,' the monarchess said immediately. 'You'll have to get the spear alone.'

'Even if Shôtoràs' power could become a danger to Elhàtor?' Aiphatòn looked to Iriänora.

But she shrugged her shoulders. 'My word won't be much use. My uncle hates me.'

'How much danger are you talking about?' Ôdaiòn gestured for him to go on. 'Let's listen to more of what the emperor has to say, Mother. I can imagine paying a visit to Tark Draan some time and doing an exchange.'

'I said *no*, Ôdaiòn!' his mother responded curtly. 'What would we want with foreign-born älfar? Just so they can die miserably like me and all the others because the magical radiation affects them too badly?'

'Fine. Let's just leave Tark Draan out of it,' her son promptly changed his tune. 'Our scouts have reported on a dam that Shôtoràs is having built and a canal that leads straight to the Tronjor and a large valley,' he said. Irïanora looked astonished at his words. She had clearly had no idea how well informed they were. 'We could use the opportunity to try and get insights into his plans. The emperor would be the best diversion for us because everyone would assume that he was searching the rooms for his spear. The sovereign would not be suspicious of Elhàtor. And if Aiphatòn makes off with his weapon, the old chap won't be using it.'

Well, those sound like preparations for war in Dâkiòn after all. Aiphatòn struggled not to grin broadly. He had judged the monarchess' son correctly. *I'll find a way of using this.*

Leïóva looked to Modôia and the pair of them communicated without words this time.

Aiphatòn could see how clearly the rejection of this daring plan was written in the black-haired confidante's eyes. *Her word carries more weight than the son's.* If he didn't convince Leïóva, he might as well be talking to a brick wall. 'Besides,' he added quickly, 'the sovereign is still holding a poor guy prisoner and I'd like to free him.'

'Where does this generosity come from, emperor?' Leïóva looked at him scornfully – and he felt the same confusion with her as he did with her daughter. They had the same intimidating aura. 'Is he a friend of yours?'

'To be honest: I first came across him in Ishím Voróo.'

Leïóva looked surprised. 'Wouldn't the fate of a random älf be all the same to you?'

'Absolutely. However, I rescued him from a band of thieves who were carrying him through the area in a sarcophagus. That oughtn't to have been in vain,' he told them, seeing the stirrings of emotion on Modôia and Leïóva's faces. 'A secret surrounds him that may also concern Elhàtor. I would need your opinion on that.' Aiphatòn fed them some more details. 'I found him shackled, bound with magical clamps I was able to remove. A half-mask over his face was the only thing I couldn't take off and it had runes on it too. We had to crush fruit into a pulp just to feed him.'

The table remained suspiciously silent after his final words.

The älfar from Elhàtor looked at each other in turn while Irïanora's brow furrowed.

'That cannot be,' Ôdaiòn eventually blurted out in bewilderment, running a hand through his brown hair. 'How did he find him?'

'I should have believed Cushròk when he told me about it,' whispered the monarchess, turning pale. 'It's happened now!'

'*What* has happened?' Irïanora understood just as little as Aiphatòn did and she gave vent to her astonishment at the top of her voice. This saved him asking the question. 'Who is this prisoner?'

'It has happened, the thing I have feared every division of unendingness since I arrived on Elhàtor,' said Modôia and looked to Leïóva for support. Her confidante lowered her head very slowly, seeming, in doing so, to agree with what the monarchess wanted to announce. 'I must order war against Dâkiòn.'

'What?' Irïanora leaped to her feet in horror. 'But my uncle hasn't done anything to justify that!'

All it took was one story? Aiphatòn had to suppress a loud cheer; at the same time, he noticed that the hostage's alarm was very clumsily feigned. *She's glad about the impending conflict too. How interesting.* 'Well, I feel honoured that you've changed your mind about helping me. But I wonder if an army needs to be dispatched immediately just because of this?' he asked, to give off the appearance of being calming.

Leïóva fixed her eyes on him. 'Is he still wearing the mask?' she demanded to know.

'Yes. I couldn't undo the protective spell.' Aiphatòn grinned. 'And the cîanoi who appeared to have the relevant knowledge died at my hands.' *Should I have kept that quiet?* he immediately thought, uneasily. *Not that the danger has been averted now.*

'Good. So we still have time to dispatch the fleet.' Ôdaiòn looked at Ávoleï. 'You know the Tronjor best. You'll lead them upstream.'

'Who,' Irïanora shouted, 'is this prisoner of my uncle's? A war is being started over him without hesitation. Do you not even want to look into what the emperor is saying?'

Leïóva turned to look at the young älf-woman. 'He has many names, but he is known as the wind-voice, provided the stories are true and Cushròk found the right creature. He is able to unleash storms that churn the sea up into such devastating waves that not one stone of our homeland will be left standing. Shôtoràs will use him against us to force us to surrender, there's no doubt about it.'

This is perfect! Samusin, you have given me a better weapon than I could have dreamt of. Aiphatòn had to be careful because he was afraid his face might give him away.

'There's no time to investigate and the description was clear-cut. Particularly since I was aware of Cushròk's mission. Who could have guessed it would be successful? We cannot delay.' Modôia gazed round at all of the älfar's faces. 'Elhàtor is going to war.'

None of those present rejoiced.

Ávoleï fixed her yellowish-green eyes on Aiphatòn. 'And you, emperor, will help us. Thus will your debt to me be paid.'

'Gladly. I suggest that I lead an advance party right away, returning secretly to Dâkiòn to thank Shôtoràs for the way he treated me.'

His words drew applause from Ôdaiòn. Aiphatòn gave a slight bow. 'And another thing: I'm getting my spear back.' He smiled. *No älf will survive this war. I'll make sure of that.*

Ishím Voróo, Älfar town of Dsôn Dâkiòn, 5452nd division of unendingness (6491st solar cycle), late summer

That's him apparently, the wind-voice. Tanôtai contemplated the moon-pale älf who was being kept in a magical sleep.

Nodûcor was lying on a very large bed in a beautifully furnished room in the sovereign's palace with a ceiling eight paces high. Little staircases led to suspended ceilings and open-plan levels with libraries and sleeping facilities. Through the enormous windows on every floor there were magnificent, ever-changing views over Dâkiòn. The fragrance of incense purified the air, cleansing it and leaving an aromatic smell behind.

Were it not for the four cîani, who had spread their books and rolls of parchment out all over the tables, chairs and windowsills, one might think Nodûcor was a privileged guest of Shôtoràs.

His glass hair caught the sunlight, his bare, sinewy chest slowly rising and falling. The magical slumber was deep.

He looks unusual anyway. Tanôtai looked over at the magic experts who were arguing quietly while leafing through their notes occasionally, looking for symbols and approaching the black half-mask to inspect it closely.

Many moments of unendingness had passed in this way.

And you can command the wind? It was Tanôtai's job to stay close by in case Nodûcor managed to wake up and try to escape. The death-dancer would be able to grab him more easily than the cîani since most of them had less muscle than the thin prisoner. *I'm intrigued by what your voice sounds like.*

The door opened.

Shôtoràs entered; they had all heard his stick clicking beforehand. 'How do things stand?' he asked, full of energy and confidence. 'Have we got to the bottom of the puzzle that Lethòras left for us?' He nodded to Tanôtai in greeting and limped over to the bed. 'He's still wearing this mask?'

The cîani in their robes bowed to the sovereign, their unease visible on their faces.

'The situation is this: Lethòras used a spell made up of different parts that are each encrypted in turn,' one of them explained. 'He fit, if you like, a series of spells one inside the other, to stop anyone opening the lock without a lot of effort.'

'I see.' Shôtoràs touched the black metal and felt the warning tingle. 'And he took this knowledge with him into the endingness.'

'Unfortunately, sovereign.'

'How long will it take you to solve this puzzle?'

The cîanoi made no secret of his own ignorance and that of his fellow guildmates. 'We deciphered the first four spells but then we reached a point where we have to be particularly careful. This particular rune symbolises death.' He reached behind him and snatched up an open book where he had marked the relevant part with a ribbon. 'If we make a mistake, this next symbol will unleash a flash of lightning that will destroy the half-mask. Along with Nodû-cor's head.'

'Good thinking by the cunning Lethòras, but bad for us.' Shôtoràs lifted the stick and tapped it against the metal, the sleeping älf's head wobbling slightly. 'We are so close to being able to call the most powerful weapon our own. After that there will be nothing left for us to fear.' He looked at the cîani. 'Will it be difficult to bend his mind to our will?'

'No. We've already woven a spell to, firstly, make him sleep and, secondly, ensure that he takes orders – just like a dog takes orders from his master. As soon as we wake him,' one cîanai explained, 'he will obey your every word. Your image is fixed firmly in his mind.'

Shôtoràs nodded absent-mindedly and turned to leave. 'Work faster,' he commanded.

'It's possible,' Tanôtai interjected cautiously, 'that we've got the wrong one, sovereign.'

The cîani stared at the death-dancer as if profoundly offensive insults had passed her sensual lips.

'Don't look so surprised. We have no guarantee that he truly is the wind-voice.' Tanôtai pointed to Nodûcor and a diamond on her wrist flashed. 'Apparently Cushròk captured him, as Aiphatòn told us. But we will only know whether he unleashes storms once he starts to speak.'

Shôtoràs smiled. 'I'm very sure. That's enough.' The silver end of the stick was pointed towards the door. 'See me out. You seem bored, and boredom leads to dangerous thoughts. I've got a better use for you than keeping watch over someone who looks dead.'

Reassured, the cîani turned back to their papers and the runes.

The sovereign and Tanôtai left the room and walked through the vaulted corridor and down the steps to the first inner courtyard. Vailóras and four of his warriors were waiting there, sitting on night-mares; one other black horse had been saddled.

'I'd like you,' Shôtoràs told her, 'to ride with them. You will be looking for Aiphatòn on my behalf. I'm sure he's somewhere in the vicinity so that he can get his spear back.'

Tanôtai screwed up her mouth. It pained her that she had not managed to kill the emperor. Anyone who could survive her dagger and that fall had proved they were extraordinary but that hardly made her failure any better. 'I'm glad you've chosen me to accompany them.'

'No doubt he has received support and care from unsuspecting locals. Spread the word that Aiphatòn died trying to kill me and seize power for himself,' he instructed Vailóras and his warriors. He stroked a night-mare fearlessly, and it approved the affection with a snort. 'If you do that, the locals ought to give you the updates you need to find him.'

'We'll do that, sovereign.' Vailóras turned his black night-mare around.

Inàste, lead him to me. Then I will burn my name into his plates of armour. Tanôtai mounted and they rode out through the narrow gate, across the wide main road and immediately left Dsôn Dâkiòn via one of the bridges.

The benàmoi guided his night-mare towards the southeast. 'That's where the closest village is,' he told the death-dancer. 'It's possible he dragged himself into one of the barns. The locals may not necessarily be aware that he is hiding in their village. So we'll be friendly,' he ordered his warriors.

I won't be. Tanôtai saw the huts, and to the side the enormous hay and grain silos looming up in front of the riders.

The crops were stored in the silos temporarily before being transported to the town's storage towers. The farmers were left with enough grain and straw to make it through the winter and they got the seeds from the sovereign in the spring. In this way the älfar stopped the residents fleeing.

'A good place to hide,' she said as they approached. 'It will take a long time to crawl over every last nook of it.'

'The farmers will do that for us,' said Vailóras. 'Nobody wants to think there's a traitor under their roof who wanted to kill Shôtoràs.'

Tanôtai grinned. 'You know how to make others take on the work and still feel like a hero during the slog.'

'I've travelled this land for a long time. I know every individual within a radius of forty miles and I have made sure that they appreciate the mercy of the sovereign. From generation to generation.' Vailóras reined in his night-mare outside the first hut and its door opened immediately. The residents had noticed the troops and were coming to ask what they wanted. 'Who would have thought that our people would be loved instead of feared?'

'*I* am feared, benàmoi.' The death-dancer leaped down from her saddle and walked up to the astonished villagers. 'If the barbarians are too slow, I'll show you why.'

After four splinters of unendingness, which they spent waiting and doing their own searches in the village, they were forced to move on empty-handed. Aiphatòn had not been hiding there.

They continued unrewarded for quite a few more moments and neither Tanôtai's unfriendliness nor Vailóras' knowledge helped. They spent a long time travelling and making inquiries, which the death-dancer did not enjoy. She found it at least as awful and boring as guarding a sleeping prisoner.

They rode through the villages in a strict sequence, beginning with the most likely ones, but they didn't find any leads on the missing emperor.

The residents of Dâkiòn's territory were horrified that someone had tried to kill the sovereign. Their anguish, as the red-haired death-dancer could clearly tell in every conversation with village elders or mayors, came from a profound sincerity: nobody wished Shôtoràs dead.

As they sat in the parlour of an isolated farmstead on the western outskirts of Dâkiòn country one evening, Vailóras toyed with the thought that Aiphatòn had started his journey home. 'In his position, it's the best solution. He knows we'll kill him as soon as we track him down. And he has already lost his spear.'

Tanôtai couldn't stand the idea of not finishing the duel she had started with the shintoìt. She touched the dagger on her right forearm guard. 'If I lost one of these, I would be desperate to get it back,' she replied. 'They're one-of-a-kind, like the spear.'

'Actually, what's the news on that?' interjected one of the warriors.

'As far as I know, a cîanoi is examining it. They want to uncover the tricks to the magic stored in it. It's extremely different from ours,' Tanôtai was repeating what she'd heard while guarding the sleeping älf's bed. 'Lethòras was reputed to be the best of our magically gifted, but he didn't know how to resist this kind of inverse charm.'

'Yes, the magic,' grumbled Vailóras as more wine was poured for him by the farmer's wife, which he acknowledged with a polite nod. 'I deliberately stay away from that.' He rubbed his black lamellar armour to remove a stain he'd got during his meal. His helmet dangled from the back of his chair and his dark blonde hair was plastered to his head.

'Surely you don't mean you don't use it?'

'I've never had reason to yet,' he admitted. He looked at his batons resting in their holders on his thighs. 'I've made the handful of defaulters pay the levy in my own way. From gold to bones, we've collected everything for the sovereign.'

His men laughed cruelly.

A squandered gift. He ought to pass it on to me if it's possible. Tanôtai stayed away from the fermented grape juice. As a death-dancer, she preferred her head to be clear at all times so that she could deploy her talents without any unsteadiness.

What's more, her magic worked differently under the influence of

alcohol. She tried to perform a dance drunk once, and the consequences were embarrassing. It had given her a broken arm and she'd
needed five moments of absolute bedrest to recover.

I want to catch him. Aiphatòn must die at my hands. Tanôtai traced
the lines on the side of her thigh, feeling the ink just underneath the
skin – it was ink and so much more.

It was made from plant sap extracts, distilled and magically treated
before being inserted with the needle. When combined with the correct movements, they released the magic – which could happen while
both fighting and dancing.

Tanôtai was aware of cases of self-inflicted injuries or even explosions, poisonings and suffocations because the steps weren't right or
the necessary precision was lacking, resulting in alterations to the
magic spells.

Magic is unforgiving.

The red-haired älf-woman tore off some brown bread and dipped it
into the pot of cream still on the table from the meal, enjoying the
mild sweetness and freshness.

While Vailóras, the country folk and the warriors chatted about
the harvest, her thoughts returned to the evening when she had struck
Aiphatòn directly in the chest.

What did I do wrong? He ought to have died. She contemplated her
right hand, whose fingertips had turned black after the explosion and
had been prickling ever since. *Should I be glad I survived – unlike
Lethòras?*

Hurried footsteps approached the main building and the door was
thrown open at the same time as a knock resounded.

Everyone turned to the door and saw a panting barbarian boy,
sweat running from his temples and forehead.

'We've seen him,' he uttered breathlessly. 'The conspirator. He was running west beside our fields and my father sent me to fetch you immediately.'

Vailóras stood up; his warriors followed suit and grabbed their helmets from where they had hung them on the backs of their chairs. 'Are you sure?'

The boy nodded. 'Father said he's absolutely certain. He said he'd never seen an älf like him before.' The farmer's wife handed him her glass of water, and he drank greedily. 'West,' he repeated. 'Following the constellation of the Ishtainor.'

'Let's look into it.' Vailóras walked past and stroked his head, and another warrior pressed a coin into his hand.

Tanôtai brought up the rear. The inks in her skin were warming up; her heart was beating faster and waking the magic from its slumber. *Thank you, Inàste!*

The night-mares were swiftly saddled, then off they went.

'Form a line,' Vailóras commanded as he rode, 'so he cannot evade us.'

The group fanned out, the black horses galloping through the night at intervals of fifty paces. Their red eyes gleamed, their hooves flashed as they hit the ground.

Tanôtai looked up at the stars guiding them. Her excitement was growing all the time; the wind caught in her red mane and made her look like a blazing fire. 'He belongs to me,' she screamed to her right and left. 'It's my right to take his life.'

Vailóras laughed. 'I will not refuse a death-dancer her wish, otherwise you'll invite me to lead off a dance with you.'

'Over here,' cried the warrior on the left flank of their formation. 'Tracks in the sand. They lead into the woods.'

The älfar turned slightly and made for the woodland, which looked like one big black mass looming up in front of them.

The route between tree trunks would mean the night-mares would have to slow down, but Tanôtai saw to her relief that the trees were still relatively far apart and there was practically no undergrowth.

You will not shake us off, she thought grimly and raced into the wood before anyone else. She briefly wondered why Aiphatòn was supposedly fleeing westwards when the passage to Tark Draan lay to the southeast of Dsôn Dâkiòn. *Because he wants to get his spear.*

Thin branches cracked on either side of her under the horseshoes, the little explosions around the beasts' ankles flashed brightly, casting such bright light on the tree bark that it looked like a storm was raging in the middle of the copse.

Tanôtai saw the tracks up ahead of her left by their prey. *The armour is making him sink into the moss.* She urged her night-mare into a trot, gazing alternately upwards and downwards.

Then she saw a reflection up ahead. A figure was scurrying forwards under the cover of the trees.

'Up there,' she called to the troops and dug her spurs into the stallion's flanks so that he started to gallop with a roar, catching up with the fleeing figure. The silhouette disappeared for several heartbeats every now and then, before reappearing again.

Tanôtai drew the needle-dagger from her left forearm guard. *I will slaughter you from my saddle like a bull running wild. My magic will make the nape of your neck explode and make your skull fly through the air.* She would only embark on a dance if he dodged her initial attacks. *But that will not happen.*

The red-haired älf-woman lost sight of him again for an instant. *Damn!* She swung the galloping night-mare around to take him past a dead tree stump – when the figure suddenly stepped out from behind the stump and planted itself directly in front of the black horse.

The collision happened almost simultaneously.

But instead of knocking the emperor to the ground and trampling him with its hooves, the animal seemed to crash into an unshakeable pillar.

Bellowing, the night-mare fell forwards, was spun around and pressed its head deep into the soft ground; with a loud crack, its neck broke. The bones poked through its black coat and the red glow in its eyes went out. Its hindquarters jutted up into the air.

Thinking quickly, Tanôtai wrenched her feet out of her stirrups. In a high arc she flew over the motionless, blood-spattered figure, who was still standing there as if the heavy stallion had been a light, harmless fly.

Tanôtai thought she saw a copper-coloured helmet on her opponent's head as well as brown leather armour and a broken flagpole on his back.

Realising this was not the emperor they were looking for, she wasted no time getting into the low-hanging branches without injuring herself.

The red-haired älf-woman held on tight to one branch, slid down the foliage and hurtled towards the ground, although with a graceful spin, she turned this into a safe, catlike landing. The magical lines on her skin pulsed and heated up.

What was that? How is he able to survive that without any trouble? She hurried back to the place where the collision had taken place, the needle-daggers in her hands.

But her opponent was no longer there.

It smelled of the blood flowing out of the animal, of resin and earth. The dead night-mare had visibly churned up the soft ground and the footprints of the enemy looked deeper than usual.

Magic. Agitated, Tanôtai listened to the sounds of the wood and picked up the noise of thundering hooves, saw the flashes and heard the alarmed cries of Vailóras and his warriors who had not realised what had happened to her.

The death-dancer ran off after the troops. 'Watch out! That is not the emperor!' she cried over and over. 'It . . .'

Suddenly she realised one explanation for the crash as well as the strange behaviour of the figure they were following. The scorching heat inside her intensified.

'Careful! Oh gods! Careful!' she shouted and made the blades light up so that she could be seen by her team. 'It's a ghaist! A ghaist!'

Then there was a loud crashing and smashing and an enraged night-mare whinnied – and fell silent.

Those damned botoicans. I thought the sovereign had made it clear to them they had no business being in our territory. Too late, Tanôtai remembered the scouts the mind-controllers dispatched to look for villages and towns they could conquer with their mass magic.

A ghaist, as the cîani explained it, consisted of magic and many souls bound together in a fake human form. The copper helmet with runes on it was a distinctive feature of this unarmed creature, who could not be stopped by anything but immense heat. The warmth made the symbols melt and deformed the copper so that the souls could not be kept in their prison any longer.

Not that long ago, the cîani had used magic spells to crush the mob-like army of one of the botoican families as they ran about in confusion outside Dsôn Dâkiòn.

They are getting cocky. Tanôtai looked at the nearest dead night-mare and the motionless warrior underneath it who hadn't got his feet out of the stirrups quickly enough. It seemed the surviving mind-controllers had learnt nothing from the defeat. *I'll cure the Nhatais of that, even if I have to go into their dilapidated town and annihilate their families. The sovereign just needs to let me do it.*

The death-dancer checked the heartbeat at the jugular but the älf had passed into endingness.

'Vailóras!' she shouted and stood up. 'Call off the chase. The cîani will have to take care of it.' She listened out for the pounding of hooves to figure out where the riders were.

But the woods had fallen silent.

Completely silent.

'Vailóras?' Tanôtai cried and extinguished the blades so that darkness closed in around her.

From her right came the voice of the dark blonde commander cursing and then there was a swift, repetitive clanking.

Who is he attacking? Not the ghaist? She ran between the tree trunks and spotted the älf facing the enormous fake human-warrior with the leather armour and copper helmet.

Vailóras was showering his opponent with blows from his batons, and his opponent was accepting the attacks without moving.

Is that blood? The death-dancer had reached the pair. Black liquid was running down the ghaist's fingers and forearms, dripping onto the moss and bracken they were standing on.

After a quick look all around her, she realised where it was coming from: among the tall blades of grass she made out the corpses of the other warriors. Their bodies had been ripped apart, arms and legs lying scattered about, one torso looking like it had been prised open at the heart and disembowelled.

Tanôtai started to stumble, assailed by the smell of fresh blood and entrails. Death spurred her on, making her plot revenge and overwhelming her mind. 'Wait, I'll be right there!' Finally she could give her powers free rein.

Vailóras turned his head towards her. 'Run back and alert the cîani,' he ordered her in a choked voice. 'This is no ghaist as we know it!'

The creature suddenly yanked its arms backwards and thrust its upper body forwards, the slight ridge of the helmet on its forehead headed straight at the dark blonde älf's face.

Vailóras swept the batons into the air with one crossed over the other, the symbols on them glowing. It seemed he had no choice but to use his magic now. He tried to catch the ghaist by the throat and hold off the attack.

But the ridge of the helmet smashed into the middle of Vailóras' handsome face, crushing the nose guard along with the bones and the delicate flesh. Blood sprayed through the air. Vailóras was hurled backwards and vanished into the speckled bracken.

No! Tanôtai raised her weapons.

The ghaist slowly turned the helmet with the narrow eye slits towards the death-dancer. The blood of the benàmoi ran down over the copper, trickling over the white botoican runes and tracing the lines, until he started moving towards her.

'I don't need any cîani to annihilate you. My magic is strong enough.' Tanôtai did a full spin and the needle blades shone like the diamonds and lines beneath her skin.

As she did so, their surroundings suddenly took on their true daylight colours.

The ghaist gave a hollow snort, its muscular arms swinging forward and back. The fresh blood, in streaks and large stains on her approaching opponent's copper helmet, armour, forearms and fingers looked unexpectedly intimidating. The creature exuded unprecedented brutality and mercilessness.

She saw the openings in the polished helmet, nothing earthly hidden behind them; it contained nothing but powerful magic and bewitched souls.

Vailóras deployed his magic and failed. That will not happen to me.

Tanôtai summoned her focus, went up on tiptoe and spread her arms out slowly from her body. 'You will not survive this,' she whispered to the ghaist and the light around them increased. 'And then I'll come for your master!'

The creature dipped its head and rushed at her.

Chapter XII

A spring tide will be stopped by a net before a ghaist is stopped by a weapon.

Wise saying of the Älfar
Collected by Carmondai, master of word and image

Tark Draan, Human kingdom of Gauragar, 5452nd division of unendingness (6491st solar cycle), autumn

Carmondai heard the whirring and felt the draught of air passing directly over his brown hair after the click.

His heart pounding, he straightened up and saw the tree next to him was studded with numerous horn arrows. If he had not stooped down to the stick, if he had stepped on the tripping mechanism while standing up, the trap would have riddled him with holes from his navel to his throat.

I'm not taking another step. 'Listen to me!' he cried in älfar. 'I know there's a hideaway here. The entrance is in the granite tree trunk and I want to come to you and open it. But the mist is too thick. I can't see the tripping mechanisms on the traps.'

His voice echoed forlornly through the wood. The clouds of mist rippled and twitched as if his words had reached inside them.

'I'm asking you: show me the way! I didn't escape my captors only to be sent into endingness by the swords of my own people!' Carmondai really hoped someone appeared. He didn't care if crazy Carâhnios died.

A very soft, scraping sound rang out, then a figure appeared at the top of the granite stump.

A fair-haired älf-woman wearing dark plate armour lifted a hand in greeting and looked around. She was holding one of the dreaded longbows in her other hand. 'It nearly slit me open when I arrived. But don't worry: I'll guide you.' She pointed to the right. 'You're less than a thumb's width away from a second tripping mechanism, so do not move your feet without my say-so.' She smiled. 'What's your name?'

'I'm Carmondai.'

'Not *the* Carmondai?' She sounded just as awestruck as Ostòras.

He held up a bundle of pages. 'I'll be happy to show you all the sketches I've drawn on the road despite my shackles, and what I've written too. As long as I survive the last steps to where you are.'

'We ought to manage that.' She laughed warmly. 'My name is Rhogàta. Take three big steps forwards.'

He did so. 'Are you alone?'

'Yes. You're lucky I was still here.' The älf-woman was watching him. 'Stop. Now one to the left and five straight towards me.'

Carmondai followed her instructions. 'Is the hideaway not safe anymore?'

'It's safe. I was going to follow Votòlor to Oakenburgh.'

I know that town. Oakenburgh was a medium-sized settlement in the south of the kingdom. In his day, there had not been anything special there to make it a destination for an älf to visit. The residents made a living from wood-cutting. The trunks of the rare blackjack oaks were floated upstream and processed in sawmills. *Why go there?* 'Is that to do with the liberation of our people?'

Rhogàta answered in the negative. 'Two diagonally to the right, then you've got to crawl five paces forward.'

'In the *mist*?'

'In the mist. Unless you'd like to touch the wire.' Rhogàta looked around again and listened out for anyone who might have followed him. 'No, there are no älfar to be freed from prison. A different mission altogether. You're very welcome to join us if you think you're up to it. I've heard you're capable of more than writing stories.' She burst out laughing. 'And this way I'll become a heroine in your stories too. As a child I used to dream of my name being celebrated.'

'It will be.' Carmondai ducked, crawled forward and when he stood up he was less than two paces from the trunk. A shudder ran down his spine when he realised he still had his rucksack on and it could have caught on the wire. 'Are you planning an invasion then?'

'Not the usual kind. The barbarian-woman who seized the biggest swathes of our kingdom is due to pay a visit.' Rhogàta held up her longbow as a clue. 'We are going to send greetings from our people straight into her heart.' She gestured around the trunk. 'Now just come along this side and I'll open up the door for you as soon as you get here.' Then she looked confused. 'Is that a bottle in your right hand?'

Before Carmondai could respond, he saw the small figure detach itself from the thick branch six paces above the älf-woman.

Feet first and in free fall, the zhadár swooped down like a bird of prey, his unusual sword raised above his head, poised to strike.

Rhogàta must have heard a noise, because she spun round as quick as a flash with her face turned upwards. Her free hand shot to the hilt of her sword.

Then Carâhnios' sword struck her, splitting her skull vertically and continuing downwards despite the armour. The zhadár's boots crashed onto the little platform, his weapon going down as far as the älf-woman's middle. Now half split in two, she keeled backwards and toppled off the tree stump. Severed strands of black hair fell into the bloody stream.

'Hey, black-eye! I subdued her for you. Look alive and collect her blood.' Carâhnios shouted the order from above, followed by sinister laughter.

What was he thinking? Carmondai had to step around the body so as not to be hit by the spray – and there was another click.

A searing pain shot across his heels and took his legs out from under him. He fell head over heels and landed on his back and the rucksack. Somehow he managed to keep the bottle safe as he did so.

'What are you doing down there, scribbler?!' Carâhnios yelled.

'Surviving, hopefully!' Surrounded by mist, all he could see was a thin shadow swooping down from above and he tried to block it with his steel shackles.

The container shattered into pieces due to the impact, the shards hurting him as they hit his face. Sparks flashed as the blade struck the connecting part of the shackles and was brought to a halt.

'Have you found another trap?' the zhadár chuckled.

Carmondai needed all of his strength to stop the blade. It was now pinning him to the ground with a huge amount of unrelenting pressure. If it slipped off the metal of his shackles, it would plunge into the middle of his chest. *It must be a tense spring.*

'Some help would be nice.' Moaning, he slid down under his hands to get out of the danger zone and slowly release the sword. He saw the curved blade like a claw dangling right in front of his nose. That's apt considering the legend.

Carmondai kept moving, his arms burning and trembling with exertion. *I can release it very soon.*

'You'll manage,' Carâhnios remarked. 'But what made that clinking sound just now? Don't tell me it was the bottle!'

There was a second click.

The hook-shaped blade was suddenly pulled forwards, catching on the connecting part of the handcuffs and dragging the älf face down over the damp, cold, mossy floor until the ground suddenly vanished and he was rolling down an embankment.

'Hey! Hey, come back!' shouted Carâhnios, outraged. 'You know what will happen if you breach the agreements. I swear I will find you!'

Carmondai could not speak. His fall ended in a pit full of decayed skeletal remains. One glance was enough to tell him they had been animals.

That was quite a trip. Carmondai groaned as he stood up and started removing the splinters from his face before making his way up the slope and following his own trail back to the tree trunk. That hadn't done the aches and pains in his old body any good, he had to limp to relieve the pressure on his right knee with its stabbing pains.

'Good. You've come back voluntarily.' Carâhnios was waiting for him in the entrance to the hideaway and, deadly serious, holding out a shard of the bottle to him accusatorily. 'What did I vow to you earlier?'

'The platform is swimming with Rhogàta's blood, it's running down the trunk and seeping into the soil. Oh yes, and it's in your beard,' he countered. 'How was I meant to collect it?'

The zhadár's gaze fell on the iron handcuffs and the grooves the sword had left behind. 'Am I seeing things – or did my shackles save your life?' He burst into such peals of laughter that he must have been audible for a radius of more than four miles in the quiet woodland. 'Now *that's* what I call Samusin's work!'

Carmondai briefly described what had happened to him. 'I assume that trap is meant to make it look like the victim has been seized and dragged off by the beast.'

'Seems that way to me too.' Carâhnios sniggered, squeezing the älf-woman's blood out of his facial hair. 'I'll admit her death was not intended to be like that. I overestimated the force.'

'From six paces in the air? Yes, it really took her by surprise. She literally burst with joy,' he remarked cuttingly.

'Let's say this: since neither of us did our best work, I'll forgive you and let you keep your blood. Especially as I know where I can get some more soon.' He pointed to the opening in the trunk. 'This is the entrance, by the way, but I've already been inside. Disappointing. Barely any different from the first hideaway.'

'I'm going to take a look anyway so that I can describe and draw it.' Carmondai looked quizzically at the zhadár. 'Is the third sanctuary nearby?'

'How did you figure that?'

'Because you said you'd get new blood soon.'

Carâhnios pointed south. 'If we hurry, we'll make it by daybreak.'

The short distances between the hideaways made no sense to Carmondai. 'Is there a tunnel between them, why are they so close together?'

'Who said anything about a hideaway? I'm talking about Oakenburgh.'

'The attempt on Mallenia's life.' He had not considered that. 'You'll be a hero if you save the life of the Queen of Gauragar and Idoslane.'

'True, true.' Carâhnios suddenly smiled that crazy grin he could have impressed demons with. 'If it arises, I'll do it. But I'd be content to catch the älf.' He pointed to the entrance. 'Now take a look, draw like the wind and then we'll get going.' He grimaced. 'Remind me, I need to go to a glassmaker. The bottles are running low.'

He would allow Mallenia to go to her death. And yet they are allies. Carmondai was more than a little taken aback and he gave up trying to understand the zhadár. The creature was different from groundlings and älfar, he had both good and evil in him. *The last drop of the new distillate seems to have pushed him much more towards the evil.*

He entered the hideaway and found a narrow staircase leading downwards. Phosphorescent moss provided enough light to make out the steps.

His plan to kill his crazy guard soon, before he lost his own life in the hunt for älfar – due to traps, villagers or one of Carâhnios' whims – crystallised. *Take any more of that elixir in my presence and you will die.*

Ishím Voróo, Eleven miles from Dsôn Dâkiòn, 5452nd division of unendingness (6491st solar cycle), late summer

The long, narrow boats with their big, triangular sails swept up the Tronjor so quickly that Aiphatòn was astonished. *You'd think they did this every orbit.*

The wind was favourable for the attackers and they had passed the rocky bottleneck. Aiphatòn's suggestion to lead a separate party on ahead had been rejected so he was forced to travel with the troops.

The ships were noticeably different from the rònkes and the escort sailboats. They had been invented purely to travel upstream and get to Dâkiòn. It appeared the älfar had had it with keeping the peace. The large three-masters were outside the mouth of the Tronjor awaiting their return.

We'll get right up to the town in just a few orbits. Aiphatòn was on
the first of almost a hundred vessels and was preparing to be dropped
off on land with a small troop. They had been given a special task that
would be vital in gaining further ground.

Irïanora was standing less than two paces away from him. The
blonde älf-woman was wearing the white armour of the Elhàtorians,
but to set her apart, she had been given red armbands. She had insisted
on taking part in the venture.

Aiphatòn would have suggested it anyway. For one thing, she knew
her way round Dâkiòn, and for another, she would be some useful
leverage. *Maybe not for using against Shôtoràs, but with the warriors
they met along the way.* The sight of the sovereign's niece could provide
the vital hesitation he needed in order to fire the first arrow. What's
more, Irïanora had friends in the town who would no doubt want her
back alive and would insist on negotiations.

Aiphatòn went and joined her. 'Is this how you pictured your
return?'

She glanced at him briefly and then looked straight ahead
again. The landing manoeuvre was beginning, the right bank drawing
closer. 'I assumed I'd never see my homeland again,' she drawled.

Now I'll sow a little uncertainty. He folded his arms across his chest.
'I've seen your antipathy towards me and your badly faked horror
when the declaration of war was made,' he said softly. 'I'm telling you:
you're *glad* about it. And you're probably wondering how to lead the
troops from Elhàtor into the trap.'

'Nonsense,' she retorted indignantly. 'A lot has changed and . . .'
She faltered. 'I've lost my heart to Ôdaiòn. How could I betray the älf
I love?'

We've got a little actress on board. 'And the älf who will enable you
to live the life of a monarchess, which you might never have been in

Dâkiòn,' he continued her sentence and laughed at her. 'I may quite clearly be the same age as you, but in terms of experience you're no match for me, Irïanora. You're being toyed with the same way you imagine you're toying with others.' Aiphatòn looked over at Ávoleï who was just swapping her white armour for brownish-green armour to stand out less in grassland. 'You're a useful playing piece to her. Nothing more. Nobody will hesitate to kill you if the situation calls for it. And Ôdaiòn would be the first to rip your oh-so-loving heart out of your body.'

Irïanora was giving him a contemptuous look now. 'You Tark Draan scum,' she hissed.

'Just like the monarchess of the town, whose son you want to take as a husband,' he countered. 'You don't fool me. In your shoes, I'd be wary if Ôdaiòn approaches you. Once he's had his fun with you, he'll cast you aside. Pray that you can still seem useful for a long time. Maybe neither your uncle nor the monarchess' son will want you. What are you going to do then?' Aiphatòn was getting ready for the ship to land. *That will have made her anxious enough and lead to mistakes. Let's see what she does.*

The flat bow of their ship made its way up the shallow gravel beach.

The crew jumped over the ship's side and made it fast with ropes as well as long iron rods that were hammered quickly into the ground.

More and more of the other vessels came alongside, deliberately running aground. The fleet of a hundred ships temporarily dropped anchor to allow the remaining river ahead of them to be explored and to avoid sailing into the defending forces' traps.

Elhàtor's secret boats could be dismantled and reassembled into scaling ladders and catapults designed to cause trouble for the defending forces. They could also be made into bridges to get across any gaps in case the sovereign ordered the entrances to be demolished. Along with the thousands of warriors, there were cîani who were thoroughly prepared for the conflict.

'Do you think they'll let you return to your subjects in Tark Draan if you get your spear back?' Irïanora whispered.

'Who's going to stop me? You? How? With your gift of bad acting?' He saw that Ávoleï was approaching them, followed by a group of twenty warriors in the camouflage armour; in her left hand she was holding a rolled-up map. 'I advise you to get yourself to safety as long as you still can. One of the soldiers will be under orders from Modôia to kill you. She wants to see Ávoleï at her son's side, not you.'

'He and the elf-woman?' she spat. 'Ridiculous. Ôdaiòn doesn't like her.' She turned to the commander.

Elf-woman? Aiphatòn hoped his surprise was not obvious, especially to Ávoleï, who had just joined them. It explained what was making him feel uneasy, no matter how attractive he found the commander.

Ávoleï spread the map out on the railing, with the exact course of the river plotted on it. 'We've reached the first safe landing point,' she explained.

Irïanora took over the explanations unasked. *Probably to justify her presence and make herself indispensable after his warnings.* Aiphatòn grinned as the blonde älf-woman pointed at various parts of the map. 'Those are shallows where whirlpools form quickly. The ships could be pushed sideways and end up with their broad sides to the waves,' she elaborated. 'I recommend you keep your distance. At least two lengths.'

Ávoleï's forehead furrowed. 'That's not the issue at all.'

'No?' Irïanora looked at her, then at Aiphatòn as if afraid she was about to be attacked by him. 'I thought . . .'

'What do you know about the supplies of petrol that have been stockpiled further up the bank?'

The sovereign's niece swallowed and placed one hand on her stomach. 'I'm hearing about it for the first time,' she admitted after a brief hesitation.

Ávoleï nodded. 'That's what I thought. So it's not for nothing we've had the Tronjor under surveillance for many divisions of unendingness.' She picked up a compressed coal-dust pen and marked several bends. 'Behind these bends, barrels have been buried in the embankment, each guarded by a platoon of around ten men.' The black-haired elf-woman nodded to Aiphatòn. 'You go with some of the warriors, investigate the right-hand bank and secure the supplies. I'll take the other side with the rest of them.'

He looked at the turns in the river. 'A simple option to put the fleet out of action.' *And that must be prevented at all costs. I need a huge battle with thousands of casualties. Burnt-out ships are no good.* It was a struggle to hide his continued surprise. *An elf-woman and yet . . . I would never have suspected it.*

Irïanora looked miserable. She had realised that she was no use for the time being. Her knowledge was out of date. 'I didn't know anything about it,' she insisted.

Ávoleï didn't even look at her as she replied. 'You also didn't know anything about the canal that Shôtoràs is having dug that flows into a hollow. We're assuming he wants to dam up the Tronjor in there and drain it. If he did so, our plan could no longer be put into action.'

'Then we've come at the right time.' Aiphatòn unrolled the paper further, his eyes fixed on the sketch of Dàkiòn, the river in front of it, the outlines of the canal and the weir. 'You're right. No boat would have been able to use the river anymore.'

Ávoleï rolled up the map. 'We'll move along the banks in parallel and maintain eye contact. As soon as we've secured the petrol supply, let's pass a message downstream so that the fleet can follow slowly,' she explained. 'In complete secrecy, we and our scouts will work our way as far as the small fishing port two miles from the town.'

He placed a hand on the map. 'But what if Shôtoràs is keeping more barrels of petrol hidden upstream from the village? As a last resort?'

'Then we'll have come far enough to be able to walk the rest of the way through the swamps. I think my warriors are just about capable of that.' Ávoleï put away the rolled-up parchment. 'Don't go too far from the bank. After more than twenty paces, the bog, swamp or quicksand starts. All three will kill you.'

'Let's get going.' Aiphatòn turned down the proffered leather armour in camouflage colours and placed one armoured hand on the railing. 'Whichever of us gets to Dâkiòn first owes the other one a favour.'

He gave Irïanora another look to remind her of his comments on her safety. *I hope she does something rash. Ideally she'll try and attack Ôdaiòn.*

He vaulted energetically over the wood and landed on the flat shingle, running off immediately without paying any attention to whether the warriors allocated to him were keeping up with him. *They ought to see how much I want my spear back.*

Aiphatòn was following the simple plan of accompanying the attacking troops to start with and then making his way on to Nodûcor alone. The wind-voice signified the end of all worries and fears. Not just for the towns. *With him, I can ensure the definitive safety of Girdlegard. Dâkiòn will fall first, then Elhàtor.*

'Not so fast,' he heard the quiet but irritated cry from behind him. 'Ávoleï still has to cross to the other side.'

Aiphatòn slowed his pace and mulled over the sequence of his plan.

With Nodûcor, he would exterminate the älfar all around Dâkiòn with storms and hurricanes, then he would go to Elhàtor and destroy that town wave by wave too. Finally, it would be important to demolish the path through the Grey Mountains that could be used to smuggle the beasts from Ishím Voróo through the valleys and ravines.

This is going to be a spectacle! Aiphatòn pictured rock faces collapsing, peaks sliding down and making new slopes. The winds would give the mountains a new silhouette. *Nobody will travel that path again, the one Leióva and Modôia took. Not monsters, not botoicans or any other creatures who have come in the hopes of conquest.*

He hurried along the embankment; on the other side of the Tronjor he could see through the ferns and creepers a sweaty Ávoleï scurrying along and scowling at him. She had had to hurry to keep pace.

Eventually I'll kill Nodûcor. And myself.

If Nodûcor were not the wind-voice as everyone supposed, there was always the war between the towns to eradicate the last älfar.

Aiphatòn almost had an attack of conscience about obliterating kingdoms that seemed to have become harmless. But the behaviour, the intrigues, the speed with which they went to war, all triggered the reassuring realisation that the älfar in Ishím Voróo hadn't changed so much that they deserved mercy. Especially not in view of their magical power.

The ten men under Aiphatòn's command dashed through the thicket.

There was a smell of decay whenever the wind from the swamp blew towards them. It was only along the river that they could breathe the air without their stomachs heaving.

Swarms of flies became their constant companions, settling on their skin and stinging them to get at their blood. It hurt, as if they were secreting venom. The bites swelled up and turned red.

We should be at the first bend soon. Aiphatòn didn't even consider slowing down, no matter how much he could see Ávoleï gesticulating out of the corner of his eye.

He was glad that the painful prickling was subsiding. Magic fields really did seem to be the reason for the agonies he suffered along with the monarchess and all the other älfar from Tark Draan. *For two hundred cycles.* He couldn't help admiring her self-control.

'The commander wants us to get there at the same time,' a soldier whispered angrily behind him. 'Go more slowly, aren't you listening?'

Seamlessly, he stopped, grabbed the rebellious warrior by the throat with his armoured glove, lifted him up and pinned him to the ground.

'You,' he whispered menacingly, 'are under my command. And you will do what I tell you. If you dare try and advise me again, you'll end up in the quicksand.' He dragged him to his feet by the neck, let him go and turned around.

Aiphatòn continued running, faster than before, to make up for the lost time that the reprimand had cost him.

This time there was no grumbling, only the soldiers' wheezing coughs.

The bend appeared ahead of them.

The petrol supply was expertly hidden. Aiphatòn couldn't see the barrels or the troops from Dâkiòn who were watching over them, waiting until they saw the fleet to smash the barrels and set the river on fire.

He ordered his warriors to crawl so they could approach unseen and unheard. 'I'll go first.'

Aiphatòn chose a different route, however: he slid silently into the water and made his way upstream by hanging from the roots, finding that the water was pleasantly warm and reduced the itching from the bites. His armour plates were light enough that there was no risk of him sinking to the riverbed like a stone.

It was only once he was in this position, with his eyes just above the flowing Tronjor, that he could make out the small recess in the steep bank on the opposite side – it lay hidden underneath the dangling ferns, roots and bushes. *They've dug out an old water vole burrow and extended it.*

He could make out definite movements inside it.

Aiphatòn's gaze swept along the embankment looking for Ávoleï.

The elf-woman was moving towards the lair, but she was going to pass over it.

She'll miss them, and they'll be alerted! He had to do something. Aiphatòn took a deep breath, then sank down and propelled himself forwards.

He glided along underneath the surface. Swimming underwater was easy with the increased weight from the metal on his body.

The current caught him, but he held his own against the pressure and the dangerous pull and reached the other side of the Tronjor.

He put his head up out of the water cautiously.

The recess was just ten paces upstream – the river had made him drift slightly.

He moved forwards quickly by hanging from the vegetation on the embankment, getting closer and closer to the burrow. He could hear a quiet conversation coming from it about the relief shift being late.

Then the warriors from Dâkiòn fell silent as Aiphatòn skilfully groped his way up to the opening. The fact that the water was hitting him in the chest with a quiet splashing sound didn't attract any attention.

The soft tinkling coming from the recess did, however.

Aiphatòn peered inside and saw ten armed figures sitting in the spacious burrow, all straining their ears; four little strings of bells dangled down in front of them from the reinforced ceiling and every single one of them was shaking. *Trip wires.* Ávoleï and her team had set off the alarm.

Aiphatòn watched as five guards got ready and grabbed their bows, while three others climbed on top of the petrol barrels and picked up chains linked to a series of bungs. The last two got torches and lit them over the little coal brazier.

Ávoleï will have to see for herself how she deals with those five. I'll take care of the barrels. He could clearly see that two of the guards had short signal-whistles between their lips. Presumably they blew into them during times of danger, transmitting the sounds to sentries further upriver. *Our plan would be done for. We could just turn back or set the ships on fire straight away ourselves.*

The archers left the cave.

Aiphatòn lay flat in the Tronjor like a predatory water lizard, cautiously drawing in his legs so that he could catapult himself out of the river.

When he heard a cry of surprise from the steep bank above him, he sprang out of the river and rammed into the three guards, sending them flying off the barrels. Meanwhile, he put one foot on the chain that linked the barrels as quick as a flash to stop any pressure on the bungs.

One warrior did manage to pull on the handle of the chain as he fell but Aiphatòn's boot blocked his attempt to remove the stopper. The three soldiers fell backwards in between the containers and vanished for the time being.

After a brief instant of shock, the torch-bearers attacked him with the burning ends of their torches.

The blows rained down uselessly on Aiphatòn's wet plates; sparks flew, hissing and glinting.

'You should have used swords.' He stood his ground with furious punches from his armoured fists and knocked his attackers to the damp floor with split chins and shattered cheekbones; both of them had swallowed their whistles.

One of the three soldiers had worked his way out from between the barrels and drawn his short swords. He jumped down and attacked at the same time.

Aiphatòn caught one blade in his metal-encased hand and snapped it, and he let the other blade slam into the plates of armour on his chest. The impact made him stagger slightly and he fell to his knees. As he did so, he did one full turn to absorb the force.

He used the momentum to hurl the broken sword fragment at a second älf who had just appeared between the barrels. Struck in the torso, the enemy collapsed, dying, and lay on the container.

Aiphatòn dealt the soldier directly in front of him a punch to the crotch with his armoured left hand, standing up at the same time and slamming his shoulder plate into the groaning älf's chin so that he fell backwards and stopped moving.

Still one to go. Aiphatòn took a spear off the wall and looked around.

He found the last warrior wedged between the barrels, wriggling. His armour had got caught.

'Aha. That's inconvenient, isn't it?' He lowered the tip of the spear to the warrior's throat. 'You would have done the same.' One stab was enough to send the last sentry into endingness. *Now the fleet is safe as far as this bend.*

Aiphatòn climbed up the narrow ladder the archers had used to leave their lair – and his head emerged into the open, directly behind one of the enemy warriors.

He pulled his legs out from under him with the shaft of the spear so that the ambushed warrior fell at his feet. Then Aiphatòn broke the warrior's neck by hitting him with the side of his hand.

Aiphatòn was cautious as he emerged fully out of the hole. He could very clearly hear the soft whizzing of fired arrows. *It seems like Ávoleï could do with some help.*

The immediately muffled cries of those who had been hit rang out from further away. The archers had let the elf-woman and her troops pass by so that they could kill them from behind.

Aiphatòn crept through the ferns.

Another archer stood less than eleven paces away from him and pulled a long, black arrow back on his bow string quite some way.

I should have taken more spears with me. He gauged the distance and threw.

The missile plunged sideways into the shoulder of his enemy's drawing arm and on into his neck where it stuck fast. The archer was dying as he fell among the tall, serrated leaves.

Aiphatòn ran over to him, braced one foot against the dead body and pulled the spear out. He then tossed it in one fluid motion at an archer who stepped out from behind a tree trunk and was aiming at him.

'Here's another!' the voice of his enemy warned, before the lethal tip of Aiphatòn's spear bored into his chest and pinned him to the tree.

He's calling them over to me. Perfect. Aiphatòn allowed himself a grin and ducked under the cover of the ferns like he had under the waters of the Tronjor earlier.

He lay still, straining his ears, and drew the dagger from the sheath on the dead body next to him along with a sheaf of arrows from the quiver.

Soon he heard the noise of stalks brushing over leather and clothing. Barely audible, an overstretched string creaked, held taut by the archer.

'There!' whispered someone.

The string whirred. An arrow hit its target nearby and another stifled cry rang out.

There are two of them. Aiphatòn raised his upper body, spotted his enemy and sent the dagger flying at the archer, just as he reloaded.

The tip struck him from behind, level with his right kidney. Moaning, he fell to his knees and dropped his bow.

The last enemy had turned away from Aiphatòn and was aiming straight at Ávoleï who was standing between the trees and preparing to throw a sword.

That's not going to save her! Aiphatòn immediately hurled the sheaf of arrows at the soldier and leaped to his feet to give chase.

The momentum of the arrows might not have been enough to penetrate the armour, but a dozen arrowheads pierced his arms and legs superficially. In the end, Aiphatòn achieved exactly what he had hoped for from his attack: one of the blades severed the bow string in the crucial instant before the archer let it go to shoot Ávoleï with an arrow.

Then Aiphatòn was close and smashing his fist into the back of his opponent's neck at top speed so that he was knocked face-first onto the ground and lying motionless with broken vertebrae before he could even utter a scream.

'So my debt is settled then,' he yelled at the elf-woman and turned around. *Where did the other one get to?*

The injured enemy was groaning as he crawled commando-style through the ferns and tried to pull the dagger out of his back.

Aiphatòn reached him and pulled him up by his mop of fair hair, yanked the weapon out of his wound and saw the blood and a pale liquid spurting out; the smell of urine spread. 'How many people are with the barrels?' he said quietly.

'Die,' snarled the warrior and tried to break the grip on his hair with both hands, but couldn't manage it. His dirty fingers slid uselessly over the armoured glove.

Ávoleï came to Aiphatòn's side, pale with anger. She rammed her sword into the injured warrior's stomach and twisted it. 'Shooting my men dead from behind like a coward,' she whispered, 'is not an act of heroism!'

The älf from Dâkiòn uttered a high-pitched sound, his eyes rolled back and his eyelids fluttered.

Aiphatòn felt the warrior go slack. *Dead.* He dropped the body. 'How many of your troops died?'

'All of them,' she replied, filled with hatred.

She's a beginner. She won't have called more than a handful of rebellious fishermen or cowardly pirates to account as commander. 'Welcome to war, little *elf-woman*,' he remarked.

'How did you know . . . ?'

'You mustn't take it to heart if you lose against warriors. See it as a game where you need to budget very carefully.'

Ávoleï looked at him in bafflement, remaining silent for several heartbeats. 'A game? That's what you call it in Tark Draan?'

'It's like with Tharc. The enemy carry out their job, we do ours. What matters' – he walked over to the tree and pulled the spear out of the trunk and the enemy's corpse – 'is that at the end of the battle, we are the victors.' He tipped the dead body to one side. 'That's the best way to honour the ones who have fallen.' Aiphatòn wiped the blood off on the ferns. 'I suggest that I continue on with my troops and you. You would only lead new warriors into another trap, after all.'

Ávoleï scrutinised him, a bead of sweat running down her right temple. He saw appreciation, awe and fear in her eyes.

It's time to sow more uncertainty. I started with Irïanora, and I'll continue with Ávoleï. Aiphatòn smiled calculatingly. 'I'll take that as agreement.' He took a step towards her.

'What?' The elf-woman shrank back a step.

'This.' He moved toward her, grabbing her by the neck and drawing her lips to his.

To his astonishment, Ávoleï did not resist his caress, she breathed faster.

Aiphatòn let her go.

She glared at him, furious and confused. 'What was that?'

'Just a foretaste of the favour that I'm going to call in from you.' He went to the embankment and waved to his warriors on the other side. 'You remember? Whoever reaches Dâkiòn first?'

The stunned looks he was getting from the troops made it clear that they had been watching the kiss.

Excellent. There will be gossip and then it won't be long until she's no longer trusted. That will weaken the army. And Ôdaiòn ought to hate me even more because it will look like I'm becoming his rival. 'The relief shift is on its way,' he told Ávoleï, turning to the surprised elf-woman. 'We ought to hurry and intercept them.'

She didn't seem to be over her shock yet. She nodded mutely.

'Let's join my platoon.' He took a run-up and jumped into the middle of the Tronjor, then swam the remaining paces to the bank.

Although Aiphatòn had not particularly enjoyed the kiss at first, he could still feel Ávoleï's lips on his mouth.

There was no longer any trace of his antipathy, truly *none at all*.

That was not something that could have been foreseen, however.

Tark Draan, Human kingdom of Gauragar, Oakenburgh, 5452nd division of unendingness (6491st solar cycle), autumn

If I were an assassin, this is where I would lie in wait. Carmondai was crouching on the roof that Carâhnios had forced him onto during the night. He was looking at the Elria Temple and the wide road that led up to it before making a sharp turn westwards. *The line of fire is clear and it's not too far away. He could fire four times before a bodyguard would be able to respond.*

The young queen would take this route to make her entrance to Oakenburgh, if he was correctly interpreting the plethora of stalls pitched along the road.

The small town looked like many others with its half-timbered houses at most three storeys high – with the exception of the mayoral building and the temple – and colourful, painted façades, the brown or white shutters and the simple red clay roof tiles.

Tranquil was the word that came to Carmondai's mind, which was a euphemism for *boring. As ever, the barbarians don't let art into their lives, their streets or their squares.*

Yet again, he didn't know where the zhadár had got to.

Carâhnios had taken off immediately after they'd arrived and ordered him to stay in the shadows on the roof to get a bird's-eye view of everything. The groundling would draw attention to himself in good time. Nobody was meant to know anything about their arrival in Oakenburgh because that would frighten Votòlor and stop him continuing with his mission.

The residents, full of anticipation, never suspected that certain death could lurk round every corner. Twine had been stretched across the streets and banners hung from it emblazoned with large-lettered greetings in honour of the Ido woman. There was a great atmosphere

in the alleyways and streets, the Gauragar standard pennants fluttering in the cool autumn wind. The woodland's blaze of colour seemed
to be reflected in Oakenburgh.

Carmondai crawled commando-style to the chimney with whitish-
grey smoke billowing out of it and hid. He stifled the urge to cough.
His sketching was coming along very well despite his reddened
eyes. Carâhnios had even taken his shackles off for this, adding the threat,
of course, that he could hunt him down any time. *At least this time his
plan doesn't entail me having to hold that bottle. Watch, wait, record.*

He was intrigued as to what kind of performance Carâhnios was
giving in front of the Gauragarians. The news of the existence of the
zhadár had done the rounds. But being changed for the worse by älfar
magic and drinks didn't necessarily cultivate a good reputation. No
amount of self-sacrifice would help.

Carmondai looked around incessantly, noting details and jot-
ting them down, from the tent stalls and the traders with trays around
their necks to the snack bars.

Musicians were rehearsing their melodies on the little square
for the fifth time but he thought it would have sounded better with
tuned instruments. Small children were being given baskets full of
brightly coloured leaves and the last blossoms of this cycle to scatter
before the queen.

Carmondai took out the sketch he'd done where he'd tried to get
her features right. *I'm excited to see how close I got.*

More and more residents appeared, their murmuring and chatting
melding together; from his position on the roof it sounded like slowly
falling rain. The stirrings on the square and along the road stoked
speculation the dignitary was to arrive soon.

The beggars also pushed their way forward to get their share of
the Ido woman's generosity and surely the cutpurses were sneaking

through the crowds, getting ready to slip their newly acquired riches into their own pockets in one swift, expert movement.

I'll make a sacrifice to Inàste if I make it out of Oakenburgh in one piece. Carmondai still didn't think it was a bright idea not to warn Mallenia. If the attack was successful and the älf and the zhadár were caught, the incensed mob would string them both up.

Provided we let it happen.

He had no interest in a fight against an angry mob, especially as he had no usable weapons on him. Besides, there would be survivors in Oakenburgh; the news would have repercussions in Girdlegard and bring more trouble with it.

Just briefly, his time in the Aklán dungeon seemed temptingly safe.

But the more Carmondai thought about it, the more a plan formed that – if it could actually be put into action – would free him from Carâhnios in Oakenburgh.

Finally a horseman raced down the street waving a banner as he shouted over and over: 'They're coming! They're coming! The queen and her entourage are coming!'

Carmondai ventured out of the smoke, staying in the shadow of the smokestack which he intensified using älfar powers. *Will I be able to see you, Votòlor?*

He was undoubtedly an observant onlooker, but it was not easy to spot an älf-warrior if they absolutely did not want you to do so.

There came the sound of multiple hoofbeats, then the first armed soldiers came riding round the bend and turned onto the main street; the flags of the two kingdoms of Idoslane and Gauragar were flapping on their upright lances.

The crosswind and the cloths fluttering everywhere would make it harder for the assassin, but Carmondai estimated three or four shots would be possible.

No matter how hard he tried, he couldn't see Votòlor or make out a conspicuously darker shadow where the assassin could be hiding, lying in wait.

Mallenia of Ido appeared around the corner with her courtly entourage after twenty soldiers. She was indistinguishable from the armed riders around her at first glance.

The tall woman had strapped on light plate armour with the coat of arms of her ancestor, Prince Mallen of Ido, engraved on it. She kept her long, blonde hair back in a braid that dangled down between her shoulder blades. Her thin crown, more like a headband made of silver wire, was not particularly eye-catching. She carried two short swords at her side.

Cheers rang out, the musicians let rip and in their excitement promptly played so badly out of tune that Carmondai grimaced in pain.

At the sight of the symbol on her armour he thought of Mallen of Ido, the brave ruler who had opposed the traitorous magus Nôd'onn and also fought against the eoîl. The young queen made no secret of the fact that she saw herself, like her ancestor, as a warrior and not as a dolled-up, expensively dressed piece of eye candy on the throne.

Carmondai looked back and forth between his sketch and Mallenia. *Not a bad likeness, I'd say. My imagination is reliable.*

A glance at the temple revealed nothing unusual and there was no sign of Carâhnios.

Maybe they've killed each other. The idea brought a smile to his face, even though that would thwart his own plan.

A delegation from the town broke away from the ranks of curious onlookers. Marching at the head of it was the mayor, as the imposing chain around his neck and chest made clear, and behind him came the representatives of the guilds and the council leaders.

Mallenia's convoy came to a halt, the mounted soldiers forming a passageway through which the mayor could walk to the queen. The flower girls and flower boys were hastily pushed to the front and scattered the mixture of blossoms and leaves, bringing a warm smile to the young ruler's face.

The line of fire is clearer than ever. Carmondai thought the two soldiers at Mallenia's side might have been vigilant but by the time they'd have raised their arms with their heavy shields, two black arrows would be lodged in the young woman's heart. The plate armour she had selected was no match for the extra-large älfar arrows. The polished arrowheads that had been designed to be used against this kind of armour would probably come out again on the other side.

'We are delighted, Queen Mallenia of Ido, Ruler of Gauragar and Idoslane, that you are visiting our town on your way through the kingdoms,' the mayor cried solemnly, and was handed an oversized key by the guild chief. 'Take this as a symbolic gift that our gates are as open to you as our hearts, Queen.' He walked at a measured pace with the guild chief through the cavalry's guard of honour.

As open as our hearts? What a trite image. Surgical instruments would have been an appropriate symbolic gift. Carmondai was surprised there had not yet been any soft whirring sound. *Carâhnios has probably tracked him down and intercepted him.*

He heard the quiet creak of a string growing taut next to him.

He turned in surprise and saw an älf standing in front of the chimney, taking precise aim over the shaft of a black arrow. He was wearing black leather armour, his dark hair tied up in a band at the nape of his neck. The polished arrowhead was presumably aimed at the queen's heart; two more arrows were leaning against the brickwork.

The assassin turned his head to Carmondai and winked once.

That winking – combined with the evil smile – said it all.

They're meant to think I'm to blame. He looked at his sketch of the queen and it looked like an accusation already.

Before Votòlor could release his finger from the string, Carmondai swung around and pulled the assassin's right leg out.

The älf recovered from the impending fall but the arrow he had accidentally released misfired.

The projectile whizzed, unnoticed by the locals, through a banner and lodged in a beam a hundred paces away.

Votòlor dropped the bow and drew a dagger out of its sheath, hurling it at Carmondai. 'You miserable traitor!'

He was too close to dodge the attack completely. Turning round was only partially successful – the tip of the blade plunged into his left shoulder instead of his heart.

Carmondai fell backwards. *Damn it! But you haven't got me yet.*

Nobody in the street noticed the silent struggle on the roof.

The assassin had picked up the bow again, taken aim and fired – just as Carmondai pulled the dagger out of his shoulder and threw it back at him.

The blade struck Votòlor underneath the shoulder, while the arrow whizzed into the chest of the bodyguard next to the queen. The polished tip penetrated the metal easily.

The man slumped forwards very slowly and fell out of his saddle, crashing to the ground next to a terrified flower girl. Shouts started up in the street.

I am definitely not dying for you. Carmondai had got to his feet and now threw himself at his opponent, who couldn't pull the dagger out. He dropped his bow and drew his sword.

Carmondai dodged a whirring blow and hit the hilt of the lodged dagger to drive it deeper into his enemy's body.

Screaming, Votòlor pushed him away.

Carmondai toppled backwards onto the roof tiles and only just escaped the next blow, the blade slicing into the fired clay.

'How can you betray your own tribe?' The assassin kicked Carmondai in the head, sending him to the edge of the roof. 'I could have killed her!' he hissed and prepared to strike again.

'Not at my expense,' Carmondai retorted in a daze.

'You're going to . . .' Votòlor didn't get any further. With a soft whistle, six arrows struck his upper body, making him stagger. Groaning, he fell sideways and plummeted into the depths.

They missed Carmondai only because he had taken cover. *I'll only avoid death if they all know that I saved the queen's life.*

He held up the bundle of white pages and waved it as a symbol of surrender. 'Don't shoot,' he shouted in the language of the humans. 'I foiled the attack on the queen, do you hear? I *foiled* it!'

'Stand up, black-eye!' came the cry.

Inàste, think of the sacrifice I'll make for you. Getting gingerly to his feet, he looked over the edge and spotted ten archers aiming at him. 'Here I am.'

A healer was already tending to the wounded bodyguard and Mallenia was surrounded by more soldiers. Amid the sudden horrified silence came the sound of many blades being rammed relentlessly into a body. Several warriors were making sure that Votòlor was dead.

'Look!' As proof, Carmondai brushed the paper over his wounds and showed them his blood. 'We fought, I pushed him down.'

'Come down from the roof,' Mallenia commanded, her face a picture of rage. 'If you make any sudden movement, my archers will shoot you dead.'

Carmondai nodded. 'Right away. But forgive me if it takes a while. It's the wounds and my age.' Suddenly he noticed a ragged beggar who, unlike the other unkempt people and the rest of the villagers, was creeping surreptitiously through the crowds.

Just three more paces and a powerful leap and the man would reach the queen.

The tale-weaver's blood ran cold. *How did it not occur to us that there could be more than one älf?*

If the second assassin were to attack, the archers would also shoot at Carmondai because they would consider him an accomplice providing a diversion – which he ironically was doing an extremely good job of right now.

I've got to warn them. 'There's another one there!' he cried and pointed at the beggar who ran away and slipped his cloak off at the same time. Black armour appeared from underneath it, and two slim maces gleamed.

The outcry from the crowd blended with the cries of the surprised warriors and the whinnying of the startled horses.

But it seemed Carmondai's warning hand gesture had been too quick, and the chaos too great: a hail of arrows whirred up at the roof.

He did not have time to take cover.

Ishím Voróo, Älfar town of Dsôn Dâkiòn, 5452nd division of unendingness (6491st solar cycle), late summer

On the evening of the fourth moment, Aiphatòn, Ávoleï and the ten warriors glimpsed the enormous mountain and the contours of Dsôn Dâkiòn through the undergrowth, shining far and wide in the light of the setting sun. The golden bridge was all aglow.

'We've done it.' Ávoleï knelt down on the dry border of the overgrown riverbed and wrote some messages that she then floated down the river in inflated leather pouches.

That was too easy and full of unexplained incidents. Aiphatòn looked back and forth between the river and the town.

They had made good progress, constantly sending news back to the waiting fleet. They found one cache of barrels after another as well as two chains that had been strung up just below the waterline. The ships would collect the barrels on their way upstream so that the petrol could be used in their attack on the town.

What they did not find, however, were the defending forces and their own scouts. They had not even encountered the expected relief shift.

Now we're outside the town and we still don't have a logical explanation for it. Aiphatòn stood up.

'We're waiting until the fleet . . .' Ávoleï looked up in surprise as he ventured out of the undergrowth below the riverbank and into the open. 'What do you think you're doing? Come back!'

'I want to know why there was nobody waiting with the other barrels,' he replied and darted across the gravel, which gave off soft crunching sounds. 'You should be having the same worries I'm having.' Aiphatòn raised his head from time to time and looked over the bank at the town that rose up all-powerful and majestic. With its bridges, battlements and towers, it clearly proved who ruled for a radius of many miles. *Is this a trick by Shôtoràs?*

The älfar from Elhàtor followed him while Ávoleï brought up the rear.

'I *have* thought about it. And I assume it's to do with the canal and the imminent flooding,' the elf-woman answered. 'They need every pair of hands to finish it.'

'Nobody would ever give up the sole lines of defence they'd had up till then for that. Even if they left just two men in the hideaways.' Aiphatòn couldn't see any lights on the allures, on the plains around

Dâkiòn or in the buildings in the small fishing port where they were headed. *That means that they are lying in ambush somewhere.* He looked past the warriors to the woodland and the adjoining swamp. 'Do you think it's possible they've set up a second garrison in the marshland where they're assembling troops to attack the ships from behind?'

Ávoleï shook her head. 'Our scouts would have noticed. They were scattered right around the town and reported every change, no matter how minor, as well as information on the dam and the canal.'

Quite true. But where are they now? Aiphatòn stopped, crouched down and took one enormous leap from the bank onto the higher ground, holding the spear in his left hand and brandishing it defiantly. *This is no ploy by the sovereign.*

'Madman!' Ávoleï hissed after him, outraged. 'You'll give us away!'

Aiphatòn's gaze darted this way and that as he waited for a cry, a bugle call, a blast of fanfare, a cloud of arrows or a platoon of horse-back riders bursting out of the ground because they had dug themselves into it.

Swallows screeched as they flew overhead and chased the swarms of midges that were buzzing around; two hares hopped cautiously among the blades of grass and nibbled them while the wind swept over the älf and cooled his skin.

There's nobody here. Aiphatòn placed a hand over his eyes, shielding them from the glare and he saw the open gates at the lower entrance as well as at the internal gateways. 'The town has been abandoned,' he informed his companions.

'That's what they want us to think.' Ávoleï pulled one of the warriors back by the shoulder just as he was about to climb upwards. 'It's a trick to get us to make stupid mistakes. Come back so that . . .'

'Let's split up.' Aiphatòn walked towards one of the entrance gates, the bridges stretching up gradually beyond them. 'You take five war-riors and investigate the trench they've started as well as the dam. The others are coming with me.'

He couldn't help grinning when he noticed the soldiers joining him and Ávoleï cursed. 'Keep an eye on the battlements,' he advised the elf-woman. 'One of us will give you a signal as soon as we've found anything.'

He raced across the plain with his warriors and reached the gate. They didn't waste any time, going straight through the open portal.

Nothing indicated an attack or a battle. There were no bodies, no blood spatters or other obvious signs.

Bridge by bridge, they jogged onwards, infiltrating Dsôn Dâkiòn.

The daystar was sinking rapidly and the sky was turning red and preparing the backdrop for the stars and moon to come out. The wind was picking up, carrying the smell of dust and burnt food.

The vast settlement gave them a silent welcome. The patter of their soles on the stones and the occasional clank of a scabbard hitting a leg or armour were the only sounds, eerily loud in the silence.

'I would never have thought when the sun came up that I would be inside the town in the very same moment,' murmured one of the sol-diers who was constantly looking around like all the others. Out of incredulity and wariness. Nobody trusted the tranquillity.

At first Aiphatòn expected the defending forces to come charging out of the gigantic basalt buildings or start throwing stones at them from the roofs to kill them, but once they'd reached the edge of Dâkiòn's lower town and were hurrying along the broad street undis-turbed, he knew that Shôtoràs had abandoned his Dsôn.

'I wonder if he built his own fleet in the swamp and is sailing to Elhàtor right now?' one of the soldiers suggested.

Aiphatòn thought this was an intriguing idea. 'Nobody would

have expected that anyway. Myself included.' He wheeled round and started to climb one of the tall watchtowers with his troops. 'Let's see if we can find out any more from up here.' The prickling in every fibre of his body had returned, and it could not be put down to the exertion. The magical field of the town was reacting with his innate magic and the alloy.

They went round and round up the tower until they reached the viewing platform.

The wind was fierce up here and the sky had darkened, accentuating the brightness of the stars.

'Take a look around.'

From around seventy paces above the roofs, the houses still did not look small.

They shimmered thanks to the inlay, the jewels and likely some special-effects spells; it was similar to what he'd seen when Vailóras brought him to the sovereign.

But behind the windows it was still dark.

Not one light, not even a small one. Aiphatòn looked towards the river, flowing along with its glittering waves. He could make out six figures moving around and spreading out near the clearly distinguishable dam. *Ávoleï has made it too. Good.*

The canal for diverting the Tronjor extended as far as the old riverbed. There was less than three paces to go before a large proportion of the river would flow into the valley. Even the flooding mechanism for the second weir was in place. Dâkiòn's architects had done a good job of preventing the fleet from Elhàtor attacking by taking the water away from them.

The plan was perfect. If it were a game of Tharc and I was the opponent, I would have to yield before the round began because I'd have nothing to counter it with. Aiphatòn didn't understand what had prompted the sovereign to get it all ready and then not actually put it into action.

'Is it possible that they wanted to lure us into the valley to drown us?' One warrior came over to him and looked at the construction on the river.

'How stupid must Shôtoràs think we are for him to seriously believe that Elhàtorians would get out of their ships to climb into a valley that has a canal leading into it from the river, visible from very far away?' Aiphatòn propped one hand against the tower wall. *Who is depriving me of my war?*

Ávoleï also seemed to assume they were alone now and her entourage lit torches. The glow of the orange flames was visible from a distance away and brought the warriors out of the darkness.

'I think there's someone there!' Aiphatòn heard the faint cry from behind him. 'There, in the second part of the town, on the bridge.'

They ran over to the soldier who made the discovery and peered around.

He's right! A decoy? Aiphatòn saw the shadowy silhouette of a petite älf-woman that looked familiar; like the last time they met, she was wearing skimpy clothes. *The death-dancer.*

'Let's seize her, but be on your guard against her magic. She is nimble and deadly.' He involuntarily placed his hand over the hole in the armoured plate – he had not yet fitted it with stuffing or a cover. A serious weak point and an oversight. *I'll have a little plate of iron laid over it later.*

They ran down the steps and spread out as soon as they reached the ground so as not to let Tanôtai escape under any circumstances.

The red-haired death-dancer was coming towards them over the bridge and saw them. She stopped in shock and ran back the way she'd come.

Aiphatòn suppressed the impulse to take up the pursuit. 'We're going after her slowly,' he commanded. 'Watch out! Because now it really looks like a trap.'

'Could all of the locals be lying in wait for us in the upper town?' one warrior said, trying to sound amused. But the idea that the sovereign's troops were standing silently in the side streets with their weapons drawn, just waiting to charge out and hack them to pieces with their swords was making the soldiers anxious.

Meanwhile Tanôtai was walking along the large road, straight towards the palace where Shôtoràs lived, her long, red hair fluttering behind her. She didn't look round, as if she didn't care whether the intruders were following her.

Aiphatòn started to jog slowly. *She's afraid of us.*

The death-dancer disappeared through the open gate into the palace.

'I'm going first.' Aiphatòn took the lead and dashed up the five steps to the entrance.

With one enormous leap, he got through the gate that was still ajar and landed in the inner courtyard he had visited once before. He did a shoulder roll and stayed down on one knee, holding the spear at the ready with both hands. *What I wouldn't give to be wielding my own spear.*

He couldn't see Tanôtai.

The courtyard appeared empty and gave onto a second courtyard directly beyond another semi-circular passageway.

Aiphatòn spared himself the analysis of carefully devised ambushes. *Anything is possible.* He stood up and moved slowly through the surreally large arch into the second courtyard.

The footsteps behind him belonged to the warriors from Elhàtor who caught up with him to protect him – he knew this without turning around. He recognised the sounds they made.

The walls towered up around him four gigantic storeys high. Large windows and galleries allowed a view of the inner courtyard and hence a view of him too.

There she is. Aiphatòn saw the death-dancer standing in the courtyard next to an älfar statue made of marble, bone and steel.

Tanôtai was leaning her tattooed shoulder blade against it and had slung her arms around the stone neck as though it were her lover and she had invited him to a secret nocturnal assignation. Her needle-daggers were stowed in the holders on her metal forearm guards. The lines on her skin looked black, as though poison was flowing through her veins.

Or anger is spreading throughout her body. Aiphatòn stopped four paces away from her. 'I want my spear back,' he said firmly and raised his weapon. 'This one isn't up to much.'

Tanôtai laughed quietly at first and then worked herself into such a fit of laughter that her whole body shook. 'Aiphatòn, emperor of the älfar of Tark Draan, ruler of a kingdom, commander of the Dsôn Aklán, son of the Inextinguishables,' she reeled off, sniggering. 'You're someone with great power and plenty of titles.'

'My spear, Tanôtai,' he reminded her. 'And what has happened to the town? Where is the sovereign?'

The death-dancer disentangled herself from the statue and slowly raised her arms out to the sides, turning on her tiptoes and gently tilting her head to the right.

With every graceful, elaborate-looking turn, more älfar appeared at the windows and on the galleries, their eyes fixed mutely on the inner courtyard and the pair inside it.

Aiphatòn saw warriors, cîani and plainly dressed townsfolk pushing and shoving each other aside to get the best view. *There must be hundreds of them and they're all unarmed.* He turned around – and saw the first inner courtyard was suddenly filled with Dâkiòners lining up in silence too.

His warriors, on the other hand, had vanished.

The prickling sensation became stronger. 'Are we to have a duel? Is that what you're after?' he tried out one explanation for this spectacle. 'Is the courtyard going to be our arena?'

Tanôtai paused and slowly lowered her arms, straightened up her neck and stared at Aiphatòn.

A huge, muscular, human-warrior suddenly leaped from the highest gallery wearing a copper close helmet and landed safely next to the death-dancer. Stone shattered under the soles of his boots on impact, dirt swirling upwards.

He was wearing simple, hardened leather armour that was covered in artistic white runes, as was his helmet. Pale, delicate smoke rose steadily out of the eye, mouth and nose slits and dispersed almost as soon as it emerged from the openings.

Aiphatòn changed his grip on the spear so that he could toss it. *I saw someone like that on the battlefield. When the botoican armies charged into each other.* 'Am I fighting him then?'

The residents of Dâkiòn stood around stiffly, staring and waiting. From time to time, whitish runes gleamed at their necks.

Tanôtai laughed. 'No, you're not going to fight. You're going to *belong* to me!'

Aiphatòn began to suspect he was no longer speaking to the death-dancer, but to a botoican. 'I'm immune to your power, botoican.'

The red-haired älf-woman gave a grotesque smirk, her charming features vanishing. 'Your tribe is vulnerable to my magic, just like every other tribe. Nobody is immune to me. Nothing and nobody, Aiphatòn.'

The warrior with the copper helmet walked towards him slowly.

'Let yourself be touched,' Tanôtai purred. 'Let yourself be touched like the others and you will be a good servant to me.'

'You've incorporated Dâkiòn into your army?' Aiphatòn was thinking through his options for escaping the trap. The quickest route out would be to go upstairs, then onto the roofs via the galleries and on from there. *The war will take a different course from the one I planned but I will get my war.*

'Surprising Shôtoràs was a wonderful moment,' the botoican confessed through the mouth of the death-dancer. The botoican must have been somewhere nearby. 'I sent this beautiful älf-woman to her homeland to have the gates opened for me. And as soon as I was inside the walls, things happened very quickly. My power is spreading like mad.' She did a few little dance steps. 'She was looking for you, by the way. She and her entourage, who were wiped out by my ghaist. They're incredible warriors, these creatures made of magic and sacrificed souls. Nothing can stop them.'

The warrior with the copper helmet had almost reached Aiphatòn and was slowly extending his hand.

'Now let yourself be touched,' Tanôtai repeated seductively and showed him her slim silhouette. 'I swear I'll treat you well. Because I've got plans for you. Your knowledge will become my knowledge and I'll give you back your spear immediately if you ask for it. Along with Nodûcor . . .'

'The wind-voice fell into your hands?' *Good thing he's still wearing the half-mask.*

Tanôtai sniggered again. 'Oh yes, as a bonus in Dâkiòn. At first I didn't know who I was looking at, but I was informed.' She tensed her muscles as though preparing for an attack. The tattooed lines glowed weakly, the light intensifying with every heartbeat. 'Nodûcor is an obedient little älf now. And the no-less-obedient cîani of this town are putting all their efforts into removing his gag so that I can start storms.' She whooped. 'And I'll annex Elhàtor, of course. With your help, great emperor. *You'll* come up with a way of conquering the island, I'm sure. It would be a shame to raze it to the ground with wind and waves. But if I can't have it, it's to be destroyed.'

The enormous ghaist's index finger came very close to the älf's solar plexus.

'I do not accept the offer.' Aiphatòn thrust the spear at the fingertip but the tip shattered as if it was made of brittle wood.

Cursing, he catapulted backwards and evaded his opponent, jumping up onto the first gallery and running past the silent residents of Dâkiòn as the ghaist lifted his head. The smoking eye slits were fixed on him.

I've got to warn Ávoleï. The fleet needs to turn around. Otherwise we're bringing the botoican the ships he needs to conquer the Magnificent. Aiphatòn jumped upwards from one storey to the next, dived onto the roof and looked down into the inner courtyard.

The warrior and the death-dancer were staring up at him.

The petrol! With petrol, we could torch them all, including the ghaist. He thought his idea was a good one. *Before he . . .*

'Catch him!' Tanôtai commanded sharply and pointed one of her daggers at him, the tip of the blade flaring with a dazzling glow. 'Catch him *alive* for me so that he can become one of you!'

And with a collective, greedy cry, all of the älfar behind the windows, on the galleries and in the courtyard started to run, push and shove to get at Aiphatòn.

Chapter XIII

There is nothing greater than the power of suspicion stoked by distrust.

Wise saying of the Älfar
Collected by Carmondai, master of word and image

Tark Draan, Human kingdom of Gauragar, Oakenburgh, 5452nd division of unendingness (6491st solar cycle), late autumn

'I want to see him. He's *my* prisoner!'

Well said! Mallenia of Ido couldn't help but admire the black-clad dwarf for standing as confidently in the stone foyer of Oakenburgh's town hall as if he were a king. She was sitting in a window alcove enjoying the rays of sunlight falling through the glass.

'I'm sure you understand that he's not capable of receiving visitors,' she responded politely but firmly. 'He was lucky the arrows didn't kill him, but let's just say this: he was close to passing into endingness.' She scrutinised the zhadár. The älfarness radiated from every single one of his pores; the aura of evil and danger was more palpable than they were with her prisoner. 'I'll have you summoned as soon as he's awake. My healers' sedatives are strong.'

The dwarf, who introduced himself as Carâhnios, but who had once gone by Balodil, had appeared during the dramatic orbit in the utter commotion of the second attempted attack. He had fearlessly confronted the älfar assassin who was dressed as a beggar.

Without him, Mallenia had to admit, it would barely have been possible for her soldiers to kill the black-eye making an attempt on her life. *I don't have to like him though.*

The guards standing around the queen in the cramped hall couldn't hide their discomfort at the dwarf with the black skin and black hair who had undergone an unmistakeable transformation due to the Akláns' influence.

A manifestation of night and evil. Mallenia, who was wearing her armour, tried to smile. But it didn't quite work. 'What do you want as a reward, my dear dwarf?'

'My black-eye back.' The zhadár glared at her and placed his blackened fingers on his belt. It had been a clever move not to turn up wearing the armour that made him look even more sinister.

'He's not *your* black-eye. He was caught in Bhará, as far as I know, and you took him with you as your companion so that the stories of what you experienced during your hunt would be written down,' she corrected him. 'That's how Fiëa reported it to me. And on top of that, the fact is, *she* overpowered the älf. Correct me if I'm wrong.'

Carâhnios took a deep breath. 'So I'm not getting him back?' he fumed.

Mallenia said nothing. *Never.*

The zhadár bowed his head. 'I'm very surprised at you, Queen,' he said, his voice deeper than before. 'You hate the älfar. They killed your relatives, you fought them relentlessly and swore not to rest until all of them were killed. But now you save an älf's life? Give me a reason that I'll understand.'

'You know he's no ordinary älf.' Mallenia was prepared for the accusation. 'This is Carmondai, who has spent the last few cycles in a dungeon. His name does not appear in connection with any atrocities in the recent history of Girdlegard. He could be accused of being involved in the construction of Dsôn Balsur and creating stories that portrayed black-eyes in a better light than was accurate,' she shot back quietly. 'But that's all.'

Carâhnios laughed bitterly. 'Do you hear yourself saying these words? You're defending an älf, Queen. An älf! Prince Mallen of Ido would box your ears for that.' After this insult he turned around and made for the door. 'I expect you to send me word as soon as he is fit to travel.'

'My advice, my dear dwarf, is to move on before word spreads that a zhadár is hunting the älfar,' Mallenia replied. 'Your intervention was impossible to miss.'

Carâhnios left the room without answering.

The queen heaved a sigh of relief. Even the guards around her relaxed, as was clear from the grinding and scraping sounds their metal armour made. *If I put the älf to death, I'd have to have you murdered too. Who knows what crimes you've committed?*

The zhadár appeared to be the more dangerous of the pair. And the fact that he had tried to collect the blood of the mutilated assassin in a bottle after the attack did not improve his trustworthiness.

He has more demonic knowledge than the tale-weaver.

Mallenia got up from the window seat and went down into the vaults of the town hall with an escort. Along with the wine cellar and the storage barrels, down here was where the dungeons were. They had chained the älf to a camp-bed in one of the dungeons; her healer was taking care of him.

Carâhnios had wounded her with his final words, because they were essentially true: the Idos did not show mercy to any black-eye.

But there were a few things about Carmondai that made the circumstances different and as long as these puzzles remained unsolved, she would hold off on executing him. *Even Mallen would spare him.*

Mallenia entered the vault and hurried to the windowless cell where they had imprisoned the älf. Ten sentries were guarding the exit and were under instruction that, at the slightest sign of unexplained fear or darkness or the torches extinguishing, they were to kill the prisoner instantly.

She walked in and saw the healer sitting next to the älf and feeding him soup. His muscular torso was bandaged in various places and his shoulder was also wrapped in a thick layer of pale, sterilised cloth.

He's awake. Excellent. 'Can he speak?'

'He can,' replied Carmondai with a smile. The dried blood was still caked on his skin in a few places, flaking off as soon as he moved. There were reddish-black clots in his mid-length brown hair too. The priority had been to save his life, not his looks.

Mallenia dismissed her healer, who obeyed in astonishment. Then she sat down next to the älf and drew one of her short swords. 'Here's a legend who wrote legends,' she said thoughtfully.

Carmondai watched her closely, his dark eyes shimmering a brownish colour in the light from all the oil lamps. 'You're not known for being a friend of my people.'

The queen nodded slowly. 'But in dying, would you potentially become an even greater legend?' Mallenia looked at the bandages – they no longer showed any red staining. 'Your wounds are closing up fast.'

'As I didn't pass into endingness, my body wants to participate in life again quickly, no matter how old it is and how much it hurts when I get up. I'm an old man, I just look like a man of fifty cycles to you.' The älf looked searchingly at her. 'That's your reason? I shouldn't become a legend? To whom? To the two or three älfar still sneaking across Girdlegard and being hunted by Carâhnios?' He shook his mop of brown hair. 'Hardly likely, Queen.'

'Well deduced.' Mallenia raised the sword. 'Your death would be more than welcome but there are circumstances that make you very interesting. There is that zhadár who is collecting älfar blood and wants to have you by his side.' She placed the sword against his throat. 'I need to find out more about him and his kind because he exudes more evil than one of the Aklán. He needs to be watched more carefully than you do.'

Carmondai simply raised his eyebrows to signify his agreement.

'Secondly, I received a letter from Ilahín, one of the last elves in Girdlegard, just after it became known that I had you here in Oakenburgh.' She leaned forward. 'In it he warns me urgently about your words, and your silver tongue that allows you to twist truths, as you have done in your writings before. Apparently I should do Girdlegard a favour and execute you.'

'That doesn't surprise me.'

'I'm surprised by the fact he is so insistent on it.' The queen looked him in the eye. 'You are so old, have so much knowledge and can give us information about so many things regarding the älfar – and we're just meant to destroy that?'

'No doubt Ilahín thinks I'll lie.'

'And you would too, and I couldn't blame you for it. But there are means of making even you tell the truth. I don't mean torture.' She gestured to the soup. 'My healer is a very experienced man. The herbs he mixes in make the truth come to light. Without using any magic.' Mallenia smiled when she saw his look of consternation. 'The elves were the first to push for your works to be collected and destroyed. Because they were a danger, because they tempted the humans into evil acts. At first I saw it the way they did,' she explained. 'But their demand is starting to seem too aggressive to me, too mysterious. And that's exactly why I want to hear more from you. If the elves have something to hide, I want to know before they invite even more of their people to Girdlegard.'

Carmondai nodded again. 'Are all of my drawings, poems and books already lost?'

'A lot was tossed into the flames, occasionally in anger, sometimes with joy but also with wistfulness.' Mallenia sat up straight. 'I secretly had some compiled instead of destroyed. Reading keeps me busy when I travel. As I know exactly what to think of your words, I can make sure the transformation of your people's deeds into heroic or even good deeds doesn't get to me. And you see: I gain knowledge from it without getting carried away by the älfar style.'

Carmondai slowly lifted one arm and reached for the soup as if to prove he wanted to tell the truth. 'That is wise of you, Queen Mallenia.'

'I just think I'm sceptical. That stemmed from the fight against your people,' she replied. 'And since the elves are your relatives and they brought ruin to my homeland once before with the eoîl, I'd like to know every little secret the älfar know about them. It is sometimes said: enemies usually know more dangerous things about you than your friends do.'

'I'll see to it as soon as I can write.' Carmondai spooned up the soup. 'I am in your debt, Queen.'

'You saved my life. I'd be in your debt for that if you weren't a black-eye.' Mallenia realised she was finding the älf more and more fascinating. It was one thing to fight against his people, but it was quite another to have a specimen in front of her who was not consumed by murderous thoughts towards her. *I can already see long conversations by the fire of an evening.* 'Let's start right now with some new information for me: what does the zhadár do with the älfar blood?'

Carmondai didn't hold back in explaining how Carâhnios went about things, and also what he was distilling for himself from the blood in order to increase his powers. The herbs ensured that no lie passed his lips.

Mallenia listened intently and found her suspicion confirmed. The last of the zhadár was definitely more dangerous than an älf.

I don't want him anywhere near me anymore. I'll let him know that and have him thrown out of Oakenburgh. He can go and hunt älfar. 'Thank you,' she said and put away the sword. 'So Carâhnios has a reason to kill you too then.'

'I'm aware of that. He has threatened me with it before.'

Which I must not allow. 'By the way, I hear King Boïndil of the Secondling tribe is desperate to have you visit him. It's about that very remedy that a zhadár . . .' She hesitated. 'The remedy that very zhadár Carâhnios gave him to drink. He wants to know what's in it and what you can take to counteract it.'

'I'm your prisoner, Queen.' Carmondai drank the last mouthful of soup straight from the bowl. 'You decide.'

Little by little, Mallenia was growing less certain as to whether the black-eye was putting on an act for her, or his meekness was down to the effect of the food garnished with herbs, or whether he had simply given up because he knew he was safe in her custody. 'I suppose so.'

The queen thought for a while.

Finally she got up and went to the door. 'Once you've recovered, you'll stay at my disposal and be permitted to move freely in my two kingdoms. Nobody will be allowed to kill you or beat you because from now on you are my property: an älf as the slave of a human. How times change,' she declared harshly. 'If you leave the confines of Ido-slane and Gauragar, I cannot guarantee your safety.'

He put down the bowl in astonishment. 'That is a great mercy.'

'You have a vast amount of knowledge about älfar and elves at your fingertips. That is a great opportunity.' Mallenia pointed to his wounds. 'By the way, they're healing because my friend Coïra stood by your bed and cast a healing spell that also bound you to me: if *I* die, *you* will pass on too. That's my protection against any more potential assassins.' She gave a brief nod. 'And so my debt to you would be set-tled.' She opened the door and went back into the corridor.

'Queen! How are you going to make sure your subjects don't mis-take me for an ordinary älf?' he called after her.

'You will be recognised.' Mallenia closed the door and sent one of the guards for the jailer as she crossed the vault. The spell supposedly binding Carmondai to her was a lie. *But he believed it.*

The jailer hurried over from the guardroom and bowed deeply to her. 'Majesty?'

'I'm very pleased with your work,' she praised him and pointed to the cell where Carmondai was. 'Oakenburgh has its own executioner, doesn't it?'

'Yes, majesty.'

'Is he skilled at torture?'

'Certainly, ma'am.'

'Is he a drinker or does he have a steady hand?'

The jailer didn't know what to make of all her questions. 'Well, I'd say he knows all the necessary methods of eliciting from the black-eye every answer that he refused to give you during the interrogation, majesty.'

Mallenia smiled. 'He was very open and spoke candidly.' She lifted her right arm, the index finger pointing at the coat of arms on her armour. 'The executioner is to brand the prisoner with the symbol of my family on both cheeks, because from now on he is my slave.'

'I see. A wonderful way of demonstrating the subjugation of the black-eyes, majesty,' he agreed, surprised and excited. 'I'll go and . . .'

'Wait,' she stopped him and turned off into the guardroom to get some paper and a quill. 'After that, the executioner is to get a thin wire, make it red-hot and write the following on the black-eye's forehead.' She jotted the words down on the page and pressed it into the jailer's hand. 'And shave the prisoner. I want the writing to be good and visible.' Mallenia turned to leave. 'My new slave is not to suffer pain at anyone's hands but mine.'

Ishím Voróo, Älfar town of Dsôn Dâkiòn, 5452nd division of unendingness (6491st solar cycle), late summer

I've got to get to the river. Aiphatòn jumped from roof to roof while hundreds of älfar followed him through the alleyways and streets of Dsôn Dâkiòn.

They kept their eyes fixed on him, running and pushing each other out of the way. Anybody who fell was trampled; nobody cared about anyone else. Urged relentlessly on by the botoican's magical command, from that point on this was the only mission on their minds.

Nobody shouted and nobody screamed anything at him, which was the most creepy thing about the scene. The shuffle of feet, the scraping of material, leather and metal, the fall of bodies and the stifled rattling breaths of those who didn't get back on their feet quickly enough, the squelching as they were then trodden over like trash by those who followed behind – there were no other sounds.

Everyone together and yet each for themselves. Aiphatòn changed direction again to leave them guessing where he was trying to go. Doing this meant they had not been able to cut him off yet.

The crowd stopped every time.

The pairs of eyes looked around until they made out their prey and started chasing after him again.

And now to the bridge. Suddenly Aiphatòn raced off in the exact opposite direction, and leaped from shingle to shingle towards an area where there were only very narrow alleys beneath him. *That will slow them down.*

He ran, dropped down onto a canopy and reached the ground. Then he was dashing towards the golden bridge. *If only I knew if it was possible to make it collapse quickly.* He wished he'd spoken to Irïanora for longer now. *She would have been able to give me some advice.*

Panting and footsteps pattering, the first älfar appeared behind him. His manoeuvre had gained him a head start of about a hundred paces, but the speed with which they stayed on his heels was remarkable.

This will not be fast enough to close a gate. Aiphatòn was running through the lower part of the town, racing towards the bridges that led away from it. He looked at the river as he ran and could make out the torches that Ávoleï and her warriors were carrying. *They are still examining the dam.*

'Hey,' he shouted as best he could while sprinting; he was running out of breath. 'Get away from there! Find a boat and set sail!' Then he had to stop shouting because it was getting too hard to breathe. *It's two miles. They'll hear me but not understand.*

He made the runes on his armour light up so that the Elhàtorians could see him and hopefully work out that he was fleeing.

Aiphatòn risked a glance over his shoulder.

His pursuers had caught up part of the way, closing the gap to fifty paces. Eight warrior-women and warriors were running out in front, having thrown off their armour without stopping so that they could run faster. Their faces were contorted; the pain in their legs must have been enormous but the botoican's mental command made them overcome the physical discomfort.

I wonder if they would still try and catch me with broken legs? As he ran past, he knocked over a large oil lamp.

The fluid spread over the stones and made them slippery.

The first two pursuers made it safely across, then the stumbling and skidding began. Hardly had one älf fallen when more of them would trip over the living obstacle until a gigantic teeming cluster had formed in front of the second gate and the lower bridge.

Aiphatòn knew it wouldn't hold up the possessed warriors for longer than a few heartbeats. *But even that could be enough for me to get into the boat and down the Tronjor to alert the fleet.*

Having crossed the last bridge, he dashed across the plain to the river. Two miles that threatened to go on forever.

To his relief, the handful of faster älfar warriors had fallen back, one lying motionless on the ground.

Aiphatòn headed for the fishing village and extinguished the runes so that he wasn't so visible to his pursuers.

He was surprised to see not only Ávoleï and her team, but also the five warriors who had accompanied him to Dsôn Dâkiòn. *The cowards fled just in time and deserted me.* 'We've got to get away,' he shouted at them.

'So it was a trap after all.' Ávoleï looked at the advancing crowd and turned pale. She completely misconstrued what she saw. 'Holy Inàste! Our plan is done for then. We will have to lay siege to Dâkiòn for a long time.'

Two of her warriors loaded arrows onto their strings and fired the missiles at the closest pursuers, who collapsed, fatally wounded.

'No. Shôtoràs and the town have fallen. But not to us.' As they hurried to the jetty where fishing boats were bobbing, he quickly summarised what had happened in the inner courtyard of the palace. 'And if the brave warriors had stayed by my side, they would have been able to tell you all this already.' He looked daggers at the five of them.

'They stayed,' replied one of the scolded warriors in a low voice. He drew his sword and stabbed the älf next to Ávoleï in the stomach. 'They became part of it.'

The stabbed warrior groaned as he fell onto the wooden planks.

The elf-woman wrenched both of her swords out of their holders and pointed them threateningly at him.

The warrior gave a distorted grin, having apparently lost his mind. 'Part of the infinite number of creatures who follow my will. Surrender and you will live – or end up like the dead.'

The botoican is speaking through him. Aiphatòn cursed and hurled his spear at the warrior, who was struck sideways through the chest by the tip of the spear and fell off the jetty into the river.

But the element of surprise was too strong: quick as a flash, Ávoleï and the four other älfar were overpowered by the externally controlled warriors, then wrestled to the ground. Meanwhile the mob of foes surged towards them along a wide front, jumping down off the embankment to get at them.

Before the ledge that led to the jetty, the crowd suddenly stopped as if there was a glass wall there.

Ávoleï was lying on the planks of the jetty. One of her own warriors was kneeling on her back and holding a sword to the nape of her neck to stop her moving.

There's only one option left. Aiphatòn was standing right in the middle of the booms, trapped between the enemies. His gaze was fixed on the elf-woman, and he tried to convey to her that he would swim to warn the fleet.

'If you jump,' the soldier behind her said, 'I will stab the commander through the neck. But if you stay and surrender to me, I will make you my top henchman.'

The warrior with the copper helmet forced his way through the glassy-eyed, motionless mob and stepped onto the jetty, placing one foot in front of the other. The wood creaked and rumbled dully under his boots.

'Ávoleï knows she's done for. Death is better than being your servant, botoican.' Aiphatòn launched himself off the jetty in a racing dive, flying through the dark night air before plunging into the river.

He glided underneath the surface for quite a few paces before needing to come up for air.

He could barely believe his eyes: the churned up water around him was foaming and splashing from all the bodies that had plunged in and were swimming towards him. *They are not giving up.*

Quicker than he'd have liked, two or three älfar had reached him.

'Back!' With swift blows Aiphatòn beat them off and they sank unconscious beneath the waves. He did the front crawl to get away and saw the mob forming a chain in the river by holding hands. The ghaist with the copper helmet was the first one in the chain.

More and more enemies joined in and lengthened the line in the water like an endless cord being unwound.

What are they up to? He again had to beat off several grabbing attackers with punches as he swam.

In the fray, one warrior-woman on the end of the älfar chain missed getting a firm hold on Aiphatòn by a hair. Her fingers slid over his wet shoulder and couldn't get any purchase.

She almost had me. Before Aiphatòn could draw his arm back to shake her off completely, it happened: a small bolt shot through him as if he had touched a powerfully magical object.

That damned energy field. Aiphatòn didn't feel any different from before and started swimming again to make up the ground. The Tronjor carried him along.

Meanwhile the chain of älfar broke up and they swam to the bank. The warrior with the copper helmet attacked Ávoleï and the four remaining älfar from Elhàtor in turn.

Thus they've become puppets of the botoican. Aiphatòn laughed grimly. *But I escaped him. We will burn them to ashes with petrol and . . .*

His arms and legs were swimming in powerful strokes. But to his horror, he was suddenly moving towards the bank on the right like all the other älfar, to get to dry land and struggle out of the river.

This . . . cannot be. He became a mere observer of his own actions.

Dripping wet, he trudged out of the waves, his legs rising and falling, carrying him towards the fishing village, surrounded by the puppets of the botoican who had no will of their own.

But I'm able to think. Aiphatòn's mind seemed to be locked inside an unruly body that was taking him through the area as it pleased.

Nothing in his movements betrayed the fact that he was not in command of them himself; he was not walking stiffly or otherwise behaving unusually. Not even a close friend or confidant would be suspicious if he approached them – until he carried out a murder or an arbitrary atrocity at the behest of the botoican.

He strode through the crowd and stopped in front of Tanôtai, who was standing next to the copper-helmeted warrior.

She sneered repulsively in a way that wasn't like her. 'Welcome. You didn't make it easy for me. You needed to be touched to gain power over you,' she greeted him. 'The transfer is more than sufficient that way.'

I'll find out where you're hiding, botoican, and annihilate you, he thought and felt the anger lines forming on his face. But his arms hung loosely by his sides and his body obeyed an enemy's will and made him stand idly by.

Besides, it doesn't make any sense to kill Tanôtai. The botoican would find himself another mouthpiece and mock me. Aiphatòn realised the infinite possibilities open to the mind-controller. *He can have me speak on his behalf and make everyone think they're my own words.*

'That was an exciting day, wasn't it? We've earned a rest.' The death-dancer scrutinised him. 'We'll come up with a plan for how you and your girlfriend are going to get your hands on the approaching fleet for me. That ought to be simple, as they think you're allies.' She pointed to the copper-helmeted warrior. 'Oh, I know: you'll take my ghaist with you as a captive and very soon boat after boat will belong to me.' She turned away. 'Let's make ourselves at home in the village. First the ships, then Elhàtor,' she remarked as she walked away. 'Even more warriors for my army!'

The älfar marched off towards the houses, pushing and shoving each other before disappearing inside.

Aiphatòn also followed the unspoken command the botoican conveyed to everyone and entered one of the dwellings. The warriors, cîani, children and adults were curling up on the floor and on the chairs and tables, wherever they found space.

Most of their clothing already looked shabby, showing stains and dirt. He saw tears in some eyes and black lines flared on a few faces, revealing their anger and hatred. *So I'm not the only one who has kept their mind.*

But none of them had the power to rise up and resist the spell that had come over them.

Not even the cîani are capable of doing that. Aiphatòn's body walked over the figures on the floor, threw two älfar out of the bed and settled down into it.

Nobody came to contest his right to the bed.

Aiphatòn tried to move his lips and say something, but he couldn't manage more than a twitch. *It probably won't work until the botoican is distracted.* His eyelids closed and he was plunged into darkness. *I will find out where the weaknesses of this spell lie.*

There came the sound of deep breathing immediately from all around him, occasionally someone coughed. A soothing peacefulness was stealing over the settlement when quiet, suppressed weeping penetrated the silence and would not stop.

A shudder ran through Aiphatòn.

He had never heard anything so moving, despairing and dreadful.

Ishím Voróo, 5452nd division of unendingness (6491st solar cycle), autumn

Suddenly the bow dipped and the narrow ship raced down into the trough of the wave, lurching as it gathered way again. Foam and spray blew across the deck where Aiphatòn was holding his ground like a statue.

To starboard and port, more boats that still had enough rigging followed them, fighting their way through the storm. They had been crossing the whipped-up sea for the last four moments, losing one ship after another, but the will of the botoican was unrelenting in its demand that they get to Elhàtor. Even the bigger, sturdy rònkes and their escort ships struggled but they fared much better in the storm.

I hope we don't sink. Aiphatòn held on tight with one hand and counteracted the movements of the hull. *That would put paid to one element of the terror at best.*

He still didn't know what he could do to fight the incredible power of the botoican. The plan to take control of the fleet had worked with terrifying ease: they had presented the copper-helmeted warrior as a supposed captive and in less than half a splinter of unendingness the warrior-women and warriors lost their free will. With nobody suspecting anything, the controlling spell spread more quickly than fire through dry grassland.

Dsôn Elhàtor, where they were headed through the raging storm, was no less unsuspecting.

Thousands live there. Thousands who will have to surrender. Even more warriors for the army. Aiphatòn still could not understand what the botoican was trying to achieve. To get an insight into his thinking and background, he would need Carmondai, who was more familiar with the stories from Ishím Voróo. *Did he say he was a member of the Nhatai family? How will I find out more about them?*

The ship passed through the lowest point of the waves and rose up again.

The wood creaked loudly under the strain, the overfilled sails looked ready to burst. Lightning darted across the black sky and the rain was thundering down relentlessly on them as if the sea spray and the breaking waves weren't enough to soak their clothes through.

The endingness seemed close enough to grasp but all of the älfar were still going about their work. While their hand movements were swift and precise, there was no shouting or agitation, as might have been expected in the face of the storm and the towering waves.

Enforced control. Aiphatòn had more freedom of movement than others, as he had noticed after a few cautious experiments in the last few moments. He was shrewd enough not to show anybody.

Presumably it took the botoican a lot of strength to maintain the spell over the agitated creatures. Or perhaps it was down to Aiphatòn's own energy which was stored in the magical alloy. As long as he hadn't received a specific order that his body was carrying out, he seemed able to control himself to a certain extent. The tiny scrap of resistance he had left. He turned his head and looked around.

On the starboard side, the crest of a breaker washed full force over one of the fragile invasion ships. The deluge of water that poured in smashed the planks of the deck, filled the triangular sail and broke the end of the mast off, which then crashed into the slightly raised look-out platform, crushing the steering wheel along with the crew. The ship instantly broke up and sank beneath the waves.

Aiphatòn looked around and made out numerous boats that looked as delicate and fragile as nutshells amid the incredibly tall waves.

A fair-haired man wearing älfar armour came and stood next to him. There were white runes visible at his temple and his grey eyes remained fixed forwards. 'Your mind is capable of greater resistance than the others' minds,' he said thoughtfully and reached for a rope to keep himself steady as the hull shot up the waves at a sharp angle.

Aiphatòn was silent – not because he had to be, but because he was surprised by how casually the man spoke to him. He hadn't noticed the man before. *Why would I have? I'd have taken him for a soldier from Elhàtor or Dâkiòn.*

'I am Kôr'losôi and I'm a member of the Nhatai family,' he explained, 'but I'm not the one controlling you. Don't even think about trying to do anything to me.' He looked at the shintoìt. 'I'm the only one who can help you, emperor. If *you* help me.' One of his hands rested on the älf's forearm and immediately a magical prickling started that was different from the painful stinging that he had felt in the towns. 'As long as I touch you, her power is reduced without her noticing. We can talk.'

Her *power? A woman then.* Aiphatòn gave up his impassiveness, especially since Kôr'losôi thought his touch was responsible for the freedom of movement. He would keep it secret that he had been able to move of his own free will before. 'She will read my thoughts.'

'No botoican can do that. We influence living creatures physically, but their thinking remains off limits to us. You needn't worry. At the most, it could be risky if she orders you to tell the truth.' He lowered his head to avoid getting a descending deluge of water in the face. 'Her name is Fa'losôi and . . .'

'*Needn't worry?*' The älf laughed bitterly. 'You want to get rid of her so you can seize control of the army yourself.'

'To dissolve it and overthrow her,' Kôr'losôi shot back. 'She is exterminating all of the remaining botoican families and it's clear she'll kill me too as soon as she has achieved her goal.' He wiped his free hand over his sea-drenched face. 'I command the fleet on her behalf. She sent along her confidant, who oversees me in turn.'

'The warrior with the copper helmet,' Aiphatòn guessed. 'The ghaist.'

'Yes. He's not a living creature, although it may look that way.' Kôr'losôi used the älf to support himself – the angle at which they were moving upwards was getting steeper. 'It's a ghaist, made of magic and souls. Through *it*, her magic and her will are strengthened. I haven't worked out how she pulls it off yet.'

'How do you kill it?' Aiphatòn asked immediately.

'Only with powerful fire. But it is too cunning and too quick.' Kôr'losôi gulped as the hull reached the point where the wave broke and they glided downwards with the ship. 'She created lots of these ghaist-creatures to have them scour the wasteland for new resources for her army.'

Aiphatòn remembered how the human village had fallen to the searchers. 'That's how they found Dâkiòn too.'

Kôr'losôi confirmed this with a nod. 'She is the only one capable of breaking an älf's will. And since you are all regarded as the best warriors, she wants you. You yourself were a bonus she didn't expect.' Kôr'losôi looked at him. 'You've got to help me! Otherwise she'll create an army that sweeps aside everything that stands in her way.'

'Is that not what the Nhatai family want anyway?' Aiphatòn did not feel any sympathy for the botoican who wanted to save himself from his own doom, having very likely bound and abused countless creatures with his spells.

But he recognised the danger brewing for Girdlegard: the botoicans could storm the Stone Gateway.

Not even the dwarves are capable of stopping the army of creatures with no will of their own. They will not countenance fleeing or retreating. In his mind's eye, he saw the älfar forming a chain and touching the first dwarf in the defensive line. From then on he would be under the spell of the botoicans. *That must not happen.*

Kôr'losôi dodged out of the way of a barrel that rolled towards them after breaking away from its fixings. It knocked two sailors behind them to the floor and broke their legs before going overboard.

The sailors didn't make a sound, clinging instead to the struts of the railing to stop themselves following the barrel overboard. It seemed they were forbidden from screaming so as not to spread any further unease. Or because the shouting annoyed the botoican.

'We botoicans just want to live in peace and protect ourselves with armed forces who obey us unconditionally,' Kôr'losôi explained. 'It might look odd to you. But we don't understand the ways of the älfar and we don't expect to be understood.'

Show me your weak spot. Aiphatòn nodded. 'Then tell me what we're going to do about her.'

'She is in her town, in Tr'hoo D'tak, where she is assembling an army to fight the battle against the last botoican families still standing in her way,' he summarised. 'We are procuring the most unique warriors in the wasteland for her right now, to ensure her victory.'

'How big will the armies be?'

'As big as possible.'

'On the way to Dâkiòn I saw forces with as many as a hundred thousand troops. One of them could have belonged to the Nhatais.'

'Yes. That was us. We defeated the Xotoina family and destroyed their town.' Kôr'losôi could barely hide his pride. 'We lost half the puppets in the process and she wants to make up for that.'

Puppets. That's all they are. 'There's no strategy in these bloodbaths?'

'No. There doesn't need to be either, especially as the creatures can't be controlled that precisely. They receive the order to destroy the enemy and they do so. Every creature according to its own ways and however it wishes.' Kôr'losôi sounded callous. 'What matters is a victory.'

Aiphatòn wasn't surprised by such wastefulness. *Since they can create reinforcements at will, they can afford it.* He saw in his mind's eye the images of the brutal battle he had watched, the carriages, the beasts, the enemies being torn to pieces with bare claws and talons. *I could find myself in a similar situation soon.* 'So let's bring her the älfar from Elhàtor and Dâkiòn and pretend we're submissive. You make sure I can move however I like at the relevant moment,' he outlined his plan. 'If I have my spear, nothing will be able to stop me.'

The crests of the waves seemed to be flattening out gradually and the rain had eased off too.

One glance at the sky told Aiphatòn that the storm was dispersing. *The elements want me to slay the sorceress and not end my life, apparently.*

'Yes. You will take her life. Then the army will dissolve anyway.' Kôr'losôi looked at him. 'Even if I were lying to you in order to seize control of the countless warriors for myself, it wouldn't work. Her power is *too* great. No ordinary botoican can control such a huge crowd of creatures from the most diverse races and species.'

'You mean we should get ourselves to a place of safety afterwards.'

Kôr'losôi pursed his lips, droplets running over them. His pale pink tongue darted out and licked them off. 'There are many souls who would like to vent their anger and their joy at being freed from someone else's will. In either case *I* do not want to be standing right next to them.' He went to take his hand away. 'Take it as read: we are allies.'

Before the botoican could even break the bond between them fully, Aiphatòn regrasped, clutching the botoican's wrist.

Kôr'losôi looked searchingly at him.

'I wanted to confirm that from now on we are allies, before I become a tool of your relatives again,' he said pointedly, fixing his black eyes on the man.

'You can save yourself the effort of trying to intimidate me.' Kôr'losôi smiled knowingly. 'Botoicans are immune to älfar powers unless it's a steady hand holding a weapon.' He grinned, confident of victory. 'I would have tried it in your position too and I'm going to overlook it.'

Aiphatòn let go of him and the prickling stopped. *That's all I needed!*

'Act submissive and let them go on believing they've broken you completely so that you get your spear back,' Kôr'losôi urged him. 'Inattention is the greatest gift they can give us.'

'Nothing can harm the ghaist?'

'Nothing short of complete destruction with fire. We can only take one chance, one that leads to guaranteed success.' The botoican fixed his gaze ahead where something was growing larger out of the flattening waves that was not rising and falling in their rhythm. 'Is that the Magnificent?'

'It probably is.' Aiphatòn didn't feel any kind of external command within himself, apart from to stand still and doing nothing. 'There aren't that many islands.'

Kôr'losôi turned towards the quarterdeck. 'Then I'll begin the preparations. Irïanora and Ávoleï will bring us into the harbour without even one defending warrior suspecting something is off. When the sun breaks through the clouds, Elhàtor will belong to us.' He hurried off to look for the älf-woman and the elf-woman. They needed to go to the bow to give the impression of being victorious heroines returning.

Aiphatòn sighed and relished the fact that the planks beneath his feet were coasting more and more calmly over the sea. *A fool like so many others*, he thought as he watched the fair-haired man go.

He had not for a moment intended to make Kôr'losôi tremble with fear, he wanted to find out whether the influence lessened if he touched the botoican or if it only worked the other way round.

It works. There was a reason he was smiling. *I have taken some of his magic for myself.*

He still needed a plan to bring about the downfall of the älfar from Elhàtor and Dâkiòn *before* he killed the botoican-woman. Kôr'losôi could be lying to Aiphatòn through his teeth to turn him into his puppet without any magic. He needed to be on his guard about that.

It was as the fleet, which had been scattered by the storm, headed straight for the mouth of the harbour from all directions that Aiphatòn had the brainwave.

Tark Draan, Älfar realm of Dsôn Bhará, formerly the elf realm Lesinteïl, 5452nd division of unendingness (6491st solar cycle), late autumn

'The crater is up there.' Ireheart pressed his heels into the flanks of the white and brown piebald pony to make it trot faster. *No other ride has ever taken so long.*

He was followed by a band made up of sixty brave dwarf-women and dwarves from all the tribes and some free people. The rain and the lashing wind couldn't stop them or their shaggy little horses.

At first, Ireheart's request to all the tribes had been rebuffed. Nobody wanted to dispatch a large delegation. But each tribe granted him ten volunteers willing to take the risk of making their way down to Phondrasôn even though Carmondai and Balodil were nowhere to be found. So the dwarf sallied forth as the leader through the highways and byways of the place of exile.

Ireheart and his valiant group claimed to be relying on their unerring instinct for managing better underground than any other tribe. Some of the warrior-women and warriors spoke älfar as well as the language the orcs used. So they could always interrogate captives along the way to gather information on Tungdil.

Vraccas, if you send us the lost, presumed dead scholar, the Children of the Smith will not know what to do with themselves in their joy. He found the role of king easier now. The kingdom in the Blue Mountains looked better and better every orbit.

Although his duties as a ruler were piling up and Goda called him an enormous fool and none of his children were able to understand how he could get so fixated on this idea, he *needed* to lead the volunteers to Dsôn Bhará and pay them the honour of personally bidding them farewell before sending them into Phondrasôn. It was extremely important to him. *Because who knows whether I'll still be alive when they come back to the surface?*

Fiëa had studiously ignored all of his messages and inquiries.

That was another reason to make an appearance and to – in a spirit of friendship – keep a close eye on the elf-woman and what she was up to in the hole in the middle of the former älfar town. *I'm intrigued to hear her excuse.*

Soaked through to their undergarments, they hurried down the crater rim via the winding paths. The palace mountain ought to tower up right next to the hole, Ireheart remembered it well. Tungdil had met Tirîgon there and greeted him like an old friend.

But there were no remnants of either the palace or the town.

There were, however, numerous tents in which people had set up camp. Even the mountain that had once been a mile high seemed to have shrunk in size by more than two thirds.

The elf-woman is really working them hard. Ireheart saw that they had built enormous diggers out of tree trunks and planks with tin fittings. They were using these to help stack the crater soil into piles with chains, ropes and idler pulleys and pushing it into the hole. As it was descending into the wide opening, the rain stopped dust flying far up into the air.

The very sight of the workers annoyed Ireheart. Had he not let her know that he needed access to the tunnels dug out of the sidewalls?

His misgivings were confirmed when they came riding up to the hole: a third of it was already filled in.

'By Vraccas! What is that pointy-ear thinking?' he ranted and jumped down off the pony to run over to the edge and look down. The soles of his boots splashed through the mud, the dirt spraying up onto his trouser legs.

And worse was yet to come: Ireheart could no longer make out an opening or even the smaller niches in the side walls that had been mentioned in the report. The debris that had been shoved in was already too high. In among it he could see clumps and even whole sheets of burnt pitch, tar, slag and scree. *What has she done?*

'At first glance, you might think the weather would make it more difficult for us. But in fact it makes our work easier – the water softens the ground and our diggers clear away the soft layer more easily,' he

heard the elf-woman's voice behind him. It was clear she was deliberately adopting this innocent, chatty tone to show him her conscience
was clear.

Well, she's come to the wrong person. Ireheart rubbed his face to
brush the drops out of his eyebrows, eyes and beard, turning round as
he did so. 'I asked you stop filling it in until we got here.'

'I heard that nobody could find Balodil and Carmondai, and the
dwarves cannot spare any warriors,' she said in apology, smiling. 'After
two escape attempts by the monsters, I felt waiting was too risky.'

'So how many tried to get out?'

'Quite a few.' Fiëa remained vague and polite. Ireheart could clearly
see in her eyes that she was dancing dangerously close to the line
between truth and untruth. She pointed into the hole. 'We drove
them back with hot slag, then we filled the passageways as best we
could with plenty of . . .'

'You blocked the passageways?' he screamed at her. 'I can't even dig
down to get into the labyrinth?' Ireheart felt the rage, a wave of heat
shooting furiously through his body. 'How are the volunteers meant
to get to Phondrasôn?'

With a splashing sound, the digger – many paces high and wide –
poured a fresh load of sludge into the hole, the grey-brown mass
flowing into the tiniest holes and filling them in.

'They won't.' The elf-woman was distant all of a sudden. The
rain drummed softly on her white armour, the splashes hitting
the dwarf in the eyes so that he had to blink. 'I've saved the lives of
the brave volunteers who wanted to go into the underworld for no
reason.'

'You disregarded my wishes,' he raged, balling his hands into fists.

'I have protected Girdlegard, King Boïndil,' Fiëa countered coldly.
'Because I am focused on more than the fate of one individual who is

in all likelihood dead. I will not allow my homeland, which is yours too, to be plagued by evil creatures yet again.'

Ireheart glared at her angrily, feeling as if his eyes were glowing like pieces of coal. *I'd be all too happy to bury you down there.*

'And just to warn you, my dear dwarf: don't even think about digging a tunnel somewhere else until you find a different entrance,' she said and bent down to him. 'I have said that I will protect my homeland.'

He took a step backwards to stop himself flying at her throat. 'You're always the same,' he cried, beside himself. 'Acting friendly, as if you invented goodness, but you murder and threaten just as cunningly as the black-eyes.' He spat at her feet, the rain immediately washing away the saliva.

Fiëa smiled patiently now, without arrogance. The rain ran through her long, white hair and trickled down her forehead. 'I understand your bad mood because you see a hope lying in ruins and now you've got to ride back to the Blue Mountains without achieving anything.' She went to place a hand on his shoulder but he dodged her. 'Be a king of the Secondlings, take care of the High Gate and hence of Girdlegard, like I'm doing. But leave the dead in peace.'

He is . . . Ireheart didn't know what to think or believe. 'I'm angry you haven't followed my instructions,' he repeated furiously.

'Whether the tunnels would still be available when you arrived was irrelevant. I would not have allowed your volunteers to climb into the hole because they would have lured the monsters here.' The elf-woman straightened up and looked at the warrior-women and warriors from the dwarf tribes. 'You heroes! Accept my thanks too, for your noble intentions and your willingness in this undertaking. But for reasons of common sense, it ends here.'

'The king must tell us that,' replied a dark-haired warrior-woman carrying a double-edged battle axe. 'Not you.'

Fiëa nodded and slowly moved away from the edge and the group. 'Stay tonight if you like. We have space left in the tents.' She gave a slight bow. 'I'll go and supervise the works. We want to be finished before winter comes and in eight orbits the honourable maga and queen, Coïra, is going to pay us a visit and see what she can achieve with magic.' The elf-woman turned and walked away.

Ireheart trudged through the mud towards his piebald pony and got back into the saddle. His anger was slowly subsiding, the rain was cooling his head. *When I think about them repopulating the Golden Plain and how we'll have even more of these know-it-alls, I feel sick.*

'We're leaving,' he announced loudly. 'There's a guesthouse not far from here where we'll stop off and spend the night. I'd rather lie with sixty snoring dwarf-women and dwarves in scratchy hay than near that insufferably posh elf-woman.'

The platoon laughed raucously and banged their coats of chainmail and shields for emphasis.

'Let's go! I feel like washing down my anger and frustration with a beer.' Ireheart took up the lead of the baggage train and they trotted back to the winding paths.

The dark-haired dwarf-woman who had replied to Fiëa rode up alongside him and looked at him in awe. She had a sturdy build and she carried the double axe on her shoulder in the same way he was in the habit of carrying the crow's beak. 'I've simply got to ask you to reconsider your decision, King Boïndil.'

'Well, we certainly aren't staying here unless Vraccas appears and demands it of me.'

'I didn't mean that, I meant you turning down the position of high king and not wanting to have the election take place for another twenty cycles,' she explained. Underneath her leather cloak he could see a blackened coat of chainmail.

'Is that what you mean?' Ireheart looked at her in surprise. 'Remind me what your name is? The anger banished it from my memory.'

'Beligata Hardblow from the clan of the Bloodshedders, formerly of the Thirdling tribe, now a freewoman.' She gave a small bow, revealing a delicate but green scar on her right cheek.

'And why should I change my mind?'

'The tribes and their clans need a high king who stands for loyalty and heroism. *You* have *both*.' She pointed her thumb contemptuously over her shoulder. 'They're just two pointy-ears but they've barely crept out of the forests and they're already revealing their old arrogance. A dwarf like you, with your age, experience and history could run against them to be our high king. Otherwise the people will soon be awestruck again and elevate them into gods of wisdom.' Beligata bowed her head lower this time. 'You'd have my vote.' She dropped back into the baggage train.

Ireheart mumbled to himself and started to brood.

I can't allow bad thoughts to have any space in my heart. Otherwise we'll soon be back where Girdlegard once was. He clicked his tongue and set the pony trotting. *Beligata is right. Unity. Among the Children of the Smith and all tribes. That is the best way.*

Nevertheless, he preferred the inn to the company of the elf-woman this evening.

A little later they had reached the farmstead and handed the innkeeper's family an entire cycle's salary, although it did mean that barrels of beer and provisions were emptied and the cupboards were cleared of sausages and cheese.

In the middle of a beautifully belted out rendition of 'A thousand tankards, a thousand drunkards', the door opened and a dwarf entered the room, soaked to the skin. His face was positively glowing with happiness as the whole troop waved their tankards in his direction and seemed to sing in his honour, making the window panes rattle.

He thanked them at the end of the song with a deep bow and had a beer mug pressed into his hands.

Before helpful hands could even push him towards the fire to warm up, he hurried over to Ireheart, who was watching all the fuss, tipsy and tickled.

Being king like this is fun. 'What have you got for me?' he greeted him and laughed. 'I'm sure you're rarely granted such honour on your arrival.'

'Not even for the most wonderful or terrible news, my king.' The dwarf grinned and bowed to the monarch. 'Baromir sent me to you so that I could let you know two things before you arrive at the Blue Mountains.'

Vraccas, no bad news. Ireheart sat up straight. 'What's wrong in the Blue Mountains?'

'Don't worry, everything is running as smoothly as a wagon on a track. The works are coming along.' The messenger lowered his voice which made him hard to understand amid the revelry. 'It's about the writings of the älf who was rescued from the palace. The human king has decided to ban them because they could lead readers astray. The idea is to prevent anyone starting to pity the black-eyes or understand their views. Only the scholars are allowed to look at them and analyse them.'

They are afraid of the quill, once the sword has been overcome. Ireheart thought about it. 'Well, I don't care, although it's nonsense. After all, anyone in their right mind who reads them knows what and who they're about. I hope the scholars aren't more susceptible than the corruptible readers.' He winked as he took a swig of beer. 'What else?'

'Here's the most outrageous thing,' the dwarf's voice cut through the din of the bar. 'There are notes about an elf settlement in the Grey Mountains. One cavalry officer is already on the way to Queen Balyndis from the tribe of the Fifthlings to let her know.'

Ireheart almost spat beer all over the messenger. The nape of his neck itched, his facial hair seemed to stand on end. Aghast, he swallowed with difficulty and wiped his sleeve across his lips. '*Pointy-ears* in the *mountains?*' He set the tankard down on the table with a bang, making the platoon's conversations and laughter fall silent all of a sudden. *Vraccas, that really is enough now! I've understood your signal to me.*

Every pair of eyes was fixed on him; the dwarves from the various mountains suspected terrible news was going to be announced.

The stately monarch of the Secondlings tossed his plait over his shoulder, stroked his silvery black beard, climbed onto the table and shouldered the crow's beak. 'With Vraccas as my witness,' he cried, letting his gaze rest on Beligata a little longer. 'Take this message to the dwarf kingdoms: if the tribes so wish, I want to be your high king as soon as possible!' He waved the tankard in the air. 'And I'll drink to that.'

The whoops of glee this unleashed made the inn shake to its foundations.

Ishím Voróo, Älfar town of Dsôn Elhàtor, 5452nd division of unendingness (6491st solar cycle), autumn

You fools. As the locals rejoiced, Aiphatòn trudged through Elhàtor next to the copper helmet who looked as if he had been put in chains. *One touch will be enough to put an end to your free will.*

The warrior-women and warriors, who had supposedly been successful in attacking and destroying Dâkiòn, were being given a triumphant victor's welcome by their homeland.

Colourful petals twirled as they rained down on them, cries of joy and fanfare sounded everywhere. Children ran along placing sashes over the fighters and pinning little bunches of flowers to them as they went uphill to the monarchess' palace with their unusual captive.

Has nobody noticed how blank the homecomers' faces are? Aiphatòn's legs were moving of their own accord, driven on by the external will. *Their silence would seem odd to me.*

From secret experiments, he now knew that he could often move of his own accord. The botoican-woman thought he was submissive like the rest of the army. That had proved useful not too long before, when he had been busy in the hull of the ship just before being ordered to disembark.

Through the hail of fluttering blossoms they approached the white palace, where banners and flags were flapping in the wind to welcome the army. This was the monarchess' way of paying homage to them.

Aiphatòn could feel the delicate petals on his bare torso, some sticking to the armour and his brown skin. He had to leave them wherever they landed.

Irïanora and Ávoleï were at the front in their white leather armour. Kôr'losôi was somewhere among the troops, equipped with a close helmet so that his human features didn't give him away. The ghaist remained staunchly by Aiphatòn's side as if he suspected how many freedoms the älf truly possessed. *Hopefully he doesn't notice my smell.*

The procession had reached the front courtyard, which was lined with crowds of älfar. The town house-like palace towered before them, its façade decorated with whalebone and dark blue marine motifs; the crowd was still clapping and screaming in excitement about the fleet's victory.

Modôia appeared on the large balcony first, wearing a white dress, and her arrival was immediately cheered. Next came her son Ôdaiòn in his ostentatious blue and silver clothes. Leïóva joined them but stayed very much in the background; her black clothes made her look like the consummate älf-woman.

Aiphatòn's legs paused and the copper helmet came to a standstill too.

Some warrior-women and warriors formed a large circle so that they towered up right in front of the onlookers, while the others marched with Iriänora and Ávoleï through the gate to get to the balcony.

They are getting into position. It's going to happen extremely quickly. Aiphatòn clenched his teeth in disappointment. *My plan could go awry. But all I need is a small opportunity.*

Then his legs started to move; he was following the commander and Shôtoràs' niece. This route took him through the gate in the reception hall and immediately up the stairs to the left. He reached the balcony above the front courtyard soon after the elf-woman and älf-woman.

The prickling was back and it hurt more than it had on his first visit. His magic-steeped body was coping with his time here increasingly badly. *I hope this isn't giving me any permanent damage.*

Aiphatòn's legs had stopped and he found himself right next to the black-clad elf-woman, who stayed in the shadows and looked around warily. It seemed the botoican-woman had him in mind as back-up against Leïóva.

When Iriänora and Ávoleï walked to the balcony's railing and joined the monarchess and her son, the frenzy of delight was stoked further and further until Modôia, who looked weak and sickly, raised her arms to make the crowd fall silent. The sun shone down on her and made her blonde hair gleam.

'What a tragic moment of unendingness,' she cried, sounding less euphoric than expected. 'Our victorious army returns with the news that Shôtoràs and Dâkiòn are history from now on. And Inàste knows that they forced us into it. Many älfar had to die and it hurts deep within my soul. But even the Creating Spirit knows: I had no choice.' She took a symbolic half-step to one side. 'Tell us what happened yourself and who this mysterious captive is that you bring to us.'

Ávoleï stepped up to the balustrade, took a quick breath and then looked out over the silent crowd. Tears welled in her eyes although there was a contorted smile on her face.

She is resisting the command.

Leïóva watched her daughter carefully, her brow furrowing.

Is she the only one who has noticed Ávoleï is struggling? They'll mistake it for emotion. As compassion towards the dead.

The locals remained intrigued. Nobody dared order the commander of the successful fleet to hurry up and begin.

More soldiers marched up onto the balcony. They had belonged to the contingent fighting Dâkiòn. Elhàtor's residents thought they were saluting.

In reality it's about forming a chain from the ghaist all the way up here.

Ávoleï wrapped her fingers around the railing and lowered her head, panting. 'We sailed up the river,' she began a disjointed story.

Aiphatòn stopped listening to her words. He wanted to use the opportunity he had been given, out of eyeshot of the ghaist. 'Intervene,' he said softly to Leïóva. 'We were put under a spell. Whatever happens, don't let yourself be touched by any of us or the botoican's power will break your will.'

The elf-woman glanced at him in shock. 'Botoican? What . . .'

'The creature with the copper helmet waiting patiently on the square, that looks like it's in chains, is a ghaist. It is under orders to conquer Elhàtor and make its inhabitants mental slaves. Dâkiòn has already fallen,' he whispered quickly.

'But what about you?' Leïóva didn't seem inclined to believe him.

'Look at your daughter. Do you think she's behaving as a victorious commander should?'

The black-haired elf-woman looked at him, disconcerted now. 'It sounds absurd.'

I understand her doubts, but they're no use to me. 'I'm only partly under his spell because I have more magic in me than the other älfar,' he explained urgently. 'The ghaist is going to attack very soon, then the soldiers will touch you, the monarchess and her son. They will grab hold of the people in the square and with their help they'll form chains and spread the influence spell into every last corner of Elhàtor.' Aiphatòn dared to turn his head slightly towards her. 'Anyone who escapes him will be hunted down and subjugated later, like they did in Dâkiòn. Like they did to your daughter too.'

'What can I do to fight the ghaist?' she whispered, not letting her fear show. He saw her muscles moving underneath her black clothes as she got ready.

'Fire.' Aiphatòn carefully turned to face forwards again. 'The hottest fire there is.'

Leïóva took a few cautious steps backwards. 'I'll fetch our best cîanoi. He'll know how to fight a botoican.' She gave him a probing look. 'If you're deceiving me, emperor, and you're actually behind all this, nothing will protect you from me.' The elf-woman disappeared into the corridor without a sound and he could no longer see her.

Aiphatòn hoped Leïóva would pull off a miracle.

In the best-case scenario, the Elhàtorian älfar would take out the ghaist and Aiphatòn could proceed with the plan he had started to form in the hull of the ship; in the worst-case scenario, the elf-woman died, no suspicion fell on him and he would stand by for his next opportunity.

'. . . we freed the copper helmet from the sovereign's dungeons,' Ávoleï cried in a choked voice. 'We brought him with us because . . .' She faltered. 'Because . . . it's a lie! I'm lying to you!' She took her hands off the railing and balled them into fists. 'You are all in great danger,' she moaned. 'We are under a magic spell and have come to subjugate you too.'

One of the soldiers on the balcony drew his sword and approached her from behind.

Ôdaiòn tried to stop him with a gesture but the warrior carried on moving towards the elf-woman. To him, the monarchess' son didn't count for anything. 'Soldier?'

'Ávoleï?' Modôia came and stood next to her sympathetically, placing a hand on her shoulder. 'Child, what's troubling you?'

Aiphatòn's eyes widened. *She's resisting!* He saw the mistake the botoican-woman had made: *she overlooked the fact she's an elf-woman. The magic works less powerfully on her. Just like with me.*

'Hey, soldier!' Ôdaiòn walked towards the armed soldier. 'Get back! What do you think you're . . .'

The warrior brought the sword down at a slanting angle, sliced through the monarchess' son's collarbone and left the collapsing princeling to die. Then the warrior lifted his arm to stab the elf-woman's armoured back.

'No!' Modôia launched herself at him – and the point of the sword ran right through her abdomen. The sword jutted out through her back. The monarchess clung to the soldier to protect Ávoleï for as long as she could.

The locals beneath the balcony were screaming in horror. They rebelled, pressing towards the square and pushing the guarding warriors together.

Ávoleï saw her murderer coming. Her whole body trembled, visibly struggling against the orders being given to her by the botoican. 'Run! Run and jump into the boats! Before they get their hands on you, slit your own throats!' She turned her gaze to Aiphatòn. 'Otherwise you'll be lower than slaves.'

The black-haired elf-woman threw herself over the balcony head first. The impact came straight away, followed by yet more bewildered screams from the crowd.

Did I scream too? Aiphatòn realised his mouth was hanging open.

He couldn't move and meanwhile a revolt was breaking out in front of the palace. The botoican-woman's command over his body meant he couldn't move his legs to get to the railing and look for Ávoleï.

What was it that had been in her eyes before she jumped? Confusion, fear and . . . His solar plexus ached, suddenly feeling cold.

By now, the soldier had shaken off the severely wounded monarchess, but he was standing around uncertainly because Ávoleï had escaped his attack. There were no more opponents he was meant to be attacking. So he turned into a statue.

The screams from the crowd soon grew quieter, as if the locals were seeking shelter in the houses, but very few had actually left the square, as Aiphatòn could tell from the sounds of the footsteps.

But since the clash of weapons didn't ring out, this meant: the ghaist and Kôr'losôi had set to work.

Aiphatòn turned his head and saw the soldiers march up on all sides and form a chain – they held hands on some silent command. The spell could be passed on as far as the balcony.

Modôia pulled herself up by the railing, her right hand groping for the three-strapped whip she wore on her belt; as she did so, she slipped the protective sheath off the blades and cut herself. She didn't even screw up her face. The blood came gushing out of the gaping wound in her abdomen and drenched her white dress. 'You won't get me.' Her eyes turned even darker, literally devouring the light. Black lines marked her face and soon her weapon cracked, ripping the head off her son's murderer.

Whirring and unbelievably fast, blow followed blow.

The blades brought endingness, whistling and softly jingling, the leather straps loudly whipping. Body after body fell to the white stone and blood spatter clung to the pale wall, furnishing it with new works of art. A number of droplets rained down on the monarchess, a frozen Irïanora and Aiphatòn. His legs walked backwards until he reached the wall without any input from him; Irïanora soon followed. *Our mistress is taking us to safety.*

The botoican-woman had apparently had enough of Modôia: a dozen warrior-women and warriors drew their swords at the same time and charged at the monarchess.

But she dealt out death undaunted. Two opponents had their stomachs slit open, a third had his skull smashed to pieces, and finally the weakened monarchess fell to the ground amid the stabs and punches. Her long blonde hair, the white dress – it was all coloured by her own and others' blood.

Aiphatòn's feet carried him forwards to the railing now so that he could look at the square.

Directly below him, Ávoleï's corpse lay on its back, not a single blemish visible. *She must have broken her neck.*

The ghaist was standing tall, his strong, bare arms outstretched and touching two warriors on the shoulder. Through them, the influence spell had passed into the other soldiers and from there into the crowd on the square.

A few hundred älfar stood dumbly in front of the palace, their eyes fixed on the ghaist. Further away, in the streets paved with tiles of bone, others lay dying with their throats slit, having taken Ávoleï's warning seriously and killed themselves before the spell got to them.

But seven chains of älfar were nevertheless moving away from the square through the alleyways to carry the botoican-woman's power deeper into Elhàtor and enslave the town.

Hopefully lots of them manage to kill themselves. Then I'll have less work to do. Aiphatòn still did not allow himself to feel pity. He had seen too much suffering caused by his people. *No älf is blameless!*

He couldn't help but gulp as he looked at the beautiful elf-woman. He remembered her last glance, which had been at him, and her lips on his . . .

A steady jet of fire made a whooshing sound as it shot out of a side street and burned its way through the crowd, completely enveloping the ghaist and the two warriors.

Burning and roasting, everyone struck by it fell to the ground and the chain was broken.

Leïóva. She has found a cîanoi who has not yet succumbed to external will. Aiphatòn could clearly feel sensation returning to his legs, although he remained where he was. As long as the ghaist was still alive, he couldn't give up his charade.

The elf-woman rode into the square on a night-mare holding a very large sword with runes engraved on it.

The hissing jet of fire continued relentlessly, keeping the creature with the copper helmet enveloped in flame. Having turned to ashes, the älfar dispersed, the little grey and black flakes swirling away.

The ghaist turned around, looking for the cîanoi whom Aiphatòn couldn't see. The leather armour crackled as it burned, the fake flesh sending tongues of flame and white sparks into the air.

Will this work? Aiphatòn waited to see what would happen. The tremendous heat surged up to where he was on the balcony.

Having just reached the creature, Leïóva swung her sword at his head with a terrible scream; the stream of fire stopped at the same time so the elf-woman wouldn't be burned. The magically formed creature kept burning.

Too soon! That was too soon! Aiphatòn had desperately hoped the sword would split the now red-hot copper in two – but the blade left a deep, straight dent, failing to penetrate the helmet.

The burning ghaist staggered and fell. It was able to get away from the trampling hooves of the night-mare and received more blows from the sword, but the blade did not destroy it. Nothing but little flames darted from the wounds inflicted on it.

'Give him some more of your fire!' Leïóva realised her mistake and moved the black horse back so the cîanoi could finish the job. 'Quickly!'

But the ghaist suddenly sprinted off, shooting tongues of flame as it ran towards some corbels and launched itself forcefully off them.

It flew several paces through the air like a comet and then sank towards the ground much too soon. It crashed onto the sloping street between the houses, the impact breaking off small segments of bone that bounced around and came tumbling after the creature. It rolled downwards head over heels and landed with a splash in the harbour.

Leïóva cast a quick, inquiring look at Aiphatòn as if he could tell her whether this was enough to destroy a ghaist.

Then bright flames shot across the water, from the quay wall to the mouth of the harbour, and danced around the rest of the fleet, the smaller ships, the rònkes and escort sailboats and it looked like the sea was ablaze.

The first explosion followed instantly, blowing up the boat that Aiphatòn had secretly bored a hole in so the petrol could flow out of the smashed barrels through its hull. Rigging and sails caught fire, and one ship after another flickered with flames.

It's working. His plan was a success. There was no escape for the älfar anymore. The fire would definitely spread throughout Elhàtor now and the residents would be wiped out. *I'll help things along however I can.*

Then he would sail back in a boat and kill the botoican-woman herself to get his spear and toss the remaining älfar into endingness with Nodûcor's powers.

A loud curse rang out below him.

When Aiphatòn turned his attention to the square, he saw Kôr'losôi standing close to Leïóva but not touching her.

The elf-woman had just slipped out of the night-mare's saddle, having rammed her own sword through her breast, and was staring straight ahead with pain etched across her face.

She followed her daughter's advice too.

He looked at the botoican, who couldn't have known how many freedoms Aiphatòn had. *Now I'll kill you.*

Then his own torso turned, hips and legs following obediently.

I . . . how can this be? His feet carried him over the dead Modôia and her slain son to the steps. His soles left red prints in the blood of the dead. Irïanora followed.

And thus it was clear: the ghaist was still alive, the heat had not been enough. The victims and Aiphatòn's plan had all been for nothing.

Chapter XIV

*Don't believe what you're told. Make up a lie that everyone falls for.
Even you.*

Wise saying of the Älfar
Collected by Carmondai, master of word and image

**Ishím Voróo, Several miles outside Dsôn Dâkiòn, 5452nd
division of unendingness (6491st solar cycle), late autumn**

Aiphatòn glanced back at the gigantic town's burning buildings, from
the smallest house to the sovereign's palace in the upper town. *What a
waste.*

The clouds of smoke soared into the sky, proclaiming the end far
and wide: Dsôn Dâkiòn, the Majestic, thus suffered the same fate as
Dsôn Elhàtor, the Magnificent, albeit much later and unexpectedly.

So the town, built by some unknown, giant creatures, perished for
a second time, set on fire by its former inhabitants. Nothing from it
was salvaged, no artworks or gold or any object that could serve as a
memento.

*The botoican-woman wants to make sure that nobody comes back here
or resettles it.* Aiphatòn was walking at the head of the convoy,

surrounded by the Majestic's warriors. His legs rose and fell, as so many times before, of their own accord.

The ghaist was leading the älfar that remained at his disposal after the suicides and the blaze. They were headed southwest towards the place they planned to stay next: Tr'hoo D'tak, the Nhatai town.

There ought to be an opportunity to kill the botoican-woman there.

After the fire in the harbour, in which the navy relief forces had all died, the flames had spread to the houses near the quay and from there to Elhàtor, as Aiphatòn had planned.

At first it had looked as though there was no way of escaping the island. But then the grotto with more rònkes was discovered.

They sailed as far as the mouth of the Tronjor in them, and then rowed and sailed as far as possible with the smaller dinghies against the current before getting out at the rocky bottleneck and crawling along the arduous route along the bank, coming out at Dâkiòn.

The marsh had cost them a lot of time and some more lives due to exhaustion. The mosquitoes from the nearby swamps transmitted illnesses and fever wiped out more älfar.

Aiphatòn reckoned they had brought at most seven thousand Elhàtorians with them. *It wasn't worth it for the botoican-woman*, he thought grimly. *Samusin could make the fever we're carrying spread through her entire army and even infect her. That would be payback.*

A loud rumbling noise sounded at intervals from behind him whenever a house collapsed in the doomed Dâkiòn and brought other buildings down with it. When an unusual metallic clanking and creaking mixed in with it, the älf guessed that the golden bridge had collapsed.

The ghaist suddenly started to sprint, moving swiftly away from the troops.

Kôr'losôi came to join Aiphatòn, so close that their shoulders touched; the monarchess' three-strapped whip dangling at his right-hand side.

'Finally,' he said, breathing a sigh of relief. 'I thought it would never disappear. After that business in Elhàtor, suspicions were running high. I think there was a fear that more elf-women and elves would be found among the inhabitants.' The fair-haired botoican looked at Aiphatòn. 'I couldn't get to you sooner to make arrangements. That would have put our plan at risk.'

The älf nodded and feigned sympathy. He knew he'd been very lucky. The disastrous events in Elhàtor were put down solely to the elf-women's resistance to the control spell; suspicion didn't fall on him. 'Where is it going?'

'It's hurrying on ahead of us, either to announce our arrival or because my cousin Fa'losôi has a specific use in mind for it.' Kôr'losôi followed the copper helmet with his eyes. 'Whatever. As long as it stays away, I feel more at ease.'

Aiphatòn thought he saw a white tower looming up in the distance. 'Is that where we're going?'

'Yes. Fa'losôi has moved her town to have more space for the huge number of warriors. Our towers can be dismantled,' he explained. 'They look enormous but they can't withstand more than the average storm.' He looked warily at Aiphatòn. 'What are you planning?'

He smiled darkly. 'I saw the ruins of a residential tower like that one. They must catch fire easily?'

'The proportion of wood is high, yes.' Kôr'losôi didn't seem to like this. 'But planning to set them on fire is far too risky. They could be salvaged. Your spear must kill Fa'losôi, *then* it will be a sure thing.'

'Then get it for me.'

'I can't. Shôtoràs and the others kept it.'

'I take it Nodûcor and the älfar from Dâkiòn are already there?'

Aiphatòn was constantly worrying about whether the cîani had managed to remove the half-mask. It would fit nicely with his new plan.

'Of course.' Kôr'losôi glanced over his shoulder to keep an eye on
the stragglers. 'We'll lose at least another fifty or more,' he estimated.
'Malaria. That's what I call irony.' He let out a laugh. 'Have you ever . . .
oh no, how could you have,' he interrupted himself.

'What do you mean?'

'The more powerful an army, the more often a family moves. Most
of our towns quickly turn the surrounding area into muddy land,
depending on the size of the army and the creatures' excrement. Rain
doesn't improve the state of affairs. Before the morass and smell
become unbearable, we move on,' he explained.

Aiphatòn also turned around briefly to check on the weaker
warriors.

There was a cowering figure every hundred or two hundred paces,
while on the horizon, Dâkiòn descended into flames and smoke. Anyone who could still move was crawling along on all fours or on their
elbows behind the baggage train. The will of the botoican-woman
knew no mercy.

'There was a time when the families aspired to build kingdoms like
the ones the älfar built before the old Dsôn fell and you were scattered
to the four winds,' Kôr'losôi told him. 'They conquered the most
enormous fortresses in just one day. No wall could withstand them.'

Aiphatòn thought about the Stone Gateway with its gigantic fortifications. *I've got to find out more.* 'Without siege equipment?' he
asked incredulously. 'I doubt that.'

'The tribes they conquered doubted it too at first,' Kôr'losôi replied,
laughing. 'All that a botoican army needs is bulk. Bulk is malleable,
flexible, you can stack it up and let it down like a rope, you can even
make it build bridges.' The botoican grinned. 'I know you can't

imagine it, but that is its very advantage.' He reflected. 'The älfar must have had acrobats who performed tricks as entertainment?' he asked.

'They performed art that had to be practised for a long time, not *tricks*. We leave those to animals.'

Kôr'losôi waved a hand dismissively. 'Well, I'm sure they built towers where someone climbed onto someone else's shoulders and that kind of thing?' When he saw Aiphatòn nod, he clapped his hands. 'That's *exactly* how our armies overcome walls and fortresses. They climb one on top of the other, and very quickly too.'

In his mind's eye, Aiphatòn saw two hundred thousand beasts, monsters, people and älfar running up the thirty-pace wide approach road and stacking themselves in front of the closed doors of the portal until they reached up high enough to take the defending forces by surprise. *They don't need to open the gate. They climb over it.*

'And then if you've got,' Kôr'losôi continued his story, lost in thought, 'over a hundred ghaists at your disposal, there's no stopping you.'

'A hundred?' Aiphatòn had been confident he could protect Girdlegard if the botoican-woman's hunger for more land and soldiers increased further and spread beyond the wasteland, but that confidence was melting like ice in the sun. 'What will happen to all of these creatures if I kill their mistress and free them from her will?'

Kôr'losôi looked pensive. 'I've never been there when it's happened. Maybe they win their freedom? Or they die? Or they just freeze mid-motion?'

We need a lot of petrol. Or the power of numerous cîani. Aiphatòn saw the single needle-shaped white tower drawing closer. 'Do you know where the armies are going to encounter each other?'

'No. We'll find out as soon as we get to Tr'hoo D'tak.' Kôr'losôi broke his connection with the älf. 'I can't weaken Fa'losôi's power for

too long. We're already very close, she might notice.' He peeled off
from the baggage train and let the älfar march past him. His lips
formed the words, *stay patient*.

Aiphatòn laughed inwardly. *Patience*. As an immortal being, he
had all the time in the world, the best prerequisite for having the
utmost patience.

But right now, time of all things was his greatest enemy.

*What will the botoican-woman do if she notices that I can resist her to
some degree?* Aiphatòn and the head of the convoy from Elhàtor
reached the town's outermost foothills where they found strange tents
made out of shabby coats, tattered sails and ragged tarpaulins. Gnomes
and smaller monsters were scurrying around, bickering and arguing
over half-rotten chunks of meat, the origins of which were more than
a little dubious.

The stench of excrement that hit them made Aiphatòn feel sick.
The swirling smoke from all the campfires couldn't cover it up. Every
beast, every man and every woman, every creature in this army seemed
to relieve themselves wherever they saw fit.

But they haven't been in this spot for long. Aiphatòn suddenly felt an
attack of nausea. The soggy ground gave way beneath the soles of his
feet as they pressed on towards the pointy white tower. It was emblazoned with green runes, no doubt proclaiming that this armed force
was under the command of the Nhatai family.

Soon Aiphatòn realised that the tall structure had been built at
the other end of the camp so that the älfar had to march straight
through it.

The small tents gave way to shelters made of wood, initially ones
with brushwood walls to keep the wind out, then walls made of small
tree trunks and finally ones with planks and eventually even foraged
stones.

The botoican-woman's power pulled off a miracle: orcs slept next to humans by the campfire, trolls and ogres lay right in the middle because they were too big for the buildings and they rested their ugly heads on their arms. All enemy beings and races squatted down close together without going at each other's throats and flesh.

Admittedly, loud arguments did break out but Aiphatòn could see that as soon as a ghaist appeared, the quarrel ended as quickly as it had flared up. They clearly served as the supervising authority, stepping in and strengthening the botoican-woman's spell with great precision.

However it is they manage it. Out of the corner of his eye, he saw one of the copper helmets using his bare hands to tear the head off an orc who wouldn't calm down and then throwing his corpse to his clan, who set about it hungrily. There wasn't even a flicker of protest at the treatment of their relative. Smacking their lips and grunting, they devoured one of their own kind.

The baggage train went on and on, past the familiar and unfamiliar beasts of Ishím Voróo.

Aiphatòn even spotted several oboona who weren't in raptures watching the älfar go past like they ought to have been.

He remembered the stories that Carmondai had told him about them and how Caphalor lost his family to the worst of them. *Now their gods walk past them and they just stare into the fire. They've found a stronger power.*

Kôr'losôi appeared next to him. 'Don't be surprised if your legs choose a different route soon,' he explained, without touching Aiphatòn. This was his way of communicating his cousin's will. 'Fa'losôi is expecting us in the tower. But first she wants to make sure that you're washed and changed.'

Aiphatòn only just stopped himself responding with a question when he saw the warning look on the botoican's face.

He and Kôr'losôi turned and left Elhàtor's älfar army who hurried on, heading for an area where black tents towered into the air. His tribe seemed to be the only ones in the crowd who, despite all the magic, were trying to maintain a vestige of dignity.

The door to the narrow, white tower – which looked out of place towering up out of the excrement and crowd of creatures – was five paces above the ground but there were no steps up to it. In the doorway stood a brown-haired woman wearing a dark green dress with white embroidery on it.

'Don't be surprised. I hinted at what would happen,' said Kôr'losôi.

Particularly strong orcs loitering underneath the entrance suddenly stood still and used their bodies to form a sturdy staircase which Aiphatòn and the botoican climbed up; the pair were hardly inside the building when the beasts scattered and the steps made of broad, armoured orc necks dispersed.

'Welcome, Kôr'losôi. Our cousin is eager to hear what you have to tell her,' said the botoican-woman, who wore her hair short and strongly resembled her relative.

'Thank you, Saî'losôi. Have you been a good confidante and aide to her in supervising the army?' He gave her a kiss on the forehead.

She returned his greeting. 'She didn't need me. So I just supplied her with food and drink.' Saî'losôi didn't look at Aiphatòn.

She thinks I'm one of the botoicans' normal tools. He looked around surreptitiously as his legs started moving to follow Kôr'losôi and Saî'losôi.

They passed through a compact corridor which brought them into a narrow shaft with a spiral staircase winding its way up the walls. It smelled of varnish and dry wood.

That's crazy: this tower is going to burn like firewood. Aiphatòn started plotting. *It's obvious they've never played Tharc or had to wage a real war.*

There was a platform on the ground fitted with a lever mechanism. They had barely stepped onto it when Saî'losôi shifted one of the levers.

Invisible chains unwound, cogs rattled and they kept moving upwards for what Aiphatòn thought was about fifty paces.

'See you soon,' Kôr'losôi said in parting. The look in his pale eyes urgently warned Aiphatòn not to do anything stupid.

The älf left the platform and as usual, Aiphatòn's body performed actions without him thinking about it. He went through a door and behind it he found a bathtub with scented water waiting for him. Towels and clean clothes had been laid out.

The bath did him good. It was only now that he realised how badly his own things stank of brackish water, salt and sweat.

He observed himself getting out of the tub, drying himself off and putting on the black robes emblazoned with the runes of the Nhatais. *It's as if I myself were giving orders to my hands.*

Then he went out and hurried up the stairs before stopping outside a large door that then opened.

Aiphatòn found himself in an anteroom where Kôr'losôi, Saî'losôi and Tanôtai were waiting for him.

The death-dancer also looked like she had been allowed a bath – she was wearing similar clothing to the shintoìt and didn't have her needle-daggers; the red-haired älf-woman's gaze was vacant and listless.

Together, they all went through the elaborately carved double doors and entered a bright room with numerous candles burning.

Incense smoke filled the air, dispelling even the slightest trace of the stink of excrement. A cosy bed had been made up with embroidered cushions, blankets and pelts, and a low table with food stood in front of it.

Unable to resist, Aiphatòn thought of Ávoleï, of the kiss, of her glance, of his encounter with her, of her scent ... Bewildered, he pushed her image aside. *I cannot allow myself any distractions.*

Diagonally behind the seats, a ghaist remained slightly in the shadows. The long, deep dent in the copper helmet gave him away – he was the creature who had escaped falling victim to the magic fire and the elf sword by a hair's breadth. His strong arms dangled down with no signs of wounds and his old, burnt armour had been replaced by new armour.

They couldn't replace the helmet. Because the souls are bewitched inside it. Aiphatòn's patience was tested again as he walked towards the bed of cushions and blankets, flanked by Kôr'losôi and Saî'losôi as Tanôtai walked ahead of him. Although the botoican-woman was controlling her, her footsteps retained their dancer-like quality and grace. The two älfar took a seat next to one another.

The botoicans sat down opposite them.

'My cousin has brought me a very special guest,' a female voice rang out, followed by a metallic clanking sound as something Aiphatòn recognised very well struck the paving stones.

She has my spear with her. It took a huge amount of control for him to keep facing forwards like the death-dancer.

A cloud of incense smoke enveloped him, a breath of wind caressed his neck – and he felt the tip of his own weapon at the nape of his neck.

'Aiphatòn, emperor of the älfar and son of the Inextinguishables. A pure shintoìt,' said the stranger behind him, impressed. 'The magical potential in you must be considerable.' She walked around him and went to take her place at the head of the table while Saî'losôi and Kôr'losôi greeted her with slight bows; she placed the spear across her lap. 'No, it's *different*. That's the right word. Different from the way it is for the cîani, who brought about the conquest of Dâkiòn and Elhàtor for me.'

Is she commanding the mob? Aiphatòn found her very unprepossessing.

She was a petite human woman with a bald head and white Nhatai tattoos on her thin skin, her veins visible through it. A black oval was painted in line with the bridge of her nose, accentuating the affixed diamond chip. Her white and dark green robes looked like they were made of silk and silver chains studded with gemstones in a variety of colours hung around her neck and wrists. 'I am Fa'losôi, your mistress. So speak: what are you thinking?'

Aiphatòn suspected she had relaxed her spell. '*That* is *my* spear.'

The three botoicans laughed at the same time.

'There, you see what happens if you allow the puppets to speak all of a sudden: they say whatever is going through their head,' Fa'losôi cried out in amusement, her pale-yellow eyes scrutinising him. 'Does that mean you'd like it back?'

'If I had it, I'd be better in battle and stay alive longer,' he replied.

'Oh, you're already thinking about combat? A superb warrior!' Fa'losôi slapped her right thigh, her jewellery jangling softly. 'Now eat and drink.'

Tanôtai moved suddenly, looking in confusion from one to another of the assembled group.

Fa'losôi took a flatbread from the plate and filled it with chunks of cooked meat. 'Don't get your hopes up,' she said as she did so. 'Your magic shackles from the navel downwards will stay in place so that you can't run away on me. But let's pretend you're not my puppets – act like you're my acquaintances and let's chat. It's a long time since I've spent time with älfar.' She poured sauce over the aromatic morsels. 'I killed most of them with my own hands. The two of you are an exception. In several respects.' She took a bite and chewed with relish, then laughed with her mouth full.

Kôr'losôi and Saî'losôi joined in the laughter. They helped themselves to some of the food too.

'Are my people getting food?' Tanôtai asked icily.

'They're not starving if that makes you feel any better.' Fa'losôi was chewing so noisily that it made Aiphatòn want to ram the spear through her throat even more. She leaned forwards and raised her goblet. 'The best wine, from the cellar of Dâkiòn's sovereign. I took the liberty as he doesn't need it anymore. Your people are making use of the provisions, don't worry.' She took a sip.

Aiphatòn didn't touch the food. *One brief pulse and I could summon the spear to me. Would there be enough time?* There was no way for him to tell how quick she was. 'Why did you kill the other älfar?'

Fa'losôi waved her wine. 'Would you explain it to him, Saî'losôi?' she asked. 'I'm too hungry. As soon as I feel full I'll take over the conversation.'

Saî'losôi put her flatbread back down on the plate. 'Fa'losôi is the daughter of Sh'taro Nhatai. Our family received a visit from one of your tribe's assassins. He killed her second cousin and simply took the head away with him. Presumably as a trophy. To this day, we don't know who the assassin was,' she explained, looking enviously at Kôr'losôi who had carried on with his meal. Her stomach rumbled softly.

Fa'losôi looked at the botoican. 'Recite my message, cousin, the one that I used to leave. And make an effort. Älfar like poetry.'

Sighing, Kôr'losôi lowered the glass that he had almost raised to his lips; this time Saî'losôi grinned.

She likes her little power games. Aiphatòn couldn't find the words to describe the disdain he felt. He would have been so glad to summon his weapon.

Kôr'losôi sat up straight and spoke as if he were reciting a poem:

'My name is Fa'losôi of the Nhatai family,
I declare
that the Nhatai family will not rest
until the murderer of my kin is found
and killed.

Until then,
every älf is
fair game for the Nhatai family.

If this message reaches the murderer of my cousin:
give yourself up and save countless älfar
lives.

Because I will come
and seize
every one
I can get my hands on.'

'It doesn't rhyme at all,' Tanôtai's assessment was disparaging. 'Even a stammering child wouldn't have been that bad. The rhythm of the individual lines is awkward and at the end it would have been better if. . .'

'Yes, yes. I admit it could have been better,' an offended Fa'losôi interrupted her. 'It wasn't a good idea to try impressing an älf-woman with clumsy words.'

'You'll have to command me to be impressed,' the death-dancer shot back drily.

Aiphatòn guffawed with laughter – and was the only one to do so. Kôr'losôi used the opportunity to keep eating fast.

Saî'losôi didn't quite know if she should continue her story. She didn't resume until her disgruntled cousin gave her the signal. 'Over time, thinking changed and during her preparations in the battle against other botoican families, she managed to make a capture that she initially regarded as a stroke of luck. Sinthoras and Caphalor . . .'

'They're long since dead,' Aiphatòn exclaimed in surprise. 'When is this supposed to have happened?'

'After the conquest of . . . well, you call it Tark Draan.' Fa'losôi relished his shock. 'Oh yes, I'm older than you. Much older. As old as Shôtoràs perhaps.' She stretched. 'I aged better than he did.' She had bitten into some bread, but she threw it back onto the plate, seeming to be full. 'In any case, they stood before me one day, on Nhatai land, and I had them locked up in my tower.'

Aiphatòn didn't believe a word she said. *As a human woman, how could she have lived this long? Even the magae and magi of Girdlegard don't live more than at most two hundred cycles.* He rested his left hand loosely on his paralysed thigh. *It would take me less than a heartbeat to stab her.*

Fa'losôi's mouth twisted. 'Those two warriors ensured that . . . let's say . . . a spell went awry. It cost thousands of lives and it wasn't just simple-minded beasts who died. No, almost all of my Nhatais were killed.'

'Only you weren't. What a shame,' Tanôtai remarked, disappointed.

She wants to provoke Fa'losôi into killing her in a rage. Aiphatòn thought he could see right through the älf-woman.

'Only I wasn't, that's right.' Fa'losôi finished her wine and poured herself some more. 'I was presumed dead and my enemies tossed me into the swamp. The Nhatais were believed to have been wiped out and the remaining botoicans carried on with their usual childish efforts to outdo each other.' The look in her pale-yellow eyes became haughty. 'Their cowardly ancestors' – she pointed at Kôr'losôi and Saî'losôi – 'surrendered and served as henchmen to the others.' She threw her hands in the air, the gemstones jangling against each other. 'But then I woke up from my magic sleep after a few years. I fought my way out of the marsh into the open air and escaped death by suffocation.' Fa'losôi lifted her bald head and smiled cheerfully. 'It took a while for me to understand what had happened. But the unintentional sleep caused by the misfiring spell strengthened my powers.' She lowered her arms and grinned as she drank. 'I couldn't help but be grateful to Sinthoras and Caphalor for trying to kill me that time. They recreated me. And in turn I rescued these two.' She pointed at her cousins again. 'Otherwise they would still be serving boy and girl to foreign masters.'

'Is serving a mistress you know any different?' Tanôtai chipped in. 'You're still slaves no matter what way you look at it.'

Kôr'losôi paused in his chewing, Saî'losôi glared spitefully at her.

'The death-dancer has a sharp tongue.' Fa'losôi looked amused. 'Huh. Why did I used to kill älfar before? I could have had so much fun at mealtimes.' She burst out laughing.

'You're going to kill us too. By deploying us on the battlefield,' Aiphatòn replied. He could barely control himself any longer. His weapon seemed to be calling to him to free it from the sorceress' fingers.

'Indeed. But at least I've talked to you first.' Fa'losôi leaned back against the cushions and placed her hands on the rune-emblazoned spear shaft. 'This isn't steel. And the armoured plates are made of an alloy I've never seen in the wasteland before.'

'My parents made it. This metal is one of a kind. Like me,' he answered. A new brainwave came to him in a flash. *Could I successfully win her trust by stealth? I wouldn't need to rush anything and I'd be in better control of the situation than the one I'm currently in.* He thought of the ghaist that was still in the corner. *An enormous imponderable.* 'If you hand over the spear, I'll lead your army from victory to victory.'

'I'm victorious anyway,' she countered cheerfully.

'But you sustain high casualties. And then the ghaist creatures scurry about looking for reinforcements. That takes time, and your enemy could pounce on you in the meantime,' he reeled off the reasons. He thought he'd found her vulnerability. 'Do you play Tharc?'

'What's that?' Fa'losôi looked curiously at him and rolled the flats of her hands over the spear, making the tip spin.

'An älfar strategy game. I was the best at it,' he lied.

'And how do you plan on commanding my troops when you don't have any power over them?'

Aiphatòn pointed to Kôr'losôi and Saî'losôi. 'I'll tell *them* what the army is to do, they'll implement my instructions and the victory will be achieved in no time. Even against a force that seems greatly superior,' he suggested. 'So you and your relatives decide what happens.'

'Are you certain, even against the *greatest* superior force?' Fa'losôi gave a cunning grin. Her emphasis puzzled Aiphatòn but he could no longer take back his promise without her losing interest. 'Why should I believe an älf seriously means what he says?'

'Because I'm immortal and would like to stay that way.' Aiphatòn sounded completely serious because that's exactly what he meant.

'And because he's a coward from Tark Draan,' Tanôtai angrily snapped at him. 'He will stand at the back and watch as others go to their doom on his orders.'

He laughed. 'That's what all generals do.'

The death-dancer uttered a contemptuous noise. 'I forgot: you were the *emperor of the älfar*. You never stood where the battle raged.' She picked up her glass.

Is it me she wants to kill now? Aiphatòn's eyes narrowed into slits, he turned to face the red-haired älf-woman. 'You will . . .'

'Are there still älfar in Tark Draan?' Fa'losôi interrupted him casually.

Kôr'losôi and Saî'losôi had stopped eating, having taken enough hasty mouthfuls. They waited eagerly for the response.

'No,' he answered and turned to the botoican-woman. 'They were wiped out by magic and an army that was second to none.'

He didn't reveal the full truth. No doubt some of his tribe had still roamed Girdlegard but they ought to have been picked off by Ireheart's crow's beak or the weapons of braver warriors.

'That fills me with a certain satisfaction.' Fa'losôi leaned forwards and poured herself some more wine. 'Because if I send you and your friends from Dâkiòn and Elhàtor to their deaths, your race will' – she paused, searching for the right word – 'pass into endingness. Belated revenge for my kin becoming the victim of an älfar assassin.' She nodded, as if she were enjoying the thought of it. 'But now you: what drove you to enter the wasteland?'

'Girdlegard no longer belongs to me. The armies are too strong, the defending forces prepared for anything and I was the only älf left. So what business did I still have there? As I mentioned, I'm fond of my immortality,' he replied glibly. 'I managed to get away from my pursuers. I jumped off the portal on the Stone Gateway and fended for myself. Here . . .'

Beside him, Tanôtai suddenly smashed the glass in her hand and at the same time stretched her arm out in one seamless throwing motion to hurl the largest fragments at Fa'losôi.

But the petite älf-woman's hand didn't open.

Gasping, Tanôtai stared at her paralysed arm. Aiphatòn looked at her face, fear and disappointment written across it.

'My will is stronger than your thought,' Fa'losôi said unsympathetically. '*Quicker* than your thought.'

One finger after another closed around the shards; they crunched as they rubbed together and cut into her flesh.

The death-dancer screamed in pain. Blood dripped, then ran down her arm and hit the cushions. Once the tendons had been severed by the blades of glass, her hand opened, the little fragments flying onto the table or falling almost inaudibly onto the fabric.

'Your flesh is mine,' said Fa'losôi coolly.

Aiphatòn was forced to watch what happened next.

Tanôtai leaned forwards and picked up the largest shard, her red blood smeared on it, and raised it to her throat as she gasped. The tattooed lines lit up all over her skin, but the magic seemed useless. Very slowly, the tip scratched her skin, cutting through the colourful lines, and the älf-woman screamed again.

'You're just a puppet. My puppet.' Fa'losôi's yellowish eyes were still fixed on Aiphatòn, as if the death-dancer was not worthy of her attention.

'As long as I breathe, I will try to kill you,' Tanôtai yelled – and uttered a strangled groan.

Her mouth closed and opened, her nostrils flared but no matter how hard she tried, her ribcage stayed as hard as stone and would not move. Not a breath of air reached her lungs; the glow of her tattoos was dimming.

'*As long as* you breathe,' Fa'losôi repeated softly. 'Do you see how quickly I can change that?'

Aiphatòn had no choice but to be the observer who was learning how to avoid becoming the botoican-woman's next victim.

Tanôtai's fury gave way to sheer mortal fear. Her complexion was getting redder and redder, the veins at her throat and around her eyes were swelling. The black anger lines didn't stand out anymore. She was still holding her cut, bleeding hand outstretched, the other resting at her throat holding the shard.

'*My* puppet,' Fa'losôi declared. 'Like everyone else.'

Tanôtai got up from her seat and started to dance, her legs still full of the grace she had once demonstrated to Aiphatòn. Only once she had so little air left that she was staggering and practically falling unconscious did the botoican-woman allow her to breathe again.

Tanôtai stopped moving and breathed hard, panting like an älf-woman who had escaped death by drowning at the very last moment. Her chest looked like it was bursting, she was pumping air into it so hard.

She dropped the shard, and came back and sat down next to Aiphatòn, gasping as strings of saliva ran from the corners of her mouth. She couldn't speak. The tattoos lost the last of their light.

Fa'losôi was silent at first, looking like she had fallen asleep with her eyes open. Then she flinched. 'All right, Aiphatòn. I'm glad to have found an astute commander in you.' She looked at Kôr'losôi and Saî'losôi as if nothing had happened. 'We'll try what he has suggested.' She got up and leaned on the spear. 'Kôr'losôi, you go with Aiphatòn and a troop of a hundred beasts to Ultai t'Ruy. A ghaist has located the town and will show you where you need to go. Apparently Ysor'kenôr *is* there with his allies.' The botoican-woman strolled over to a side door. 'Attack them. I want to see what you can accomplish against the *greatest superior force.* Seeing as he's such a good Tharc-player.' Laughing, she stopped on the threshold. 'Oh, as a little incentive: if I'm satisfied, you'll get your toy back. I've heard it's meant to be good for warding off endingness.' Fa'losôi left the room.

I am going to find out whether presenting my suggestion to her really was a brainwave. Aiphatòn felt the external power taking hold of him, then his arms dangled down.

Tanôtai groaned, her hands lowering. Her wound was still bleeding.

Kôr'losôi grimaced. 'Setting out with a hundred beasts,' he moaned in a low voice. 'Not the best idea, cunning emperor.'

Saî'losôi, on the other hand, looked relieved. She looked at Aiphatòn. 'Do you also play Tharc with a hundred against a hundred thousand?' She stood up, giving Kôr'losôi an encouraging clap on the shoulder. 'And I used to be jealous of your travels.' The botoican-woman snickered as she left through the door the group had entered by.

'I sincerely hope,' Kôr'losôi practically whispered, 'that this game actually exists and that you are as good at it as you fooled Fa'losôi into believing you are.'

Tanôtai still could not speak, and she had a faraway, blank look on her face, as she had had at the beginning.

Aiphatòn was about to respond when the copper helmet, whom he had already forgotten about, ran off after the head of the Nhatai family. *I almost gave myself away.*

'Since I'm the only one who knows Tharc, I'll win,' he whispered when they were alone, barely moving his lips. 'It will be enough if we annihilate a few thousand with our hundred monsters before they get crushed.'

Kôr'losôi stared at him in horror and stood up. 'A vital detail has escaped you, however: the *greatest* superior force,' he hissed. 'If you knew what she meant by that, you might not think your suggestion had been so successful. Unless another part of Tharc is forcing your enemy to surrender through *inferiority.*'

Aiphatòn's legs were moving, the botoican-woman was sending him out of the room. Tanôtai was still sitting on the cushions. *Like a puppet.* 'It's just a test.'

Kôr'losôi came right up close to him and he looked anxious. Anxious and angry. 'Ysor'kenôr's army is overwhelmingly made up of mongrels that he bred himself, a mixture of trolls and ogres and giants. He calls them malméners,' he revealed. 'What do you think these mountain-sized creatures are going to do to our orcs?' He walked past him.

Aiphatòn started to brood. These things never happened in Tharc.

Chapter XV

Beware of the shadow that is also visible in the dark.

Wise saying of the Älfar
Collected by Carmondai, master of word and image

Ishím Voróo, 5452nd division of unendingness (6491st solar cycle), late autumn

'It was not a good idea.' Kôr'losôi wouldn't stop complaining. 'In fact it was the worst possible idea.' At the head of a group of orcs a hundred strong, he and Aiphatòn were speeding through the grassland at a brisk pace, the rippling green stalks occasionally reaching up to their hips. The stalks grew as much as a finger's-width thick, the reed-like plants hitting them painfully in the thighs and shinbones. The sap that sometimes seeped out left streaks on both armour and fabric.

They were taking the path south-westwards to where the town called Ultai t'Ruy was located, as they had heard from the ghaist that Fa'losôi used as a scout.

'*Greatest* superior force.' Kôr'losôi cursed and placed a hand on the älf's shoulder.

His whining is the whining of a coward. Aiphatòn remained silent.

He would not start to worry about his plans until they got close to the enemy camp.

The botoicans hadn't drawn up any maps of Ishím Voróo because they moved around with their armies in a nomadic fashion, settling down wherever they liked. That made preparing for the skirmish difficult.

Aiphatòn felt the botoican-woman was giving him just enough freedom, like a dog on a long but very secure leash that could be yanked on at any time to call the mutt back. 'I've never been more relaxed,' he admitted to Kôr'losôi.

'What?' The botoican, who was wearing the white armour of Elhàtor because he liked it, cursed again. 'You are genuinely crazy. Malméners are enormous. Those hairy brutes! Like three orcs stacked on top of each other. They snap trees between their fingers and twist the trunks to tie them in knots.'

Aiphatòn didn't set too much store by these words. They came from sheer fear. 'We are on the safer side. All we need to do is find ourselves a cosy spot and direct the greenskins.' *But if an arrow were to get you, that wouldn't be such a shame.*

The black robe the botoican-woman had given him fit perfectly. If it hadn't been her who had given him the gift, he would have liked the outfit.

'These beasts that Ysor'kenôr created for himself have got keener noses than the most experienced bloodhounds and they detect scents upwind.' Kôr'losôi still wouldn't be pacified. 'But they're reared to be so obedient that it only takes him one tiny thought to command them. They are perfect. What the last botoican of the Rhâhois lacks in powers, he has made up for with his subordinates.'

Aiphatòn was gradually realising why Fa'losôi amassed so many warriors. *And I promised her I'd achieve it with less. She is sitting in her tower right now, sick with laughter at me.*

He was sticking to his plan, however: he would pass the test, get his spear and send the älfar into a decisive battle first, to dispatch as many of them as possible into endingness. Then there was the botoican-woman to be dealt with. *She doesn't realise how much magic there is within me and the weapon. And for that very reason, I could overpower her.* He reflected. *Best to wait until the battle is over.*

'Do you hear that?' Kôr'losôi turned his head slightly in the wind.

Aiphatòn had heard the quiet rumbling sound coming from up ahead. 'It could be falling tree trunks. Maybe they're building catapults?'

The group jogged up a gentle incline to get a better view. Under orders from Aiphatòn, Kôr'losôi made the orcs slowly creep up the last few paces before the summit so that they weren't visible from the other side. The blades of grass weren't as high here, but still provided enough cover so long as they were careful.

Aiphatòn was looking down into a gently sloping crater no more than four paces deep at its lowest point, but with a diameter of two miles. Tree stumps rose up out of the mossy floor, a reminder of the wood that must once have stood there, and it smelled of fresh resin and turned over earth.

The malméners, whom Kôr'losôi had described accurately earlier, were roaming across the cleared expanse as if they were looking for tree trunks that had been overlooked. Their heads were lowered and their eyes, as big as plates, stayed fixed on the ground.

'There are only fifty of them,' murmured Aiphatòn, his gaze roving around. *Something is off here.* 'That's not even a *greater* superior force,' he couldn't help adding. 'Fa'losôi needs all these soldiers just for them?' To the north, he thought he could make out a narrow path. 'And where has the botoican got to?'

Kôr'losôi looked confused. 'The ghaist said that this was where . . .' He lifted his head slightly to assess the situation better.

'How intelligent is a ghaist if it's not being directed by its master?'

'That depends. Most of them are about as smart as a dog but if the souls used were particularly clever, it comes close to a human.' Kôr'losôi didn't seem to grasp what the älf was trying to get at. 'Am I mistaken or are the malméners looking for something?'

A vague explanation for what they were seeing was forming in Aiphatòn's mind. 'We need to get closer. I want to know what they're searching for.'

'Never!' Kôr'losôi made a defensive motion with his hands. 'We'll make the greenskins . . .'

'They're too stupid.' Aiphatòn had to admit that the enemy out-classed them. The orcs would be torn to pieces, and just a dozen of the enemy beasts would be enough to do it.

'You might be a warrior, emperor, but I'm nothing more than a puppet-master.' Kôr'losôi looked at the malméners again, who were staggering about like tree trunks brought to life. 'We would need all of the älfar to defeat those brutes down there.'

'Trust my Tharc skills.' He pointed to the right. 'Send thirty green-skins back so that they come round the hill and encounter the enemy as if by chance. If these simple-minded giant-beasts are as dumb as you say, the majority of them will attack the greenskins immediately. As soon as that happens, you send the next thirty in from the other side.'

'They won't survive for long,' Kôr'losôi interjected.

'They don't need to. If the sixty are as good as annihilated, send another twenty in on either side and make them run away immedi-ately so the malméners give chase.' Aiphatòn went over his strategy again in his mind.

'What is that meant to achieve?'

'I can go down and take a look around without them pouncing on me right away.'

Kôr'losôi scowled as the orcs crept back and positioned themselves at the foot of the hill. Being sent to their deaths didn't seem to bother them. 'At some point, you're going to explain this Tharc game to me,' he whispered. 'So that I can understand whether what you're doing right now is a good idea.'

The two of them watched as the greenskins marched around the mound and launched themselves at the enemy with loud roars, as if these were just harmless gnomes whom they could slay with the flats of their hands.

The extremely simple-minded malméners started by storming over to the first group of orcs, then split up when the second detachment of greenskins advanced. Just ten enemies remained on the cleared field, looking indecisively at the ground and over at the skirmish as it calmed down and drew to a close.

It turned out the way I'd hoped it would. Aiphatòn gave Kôr'losôi a clap on the shoulder. 'Now the final forty.' He got ready to run down the hill.

The botoican dispatched the last battalion, instructing them to run away immediately.

The gigantic malméners promptly fled the clearing and chased after them – including the ten indecisive ones who were screaming at each other as if trying to remind themselves of their mission and keep themselves under control.

I'll be quicker than them. Aiphatòn ducked, then hurried down the hill through the knee-high stalks.

He reached the outer edge of the crater unnoticed and stayed in a crouched position as he examined the point where forest gave way to grassland.

It was in that exact spot that he noticed a ditch-like indentation, as wide as a forearm and as deep as the blade of a dagger.

Aiphatòn glanced right and left. *That ditch keeps going and stretches right around the missing forest.* When he looked forward again, he saw two malméners coming towards him and spotted some more indentations. *That makes sense.*

Aiphatòn got up and started running, right between the two beasts who were moving far too slowly to be a danger to him; symbols branded on their chests showed that they belonged to the Rhâhois. Since he saw no need to kill the malméners, he kept them at arm's length. *There's a favour they're going to do for me.*

He jogged across the hollow, looking at the marks and swerving from time to time when the enemies yelled and threw stones at him. These beasts were cut out for the battlefield, not for fighting nimble adversaries like him.

During his inspection, he occasionally noticed a magical radiation being emitted from something in the area, but it was nothing like the torturous magical fields in the towns. He explored the area, trying to pinpoint its exact location.

Aiphatòn grinned as he watched two malméners trudging up the hill. They had probably picked up Kôr'losôi's scent. The white armour meant he was easy to see against the green; he would not be able to escape. The botoican had no more orcs he could summon as a diversion. *That's one less Nhatai. They're doing the favour I wanted them to do for me. A good Tharc player thinks many moves ahead.*

The älf scoured the ground as he ran. The more semi-circular and right-angled indentations he found, the more he was convinced: Ysor'kenôr had built a town here as a trick, probably with pictures in heavy frames and thin brick walls and roofs made of hastily bound branches and slats to keep up appearances; and he had a handful of his impressive beasts walk around to boot.

The ghaist-creature had been taken in by the sight from a distance but the botoican-woman hadn't let her scout go any closer so as not to be spotted. That's how the trick worked. *But why go to so much effort?* Realising he might not be the only one who knew how to play Tharc, Aiphatòn smiled.

He wanted the Nhatais to relocate their town! A good strategy. He assumed the enemy army was already on its way to Fa'losôi to ambush her in her own residence instead of seeking conflict in the usual battlefield carnage. *He isn't sticking to the established rules of the game. That makes him even better.*

A loud human scream cut through the air.

Aiphatòn smiled. Due to the power of the malméners, Kôr'losôi had stopped being a puppet-master.

He suddenly noticed the magical radiation was unusually concentrated so he stopped and looked around more carefully.

A sparkle in the churned-up moss caught his attention.

Is that the object the monsters were looking for? He stooped down, rummaging in the soft, damp carpet of green until he caught hold of a triangular silver amulet.

He immediately felt a warm but pleasant prickling in the tips of his fingers and the runes on his gloves glowed blissfully.

This is highly magical. The runes undoubtedly belonged to the Rhâhoi family. On the polished surface, numerous jewels were glimmering. *No matter what Ysor'kenôr needed it for, he'll have to do without it.*

Aiphatòn stowed it underneath his black clothing and jogged on again to get away from the enemy.

Tracing a wide arc, he returned to the path that he, Kôr'losôi and the troops had taken. Their tracks were easy to make out, thanks to the trampled stalks of grass.

The malméners were unable to keep up with his speed despite their long legs and they fell behind straight away.

After half a mile, he passed by where the last of the orcs were being torn into little pieces.

Thus they've fulfilled their duty. Aiphatòn stayed a safe distance away from the crazed, gigantic monsters jumping around on the cadavers of the defeated orcs and trampling them flat.

Aiphatòn wasn't worried about his future, despite the defeat. By the time he reached the white tower, he would have thought of a good story to explain Kôr'losôi's death and present himself as a skilled general. On top of the knowledge that Ysor'kenôr might invade their army camp at any time and that he protected them from imminent defeat or at least an attack, his spear was drawing nearer as a reward.

Aiphatòn could feel the amulet underneath his clothing. It rubbed against his tanned skin as if it were trying to draw attention to itself. Nobody knew that he had taken it – neither Kôr'losôi nor any ghaists – so it remained secret from Fa'losôi too.

I will find out what it does. He hurried across the grassland, his thoughts returning to the incident in the tower when the botoican-woman had demonstrated to Tanôtai how deft her responses and actions were as soon as someone tried to attack her.

And he suddenly thought about Ávoleï again, which surprised him.

Was it because she had been an elf-woman? His shock at himself continued when the images took him unawares.

He remembered her laugh.

Her kiss.

That look she gave him before throwing herself over the balustrade in Elhàtor to escape the spell.

Whatever might have happened with her – it didn't happen and never will. It's better like this, although I wouldn't have wished death on her. Engrossed in memories and strange thoughts, it took Aiphatòn a long time to notice the two black columns of smoke looming straight as an arrow over the grassland. They were both above Fa'losôi's town and a third was just working its way skywards.

Ysor'kenôr had made his next move.

Ishím Voróo, Tr'hoo D'tak, 5452nd division of unendingness (6491st solar cycle), late autumn

Saî'losôi lay in the copper bathtub with her eyes closed and let the water laced with essential oils wash away the dirt the moloch had left on her.

She breathed in the fragrant steam, enjoying the aroma of flowers and spices. And yet she fancied she could still smell the acrid stench of excrement, decaying corpses and fermenting swamp.

She was haunted by the grumbling, panting and roaring. The crowds of älfar made the monsters uneasy because they were afraid of black-eyes. What's more, it seemed the race of tall creatures emitted a weak radiation because of their own innate magic, which made the botoican spell less reliable.

So Saî'losôi had walked around on Fa'losôi's orders, accompanied by two ghaists, and pulled the invisible chains around the beasts' minds tighter while the more powerful botoican-woman and the cîani made an attempt to force Nodûcor's half-mask off.

Saî'losôi hated what her cousin called a town. This village was unwieldy, the paths too wide, the air foul.

And she hated her cousin – something she had in common with Kôr'losôi.

The time for a decision is drawing near. Tr'hoo D'tak was a matter of pride only for Fa'losôi, not for her. Not for any of the Nhatais. Saî'losôi had been treated better by other botoican families than by her own flesh and blood.

She thought her cousin was completely insane – lingering in a half-death seemed to have made her take leave of her senses. She was behaving more and more strangely, her actions verging on incomprehensible. Saî'losôi knew that she became dispensable after the last battle – another thing she had in common with Kôr'losôi. *I've got to act before she kills me on a whim.*

It appeared her cousin Kôr'losôi had joined forces with the älf, the former emperor, which she thought was a mistake. No puppet was a match for Fa'losôi, the death-dancer's failure clearly demonstrated that. *Not even Aiphatòn will be quicker than her.*

The brown-haired botoican-woman wondered how Fa'losôi had managed to escape the marsh she had supposedly been lying in after the älfar, Shintoras and Caphalor, appeared to have finished her off.

That incident took place a long time before she was born. The fact this relative of hers, who was her cousin many times removed, had survived lying in wet earth was a puzzle. It had been a long time since there were any witnesses around who might have been able to confirm the story.

Kôr'losôi had simply accepted her return because he was no match for her and he benefitted from her swift rise to power. Or at least he did at first.

Meanwhile Saî'losôi paid close attention to many little things about her cousin, trying to uncover the secret. Her certainty grew day by day that there was a demon involved, which explained the madness and the volatility.

The wasteland had known more than one such creature to get up to mischief and enter living beings to gain possession of them and control the destinies of entire tribes.

Even the älfar used one of them when they battled Tark Draan. Saî'losôi opened her eyes and fished the sponge out of the water to rub it over her rune-adorned skin. *Why wasn't it possible that a demon had taken on Fa'losôi's form?* That would explain her immense power, if control and influence spells were at work.

Saî'losôi knew there was an antidote to anything and everything.

Even for demons.

Unfortunately, she wasn't an expert in the art of exorcism. Her cousin kept a very careful eye on the cîani, otherwise Saî'losôi would have used some pretext to grab one of them a long time ago. This possessive behaviour confirmed her theories.

If Kôr'losôi acts oddly and arouses her suspicions by making a pact with the emperor – I'll wait for my chance. And it ought to come soon.

A gentle jolt passed through the bathtub.

There were barely noticeable ripples in the water and the thin foam sloshed up over Saî'losôi's arms and neck.

She stopped moving and listened. *Was the platform falling? Or was it . . .*

The second jolt made the whole room shake hard, the water flowing over the copper rim.

Saî'losôi cursed and stepped out of the bathtub, wrapping herself in her green dressing gown, wet as she was, to go and check if everything was all right.

She feared an earthquake or that the ground beneath the Nhatai tower was softening. Subsidence could create strain in the beams, which warped and broke easily. She had experienced it once before and that time she was able to stabilise the building before it could fall, with help from a pack of beasts, while the residents had moved their worldly belongings to safety.

Ideally, I'll be able to see from one of the balconies what's causing the groaning and cracking in the timber frame. Saî'losôi ran out of the room and along the narrow corridor, opening a door to the open air that was about forty paces above the ground and gave onto a viewing platform.

One glance was enough for her to realise that the ground sinking or even an earthquake would have been less of an issue.

Ysor'kenôr!

The revolting town that stretched out in front of the botoican-woman was being attacked from two sides. The surviving member of the Rhâhoi family had had his malméners advance from the south and southwest in wedge formation and they had already cleared two paths.

At the point where the heads of the two platoons met, they formed a cluster, launching carved tree-trunks lengthwise all over the town.

The extremely heavy tree-rolling demolished any and all huts or beasts standing in their way. Two of them had rolled right up to the tower and smashed into the lower part of the stone wall.

Are those catapults? Saî'losôi thought she could make out enemy creatures assembling the roughly hewn components of catapults under cover of the group. The throwing arms were aimed at the tower, stones the size of oxen placed in the slings.

Meanwhile Fa'losôi's army set upon the enemy from all sides in a chaotic tumult. With no rhyme or reason, they obeyed the control spell that ordered them to tackle everything that attacked them or represented a danger to the town.

Ysor'kenôr's army had been recognised as an enemy by their befuddled minds. But since the enormous adversaries were in the middle of their camp, the defending forces themselves were in the way – and they tore through everything that stopped them getting at their opponents.

Orcs trampled gnomes, trolls knocked people down and sprinted over them, and the älfar unit used their cîani's magic fire to burn a path of destruction right through all of the monsters, large and small.

I've got to sort this out before Fa'losôi intervenes. Saî'losôi made the gnomes drop back, then the people, to bring the orcs and älfar up towards Ysor'kenôr's group faster. The trolls and ogres acted as marshals in this, creating pathways.

Then she noticed there were two standard flags with Ysor'kenôr's personal coat of arms in different places on the battlefield. Was this to create confusion, to leave the enemy uncertain as to where the Rhâhoi man was, or could the opposing side have more than one powerful botoican?

Where can my cousin be? Saî'losôi didn't dare leave the balcony to look for her because that would make the defending forces descend into chaos again. It was a risk, bringing the älfar's magic radiation close to the orcs and encouraging their wild natures. *But maybe it will upset Ysor'kenôr's power too.*

In the meantime, the wedges of malméners had banded together and taken control of a quarter of the town by advancing right and left. In the distance, even more troops were marching closer; Ysor'kenôr made sure they were rolling into the town in waves.

That son of a bitch! The botoican-woman felt an ache in her temples; her exhaustion was making itself felt. The ghaists were desperately needed but their creator was Fa'losôi, therefore she was their only commander. Saî'losôi could only hope that the creatures would step in of their own accord.

The älfar had reached the northern edge of the pack and were launching themselves at the malméners. The cîani used their magic to transform the house-sized monsters into roaring flames, and the archers killed the burning, helpless enemies within a few heartbeats. Two of their siege machines had also caught fire.

The orcs, on the other hand, were doing a much clumsier job of it. Their attacking unit ran at the enemy and got stuck in their ranks, getting killed and trampled on.

The wind carried the sounds of screams and animalistic roars, and the hail of weapons and arrows to Saî'losôi. Never before had she found herself so dangerously close to the fighting.

It's taking too long. Her breath caught in her throat as the burning catapults, despite being damaged, fired a first salvo.

Four stones flew in a high arc, spinning as they did so, as if they were trying to show themselves to the botoican-woman from every angle.

One missile whirred past the tower less than four paces from it, at the height of her balcony. Saî'losôi automatically leaned sideways, as if the building would tilt with her and dodge it.

The second stone was aimed far too high, only ripping the roof off.

The botoican-woman shrank back against the white wall to escape the falling debris – and threw herself flat on the balcony when she saw the third shell coming towards her.

Five paces above, the heavy missile thundered through the wall, smashing beams and supporting structures, snapping guy ropes and leaving a hole behind.

This time the tower shook underneath Saî'losôi, who had put her hands over her head. She felt the fourth impact much further below her – it must have torn away sections of the external wall to the right.

I need to get out of this trap. She got up, trembling with fear, but managed to keep setting the älfar and orcs on the malméners.

Two catapults went down in flames and a hastily fired stone did not have enough momentum and landed in a pack of gnomes, crushing three dozen of them and rolling through the crowd, leaving a trail of destruction in its wake.

The double rumbles of a wooden swinging arm heralded new missiles. These stones flew straight at the centre and foundations.

As the shells hit the tower and forced it to bend like a reed, Saî'losôi made a handful of trolls run towards her. *I can do this.*

She clung to the railing and ordered her approaching rescuers to form a ladder with their bodies against the wall. In this way the botoican-woman managed to keep the swaying under control.

She vaulted bravely over the balustrade and dived onto the highest troll's neck, clinging to his stinking hair and making him jump onto the ground.

At the same moment, new missiles hurtled at them. They scattered the beasts stacked on top of each other and dealt the final blow to the building.

Saî'losôi landed safely on the soft earth with the troll but she needed to get out of the way immediately to avoid the falling building. 'To the left, to the left!' she thought and screamed at the same time. The monster obeyed.

With a cracking sound, the tower tilted. The wall panels came away, and masonry rained down stone by stone on the Nhatai troops, crushing humans and pulverising gnomes. Even the ogres and trolls fell to their knees under the weight of debris and were severely wounded.

The swamp quaked at the impact.

Beams and planks shot out and fetid mud sprayed many paces upwards and outwards. The tower collapsed, smoking, and fell onto the mucky ground like a dead, burst mayfly.

The survivors crawled out of it like maggots.

'Cousin!' From the troll's neck, Saî'losôi scoured the ruined building, the different storeys and destroyed floors. *There she is!*

Amid the disarray, Fa'losôi lay trapped, surrounded by various älfar, Tanôtai and some servants. None of them were moving.

Don't be dead! I need you alive to achieve victory! The clouds of smoke blocked Saî'losôi's view of the battlefield. She ordered the monsters to launch themselves at Ysor'kenôr's troops with all their might.

Her troll suddenly uttered a muffled groan and held his side, his knees swaying before he collapsed.

Saî'losôi jumped off in time to avoid getting buried underneath him. She didn't see what kind of missile had killed the creature but it meant that some enemies had got far too close.

'Fa'losôi!' she screamed, as she balanced her way across the rubble and approached her cousin. The sounds of fighting beyond the grey clouds were getting louder and seemed to be moving forward as Saî'losôi did.

Finally, she reached the motionless woman. Her jugular vein was throbbing gently.

Tanôtai groaned and sat up.

Good! Oh, that's good! Saî'losôi commanded the death-dancer to clear away the debris then helped her tackle it. Tanôtai picked up a stick and then swapped it for an iron rod to use as a lever with bigger pieces of debris.

Suddenly the ghaist with the dented copper helmet appeared and started to help. Its supernatural powers ensured that Fa'losôi was quickly rescued from the tangle of beams. Then, as quickly as it had come, the ghaist disappeared again, burrowing down through the ruins of the tower.

It could be looking for anything down there.

'Cousin, it's me: Saî'losôi,' she cried, stroking the unconscious woman's dirty cheek. 'Wake up! I'm begging and pleading!'

Her eyelids fluttered, then Fa'losôi coughed and inhaled, her breath rattling. The dust had settled in her lungs. 'What . . . happened?'

Saî'losôi was relieved, although the yelling and shrieking and dying seemed to be just beyond the clouds of dust now. She drew her dagger as if she could halt a superior force with the blade. 'You've got to rally the troops and launch a counter-attack. Ysor'kenôr has led his army right into our town. He might even have brought a second botoican with him!'

Fa'losôi touched her shorn, rune-adorned head, a rivulet of blood streaming out of her nose and running red over her lips. 'I . . . can't remember,' she moaned. 'What troops? Aren't we in Ikârion?'

Saî'losôi felt a chill all of a sudden. 'That was almost eighty days ago, cousin!' she replied in a guttural voice, grabbing her by the shoulders and shaking her. 'Try and remember! You've got to think straight. My powers are exhausted. You are Fa'losôi, the commander of the Nhatais, and if you don't pull yourself together right now, you are going to die, along with me, unlike the Rhâhois' beasts!'

Fa'losôi looked around in confusion, wiping a hand over the blood under her nose, which was followed by a fresh stream from both nostrils, bigger this time. 'My head . . . is pounding and burning,' she said haltingly. 'I . . . do you have anything to drink? I wouldn't mind wine.'

'Wine? Is this one all right with you?' Saî'losôi cursed and slapped her across the face. 'I'll keep giving you this wine until you remember!' the brunette screamed in terror. 'By the ancestors of the Nhatais, I swear I'll kill you myself before one of Ysor'kenôr's people can do it.' After three swift, ringing slaps, her cousin wailing as she tried to block them, her gaze changed and seemed to clear. 'Oh, do you remember now?'

Fa'losôi gulped and touched the diamond chip on the bridge of her nose. She closed her eyes. 'I need to concentrate.'

'Good! Great! Now . . .'

Saî'losôi was annoyed by a powerful, pale-green light that fell on the botoican-woman from one side.

She turned her head to look for the source and brandished her dagger.

'Endingness awaits you.' The death-dancer got to her feet next to her. She had taken off the black robe and was wearing nothing but the loincloth. The object that Saî'losôi had thought was an iron rod turned out to be Aiphatòn's rune spear.

All of the symbols were gleaming and illuminating Tanôtai, who was holding the weapon in her uninjured hand; the lines on her skin were glowing too, the jewels sparkling. The long, narrow blade was pointing at the brown-haired botoican-woman – and stabbed at her.

Saî'losôi couldn't parry the spear with the dagger; her weapon slipped over the metal. The thin dressing gown did not put up any resistance and the tip of the spear plunged right into her solar plexus.

She opened her mouth to scream but couldn't breathe.

'That's what happened to me,' remarked the red-haired älf-woman, twisting the shaft so that the blade caused greater damage inside her enemy's body. The runes were flickering as if they were exhausted or were overwhelmed by the contact with the botoican-woman's magic; then they went out. 'But I'm breathing again. You never will.' She yanked the spear out of the dying woman, droplets of blood falling on the woman's gaping robe and skin. 'Your death is called Tanôtai,' she said in älfar, the dripping red blade swinging towards Fa'losôi, who was still lying there with her eyes closed. 'And your death also bears my name.'

The slim death-dancer's muscles tensed.

Heat spread through Saî'losôi's stomach and burned into every last nook of her body. This was followed by a second wave, this time of ice. Her eyes were fixed incredulously on Tanôtai, who was taking her time to stab Fa'losôi. *Or . . .*

'Isn't it a shame that you're failing for a second time?' A smile played around the corners of Fa'losôi's mouth, her eyelids still closed. 'So close to freeing your people from my will.'

She's awake at last. Saî'losôi fell sideways silently, the world swimming and dimming. She guessed what was happening more than she could actually perceive it.

Tanôtai uttered a despairing groan and couldn't move.

'Here we are again, my puppet. Like at dinner when I invited you and Aiphatòn.' Fa'losôi opened her eyes, her gaze riveted triumphantly on the älf-woman. She didn't seem interested in either the outcome of the battle or the approaching enemies. 'You älfar are a race I will never understand. But why worry about the dead?'

Out of the thinning clouds of dust and smoke, arrows whizzed in their direction.

Saî'losôi felt an impact in her back, next to her spine. But the chill from her mortally wounded solar plexus masked everything.

Fa'losôi stayed on the ground, ducking lower behind the beams. 'Well, this is getting annoying now.'

Two projectiles struck the upright death-dancer in the thigh and shoulder. Her face was covered in anger lines, but her mouth remained shut. Tears of disappointment and pain ran down her cheeks.

'You would definitely have been a motif for your tribe's painters and sculptors to fight over,' Fa'losôi remarked thoughtfully. '*The frozen death-dancer*. That could have been the title of the work they created in your honour.'

Another arrow whirred towards them and pierced the red-haired älf-woman's right side.

Tanôtai stayed standing, the tip of the spear still aimed unrelentingly at her opponent. Blood ran from her wounds and painted symbols on her skin, as if trying to cover the tattooed runes that did not have the strength to light up.

'So close to your goal and rashly claiming my death would bear your name.' Fa'losôi watched as the red-haired älf-woman was penetrated by two more arrows that plunged into her neck and upper arm. 'Your death will have no name,' the botoican-woman decided. 'Some unknown archer will release the arrow that strikes your heart or goes through your skull.' She turned to Saî'losôi. 'Can you still hear me, cousin?'

Yes. The dying woman managed to make two fingers twitch.

'Then take my thanks with you into the beyond,' Fa'losôi bid her farewell. 'You have put yourself in danger to rescue me and it has killed you. That was noble.' She laughed softly. 'Although you needn't have worried, you could have let it be.'

Saî'losôi didn't understand what her cousin meant.

Any more thoughts she had froze like ice.

Her body gave up and she did too.

Chapter XVI

The best victory is always the next one.

Wise saying of the Älfar

Collected by Carmondai, master of word and image

Ishím Voróo, Tr'hoo D'tak, 5452nd division of unendingness (6491st solar cycle), late autumn

Just as night fell, Aiphatòn approached Tr'hoo D'tak from the east so that he would have a better view of the town away from the columns of smoke. The dwellings were reasonably sturdy here.

He climbed onto one of the huts to take an awed look round. *The tower is gone. And the enemy catapults over there are on fire.*

The bloodbath was in full swing and would end in defeat for Fa'losôi's forces.

The bright red flags of the foreign family had already laid claim to the entire western half of the town. The ruined tower lay partially burning, partially smouldering along the town's north-south axis and looked, with its shiny protruding beams, like a gigantic animal with its ribcage exposed. The attackers may have lost the catapults they'd brought, but they had achieved their goal.

Ysor'kenôr knows what's he doing more than the Nhatais do. Aiphatòn could still feel the magic shackles, albeit faintly. At least one of the botoican family members was still alive. *I'll change that soon.*

The älfar units from Dâkiòn and Elhàtor fought quietly and with a will of iron. Swarms of arrows whirred across the battlefield, carrying death deep into enemy ranks. The cîani were unleashing havoc among the malméners.

It was magic similar to what he knew from Lot-Ionan, but he would never have expected his people would be capable of it. It was clearer than ever before: northern Ishím Voróo and the time that had gone by had both transformed the älfar.

Girdlegard would have been easy prey for älfar like this. Praise be to all the gods that neither Shôtoràs nor the monarchess had been eager to make conquests. Aiphatòn could see the ghaist-creatures were tough opposition. With their white flags on their backs, they ploughed through enemy lines, tearing apart every creature that crossed their path. They didn't even shy away from the malméners.

But the Rhâhois' troops were too numerous and too enormous, and they made up for their stout statures and lumbering gaits with their strength.

From where he stood, he could make out two eye-catching banners hovering above the enemy army, far apart from each other. They had the same Rhâhoi insignia on them as the one he had seen branded into the malméners.

So perhaps they've got two puppet-masters, he reasoned. The Nhatais had not counted on that.

The enemy botoicans controlling their contingent had a head for military strategy. The weaker auxiliaries marched along behind monsters the size of trees, stabbing wounded enemies to death. Their certain victory did not make them at all cocky.

And that annoyed Aiphatòn. He would have been pleased to see the Rhâhois advancing in a more frenzied, rash way and suffering more casualties.

The älfar now found themselves at the centre of the devastation. The opposing army seemed to have magicians at their disposal too; the air shimmered with the cîani's jets of flame fizzling out or getting redirected at the älfar troops.

Ysor'kenôr and his second in command know exactly what they're doing. Aiphatòn watched the downright one-sided destruction unhappily. *They mustn't make it too easy for the Rhâhois.*

What's more, he was growing increasingly afraid that the enemy would spare the älfar troops at the last moment so that they could use them themselves after the victory over the Nhatais. That would achieve nothing.

Things ought to be moving more quickly. I need a quick, brutal battle that does not allow any mercy. His gaze swept over the swampy plain again, the stink of putrefaction and fresh blood mingling together in a nauseating way.

Aiphatòn assumed that Ysor'kenôr and the second botoican were near a flag with insignia, slightly elevated so as to have a better overview and direct the army.

We'll see whether there really are two botoicans or if it's a trick. He planned to put one of them under a little pressure. *Then, out of fear, they'll urge their people to move faster.* After that, he wanted to kill the puppet-master and take another piece off the Tharc board.

As the älf couldn't make out any platform that might have been constructed like one of the catapults, he assumed the enemy commanders were each on the shoulders of one of the enormous malméners.

They're hardly going to be right in the middle of the densest fray. The danger of falling victim to a charm or an arrow is just too high.

Aiphatòn picked out one of the gigantic monsters towering up out of a crowd of shorter auxiliaries in the southwest and not moving. He couldn't tell if someone was on its shoulders but one of the flags with insignia was fluttering less than fifty paces away. *That's where one of them might be.*

He jumped down off the dilapidated hut and kept to the outskirts of Tr'hoo D'tak to avoid going straight through the battle and encountering a ghaist.

The closer he got to the district of the doomed town that had fallen to the Rhâhois, the more often individual enemy fighters or smaller units attacked him.

Aiphatòn didn't waste time on them; he slayed them with his armoured gloves or used their own weapons to kill them. Since he still hadn't got his spear back and couldn't summon it from this distance, he used whatever weapons the enemy left for him.

In the end he broke through the surprised rearguard made up of orc-like beasts. On top of the fact that night had fallen, they shrouded themselves in darkness for protection, to avoid giving enemy arrows a target. He hurried over the corpses but didn't slip or utter a sound and they soon lost sight of him.

Aiphatòn was drawing closer to the single malméner who towered up as rigid as a monument over the auxiliaries. A group of forty lance-bearers was guarding him, his legs soaring into the air behind them like pillars, but the älf wasn't worried about them.

Sure enough, on the monster's right shoulder, Aiphatòn spotted a male figure wearing armour and sitting with his back to him in a saddle contraption with a high, metal-plated backrest. *Just as I thought.*

A commotion erupted and started moving towards them from the northeast. Horns were being blown in alarm.

The lance-bearers refocused their attention, looking away from the invisible älf. This made it even easier for him to get close to the brute with the commander on his shoulder.

Aiphatòn saw a ghaist approaching. *Fa'losôi sent it because she understood that only the death of the puppet-master could ward off defeat.* The long groove on the copper helmet revealed that he was dealing with the most dangerous one.

Then Aiphatòn noticed more of the magical creatures, who were so easy to spot with the towering white flags on their backs. He suspected the botoican-woman's aim was to create as big a diversion as possible to get their best warriors where she needed them. On the other hand, it could also mean that –

Ysor'kenôr himself was in front of him.

The most important playing piece in the game isn't yours yet. The Rhâhoi man needs to wipe out the älfar for me first. Aiphatòn picked up his pace and cast darkness over the lance-bearers.

He killed one of them with a blow from an armoured glove and stole his weapon, which he immediately hurled at the botoican – but not to kill him. *That should unleash enough terror to provoke him.*

The tip flew through the night air and the spear plunged through the reinforced backrest as planned.

The scream that drifted down from the monster's shoulder told Aiphatòn that the blade had bored through as far as the commander. The curse that followed revealed that Ysor'kenôr was still alive. *Excellent. Now he'll drive his troops forward.*

But there was no sign from the battlefield that they were redoubling their efforts. The Rhâhoi man didn't seem to want to alter his successful strategy.

The malméner turned around and aimed a kick at Aiphatòn, but he had no difficulty dodging the toes. Two surprised pike-bearers weren't as lucky; they were caught by his foot and flew screaming through the air.

I'll make you lose your mind with fear, botoican! Aiphatòn drew the sword of one of the dead and rushed forwards, the darkness still enveloping him like a protective blanket. *This time I'll force one of your own kind to fulfil my wish!*

He skilfully dodged the indiscriminately kicking feet, came up behind the malméner and severed its heel tendons with powerful blows.

The ligaments snapped with a crack, the brute staggered and uttered muffled cries, then his knees buckled. The lance-bearers ran away to avoid getting buried beneath the falling giant.

But Aiphatòn was right on his heels. He jumped up and cut the tendons in the knee joints too, to stop the malméner getting up again.

The brute fell, breaking his descent with his elbows and emitting such a resounding howl that bystanders covered their ears to protect their eardrums.

Aiphatòn walked around the malméner and looked at the empty seat: either the figure he presumed to be Ysor'kenôr had got himself to safety before the fall or he had gone down with it.

He took a quick look around. *He can't have gone far.*

A wind sprang up that pushed the clouds of smoke towards the ground and made his eyes water. Yet Aiphatòn fancied he detected the smell of flowers.

By now the ghaist creatures were being pelted with bulging pig's bladders by their opponents and the smell of petrol was spreading. Flaming arrows flew at them. Ghaist after ghaist turned into a running torch that slowed down the higher the flames leaped around them. Ysor'kenôr knew the magical creatures' vulnerability and was prepared for it.

The ghaist in the copper helmet with the long groove couldn't dodge the pouches either, but he was able to avoid being set on fire.

Aiphatòn saw a shadowy figure flit across the field and disappear among his soldiers' shields. *There you are!* He raced after the shadow without casting off the darkness. *Do you really feel safe behind the shields?*

A big leap allowed Aiphatòn to soar over them and hit the heavily armed figure right in the back.

The man fell to the ground screaming and rolled over, the heavy, full suit of armour rattling and scraping. The face remained hidden behind the helmet's shut visor.

He stabbed at the älf with his dagger. Meanwhile the wind was getting stronger, little golden tiles dancing wildly in the air with petals and feathers.

Aiphatòn caught the weapon with his armoured hand and crushed the blade effortlessly, dropping it onto the churned-up earth. 'If you don't want your death to be called Aiphatòn,' he said in a deep voice over the murmur of the breezes chafing at his plates of armour, 'keep your guards back.' He wrenched the visor open and looked into the face of an unprepossessing man with a dark brown moustache. 'Tell me your name!'

So as not to endanger the life of their commander, the guards remained at a distance and even started to retreat slowly.

'Ythan'kenôr,' he answered, panting, and immediately he understood. 'You're not one of Nhatais' puppets! Let me live and my brother will reward you after the battle.'

'I thought *he* was the last of the Rhâhois?'

The botoican grinned. 'So long as our enemies think so, that's all right.'

Aiphatòn cursed in the silence. *I'm dealing with very good Tharc players here.* 'Is he commanding the troops or are you?'

'We both do,' Ythan'kenôr shot back quickly, shouting to be heard over the wind.

'Then I don't need you. One is enough for me. But if it's any consolation to you in death: Fa'losôi Nhatai will follow you.' He raised an arm to slay the unremarkable botoican before the distant guards could intervene.

As he did so, the amulet he had found on the deforested land slipped out from underneath his dark clothing.

Ythan'kenôr spotted it and seemed to recognise it. 'You've got it?' He had an evil look in his eyes and his left hand jerked upwards to touch it. 'I'll show you its power . . .'

Aiphatòn hammered his fist right into the man's face, shoving the bone at the bridge of his nose up into his brain. Ythan'kenôr uttered an unintelligible sound.

The piece of jewellery glowed and a bright light flashed at the same time.

Aiphatòn felt his plates warming up. The dreaded, painful prickling flooded his entire body; the magic in him was reacting with the energy released – and then it was over.

Neither pain nor . . . He blinked in surprise at the dead botoican. *What happened?* He got to his feet and didn't feel any different.

The darkness danced around him protectively; not even the powerful wind could blow it away. There was a jarringly fresh, intense scent on the wind. The swamp, blood and excrement didn't seem to exist anymore. The botoican's guards had bolted, presumably because their mental shackles had fallen away. There was no reason for them to attack the älf and meet with certain death in the attempt.

Aiphatòn turned his attention to the battlefield.

The first enemy units had come to a halt because they were no longer receiving any orders from one of their masters.

The älfar in particular were exploiting the confusion to kill their enemies. Their military fortunes seemed to be on the turn, or at least until the brother got the whole army under his control.

Some Nhatai ghaists had perished in explosions in the distance. Craters had formed and the corpses of the Rhâhoi army were ablaze all around them, while another ghaist blew up in front of the älf's eyes. The fiery shockwave knocked creatures within a radius of thirty paces off their feet.

Dazzled, Aiphatòn had to shut his eyes, bracing himself against the approaching draught of air that descended on him.

Once the glow of the blast had subsided, the wind kept on blowing.

The fallen malméner had a broken, stray spear sticking out of his eye that had found its target by chance. *At least the ghaists are slaughtering more of them.*

Aiphatòn held one glove protectively in front of his face. Although it was a clear, starlit night and the moon was a silver glow, a storm seemed to have sprung up, and it was constantly changing direction.

The strong, fresh smells of fruit, green foliage and morning dew were replaced by the fragrance of flowers while light and dark-coloured feathers twirled over the battlefield along with petals. Tiny gold tiles and fine, glittering splinters of glass mingled with them – they hurt on contact with bare skin. A heartbeat later, the smell of iron and earth prevailed, then the air shifted and suddenly smelled of stone and rain. Thin blades of basalt and obsidian clinked as they shattered on Aiphatòn's glove and plates of armour.

The wind intensified and the cuts became more painful.

Blood ran from the many slits where delicate glass had pierced Aiphatòn's skin and sliced it open. *The splinters are going to flay me alive!* He threw himself onto the ground and tried to work out why this was happening. *A hostile spell that Ythan'kenôr cast with the help of the amulet to rescue his victory?* He pulled a shield towards him and used it as cover. *But he didn't touch the amulet. Or did he?*

The brewing storm came whistling angrily under the metal-plated wood and tore his protection away.

Aiphatòn screamed as the splinters and tiny blades hit him again. He held both hands in front of his face and crawled forwards until he reached the monstrous corpse of the malméner. He got under it as best he could.

And then finally he realised.

It's Nodûcor! Fa'losôi removed the mask with the help of the cîani and forced him to summon the winds.

The storm turned into a hurricane, powerful enough to tug at the enormous corpse Aiphatòn had hidden underneath.

The splinters of glass and blades of obsidian and basalt shredded the monster's skin with grating, scraping sounds, blood trickling down onto the älf. The bones crackled as they were ground down until the gusts of wind blew into the cadaver and swept it away with them, making a hollow whistling sound.

Aiphatòn immediately felt the impact of the terrible force that raged and roared from every direction. The wind of mortality swept in from the north, the wind of freedom shot out of the south, the wind of war blew from the west, and the east wind carried inspiration.

They've all come to speak to Nodûcor, like the legends say. He felt his skin getting thinner and thinner, the blades penetrating any exposed flesh, and he heard tinkling and rustling as they bounced off his armour.

I must not die as long as the botoican-woman and the wind-voice are still alive. Aiphatòn tried to look around and screamed in pain. *The plates are not going to save me.*

A figure came walking through the raging storm, enveloped in flickering flames and as erect as if it were made of indestructible stone. The little splinters scraped against the dented copper helmet and poured into the slits like hail, but that didn't bother the warrior.

Indignant, the wind whirred and the flames around the ghaist creature went out.

It turned its head, spotted Aiphatòn and hurried over to throw itself on top of the älf and protect him.

Aiphatòn smelled the petrol, felt the unbearable heat coming off the ghaist and thought he could hear sizzling. But he took the opportunity to huddle beneath his unexpected new shield.

Overcome by the exertion and pain, he fell into a state somewhere between sleep and unconsciousness.

Aiphatòn did not know how long it took for the hurricane to die down and the four winds to withdraw. He didn't wake until the ghaist on top of him stirred and got to its feet.

There was nothing more than a weak gust of wind blowing now and the sun was rising over the plain.

The peaceful silence was incongruous with the damp smell of swampland, mutilated bodies and blood.

Aiphatòn blinked; his eyes were painful and burning. His whole body hurt, as if it were made of raw flesh. He sat up cautiously and clenched his teeth to stop himself screaming.

Before he even looked around, he examined his wounds.

He was barely wearing any clothes anymore. The skin on his arms was already healing underneath an unbroken crust of dirt and blood. The cuts felt like they had closed up and he was itching all over.

He was as pleased as he was astonished by this swift recovery. *My magic has become stronger – because of the amulet? Or is this a feature of the wounds that the winds cause?*

The ghaist was standing next to him and looked like it was waiting.

Aiphatòn lifted his head and surveyed his surroundings through streaming eyes.

There was nothing left of the Nhatai and Rhâhoi armies. Everything had been pulverised and dashed to pieces on the battlefield. The splinters of glass had squeezed through the tiniest holes in their armour and the blades of basalt and obsidian had sliced up everything there was to slice. There weren't even any complete cadavers – there were at most bones polished clean and scattered by the storm.

Aiphatòn stood up and continued to look around, unable to wrap his head around it.

The blood of thousands – as well as flayed skin and slivers of bone, tooth and intestine – had mingled with the churned-up sand, been lifted by the wind and scattered over the town. The coating reminded Aiphatòn of the crust over his wounds.

The sky has shed crimson rain over the land.

The plain smelled like an abattoir. Weapons and armour were strewn about, the leather torn off the hilts and shafts, the straps shredded; more than a few blades were snapped.

Älfar, orcs, trolls, gnomes, malméners and whatever brutes had served in the armed forces of the warring families were no more.

Although it meant Aiphatòn had almost achieved his goal, he felt afraid of the thin, pale älf he had freed. *Nodûcor must die.* He swallowed. *Nobody is a match for his powers.*

Several figures were walking slowly across the plain towards him.

Two copper helmets shone in the light of the rising daystar and next to them he recognised Irïanora, Nodûcor, Fa'losôi and an älf wearing a light blue robe with an elaborate shell embroidered on it, which signified he was a cîanoi from Elhàtor.

Fa'losôi's robe was grimy and tattered. She was holding Aiphatòn's spear, using it as a cane. If he was interpreting the look on her face correctly, she appeared far from pleased.

It took them a while to march through the remains of the warriors.

Their trouser legs and the hems of their robes were saturated with moisture; the blood had worked its way up the fabric and penetrated into the seams on the soles of their shoes. Both Iriianora's beautiful dark blue and silver robe and the blonde älf-woman herself were covered in dirt. Only Nodûcor's light, black leather armour looked immaculate.

Aiphatòn didn't notice it until the botoican-woman was standing in front of him. *She has discarded the mind-shackles she usually restrains me with.*

He could barely contain his joy. However, surrounded by three ghaist creatures and bearing in mind the unfortunate Tanôtai, he refrained from any attempt to snatch the spear immediately and attack. Instead of setting upon her, he gave a slight, submissive bow.

'Don't you dare congratulate me on my victory,' she said sharply.

'So was that not how it was meant to go?' he couldn't help asking.

Fa'losôi rammed the spear blunt-end down into the soft sand and let go of it. 'Did I come up with the idea of literally crushing my laboriously assembled army in a storm of flowers, glass, blades and perfumes?' she snarled, wiping away the blood underneath her nose; more blood immediately trickled after it. 'The wind-voice shouted too loudly.'

Aiphatòn looked at Nodûcor, who suddenly looked harmless without the black half-mask around his chin and mouth; his skin was scarred in some places, grazed in others. *He looks like a scholar, not like someone who gets two-hundred-thousand-strong armies pulverised.* 'What happened?'

The wan älf didn't respond.

Fa'losôi let out a nasty laugh. 'He can't speak. As soon as he opens his mouth to say anything, what happens is what we experienced last night. If he has to communicate, he'll write it down.' She fixed her eyes on Aiphatòn. 'I'm surprised. In the best way,' she admitted.

'I thought I'd kill Ysor'kenôr for you so that his army would be without a leader,' he lied. 'But you had the same idea when you sent the ghaists. Did you know there were two of them? He also had a brother who was helping him.'

'No. But that's not what I meant.' Fa'losôi scrutinised him. 'You've been free of my influence for quite some time and yet you stayed and killed one of the Rhâhois.' She slowly lowered her symbol-adorned head. 'How did you manage to break my control?'

I'm free? Or is this a test? 'Kôr'losôi,' he answered on an impulse, to buy himself time. 'Your cousin wanted to talk me into a pact against you so that I'd kill you. He weakened your influence as often as he could.'

Fa'losôi raised her eyebrows. '*That* explains it! I knew Kôr'losôi was plotting something but I didn't think he was good enough to break your bond with me.' She put her hands behind her back, her necklaces and gemstones clinking. 'And *what* did you stay to do, emperor?'

Aiphatòn laughed. 'I planned to ask you for the commandership of the älfar.' He pointed at the bedraggled-looking Irïanora as an example. 'I could have used her. And an army that is well-led can achieve greater victories. *Quicker* victories with *fewer* casualties.' He looked around pointedly. 'You'll have to start over again and I've only got –' he looked at the survivors – 'three älfar left.'

'I remember what you said about the Tharc game.' Fa'losôi smiled. 'And you've convinced me: from now on you are to be by my side without my control spell.' She nodded to the cîanoi. 'Let him see to your wounds quickly and then let's head east. Nodûcor's voice is a little hoarse; that's got to change. He needs to use it more, I think, so that he knows how to say the right words.' Fa'losôi gestured to the rune spear invitingly and patronisingly with her right hand. 'Take it. It's yours.'

Aiphatòn struggled to keep up the pretence of friendliness as he slowly reached out a hand and grasped the shaft. 'Ordinary spells don't work on me.'

'You're in the wasteland. You ought to have realised that things are different here.' Fa'losôi nodded to the cîanoi. 'It's possible to understand how magic works and functions and what paths it takes.'

It will roast him alive, just like what almost happened to the healer on board the Mistress of the Sea. Healing me is a suicide mission.

Meanwhile the älf in the pale blue robe was touching Aiphatòn's forearm and murmuring a healing spell; the layer of scabs crumbled off. A prickling sensation wrapped around his wounds and spread through him, soothing and alleviating his pain.

Aiphatòn gazed at the cîanoi in surprise. *This man sets about his work much more carefully.*

Then he turned back to Fa'losôi. 'What are we going to do in the east?'

'The true Ultai t'Ruy, the Rhâhoi family's capital city, must be there. Given the brothers tricked us, I want to make sure that it's destroyed. *One* botoican-woman in the wasteland is quite enough.' She looked at the soaking wet, filthy hem of her robe, no green or white still visible. 'Some new clothes would be . . .'

No botoican-woman at all would be even better! Aiphatòn thrust the spear, plunging it into Fa'losôi's chest but not killing her with his well-aimed stab. 'Keep the ghaist creatures back,' he commanded the panting botoican-woman whose legs were giving way. She clung to the shaft – without it she would have fallen to the ground.

Sure enough, the copper helmets didn't move.

Irïanora, Nodûcor and the cîanoi shrank away from him, the sorcerer still murmuring his healing spell because he had not received an order to the contrary from the botoican-woman.

'I have . . . no power over them anyway,' Fa'losôi replied, grinning weakly as her breath rattled. 'Are you afraid . . . that after my death they'll follow any botoican that comes along?' she choked out. 'You're so easy to fool,' she whispered, and her bald head sank onto her chest with a creaking sound. Her hands slipped away and Fa'losôi slumped forwards.

Now I'll fulfil the vow I made to Ireheart. Aiphatòn pulled the spear out of the body that collapsed at his feet and pointed the tip in one fluid movement at the surprised cîanoi.

The blade struck the blue-robed älf in the heart. He collapsed on top of the botoican-woman with a stifled groan and his eyes paled.

Nodûcor watched the dying älf, fascinated and completely calm. It seemed he was completely convinced he would escape death.

'Murder!' Iriïanora suddenly screamed at him, outraged. Her mind had been freed from all influence. 'Why are you doing this after freeing us from the botoican-woman? Do you want to kill me too?'

'I swore to wipe out the älfar. *That* is the *real* reason I left Girdlegard,' Aiphatòn explained, turning to the aghast Iriïanora. 'We must be eradicated.' The healing spell was still prickling through his body, but he ignored it.

'Then start with yourself!' The blonde älf-woman stooped down and drew the cîanoi's dagger.

One blow with the blunt end of the spear was enough, the weapon fell out of her hand and lodged in the damp earth.

'We are a cruel tribe. And I've been no better for two hundred cycles. Your towns would have made a nuisance of themselves sooner or later and the generations to come would have regained their old tyrannical ambitions and set themselves up as ruthless rulers.' Aiphatòn placed the tip of the spear against the älf-woman's solar plexus. The cîanoi's fresh blood left a dark stain on her blue robe. 'Your death . . .'

'Stop!' Irïanora was breathing fast, her dark-tinted eyes open wide. 'Please! Spare me. Together, *we* could make the älfar tribe rise from the ashes and make it better. You, a shintoìt, and I, a modern älf-woman filled with magic. If you were able to imagine what . . .'

The schemer fights to the last. 'With your death and Nodûcor's, I'll have fulfilled my vow,' he interrupted her. 'Afterwards I'll gladly depart into endingness by my own hand. But *your* death is called Aiphatòn!'

He stabbed with considerable force so Irïanora wouldn't suffer. But the blonde älf-woman must have been wearing hidden armour under her blue and silver dress – the tip only just went through the material, then stopped.

'Are you sparing me?' Irïanora scoffed. 'Would you rather continue your murder spree on Nodûcor and practise until you get it right?'

'No armour will protect you, whether it's made of steel or magic.' Aiphatòn deployed his magic, pulling the spear back by half an arm's length and ramming the dazzling runic weapon at her exposed throat. *This time you're passing into endingness.*

Irïanora didn't move, standing surprisingly tall as she faced the weapon.

Again, the razor-sharp and usually reliable blade didn't get any further than her dirty skin. No matter how hard Aiphatòn worked his magic, bracing both feet against the ground to force the spear tip into her, nothing happened.

'Put your weapon down,' the älf-woman eventually told him in a polite voice. 'You can't kill me. Your subconscious is refusing to.'

Aiphatòn lowered the spear. *How can this be?* The prickling in his body intensified and became painful, like on Elhàtor and Dâkiòn. From the spot where the cîanoi had touched him, the pain gnawed its way up his arm into his shoulders. *But the botoican-woman*, he turned his head to look at her corpse, *is dead.*

'You're so easy to fool,' Irïanora repeated the words Fa'losôi had whispered before her death. 'And *what* do you deduce from this?'

'She taught you her power.' Aiphatòn would have liked to do something about the burning sensation creeping up his throat and the back of his neck. 'You've just proven to me twice over that no älf should remain alive.' *What can I do?* As soon as he used his magic, the pain would get worse. Just the thought of killing the älf-woman made the spear feel as heavy as a thousand stones.

'That would be one explanation.' Irïanora smiled indulgently. 'The fact you haven't hit upon the other one is a point in my favour.'

Nodûcor was still staring at the cîanoi's body, as if the other two älfar didn't exist.

The ghaist with the dented copper helmet walked forwards slowly and stopped next to the älf-woman.

'So that's not a ghaist?' Aiphatòn expected it to remove its head-gear and reveal another botoican underneath it.

But it remained still while white smoke gently drifted out of the slits and curled upwards.

'Explain it to me.' His vision was blurring.

Irïanora raised her right arm, the index finger pointing at the creature. '*I* am Fa'losôi Nhatai. The creature you, Kôr'losôi and Saî'losôi thought was a ghaist is actually the puppet-master. And I'm controlling the älf-woman as well as the wind-voice.'

Aiphatòn felt nauseous and was overcome with dizziness. 'But I . . . why did you let me kill the botoican-woman?' His eyes were playing new tricks on him. Ávoleï's face suddenly flickered across Irïanora's features as if the young elf-woman was trying to battle the magic from the grave.

'For one thing, she wasn't a true botoican-woman, just a woman who looked like me when I still lived as a human. For another, the collapse of the tower didn't leave her unscathed. She would have died soon anyway. I didn't need her anymore. When I noticed that you were more resistant to my influence spells than all the other älfar, much more resistant even than the elf-women, I wanted to find out how far that freedom went.' Iriänora lowered her arm. '*Now* I know. And I've taken precautions.'

The burning sensation had reached the top of Aiphatòn's neck and was creeping into his skull and from there into his brain – gradually it turned into a warm, pleasant feeling. He shuddered.

He found Iriänora increasingly attractive and enchanting. *Why did I not notice she was incomparably beautiful before?* When he shut his eyelids over his burning eyes and opened them again two heartbeats later, she had come right up to him. 'How did you become a ghaist?'

'That's *actually* Sinthoras and Caphalor's fault. They ensured that the creation of a ghaist went awry on me. My body perished and my soul ended up in this creature along with thousands of others.' Iriänora laughed. 'My own family threw me into the swamp because they had no use for this apparently faulty being. Eventually I managed to assume control over those raging souls and freed myself. But that's not a story I like to be reminded of.' She placed her forearm on his shoulder, her fingers touching the nape of his neck and tenderly caressing it. 'Time can be so long and yet it can pass quickly if you celebrate victories.'

Beautiful! He looked at her gently curving mouth, listening carefully to the irresistible sound of her beguiling voice. 'Allow me to help you celebrate victories,' Aiphatòn said longingly. *Everything about her is beautiful.*

'So you shall. And to make absolutely certain you do, I've had the cîanoi work a spell that makes you my slave. As long as you live and as long as Iriänora lives, you will not be able to raise your hand against my new self. Soon you will believe it was your own, most heartfelt desire to fulfil my every wish. No matter the cost. Or whoever may die.' Iriänora smiled and kissed him lightly on the cheek.

In the same heartbeat, the last sharp pain in his head gave way to a blissful feeling and Aiphatòn basked in it. *Only she can give me peace.* 'Whoever may die,' he whispered.

Iriänora ran a hand lovingly over his head, through his dark hair. 'My best puppet. Effortlessly obedient.' She looked at her dirty fingers. 'A bath would be lovely.'

Aiphatòn breathed in happily. He was content just to gaze at the älf-woman and be near her so that he could carry out her wishes. 'A bath?' He looked around. 'That won't be easy.'

Iriänora couldn't help laughing again. 'No, that's not something I'll ask of you.'

'What shall we do then?' He looked at Nodûcor. 'With him on our side, nothing can resist us.'

'We're going east, but you'll have forgotten that at the sight of my enchanting face. We're paying a visit to Ultai t'Ruy.' Iriänora let go of him and started to walk away. 'And then? The last botoican-woman ought to have a kingdom befitting her status.' As she walked, she spun around once and smiled at him, her blue dress flying out a little. 'We could have Dâkiòn rebuilt. With my abilities, we'll make ourselves a new army of slaves. What do you think?'

Nodûcor was shuffling along behind them, his gaze remaining fixed on the corpse of the cîanoi, as if he was looking at a dead body for the first time. He didn't seem to care where they were going.

'I look forward to it.'

The blonde älf-woman smiled at him, then her gaze wandered down to the middle of his chest. 'What have you got there?'

Aiphatòn remembered the amulet. 'Oh, I found it where the

malméners were. It was lying in the moss.' He pulled the chain over his head and held it out to her. 'Take it if you like.'

Irïanora came closer and examined the piece of jewellery without touching it. 'No need. It's been discharged. It was a power repository but now it's merely a nice trinket.'

Aiphatòn put the amulet away again and placed his spear on his shoulder, balancing the weapon so that it hovered horizontally, then put one lively foot in front of the other. He was fascinated by Irïanora's charm and could hardly restrain himself.

They were flanked by two ghaist creatures while the third brought up the rear.

Making straight for the east, they walked over the metallic-smelling red sand and the stalks of grass gradually turning brown.

The cool wind blew on them and this time it didn't carry any feathers or glass or basalt blades. Winter was coming faster and it seemed keen to spread ice and snow over the battlefield behind the travellers.

Samusin, God of Balance, thank you! 'I would be delighted to lay an enormous kingdom at your feet,' Aiphatòn blurted out. 'Nobody else deserves to rule over the tribes! Over all the tribes in existence!'

'Oh, you speak the truth, although being in love is making you gush.' Irïanora's laugh rang out as clear as a bell. 'Let's destroy the town first and renovate Dâkiòn enough for us to spend the winter in a cosy home. We'll see what the coming years have in store.'

It's admittedly not much, what she lets me do, but it's still a start. 'The foundation stone for our kingdom.' Aiphatòn exercised great self-control in not reaching for her hand. 'Your kingdom, my love.' He couldn't imagine anything better than sharing immortality with Irïanora.

I will fulfil her every wish. Aiphatòn smiled demonically. *Anything I fail to find in Ishím Voróo, I'll get for her in Girdlegard.*

He knew two ways into Girdlegard.

Tark Draan, Human kingdom of Gauragar, Oakenburgh, 5452nd division of unendingness (6491st solar cycle), winter

Carmondai was sitting wrapped in a blanket next to the window. He was on the fourth floor of the town hall tower where he had spent the last few orbits working on new poems.

He was glad to see his surroundings and the woods disappearing more and more beneath the falling snow. *I couldn't have stood the damp, mouldy walls of the dungeon much longer.* Everything reminded him too much of his imprisonment by the Aklán. And yet he was even worse off now than he had been with the triplets.

Oakenburgh stretched out peacefully below him. The people were trudging through the snowdrifts. Huge quantities of firewood and coal were being brought out of the woods on sleds to heat the half-timbered homes.

Winter is here. Carmondai opened the window to let the sounds into his room. *And it's magnificent.*

The cool westerly wind sent the white splendour swirling in at him, and the high-spirited shouts of children doing battle with snowballs reached his ears. The air smelled of open fires and baking, and sometimes resin, when needles caught fire and released their scent through the chimney.

Carmondai sucked the cold air into his lungs and broke off one of the icicles hanging in a row from the window frame.

He rubbed it over his ravaged cheeks and forehead.

The frozen water cooled his sensitive skin, which still hadn't recovered from the treatment it had received. It hurt to speak and accidentally furrowing his brow meant he immediately had to stifle a scream. The healer who had been so excellent before couldn't give him anything for the pain – or didn't want to.

Once the queen had departed, the people of Oakenburgh's contempt and appetite for murder came to light. The branding and the warning on his forehead prevented any attacks taking the form of punches or knife wounds, but he was spat on, insulted and had excrement and rubbish poured over him.

Since then, Carmondai had preferred to avoid these humiliations by declaring the town hall tower his new quarters. He didn't dare flee so long as he didn't have a safe plan for how to leave Girdlegard. Too many enemies were lurking, from the elves to the zhadár, who all wanted him dead. Perhaps the last älfar were lurking too now, in order to have their revenge on him for preventing the assassination. And besides that, others were trying to get their hands on him alive: dwarves, human kings, scholars. *So this position in Mallenia's shadow is safer.*

He felt tired.

Very old and very tired.

I underestimated Mallenia. He broke off another icicle to keep cooling his skin; the first one had melted. *Death would have been a relief in comparison to this. That's her form of revenge: calling it a mercy.* He looked around, gathering impressions so that he could commit them to paper straight away.

As he did so, his gaze fell on the window pane where his disfigured face was reflected.

Carmondai swallowed. He was still far from used to this new external appearance of his.

On either side of his face, the Ido coat of arms stretched from his cheekbone to lower jaw, forever designating him a possession of the ruling family.

With a red-hot wire, the following had been etched into his forehead: *Anyone who harms this älf will have the same harm done to them.* His mid-length brown hair was gone, replaced by grey stubble.

Now I really look old. Or is it the sadness that my divisions of unend-ingness carved into my face overnight? Carmondai touched his hardened features with their bright red wounds. *What have I become?*

A slave in order to survive, was the answer the reflection gave him. The lapdog of a queen who let him live in order to degrade him more deeply than any other punishment could ever have done. The iron had burned his courage and pride out of him.

Furious, he slammed the window shut so that the panes rattled.

A loud, nasty laugh rang out.

'The warning,' said a sinister voice behind him, 'could have been a bit more clear-cut. You might come across people who think it's worth stabbing you in the arm or leg with a dagger, even though they then have to endure it themselves.'

Carmondai didn't need to turn around to know that Carâhnios had slipped unnoticed into the room. 'My forehead wasn't big enough.'

'But they did shave your head,' he said, chuckling. 'Lots of things could have been written so that nobody does you any harm at all.'

The älf shifted his gaze away from the window pane – which threatened to show him his face again – and turned to the zhadár. 'Are you making progress on your hunt?'

Carâhnios bared his black teeth. Darkness swirled around him like heat haze or a sun's corona; he practically radiated shadow. Carmondai understood Mallenia's dislike of the zhadár now. 'Unfortunately I haven't achieved any more success since our intervention in Oaken-burgh. Either we've already caught them all or they're getting better at hiding from me.' He kept one hand concealed behind his back.

'Then I wish you better luck. I can't go with you,' he declined the implicit request. 'As you can see, Mallenia sees me as her property.'

'But you can move freely.'

'I can move around Gauragar and Idoslane. But as soon as she returns to Oakenburgh, I'll stay close to her. It is her wish that I do not stray from her side.' He pulled the blanket tighter around himself.

That was a lie, but he was desperate to be near her after he recovered to prevent any more assassination attempts on her. The spell bound her life to his.

He may have been in a terrible situation for now, but there was one thing he knew: times changed. *Constantly.* The thought comforted him.

The zhadár guffawed, one hand still behind his back. 'They took your dignity and courage away.' He was giggling like a lunatic.

'How many times have you taken the remedy?'

'The new one?'

'Yes.'

'Three times,' he whooped and raised his free hand. The black haze danced around his fingers. 'Do you see that?'

'A side-effect, I'd say. You needed a different formula for älfar blood than for elf blood. But I'm not an alchemist.' Carmondai reached for paper and ink to draw the effect – and suddenly couldn't see a thing. *What . . . ?*

Two heartbeats later, everything brightened up again.

'Hey, black-eye! That was me!' Carâhnios crowed. 'I can plunge a room into darkness just by thinking about it. It even works in the open air, in broad daylight.'

'Like Arviû,' the älf blurted out, remembering the archer whose älfar power changed after a sudden loss of sight. The zhadár had experienced a similar effect.

'I'm capable of so much and I'm constantly testing out my power.' He took a step towards Carmondai. 'But I need more blood.' He removed his hand from behind his back and in it was one of the familiar bottles.

He didn't come to take me with him. Carmondai shrank back, the blanket falling to the floor. Underneath he was wearing a simple woollen robe to beat the winter chill.

He didn't carry a weapon on his person in the tower room – his sword lay on the floor next to the bed and the dagger remained next to the pieces of apple on the table. His injuries may outwardly have healed but his power was still far from restored.

'You said you'd kill me last,' he remembered, hoping it would save his life.

'I can't find Aiphatòn anywhere right now. So I'll deal with you first,' Carâhnios snarled and immediately laughed at much too high a pitch. He drew his dagger with his free hand. 'Don't put up any resistance and this will be quick.' His black eyes never left Carmondai. 'But if you'd like to give me a laugh, try it. Please.'

Without warning, Carmondai tipped the ink out at him – and found himself standing in blackness as if it had been sprayed in his own face.

He soon felt a blow to the backs of his knees and he fell, disoriented, against the table and then onto the wooden floor.

With two powerful blows to the back of the neck, Carâhnios almost knocked him unconscious, all of his limbs suddenly weighing more than an enormous gold block.

'Taken out like a fish on a hook,' the zhadár said cheerfully next to him. 'Shall I gut you now, little fishy?' He sniggered. 'It would be so easy.'

Carmondai felt a slight pinch at the neck instead and then the mouth of the bottle was pressed against the wound. He could hear the muffled sound of his blood spraying against the glass in time with his heartbeat. His eyelids closed.

I'm passing into endingness in such an undignified way, he thought as he drifted off, unable to move. How he would have liked to say something impressive. *But what for?* There was nobody recording his last words for posterity. *What a bad joke on the gods' part.*

Before he slipped into unconsciousness fully, he felt a few firm slaps to the cheeks.

The pain in his sensitive, burned skin roused him. Then straight away he had some ice-cold snow thrown into his face, which made him open his eyes wide.

To his surprise he was lying on the bed and could feel a bandage on his neck. *He left me alive?*

Carâhnios was standing in front of him brandishing a bottle with quite a lot of blood sloshing around in it. 'Two units. That's enough to start with,' he decreed and carefully sealed it with a cork. 'Rest up, eat well and you'll be back on your feet in no time, little black-eye fishy.' He sniggered. 'You thought I'd kill you? Oh, that was amazing, feeling how scared you were.'

Carmondai sat up carefully; the melted water was cooling his face as it trickled down. He couldn't speak yet. Dizziness spread over him as soon as he moved too quickly.

'If I don't find any more black-eyes, I'll come visit you often, my inexhaustible source. I know where to find you, don't I? Wherever the little Ido woman is.' Carâhnios laughed as he placed the dagger to his own throat and gave himself a little cut – black blood flowed from it. He immediately held a piece of cloth against it. He appeared to have cut the cloth out of the pillow for himself. 'There. Now the condition written on your forehead has been met: *anyone who harms this älf will have the same harm done to them.* The queen can't do anything to me.'

He left the room without another word.

Weakened, Carmondai hauled himself to his feet and surveyed the mess his brief skirmish with the zhadár had left in its wake. With some difficulty, he went over to the open window to breathe in the fresh air.

He will make good on his threat. And there's nothing I can do about it so long as he has those powers at his fingertips.

He looked outside and saw the groundling riding away on his white pony. He was passing the queen's retinue, who had just arrived in Oakenburgh to check on their valuable slave. *I'll add him to the list of everyone out to get me then.*

He looked directly downwards, to where the ground lay a good fifteen paces below.

He could simply lean forwards and fall.

Everything would be forgotten, the pain, the scars, the humiliations and fears.

But a single feeling stopped him.

Samusin must have something in store for me. Anyone who goes through such dark times will be exalted by him all the more. Carmondai looked up again and surveyed the woods, darkness and snow descending on them. *What a beautiful contrast.*

He went over to the table and tidied up the mess. He took some new ink and began the next drawing and on another page wrote the lines of a poem that had come to him.

Even pain and suffering served as inspiration to an artist.

Sometimes these produced the best pieces of work.

Epilogue

A man in love is worse than a grieving man. Because he expects something in return for his actions.

Wise saying of the Älfar
Collected by Carmondai, master of word and image

Tark Draan, Human kingdom of Gauragar, Grey Mountains, 5452nd division of unendingness (6491st/92nd solar cycle), winter

The storm paused for the first time, allowing the two tired travellers of different heights a view of the mountains around them, as if it wanted to reward them for having struggled on to get to this point.

The sun was rising over the vast peaks and broad mountain ridges glittering radiantly with ice and snow.

The brightness was getting unbearable. The unrelenting whiteness intensified the sunlight and forced both humans to squint, having stopped in the middle of nowhere in the Grey Mountains to puff and pant. They did it every ten steps to draw air into their shrivelled-feeling lungs.

And yet they didn't want to take their stunned eyes off it, they wanted to take in the beauty of the sparseness.

The rock appeared to take the shape of various creatures – here a peak looked like a dragon's head, there a gnome seemed to be peeking out of the rock face. The wind blew the snow off the higher slopes, forming white banners that stretched far across the sky as they scattered and dispersed.

'Look! They've hoisted the banners to welcome us, Endô,' said the girl, out of breath. Her thick clothing was too big for her; the hems had been shortened using a knife. 'I'm sure we're in Tark Draan already.'

Endô smiled and placed a hand on her shoulder. His cloaks had also once belonged to a significantly taller creature. The hoods had enough space for two or three heads. 'Definitely.' He looked around, putting a hand in front of his eyes and peeping through a narrow slit between his fingers to avoid blinding himself permanently.

'Shall we keep going, Uncle?'

'Soon.' He took a few steps forwards. Then, to his relief, he noticed the runes that had formed in ice on a precipice. 'The next symbol is up there, Sha'taï.'

He walked on, panting, and his niece followed.

'Don't forget to close your eyes almost completely. Otherwise you'll go blind,' he warned her. Endô took her by the hand and they tramped across hard ice.

This time they got twenty paces before stopping with a groan and taking a break.

Endô didn't know who had carved the älfar runes into the rock but he desperately hoped they were leading him and Sha'taï to a destination that would make a better life possible for them.

He dimly remembered a story he had heard a long time ago, about an älf-woman who had come from Tark Draan, but it seemed too far-fetched to him at the time.

Hadn't she declared herself ruler of Elhàtor? She might as well have been the ruler as any other black-eye. As long as the signs took them to a place where they could live, it was all the same to him.

The symbols had been formed by seeping water that had filled slight indents in the stone and then frozen. Hence the mysterious signposts became visible in the lower-lying regions, only in the winter, and led walkers along a dangerous path.

They had come within a hair's breadth of getting stuck. An entire section of icy pathway must have caved in during the summer and it took them a long time to spot the next rune.

In one chasm they had also found the stiff bodies of monsters who had been stabbed to death. They had taken their frozen provisions and cloaks from them, which meant uncle and niece were better protected from the storms in the mountains.

'We're moving on,' he heard Sha'taï saying as she gently dragged him forwards.

She didn't seem to make any allowances for the fact Endô still needed a little longer to regain his strength. 'Good, good.'

He didn't reveal to her that he had known one of the monsters.

Cushròk was the commander of a notorious band of soldiers deployed when unsavoury things needed doing without the name of the client being made known.

He didn't know what they had been up to in the Grey Mountains.

The wounds didn't match their own weapons so they probably hadn't killed each other. Therefore, there was definitely life among the steep slopes and hidden caves – beyond the odd herd of ibex – and that life was not well disposed towards visitors.

Endô remembered the message that Cushròk had sent him word for word. He had probably sent it to everyone in Ishím Voróo whom he acknowledged had greater power than him.

Endô's mistake had been not to reply. But unlike most of the others who had received a similar letter, he could still beat himself up about his oversight.

> *My dear Endô,*
>
> *I'm on the verge of obtaining a magic weapon of obscene power.*
>
> *You ought to be aware that I'm doing this on the orders of others who know how to handle the weapon.*
>
> *However, I think it would be fairer if the existence of this weapon became more common knowledge.*
>
> *I am a soldier and will pledge my word to whoever pays best.*
>
> *If you want this weapon of destruction to end up in your hands instead of someone else's, possibly an enemy's, send me more than a thousand gold coins of the heaviest kind. I'll bring the weapon to you as soon as I have received the payment – and so long as it amounts to more than the sum I receive from everyone else to whom I'm also sending word.*
>
> *Regards and prosperity,*
> *Cushròk*

Since the soldier and his band were lying dead in the icy landscape, it seemed one of the recipients or the original client had taken the message badly. Ignorant people have set out to commit murder and theft for far less than a thousand coins and been known to come back with something more valuable.

As for where the weapon had finally ended up, Endô knew from personal, painful experience.

His lungs felt like they had shrivelled into peas again; black rings spun before his eyes and he had to stop walking. 'Wait,' he asked Sha'taï.

'Again?' She may have been panting hard, but her youth seemed to make her less susceptible to the altitude and thin air.

What would have happened if he himself had paid Cushròk the most?

Would he be sitting on a comfortable throne in Dàkiòn, ruling over the Majestic? Or would the soldier have kept the weapon for himself after all and used it against all of the tribes?

Endô was panting as he moved off again. His eyes were open just a thin crack to check for the path so he wouldn't veer off and plummet downwards. 'I told you to close your eyes!' he barked at his niece.

'But . . . it's glittering so beautifully,' she defended herself, caught in the act.

'You're going to go blind,' he said with anxious emphasis, feeling his lips cracking. The dry air and the cold attacked the skin, while the sun gave them severe sunburn.

Endô thought the mountains worse than the most gloomy moorland, the most isolated grassy plain, the most desolate wilderness, or any other area he had visited before.

Sha'taï muttered an unintelligible response.

They continued their trek with its monotonous rhythm in silence: ten paces, stop, ten paces, stop, ten paces – until night started to fall.

Pressed close together, they hunkered down in a narrow niche and prayed for the winter to spare them.

Due to the hardship and the altitude, Endô fell into a sleep that brought little refreshment. He started out of his sleep several times, his hand on his sword.

But there was nobody in the frozen wasteland of rock. Apart from them.

*

It snowed towards morning.

Thick flakes fell on uncle and niece, shielding them from the bitter, deadly frost with a thick, white coating like a cool cloth.

Sha'taï woke him as the sun rose and shone through the loose, soft white coating that lay on top of them a hand's-width thick.

Endô shared out their provisions – they had to suck on them to thaw them out – and treated himself to a little more rest although the girl was pestering him and seemed oddly restless. 'What's wrong? Did you have a nightmare?'

Sha'taï looked nervously at him, as if she had to keep a secret and no longer could. 'We're near a valley,' she spluttered.

'We're surrounded by them. And by ravines and precipices and . . .' Endô saw her glowing face. 'You snuck away during the night!' The belated worry made him angry at his niece. 'What were you thinking? You could have . . .'

'The moonlight was pleasant and the glittering can't even dazzle you then,' she interrupted him slyly. 'You were asleep and I thought I was dreaming of juicy apples until I woke up and the smell was still there.' Sha'taï pointed north-eastwards. 'The path leads to a peak that looks like a crown. Below it is a valley with no snow in it! And there are trees there! I've seen them!' she whooped.

Endô feared the thin air had affected his niece's mind. 'It's the depths of winter and we have the gods' mercy to thank that we're still alive . . .' He suddenly fell silent as she took his hand, opened it and put an apple into it.

'I took this,' she admitted happily. 'I actually wanted to surprise you and let you find the valley but since you don't believe me: see for yourself.'

Endô stared at the apple as if it were the world's greatest treasure. Although his lips cracked even more, he opened his mouth and bit cautiously into the apple.

The fruit was neither frozen nor foul-tasting. The bittersweet juice flooded his mouth. Endô chewed carefully – the taste of the fruit was a revelation on his tongue and palate.

He quickly took another bite, although his open cuts stung. 'Is it a magic spell or the work of mountain demons?' he asked with his mouth full. 'Are we to be lured into a trap only to end up as their meal?'

'It looked very real.' Sha'taï shrugged her shoulders. 'I wasn't able to examine it more closely because I've lost my talisman.'

'You don't need it. Your powers are strong enough. Why else would you have been entrusted with the mission?' Endô pulled himself together. 'So *you* are leading *me* now.' He smiled and held a hand out to her. 'And don't forget about your eyes.'

Sha'taï grasped his fingers and pulled him along behind her.

The path went steeply upwards and the travellers had to climb up. The snow had covered the girl's tracks but she made straight for her destination without hesitating.

Endô did her a favour and didn't take any more breaks, even though his heart was beating madly in his chest, the blood was rushing in his ears and the black rings in his vision were no longer going away.

But on the other hand, it smelled of apples and there was the steady sound of a waterfall roaring.

'Here it is!' Sha'taï dragged him forwards.

'You walked this path here and back by yourself?' Endô had made it, coughing and groaning, onto a little platform with steps leading down from it.

When he cast a glance at the valley stretched out in front of them, two miles long and half a mile across, he burst into tears of relief. Even if it were the work of demons, he would still have been glad. He would serve any ghost who ruled over it.

Fruit trees grew on the terraces that had been laid out, the fruit shining rosy-cheeked in the sun; overgrown fields were testament to abandoned grain cultivation. The ruins of stone buildings rose up from the floor of the valley; a fire must have raged through there. Only two structures seemed to have been spared the destruction.

Endô looked at the small lake at the bottom of the waterfall he had heard roaring in the distance. He wondered whether there were any fish in it. His heart raced with joy even more.

A warm gust of wind flowed from the valley into the travellers' faces. The source of the wind appeared to be the numerous holes in the porous rock.

'Saved,' he whispered and wiped the tears from his cheeks, the sun-burnt skin peeling as he did so. 'Let's go and see what the former residents have left for us.' He stroked Sha'taï's hair. 'If they've got grindstones, I can bake us some bread.' He threw the soldiers' provisions over his shoulder in disgust.

His niece let out a loud peal of laughter and raced down the steps.

Endô took a breath in and followed her.

After a few steps he was overcome by dizziness; his heart hurt in his chest, as it had done many times on the journey. The altitude was seriously bothering him, but he just needed to sit down calmly and wait it out.

'Where have you got to?' Sha'taï called to him, having almost reached the bottom.

'I'll be there soon, my dear. I'm going to enjoy the view a little more,' Endô replied, slowly kneeling down so that he could sit.

As he moved, the walls and the steps spun, the black rings forming again. He reached his arms out to keep his balance, but his right foot slipped and Endô fell forwards.

The staircase seemed to be getting longer and longer, the edges harder and steeper as he rolled down, his niece's fearful screams in his ears. He couldn't get hold of anything – after every roll, the next somersault followed.

Then Endô saw the blue sky above him and he stretched his arms out to his right and left. His fall finally came to a stop.

Only his head jerked back with one final, severe swinging motion.

Endô's neck broke against the edge of the step with a dry crack.

At the same moment, every thought of the past and future faded because the present had brought him death.

Girdlegard, Human kingdom of Gauragar, Grey Mountains, 6492nd solar cycle, spring

Belogar Strifehammer's bushy brown eyebrows rose very slowly as he looked north from the Jagged Crown and recognised the small valley not far from him and his companions. 'By Vraccas!' As the dwarf from the Boulder Heaver clan from the Fifthling tribe shouldered his mace, the coat of chainmail under his thick layer of cloaks clinked softly. 'There it is, the secret settlement.'

Phenîlas pushed past the upright rocks that had given the peak its name and clapped the dwarf on the back. 'An amazing miracle from my goddess and your god,' remarked the elf. 'My tribe were wrong to keep it to themselves.'

'And *my* tribe should have discovered it,' muttered Belogar.

'Actually we did that,' piped up Gosalyn Landslip, whose breath had formed ice-crystals under her nose. 'But we forgot it rather than keeping it secret. So we're equally to blame.' The dwarf-woman squeezed between him and the elf to start the descent. 'Let's check what's left. My queen and High King Boïndil are eager for news.'

'Wait,' came a breathless voice from the Jagged Crown behind them. Rodîr Bannerman appeared, needing to lean on his spear and then against the stone. 'I can't go on.'

The dwarves and the elf grinned.

'You people just aren't cut out for the mountains.' Belogar sounded paternal. 'I warned you and your soldiers about coming with us.'

'Besides, we chose the easy descent through the mountain,' Gosalyn added, laughing. 'You only had to walk the last half mile through the snow.'

'And I'm very grateful for that,' the warrior replied, panting. 'But it's pure torture.' He looked in the other direction. 'My troops will be here very soon.'

Belogar pursed his lips, which were surrounded by a sprawling beard. 'What wouldn't one do to strengthen the newly won friendship between our peoples?' he teased.

Phenîlas smiled kindly and contemplated the mountains. He adjusted the white fur coat over his light leather armour. 'I can see the beauty but I admit I feel better in the Golden Plain. Ice and snow are not for my people, I'm afraid.'

'Thanks be to Sitalia,' murmured Gosalyn.

The elf laughed sympathetically. 'Yes, thanks be to Sitalia. Vraccas knows why *you'd* be here.'

Rodîr approached them. Twenty warrior-women and warriors were coming over the summit, bearing Gauragar's colours on their shields and pennons.

'They look exhausted,' Belogar remarked.

'And they've got sunburn,' Gosalyn chuckled. 'Didn't I say you should make sure their faces were covered?'

'I didn't think it was worth it for half a mile,' Rodîr admitted.

'If we had walked faster, you wouldn't look like a virgin who has just been told a dirty joke,' Belogar replied and laughed. 'Oh, that reminds me, an orc comes up to a dwarf to ask him for directions . . .'

'Not now, my friend,' Phenîlas interrupted him and moved on. 'The valley awaits us. Treat us to it there.'

'You'd better not.' Gosalyn winked at the disappointed dwarf. 'Everyone knows it anyway. The pointy-ear is just being polite.'

She followed the elf. Rodîr caught up to them while the rest of the human warriors followed shortly afterward.

High King Boïndil had insisted on dispatching a group to visit the legendary settlement where elves and dwarves were reputed to have lived together. There were certainly references to it in the ancient writings of the Fifthlings, but the turmoil of the preceding cycles had caused them to fall into obscurity.

The elves of the Golden Plain also wanted absolute certainty and had invited the humans to share in this flourishing settlement. No tribe ought to have secrets from other tribes anymore, the reasoning went.

Belogar saw it a little differently. There definitely wouldn't be any tunnel tours through the Kingdom of the Fifthlings or sight-seeing of the treasure trove. Friends remained friends, they didn't become family or even a member of the clan.

They assembled on the small ledge with a broad, steep staircase leading down from it, past the terraces of fruit trees and fields of grain. A fire had razed most of the buildings to the ground; just two remained habitable. Insects were buzzing around, the trees were in full bloom.

'I see elven and dwarfish runes on the walls,' Phenîlas said and he was moved. 'They've been eroded by time and the flames, but I'm reading about friendship and alliance.'

'Fantastic,' Rodîr gushed. 'The warm wind that is protecting the valley from ice and snow is coming out of the holes in the rock!'

'An array of different chimneys coming up from inside the

mountain,' Belogar realised. 'It works the opposite way to the flues we built to bring fresh air into our kingdom.' He nodded. 'We did a good job.'

Phenîlas started to walk on, hesitated, and looked encouragingly at Gosalyn and Rodîr.

They understood his glance and the soles of their shoes lowered onto the first step at the same time. Side by side they strode downwards, Belogar and the warriors following them.

Having reached the ground, Rodîr ordered his battalion to spread out and secure the area.

Belogar laughed at him. 'You think there are monsters here?' He loosened the clasp of his cloak and let it slip to the ground. It was too warm.

'Did you believe in the settlement?' the man shot back calmly. 'Anything could be hidden out here.' He pointed to the small, dark pond with waterlilies dancing on the surface. 'A beast could live in there.'

'Caution never harmed anyone,' Phenîlas conceded.

'So true.' The dwarf-woman looked around, one hand resting on the handle of her axe. 'It's beautiful here. If I didn't have a home, I'd move.'

'Oh, I know what you're thinking,' Belogar interjected, 'but it's not up to us to decide whether this settlement will ever be inhabited by dwarves and elves . . .'

'And people,' Rodîr chipped in, friendly but firm.

'As far as I'm concerned, it could be inhabited by unicorns and fairies too,' Belogar raved. 'We've got kings to make that decision, who will wrack their brains about it.'

'They certainly will.' Rodîr was amused by the dwarf as he leaned on his spear. 'Tell me, what made you think of unicorns? That image is practically idyllic.'

'Yes. Especially if *he* is sitting on it,' Gosalyn cried, pointing at Belogar and laughing uproariously.

The dwarf rolled his eyes and trudged off. 'I'm taking a look around,' he growled into his beard. 'In case nobody noticed amid their raptures' – he pointed at the fields using his mace – 'it's been harvested in places.'

Two soldiers suddenly called the commanders over: in one of the houses that was in better condition, they had stumbled across a discovery.

'Didn't I say?' Belogar couldn't help relishing the moment.

'Watch it, you're getting unbearable,' Gosalyn muttered as she walked past.

They went inside the hut and saw a dark blonde girl who had lain down to sleep in front of a window the size of a wagon wheel with various symbols painted on it. Her hair was dishevelled and her dark red vest looked threadbare and too small.

The intruders' entrance didn't wake her, her chest slowly rising and falling.

Belogar pointed at several thin flatbreads on the table. 'She's a little baker.' He tasted some. 'Not bad at all. She took salt from the walls . . .'

Gosalyn grabbed his arm and pulled him back. 'I would say she's eleven or twelve cycles.'

'She's not an elf-woman.' Phenîlas crouched down carefully and examined the sleeping girl, then reached out a hand to shake her awake.

The girl started, scrambling backwards and banging her head on the rune-patterned window, which immediately unleashed a cacophony of metallic noises. Without opening her eyes, she reached out her right hand, groping around, and with the other she whipped out a dagger from under the pillow. The words she uttered were incomprehensible.

'She's blind.' Rodîr sounded sympathetic.

'She just has her eyes closed. And she's not from Girdlegard.' Belogar's expression darkened. 'Nobody speaks that language back home.'

'She might be snow-blind. Look at her skin and eyelids. They must have been badly sunburned.' Phenîlas looked kindly at the dwarf. 'So you've travelled a lot and you know every dialect?'

Belogar huffed. 'No.'

'What he is trying to say in his bad mood,' the dwarf-woman stepped in, 'is that she must come from the Outer Lands.'

They contemplated the panting, dark blonde girl who was brandishing the dagger to and fro defensively.

'She's got guts.' Phenîlas spoke to her in elvish, Rodîr in the language of humans and Gosalyn tried dwarfish.

But the little girl kept shaking her head, answering incomprehensibly, although she did put the weapon away. She had realised they weren't a danger to her.

'We're not educated enough.' Rodîr approached her, touching her gingerly on the head and stroking her wild hair soothingly. Then he took his glove off and conveyed by touching her face that he wanted to see her eyes.

'She is from the Outer Lands,' Belogar stressed again. 'Nothing from there makes it to our homeland.'

The girl opened her eyes a crack, exposing inflamed redness. Her eyes started watering immediately and she groaned, holding her hands over them.

'The poor thing. She needs help!' Rodîr got up. 'I'm sure the dwarves must be good at treating snow-blindness?'

'Oh yes.' Belogar raised his mace. 'She'll feel better *after this*.'

At the sound of these harsh words, the girl clung to the human warrior's hand for protection. 'You seriously want to kill a child?' he asked indignantly.

'A child from the Outer Lands,' the dwarf cried, losing his temper. 'By Vraccas! What good has come from there in recent cycles? Aiphatòn? The kordrion? The demon? Monsters and älfar?'

'*Tungdil* came from there,' Phenîlas of all people softly replied, and crossed his arms over his white armour. 'From the Black Abyss. And he saved you all, as far as I know.'

Gosalyn was going to intervene to calm things down, but Belogar dismissed her with a harsh glance. 'No, I'm not going to give in. This child will not be taken to the kingdom of the Fifthlings.'

Rodîr nodded. 'Fine. Then I'll take her to my queen. Our healers will take care of her. We'll see what she can tell us.'

'My name is Sha'taï,' she said haltingly in a high-pitched voice and cleared her throat. 'Do you understand me now? If you do: I had to flee from my family's enemies. The town was destroyed and my uncle brought me . . .'

'Silence!' Shuddering, Belogar took a step backwards and fear showed on Phenîlas' delicate face. 'That was . . . älfar,' he whispered in disgust. 'This child speaks älfar!' He snatched up his weapon and made to strike.

Gosalyn stopped him. 'No,' she screamed. 'That's not your decision to make!'

The dwarf wrestled with her and shoved her aside. He knitted his bushy eyebrows. 'There's nothing to decide. She's one of them! Or she's a demon. Some kind of new trick!'

'She's not an älf-woman, you can tell at a glance,' Phenîlas cut in, his face pale. 'She probably comes from an area that belonged to the älfar. As Girdlegard once did.'

Belogar spat, not even considering lowering his weapon. He didn't take his eyes off the little girl. 'I thought the black-eyes had perished?'

'That remains to be seen.' Rodîr pulled the child to her feet and pushed her behind him, the guards coming to his side and forming a rock-solid wall. 'It's all the more important that we bring her to Queen Mallenia now. In the interests of all kingdoms and tribes of Girdlegard. The little girl will tell us about the älfar and can warn us if they are going to attack again.'

Phenîlas nodded. 'I'll guard her. She can't do anything to harm us, my dear dwarf. She's just a child who escaped the älfar and came to this settlement.' He placed a hand on his shoulder. 'This settlement once represented peace between us.'

Belogar was furious but he reluctantly lowered the mace. 'You'll have to take the outer path,' he thundered. 'I'm going to keep my word: this child will not set foot in the kingdom of my tribe. Gosalyn and I will direct you so that you make it to Gauragar safely.'

The elf slowly bowed his head. 'So be it. The Grey Mountains belong to the Fifthlings.' Rodîr wanted to protest but Phenîlas' warning glance made him remain silent. 'We'll set out tomorrow morning to have Sha'taï treated and learn more about the Outer Lands. But let's explore the settlement now. That's what we actually came here to do.' He went outside with the human warriors.

'I don't have a good feeling about this. High King Ireheart needs to hear about it. About everything. He'll be able to get the lankies and the pointy-ears to see sense.' Belogar looked anxiously at Gosalyn. 'We've got to find that path from here to the Outer Lands and destroy it.'

'Agreed.' The dwarf-woman looked out the window at the staircase they had used to get down into the valley. 'I'll lead the group by myself. You go straight back to Balyndis. We need more troops for the search and we need our best architects to seal the hole with mountain scree. For good.'

Belogar and Gosalyn walked outside and went over to Phenîlas and Rodîr to explain why the dwarf was immediately and unexpect-edly going away.

The elf and the human pretended to be sympathetic and wished him a safe journey and all possible aid from the gods so that the path could be found and destroyed. But as they parted, Belogar saw a fine film over the young human warrior's eyes that seemed to disappear the next time he blinked. *That must have been his danger-blindness.*

He trudged up the steps, putting his cloaks on again as he did so because ice and snow awaited him.

Halfway up, he turned and surveyed the tranquil valley.

Phenîlas and Rodîr were conferring together a slight distance from the fire that was just being fanned, while Gosalyn was taking a bucket to the waterfall to scoop water out of the pond.

The soldiers from Gauragar were preparing the provisions they had brought with them.

Sha'taï was sitting in their midst, receiving a friendly laugh and encouraging words to show her she didn't need to fear her rescuers. Occasionally someone ran a hand over her dark blonde hair, the way people did with children.

Belogar's mistrust remained undiminished. *I should have killed her.*

He hurriedly continued his ascent. Nobody else would ever get into Girdlegard on this path. That much was as good as settled.

Afterword and Thanks

With that, they are told for now, the great fortunes and legends of the älfar.

The last älfar have either been wiped out or no longer have their own free will and have become slaves to a stronger power – whatever the shackles that lie on heart and mind.

I admit it wasn't easy for me to take the villains who have style, profound wickedness, cruelty, brilliance and a taste for art, and turn them into a declining, doomed people.

No, it *truly* wasn't easy.

But history and stories simply don't make any allowances for sensitivities. Anyone who misbehaves for long enough gets the come-uppance they deserve at some point.

The älfar had the misfortune to come across an opponent who was not their equal, but who had the more treacherous tool at their disposal.

It was difficult even for the author to acknowledge that until the bitter end.

Oh well . . .

People will suppose there might be a reunion between Aiphatòn, Carmondai and possibly an älfar assassin in the fifth Dwarf volume.

But don't worry, it won't be too long.

*

My thanks once again go to the wonderful test-readers Tanja Kar-
mann, Yvonne Schöneck and Sonja Rüther. They found the demon in
the detail.

This time, editor Hanka Jobke had to do battle with the black-eyes
and, with her notes and queries, she gave the villains a better send-off.
Thank you!

Carsten Polzin should be mentioned for his great care, and once
again, Piper Verlag for all of the liberties an author could hope for,
from making up the title to the cover design – thanks also to the Guter
Punkt Agency who implemented my idea so successfully.

And last but not least, the most enormous THANK YOU to
everyone who followed the älfar to the end!

Oh, anyone who wants to know what the frekorian soldiers, ghaists,
botoicans, the wind-voice and other topics touched upon are all about
is advised to read the *Forgotten Writings* anthology.

You'll find what you're looking for.

ALSO AVAILABLE FROM

JO FLETCHER BOOKS

Jo Fletcher
BOOKS

MARKUS HEITZ

ONEIROS

In Leipzig an undertaker named Konstantin Korff harbours a cruel secret.

In Minsk an unscrupulous scientist performs questionable experiments.

And in Paris a plane that is about to take off crashes into an airport terminal with all its passengers already dead.

Except for one.

Jo Fletcher
BOOKS

MARKUS HEITZ

AERA

The Return of the Ancient Gods
An Episodic Novel

NOVEMBER, 2019

I've never believed in any kind of god.

But that's a problem when they start manifesting.

Because I don't think these really are the gods we've worshipped - Zeus, The Mórrígan, Thor, they can go to hell. We're in the middle of an invasion, and I'm the only one who believes in that reality.

My name is Malleus Bourreau, I'm an atheist, an investigator, and I will find the answers.

Jo Fletcher
BOOKS